LAST DAY

By **MARK PATRICK**

@mpatricknovels

markpatricknovels@gmail.com

www.markpatricknovels.com

PART I

THE ACCIDENT

1

THE SUN WAS TOO BRIGHT for this old-fashioned print journalist. One would wonder how many typical newspaper writers even knew what a sunny day looked like. Alec Rossi, a master of his craft, was living a life in darkness.

To better see what was in front of him, Alec squinted, creating a slight blur in his vision. With his right hand, he emulated the curved brim of a ballcap to shield the sun. There was a vast expanse of metropolis buzzing all around him—buildings and busy streets and sidewalks filled with pedestrians scurrying home.

However, standing on the overpass ledge, as rush-hour traffic zoomed by on the interstate beneath him, Alec saw nothing. His life, for all intents and purposes, was over. He was just waiting for the right moment to jump.

As his eyes adjusted, he saw a tanker truck barreling north, and he knew instantly it was his destiny; it was his ticket out of this world.

It closed to within 400 yards and he readied himself for the end.

LAST DAY

Three. ... Two. ...

• • •

The medication was hiding in a drawer beneath two years worth of clutter. His therapist had prescribed it long ago and Alec's personal prognosis was that he was fine without it.

For two years, that self-diagnosis went along without a hitch, but like an avalanche collecting snow, Alec's life was falling apart fast.

"You want another," the bartender asked.

Alec tapped the brim of the glass and the bartender obliged.

It was his fifth double Jack on the rocks in the last three hours, and he was nowhere close to being done. Alec's goal was to not remember, but everywhere he looked, memories appeared, hidden in even the simplest of objects.

A neon sign, flickering from years of overuse, burned the Yuengling Lager logo into his retinas as he stared at it, wishing the wall would just open up and envelop it.

Three months ago, Alec would not have even noticed the sign. Now, it ushered in an overwhelming sense of regret. Still, it didn't stop him from ordering a pint of the painful brew.

He lifted the mug to his lips and downed three-quarters of it in one tilt. Not only did he resent the thought of it; he also hated the taste. Nevertheless, it was his father's favorite, so to honor him, Alec forced one down every time he was out.

Roman Rossi meant the world to him. They were close from the moment Alec was born until the day Roman passed away. They still went to Orioles games as recent as last summer, and it was a blast. The Orioles made the playoffs for the first time since 1997, when Alec was a freshman at the University of Maryland. He remembered how happy that made his father. They went to Game Four of the American League Divisional Series against the Yankees and celebrated like they were both kids when the Orioles walked off with a win in thirteen innings.

"What a game," he said quietly to himself, tapping his finger on the beer mug.

He smiled as he recalled his father talking about the World Series Championship in 1983. There were some days when Alec truly wondered if that moment ranked higher than any other moment in his father's life. Under his father's roof, there were three things that reigned supreme—"God, baseball and food," he would always say. As Italians, the former and the latter were musts. His dad added the baseball part to get everyone to chuckle. Alec couldn't help but let one out at the bar while thinking about it.

Still, no matter how many smiles the memories could deliver, Alec always found himself dwelling on Roman's last day. His older sister, Holly, called him out of the blue one day in June to say that he needed to come home.

"Dad's in the hospital," she said.

"What happened? Is he okay?" Alec asked.

"They think it was a heart attack, but he's awake and alert now. They're going to run some more tests, but he's asking for you."

"But he's alert and okay, right?" Alec asked.

"Yes."

"Then tell him I'll get there as soon as I can, but I have to cover this press conference on the murder of that Loyola student. This is big and it sounds like dad is going to be okay."

There was a pause, but Holly understood.

"Yeah, he's fine. Just hurry up. It'd make him feel better to see you."

Alec clicked off his cellphone as the press conference with the victim's father started. It was the worst mistake of his life—at least up until this point. An hour later, Roman suffered a second heart attack and the doctors couldn't revive him.

Never got to say, "Good-bye," he thought, taking another swig.

Alec's gaze shifted from the neon sign toward an old man drinking a bottled beer by himself. As Alec turned his head, he felt the slow-motion effect of alcohol take over. His phone vibrated in his pocket and he took a quick glance at the lit screen. It was just an Associated Press news alert about a Supreme Court case. Disappointment fell over him once again. Every time the phone came to life, there was a glimmer of hope that maybe—just maybe—it was Abby texting him.

It had been fifty-three days since his ex-wife left for Seattle. Alec was oblivious until the day he came home unexpectedly to find her packing suitcases. She had no plans of telling him anything. She just wanted to leave.

Sometimes Alec wondered if that would have been easier to accept. Perhaps the thought of her being taken was better than the knowledge that she just got up and left. Plus, in that case, he would have never known about Blake, some snobby dot-com jerk who filled his bank account with millions in 1999 and sold his business before it fell to the ground.

That's whom Abby left with. She said it was love, but Alec knew it was all about the money.

Funny, he thought. *That's what The Sun said.*

The Sun was *The Baltimore Sun*, Alec's now former employer. Just four hours ago, he was called in to his executive editor's office and handed a two-week notice and a dismal severance.

Twelve years of loyal dedication to the only newspaper he had ever written for were thrown out with the same care a heavy smoker gives to a cigarette butt.

With his wife, father and career all gone—essentially his entire life—Alec felt nothing. It was a deep depression, a depth in which he had never reached before.

His prior run-ins with mental instability revolved around his drinking problems; and his drinking problems were a by-product of his career as a police reporter for *The Sun*.

Death and sadness were all around him, in every story he wrote. Murders, overdoses, rapes, assaults; he covered it all. He reported on the worst of society, and its filth left scars invisible to the rest of the world; scars that even he himself chose not to see until the day he finally went to see a therapist on his own volition. After a few sessions and a prescription, his troubles faded.

That was two years ago, and two years worth of repressed emotion built up and exploded this morning when the third part of his life was taken from him.

Losing his wife and father were traumatic experiences, but his career kept him going. It was the last thing on this Earth that he loved.

Alec gulped down the last of his drink, dropped a fifty dollar bill on the bar—an overpay, but money was useless to him now—and he walked out the door.

Within minutes, he was standing above Interstate 83 in the heart of downtown Baltimore, his lifelong home. There was nothing left for him, so with one last look at the city skyline, he aimed for the tanker truck coming his way.

Three. ... Two. ...

One never happened.

A loud screech interrupted Alec's countdown, and its ear-pinching shrill was followed by several more. Below him, a red Toyota Prius swerved into a black Honda Accord, causing the Honda to veer sharply into the concrete wall on the right side of the road. The Prius spun out of control in the other direction and farther down the highway, crashing into the concrete barrier that separated northbound from southbound. Other drivers slammed on their brakes, with a few minor fender benders, but the tanker truck—his ticket to leave everything behind—jack-knifed, flipped and scraped across the highway until it came to a stop up against the Prius.

Alec was in disbelief. What he had just witnessed was a shock to the heart. The adrenaline rush gave him a moment of clarity and he backed away from the ledge. He couldn't believe he was about to jump off a bridge, onto a busy highway no less.

As he climbed down, he scanned his surroundings. Nobody else was walking on the bridge—although a few drivers may have spotted him climbing off the ledge. He wasn't sure of that. Nevertheless, he decided that it would be best to get out of there quickly and he ran for his condo.

He heard the wail of sirens reverberating throughout the city as he distanced himself from the bridge. About five minutes later, when he was a few blocks from his place, he heard a loud explosion. It echoed off of every building downtown. Scared and drunk, he sprinted to his condo without looking back.

He never wanted to look back.

2

IT WAS NOT A GOOD DAY, but then again, for Chase Valenti, that seemed to be a running theme in his life. Late for yet another class, he sped west on Boston Street. The Johns Hopkins junior was stuck taking a summer course after failing a pair of classes during the traditional academic year.

Valenti was on the verge of failing once again, and a great part of him wondered why he was still trying. He had been a failure thus far in everything since he left the halls of his high school in a suburb outside of Cleveland.

He *was* a star attackman for the highly touted Johns Hopkins men's lacrosse team, but he got suspended during his sophomore season and was eventually kicked off the team for disciplinary reasons. That was the hogwash the media relations department served up to all the media outlets.

Behind closed doors and on campus, "disciplinary reasons" covered up his failed drug tests for smoking marijuana. What the test didn't disclose was that he was also a big-time dealer on campus. It was the second failed test in two years, and added on top of it was an attitude problem that had him in the doghouse with the head coach. It didn't matter that he had twenty-five goals three-quarters of the way through his sophomore season; the coach wanted him gone and the second failed drug test sealed it. He lost his scholarship and would have left the school if it weren't for the fact that his parents picked up the tab. Spoiled did not begin to describe Chase.

As he swerved in and out of lanes, he looked at the clock on the dash. Five minutes after five, which was five minutes too late for his class. And it was not like he was busy or stuck in traffic. The only reason he was late was because he and his roommates decided to light up another joint.

"Stupid," he admitted aloud in the car as he smacked his clenched right fist on the steering wheel.

Chase wanted desperately to be successful at school, but he couldn't help wonder if he was meant for a darker world. He ran a smooth drug operation on campus and he was bringing in large amounts of cash each week. Much more than the average college student working a part-time job on campus.

He turned sharply onto Fleet Street, drove to South President Street and traveled the length until he got to the on-ramp for Interstate 83.

As he got on the interstate, he saw it. Several cars were slamming on their brakes as a tanker truck jack-knifed, flipped and slid across the road into a red car.

Chase slowed down and came to a halt behind other stopped cars. Numerous people jumped out of their vehicles to call 9-1-1 and attend to the shaken-up driver in the Honda on the right side of the highway.

Fifty yards beyond that, the tanker truck lay on its side next to the badly damaged red car, with its backside pinning it up against the concrete barrier.

He got out of his car as traffic stacked up behind him. Jogging toward the wrecked vehicles, Chase ran past the Honda and saw the red car's engine catch fire. He heard the screams of a woman, but with the smell of gasoline in the air, he stopped and pulled out his smart phone. He opened the camera application and began recording.

He steadied the phone and zoomed in on the car. Even through all the pixelation, he saw a woman struggling to break free. Selfishly, he kept the camera rolling.

Somebody else will save her, he thought.

That wasn't the only thought he had. Chase knew once someone went to save her, he'd have the whole thing on video. He could sell it to the highest bidder. A payday was coming.

After about seventy seconds of focusing on the woman, he noticed the driver of the truck miraculously climb out of the passenger side, which was now facing up. Chase panned his phone to capture the driver squeeze through the window and jump to the pavement. It was a fourteen-foot drop and the driver's right knee buckled, but he got up and ran toward Chase.

The driver heard the woman yelling, and as he ran past the back of his truck, he could see her frantically moving in her car, but he also saw the flames dancing and the gas spilling out of his truck.

That made him run away faster.

Chase captured this all on his camera and then turned toward a pair of men who were arguing. The one broke free and ran toward the red car, but the other man stopped him again. Both men saw the gas spewing out of the tanker onto the back of the car, and they both turned to run the other way.

Chase followed them with his camera for about twenty seconds and then panned back to the car on fire. He zoomed in once more, and again, he saw the woman fighting like hell to get free.

It was at this point that Chase realized that no one was going to help her. He panned the scene to capture a young woman standing outside her car just mesmerized by what she was witnessing. Next to her car was another man stepping out of his minivan only to have a woman from inside grab his arm and pull him back inside.

About thirty-five seconds later, Chase heard sirens and he turned to capture a police car and fire truck both stuck behind an abandoned car that had pulled over to the shoulder on the right. The driver had run off—perhaps to get help, but Chase wasn't sure.

. . .

It was hard to see with the smoke and flames shooting out of the hood of her car, but the woman managed to make out a few details through the gap where her driver's side window used to be. The glass had shattered after the tanker truck slammed into her car, pinning the small vehicle up against the concrete barrier. The backside of the truck was now pressed against her driver's side back door.

The gas fumes invaded her nose and made her queasy, and the smoke from the car fire wasn't making it any easier to breathe. As she struggled to free herself, she could see a constant flow of gasoline streaming out of the tanker truck. She knew time was precious at this point and the adrenaline was kicking in.

Glass was everywhere and she had cut her hands numerous times trying to free her legs from the steering column, which was severely bent downward. That occurred when her car smashed head first into the barrier after several spins across the highway.

She kept squirming, but she knew it was hopeless without some help. She started to think about everything she hadn't done in her life. There was so much left to do, but now, all of a sudden, no time to do it.

Then, she saw a man run away from the tanker truck. He looked back as she screamed—pleaded—for his help, but he kept running. As she continued to cry for help, she saw a pair of men run toward her, but they too stopped and ran the other way. She continued to look out toward the onlookers; there were so many. She saw them all, including a young man who appeared to be using his cellphone. She screamed one last time as she caught a glimpse of a fire truck's flashing lights.

I'm saved, she thought, as the smoke and gas fumes took over causing her to lose consciousness.

. . .

Chase, who was focused on the abandoned car, once again panned back to the car on fire. He continued to record as the woman appeared to be slumped over the steering wheel. Never did he think about the severity of the situation until a flame reached out and made contact with the stream of gasoline. The concussion of the explosion sent Chase to the ground, but he quickly refocused his camera on the large fire and plume of smoke towering into the sky. The blast broke the windows of nearby cars and the buildings close to the highway.

At no point in time did Chase think about how he could have been the one to save the woman. He was too obsessed with the fact that he caught the whole amazing scene on video. He was still thinking about YouTube stardom.

Everyone around him, though, could not believe what they just saw. The two men, who initially went to help, but turned away, fell to their knees. The truck driver was an emotional mess in need of medical attention, and the woman, who stood outside her car and watched the whole event, screamed hysterically. Many others, who were farther behind and never saw the trapped woman, left their cars and ran in the opposite direction.

The fire fighters broke into the abandoned car and moved it out of way, but at this point it was too late. They battled the fuel-propelled blaze for an hour, and when it was just smoke, all that was left was the shell of the tanker and the frame of a small car.

By that time, Chase's video had already garnered 100 views on YouTube. It gained another thousand over the next two hours, and when the local and national news outlets contacted him for a copy, it officially went viral, hitting a million views by noon the next day.

But it wasn't the way Chase wanted to become famous.

The world did not tab it as "The dramatic explosion caught on camera."

Rather, it was the handful of cowardly people who did nothing to save a life.

In their most regretful moments, they would reflect, replay the moment and pray that if put in that same situation, someone would save them.

3

THE ROOM WAS DARK save for the soft glow of the screen behind Evrett Eckhard. He swiped his fingers across the tablet he held in his hand, zooming in on the drafted blueprints of a large building. The image on the screen did the same.

"And as you can see here, we went with the circular rotunda we had mentioned at the last meeting," he said.

A few of the men seated before him nodded in agreement. Evrett continued explaining the aesthetic elements of the office building he had designed. He was in his element.

Evrett savored these moments as his presentation ended and the lights brightened in the conference room. He had worked for more than ten years to get to this point. As he shook the clients' hands, one thought ran through his head: He couldn't wait to tell Sam.

"Nice work in there," said David Marks, patting Evrett on the shoulder. The two men walked down the bright hallway of Griffin, Graham, and Marks, Inc., more commonly known as GGM.

LAST DAY

"Thank you, sir," Evrett responded.

David nodded and continued down the hall, leaving Evrett to enter his office alone. He shut the door, placed his iPad on the small sofa and made a quick motion with his arm.

Nailed it, he thought. Three months of work had paid off. After four designs, three rejections and countless hours of effort and sweat, the clients had left GGM satisfied. Better yet, his boss, David, had left the meeting pleased with his efforts. Evrett looked at the clock. It was almost five.

His office was organized and exceptionally neat for an architect in his position. He was not one to leave sketches and drafts lying around. Evrett liked to keep things managed.

He stepped closer to the window and peered out at the streets of Baltimore. The July sun painted the city in a golden haze.

Evrett sat in his leather-bound office chair. While he played with a small Oriole Bird bobblehead, he used his cellphone to make a call. The screen read, "Sam."

After a few rings the call went to voicemail. Evrett didn't leave a message. His wife would call him back eventually. He flicked the bobblehead another time.

The last few years of his life had been a whirlwind of differences. He had heard several older drafters and assistants at the firm say that the thirties were often some of the best years of your life, but at twenty-nine, those years loomed dark on his horizon. Evrett had spent his twenties working at GGM since his internship when he was a senior at the University of Virginia. He was driven to make partner, a goal that required commitment and determination, along with long hours and little social life.

It must have been serendipity that made Evrett agree to go to happy hour that one night. The Irish pub at the Inner Harbor was not nearly as packed as he had imagined it would be, and that was a good thing. He despised crowded environments, and the Inner Harbor was typically filled with tourists and businessmen and women partaking in happy hour. Evrett was among them for the first time, as coworkers finally coaxed him out of the office by five. And he was glad they did, because it was on that evening he met Sam. She changed everything.

13

Three years later, they were married, living in a townhome that on the outside was nothing close to the modern structures Evrett designed on a daily basis, but on the inside—after a year of renovation—it had his own personal touch.

The phone vibrated, breaking Evrett's train of thought. He answered.

"Hey, honey."

"Evrett, you would not believe my day," Sam said.

"Why? What happened?"

Evrett noticed a strain and hesitation in her voice. It wasn't unusual for Sam to call on her way home from work with some story to share, but this time, her voice was different.

"Well, first of all, promise you won't be mad."

"Sam…"

The face of her boss, Harrison MacLain, immediately popped into his head. He was often the cause of any distress Sam had at her job at the advertising agency. Many times, a glass of wine at dinner would lead Evrett and Sam to concocting ridiculous scenarios that found Harrison meeting a grisly end. Their favorite involved a pelican and a paddleboat.

"What did Harry Ass MacLame do now?" Evrett joked.

He could hear his wife snort as she laughed and her mood lightened.

"You know, I just had enough. I couldn't take one more day working next to that man."

"What did you—"

"I quit," she interjected.

Evrett was shocked by his wife's revelation. They had spoken about her leaving the agency, but it always seemed like a fantasy.

"You quit? You actually quit?"

"I did. I just," Sam said, stumbling over the right to thing to say. "I needed to leave that place with my dignity intact."

For five years Sam had been working at Media Matters, a small advertising agency on Water Street near the Inner Harbor. And for those five years she also had to deal with the insufferable Harrison MacLain. Had he been in the room when Sam interviewed, she surely would have passed on the job. Harrison was a man who thought highly of himself, a thirty-seven-year-old college frat boy.

Sam designed the Web content for the agency. Her days were filled with brainstorming creative ways to sell whatever products and services their clients sent her way. She loved the artistic side of the job, finding new techniques to interest and entice the masses. Sam was quite proud of a recent campaign of ad emails where she had used a beach theme and sunscreen bottles. The recipient could choose what service suited his or her needs by clicking on the desired "SPF." *How appropriate for July*, Sam had thought.

Before it could be sent out, Harrison had to give final approval.

"Why not spice it up a bit?" he had suggested. "Maybe a chick in a skimpy bathing suit."

"This is 2013," Sam had retorted.

It was this blatant sexism that seeped out of Harrison's pores. He tiptoed a fine line between seemingly harmless humor and sexual harassment. After a verbal exchange of disagreeing opinions, the ads went out; a slightly out-of-focus image of a swimsuit model serving as part of the background.

"Hold on, I'm crossing the street," Sam said.

Evrett began to pack up some of his things while he waited for his wife on the phone.

"Okay, can never be too careful, you know?" she said. "So, today I was in a meeting with Harrison, Jared, and these guys from Axis Travel. You remember, they're the ones I've been doing the picnic themes for."

"Yeah, the picnics in different parks…"

"Landmarks," she interrupted.

"Oh, yeah. The landmarks."

They chuckled in unison. Sam continued.

The meeting had been going well. Sam had just finished show-casing all the advertisements she had designed using stock images and backgrounds. There were couples in silhouette enjoying a picnic at the Grand Canyon, Mount Rushmore and Washington Monument. Recipients would be able to click on the picnic basket in each ad and be taken to the main Axis Travel website.

The two men from Axis, both in their late forties, had nodded in approval. Harrison then leaned forward, placing both elbows on the conference table.

"Samantha is a real talent. If only she could make better wardrobe choices. Maybe show off a bit more than her mind every once in a while."

One of the clients snickered briefly. Sam fumed. It was clear Harrison was impressed by the work she did, but he could never let her savor the feeling for too long. The attention had to be on him.

"I could have thrown my laptop at him, I was so angry."

Evrett heard Sam's car door slam shut, followed by the sound of the keys starting the ignition.

"What did he say when you quit?"

"Ah, he went on about how I was making a big mistake, and that in this economy it would be difficult to find another job doing what I was doing and making what I was making. Hold on, I'm going to switch over to the Bluetooth."

The thought of finances began to creep into Evrett's mind. Sure the economy had seemed to be turning around, but that didn't mean there was an overabundance of jobs available. How long would Sam be without a job? Having quit she wouldn't even be able to collect unemployment. They had recently been talking about starting a family, but didn't have the opportunity to sit down and work out all the numbers. Evrett was a planner, and this had certainly thrown a curveball his way.

As these thoughts and more raced through his head, Sam's voice snapped him back to the conversation at hand.

"I know what you're thinking, but don't worry. Let's look at this as a positive. It will give me some time to clear my head. I've been working since I was sixteen. I could use a break, and we were talking about the possibility of me staying home when we start adding some more mouths to feed."

"No, no, you're right," Evrett said. "I was just. Well, you know me. I don't do well with surprises."

It was true. Evrett liked knowing what was waiting around the corner. He had left Pennsylvania with a plan. He attended school, landed an internship, turned it into a job and moved permanently to Baltimore. His office trash can was filled with crumpled Post-its of completed itemized to-do lists.

Sam was the adventurous one. She added a hint of much needed spontaneity to his life.

"I know quitting is a big deal."

"Sam, it's fine. I'm happy. Thrilled really."

"You are?"

"Oh, yeah. Look, I want you to be happy, and we both know that Harrison's a jerk and never going to change. We'll be fine. I'm doing really well right now at work. Sure things might be a little tight, but we'll make it work."

"You always know what to say."

"Although, you could have sued instead of quitting. We wouldn't have to worry about money then!"

Sam laughed. Evrett loved to hear her laugh, but this time the Bluetooth made her voice sound a bit distant.

"You're right, let me turn this car around!"

"No, I know you'd never do that."

A few months ago they had had this discussion. While offensive, Harrison was an equal opportunity offender. Sam was certainly not the only target. At least once a week he said something rude to an employee, male or female. It never felt to Sam that she would have had much of a case, and human resources, all one man of it, had reassured her of this.

"I can just take delight in knowing that that place will miss me when I'm gone. All right, enough about my day. How did yours go?"

"Just fine. My meeting went much better than yours apparently. I will be reporting to work tomorrow at least."

"Har har. Well, get your stuff packed up soon. I'm hungry. I'm already on eighty-three."

"Okay. I'll be leaving shortly."

"Good, I'm thinking Chinese tonight, what do you—"

Sam stopped mid-sentence and interrupted herself.

"Shit, there's a man on the bridge, I think he's going to—"

The sound of screeching tires and metal crashing into metal

pierced Evrett's eardrum. He heard her scream and pulled the phone away from his ear. A second of confusion passed.

"Sam!" he shouted, but there was no one there. The phone was silent.

The only thing that replayed in his head was "There's a man on the bridge."

He sprinted out of the building and to his car, as his heart pounded. All he kept saying to himself was, "Let her be okay," as he re-dialed her number over and over again.

It was the most helpless feeling in the world.

4

SMOKE BILLOWED UP TOWARD THE CLOUDS becoming a part of the city skyline. Evrett abandoned his black Audi A4 near Pratt Street. Traffic was starting to back up in the Inner Harbor, and while this wasn't unusual during rush hour, today it was worsened by whatever had happened on the other end of the phone. As Evrett ran toward South President Street, he saw the rows of cars sitting still and decided to head north on Calvert instead. He knew there was an overpass a few blocks away, eight to be exact, but he was in no state to be counting. He kept his eyes focused toward the north. Off in the distance, the sky was dark with the ominous pillar of smoke.

He had re-dialed Sam's number five times as he raced up Calvert, but she did not answer.

Please let her be all right. Please let her be all right, he repeated in his mind, as if saying it one more time might make it so. The scraping sound of the metal mixed with her scream drowned out his thoughts. It had been such a primal sound.

"There's a man on the bridge," she had said.

What bridge? He envisioned her commute home to Hampden, their neighborhood north of the inner city. She had only left work a few minutes before, so she could not have been far on Interstate 83.

He tore his suit coat off and tossed it on the hood of a taxi stuck in the traffic. The cabby yelled to get Evrett's attention, but he did not stop—could not stop.

Running was one of the many loves Sam and Evrett had in common. Each weekend they would make time to lace up their Sauconys and run together through their neighborhood or in one of the many parks in the city.

Now Evrett was running to save the one he loved. The adrenaline coursing through his veins numbed the pain he should have been feeling with his feet stuffed in leather dress shoes. His navy blue tie flapped back and forth over his shoulder as he picked up speed.

At each intersection Evrett quickly glanced from his left to his right, partly trying his hardest to dodge oncoming traffic, but also to see how close he was to the highway. He could hear the shrill screech of police sirens and the deeper groan of the fire engines that surely were on their way to the scene of the accident.

Accident. Samantha was one of the safest drivers he had ever met. She never texted while driving, played with the radio or rolled through a stop sign.

"You always must have respect for the road," she would tell Evrett. It was something her father had taught her when she had learned to drive.

The thought of her in an accident seemed preposterous. It must have been someone else's fault. Another car must have swerved in front of her.

Or maybe. There's a man on the bridge.

He couldn't shake those words as he ran past the Battle Monument. A slow moving SUV honked at him. The sound startled him, but Evrett did not lose his pace. He now found himself in the shadows of the taller buildings that lined the street, blocking his view of the smoke. In another block, he would be at the overpass.

It was then that he saw it. Orleans Street, the one he knew crossed over 83, was only a little more than a block away. Evrett's heart fell at the sight of the brown and grey overpass hovering above Calvert Street, casting its shadow on the townhomes below it. There was no way for Evrett to make it up on the road from the street he was on.

Before continuing any farther, he darted toward his left. Evrett's legs moved faster than they ever had before in his life. His heart beat loud in his ears. He hoped this mistake in directions would not delay him too badly. He was so close now.

He tore through the small park that lay near the Medical Center he was now passing. Two sets of concrete steps connected it to Orleans Street. A man sat nearby casually drinking a cup of coffee. It was hard to imagine that the world hadn't stopped for everyone.

The sky was wide and open in front of Evrett. Two blocks ahead he saw the massive black clouds. Three police cars, lights flashing, had formed a blockade. Several motorists had abandoned their cars and were wandering in the street trying to get a better look at what was going on a block ahead. His view of the expressway was still obstructed by a large parking garage.

"Stay back!" a police officer shouted out into the crowd that was now gathering.

Evrett saw an opening to the left of the last police car. He squeezed around the hood of the car as one of the officers turned to notice him.

"Hey! Stop! You can't go out there!"

Evrett could count on one hand the number of times he had come in contact with the law. Once in college, campus security had been called to his dorm room. It was his roommate's party that had gotten a bit noisy and out of hand. Evrett had sat quietly on the futon while the campus officers forced everyone out of the room.

This time, he was the rebel. He kept going, ignoring the calls from the officer. It didn't matter to him what consequences would come of his actions. He needed to see Sam.

In his head he saw her standing by the side of the road, leaning on the guardrail with a blanket wrapped around her shoulders. Her red Prius, a bit worse for wear, was a few yards away from her. The car behind her had rear-ended her. As Evrett approached the side of

21

the overpass, she looked up and saw him. Breathing a sigh of relief, she waved and he could see a smile across her face.

Nothing in his imagination prepared him for the sight that truly awaited him. Finally, Evrett saw it.

From the south side of the overpass he could see the whole gruesome scene. Flames and thick black smoke roared from the wreckage of a tanker and what looked like a sedan. Another car had been involved in the collision, but it was a little farther back on the other side of the highway. A third vehicle was being towed to clear the shoulder, as fire fighters continued to battle the once mighty blaze.

It was much smaller now, but Evrett could still feel the heat from the fire on his face as he scoured the scene for any sight of Sam or her car.

Maybe she missed it. Maybe she kept driving. Evrett stepped back to race to the other side of the overpass, hoping to see Sam's car perhaps parked off to the side of the road. He was sure she would have pulled over to see if there was anything she could have done to help someone.

Something caught his eye, though. A long piece of what used to be a car's fender was lying away from the wreckage. Its edges were scorched and a part of it was on fire. Still, Evrett could make out the color—red. Attached to the middle of the shard was a license plate. The letters and numerals were legible and they cut him deep. It was Sam's plate.

The horror crashed over him like tidal wave. The realization that it was her car engulfed in flames washed over him, saturating every level of his consciousness. He was lost in the moment as he fell to his knees on the sidewalk. Two police officers were hurrying toward him, shouting for him to get back away from the edge. He was deaf to their cries.

Her car… Her… Sam, he thought as tears began to fall from his eyes. The fire fighters were hosing down the wreckage now, but it was too late. No one could have survived such an explosion. In a matter of minutes, the plans they had made for their lives together ceased to exist, wiped clean away. She was gone.

• • •

LAST DAY

Evrett could remember moments in his life when he had been truly happy. Some were during his childhood, moments spent running through cornfields on his grandparents' farm or playing Frisbee with his golden retriever, Geordi. Dateless moments that now seemed to his adult self to exist in a perpetual state of summer. He couldn't tell if he was nine or eleven.

And then there were those more specific memories. He remembered his tenth birthday, when his father had taken him to an Orioles game, just the two of them. He remembered his first time alone behind the wheel of his 1993 Toyota Camry and the limitless feeling of freedom that came with it. He remembered his toast at his sister Molly's wedding, eight years earlier.

But all of those moments paled in comparison to when he had been the happiest. He and Sam were driving in a Jeep they had rented in Hawaii for their honeymoon. They had decided to spend the day driving along the coast of Oahu, stopping at the different small beaches tucked away in the less tourist-filled sections of the island. As they left the North Shore, the sun began to set and Evrett turned to glance at his wife. Her long wavy hair blew around her face in the salty summer breeze. Behind her, the coast rushed by in a haze of motion, the blue Pacific stretching out endlessly. She smiled and it was a smile that let Evrett know she was thinking the same thing. This was what life was supposed to be. It was a perfect moment.

• • •

She was gone. Chaos was all Evrett could feel. Their earlier phone conversation seemed forever ago. The two police officers pulled him to his feet, the larger officer placing Evrett's arm over his shoulder. His senses began to function again and the smell of gas and smoke burned his nose and lungs.

"You need to come with us, sir," the shorter officer said, leading him back toward the barricade.

Evrett made no effort to respond. He was miles and years away, holding on to a fleeting memory that would now begin to dull. He needed no confirmation; he knew in his soul that Sam was gone. He could feel the loss of her.

"Sam!" Evrett cried. He broke free of the officers and again raced to the edge of the overpass. His eyes took in the sight of the accident once more. The bystanders huddled below on the expressway looked up at him. Did they know? Could they fathom how profoundly his life had changed in a matter of minutes?

No, he thought.

To them, he was just a man on the bridge.

PART II

THE REBUILD

5

SUNFLOWERS WERE RUINED for him. They had been Sam's favorite flower, a prominent piece in her wedding bouquet. Now Evrett stared at a collection of funeral arrangements, laced with sunflowers, which covered his dining room table and spilled over on to the floor. Their smell now reminded him of death and the fact that she was truly gone.

The days that followed seemed to drag on and on. To Evrett they felt like moments in some freakish nightmare, stitched together haphazardly. There was so much to deal with when a spouse passed away. Being so young, nothing had been planned. And why would it have been? Evrett and Sam had just started their life together. They were going to grow old together. Surely there would be time to make wills and funerals arrangements. Life apparently had another plan.

Silence was all he could remember of the first night. The police escorted him to the station and later brought him the confirmation of what he already knew.

Afterward, he sat alone at their kitchen table with his iPhone in front of him. He had calls to make, family and work to inform, and a funeral to plan. But there the phone sat, and Evrett made no attempts to use it.

Thursday morning found him in the same spot. At some point he must have fallen asleep. A sharp pain throbbed in his neck as he walked up the stairs and down the hallway to their master bedroom.

In a fog, he slowly undressed and got ready for a shower. The hot water would sooth his aching neck. He noticed his feet and legs also hurt.

Weird, what was that?

Evrett didn't have to finish the thought. The world beneath him seemed to pull away, like he was standing on the sand while the tide went back out to sea. He shrugged under the weight of yesterday and his neck hurt even more. Looking back at the queen-sized bed he noticed the blankets were tightly tucked under the fluffy comforter. Sam had made the bed yesterday, the same as she had done for the last few years. She would never make it for them again.

Thursday was filled with white noise. Evrett made the necessary calls and he suffered through the heartbreaking sound of her mother's wail on the other end of the phone. He tried to remain strong, not just for them, but for himself as well. If he allowed himself to cry today, he might not be able to stop.

Parents and siblings were informed, and Evrett moved on to the cumbersome task of arranging the funeral. After contacting a few nearby funeral homes, he finally found one that would be able to have the burial that Sunday. He would have to have a luncheon.

There was no time to mourn.

In all the prepping and planning of the day, eating hadn't crossed Evrett's mind until eleven that night. He searched the fridge and pantry, but found nothing appetizing. Evrett decided he could force down a bowl of cereal. In bed, he turned on the news while he crunched on the Honey Bunches of Oats. The sound of Evrett's chewing muffled the voice of the eleven o'clock news anchor.

"Local officials say the homeowners were uninjured in the blaze. There were no working smoke alarms in the house," said the news anchor, a brunette woman in a grey suit.

Evrett placed his spoon back in the bowl of cereal. The next story's graphic caught his attention.

"More information has been released regarding yesterday's fatal accident that closed down Interstate Eighty-Three for several hours.

"The identity of the woman killed has been released. She was Samantha Eckhard, age twenty-eight, of Hampden, Maryland."

Evrett was taken aback. The newscast had a picture of Sam, a headshot from her company bio on the Media Matters' website.

Before Evrett could convey any emotion, the picture was gone and the anchor continued on with the news story.

She recounted the horrifying events that led to the accident. Video taken from a helicopter showed the flames and smoke engulfing the tanker truck and Sam's Prius. Evrett couldn't help but stare at the screen. Somewhere in that burning wreckage lay his wife's body.

"A video recorded at the scene of the accident has gone viral since it was uploaded to the Internet yesterday evening. The footage, shot by a student from Johns Hopkins, shows the moments before the fatal explosion."

The telecast cut away from the news anchor to the video of the crash scene. The sound of the video was covered by a voiceover from the news anchor. The screen flashed short segments of the YouTube video. A truck driver leaping from his truck, two men running toward Sam's car, an abandoned vehicle blocking the fire fighters and the pixelated image of the woman in the Prius—Sam. The final segment showed the chaos of the explosion and the recorder's frantic attempt to catch it all on video.

"The full video has been posted on the WBAL website. While gaining millions of views, the footage has also sparked a national debate on what role bystanders play in these tragic events."

Video cut to a woman in her late forties. She responded to a reporter who was off camera.

"It's just horrible. What happened to being a Good Samaritan?"

Below her name the screen read Debbie Siemens, Keswick, MD. The newscast cut to another interviewee, this time a man named Tobias O'Connell.

"From the looks of things, there wasn't much anybody could have done. Are you supposed to risk your life for someone you don't know when the risk is that big?"

Evrett sat upright in his bed. The cereal bowl trembled in his hands. He felt sick and a moment later the cereal he had forced down came back up. He threw the bowl toward the television, shattering it on the dresser.

Nothing. They did nothing. That was incorrect. One person had done something—he recorded it.

The thought of his wife's last moments, her final breaths, caught on camera and replayed on people's phones and computers and television screens tore at his mind. And there it was slapping him in the face on the evening news.

Evrett leapt out of bed and slammed the power button on the television. He couldn't take any more.

• • •

When Evrett was eight his pet guinea pig, Jeffry, died. Jeffry was three, relatively young for a guinea pig. One day Evrett and his mother came home from school to find the small brown and white animal motionless with his head in his food dish. Evrett couldn't remember the specifics of what his mother told him, but it wasn't far from the standard "he's passed away" and "in a better place" that most people say when confronted with the explanation of death. Whatever she said, it hadn't made him feel much better. His pet was gone and Evrett didn't understand why. They buried Jeffry in a shoebox in their backyard by the shed. Evrett's father built a small cross out of some scrap pieces of wood he had in the garage.

Growing up, Evrett attended other funerals—his grandparents, a few great aunts, even a high school classmate. The process of mourning and saying goodbye was an awkward one. In the receiving lines at the viewings, he never could find the right words to say to those left behind. Were there really any right words to say in these situations?

Now Evrett found himself on the other end. The wake was Saturday evening. Evrett stood off to the side of Sam's closed casket. One by one, he shook hands with the people who came to pay their last respects to his wife. It was a flood of condolences and lengthy hugs. Some offered words of comfort while some expressed their confusion and shock.

"I just don't know why God would allow something like this to happen," his Aunt Bernice said. She wrapped her arms tightly around Evrett as he bent down to hug her.

"I know," was all he could muster in reply.

Aunt Bernice held his face in her hands and kissed him on the cheek before moving down the line to Sam's mother and father.

And so it went, one after another. By the end of the night, Evrett was exhausted. He hadn't been eating or sleeping well. Who could blame him?

Sam's parents said goodbye and climbed into their Nissan Santa Fe. Sam was originally from Timonium, about twenty minutes north of the city. Her parents, Jim and Linda Fielding, still lived in the same Cape Cod from her childhood. His parents, Dylan and Joanna, were staying at the Double Tree a few blocks away from his house.

That night Evrett lay awake in bed, staring at the ceiling. He didn't want to face tomorrow. The wake had been hard enough to get through. He thought about standing next to the casket. He knew it had to be a closed casket; the nature of her death had decided that for him. His grandmother on his father's side had had an open casket, and while he remembered she didn't look quite like herself, he never really considered how lucky his grandfather had been—he had seen her one last time.

Evrett tried desperately to remember what Sam was wearing the day of the accident. They normally left for work around the same time, and Wednesday had been no different. In the rush of the morning preparation, had he forgotten to take notice of his wife?

No, she had worn one of his favorites, her light green blouse and grey slacks. He always liked how it brought out the green tint of her hazel eyes.

She'd never wear it again, nor would he ever see it again. It too had been engulfed in flames.

He had to stop himself from ever thinking about the fire. It was the worst part. Evrett's thoughts returned to the green blouse. It had short sleeves and a small ruffle around the neck. It was modest, but clung to her, accentuating her athletic body. The memory of their final conversation crept into his head.

"Samantha is a real talent. If only she could make better wardrobe choices. Maybe show off a bit more than her mind every once in a while."

He heard Harrison's words through Sam's voice. A ball of anger formed in his throat. *How dare he?*

Harrison hadn't even come to the viewing. After five years of working together—five years of projects, deadlines, company picnics and insults—Harrison MacLain had better show his face and pay his respects.

That dick.

The clock on Sam's nightstand read 3:27 when Evrett finally fell asleep.

• • •

It was Sunday evening and all Evrett could smell were sunflowers. The funeral service, burial and luncheon were all over. In the course of five days his wife died and was laid to rest in a cemetery plot a few miles away. He was approaching the hardest part of it all— the slow climb back to routine. The friends and family had all left, most would be returning to work the next day. GGM had given him seven days of bereavement leave. This would allow him a few more days to be alone with his thoughts and time to take care of tying up the loose ends of Sam's life. How could seven days, let alone seven years, be enough time for him to return?

He had never seen so many flowers. Evrett had even left some behind at the cemetery. The arrangements covered the kitchen table and the large granite counter that served as a breakfast bar.

Sam had liked gardening. In the little stretch of yard they had between their house and detached garage, she had planted several different types of bushes and flowers. Roses, azaleas, and of course, sunflowers formed a border between the grass and fence. Each spring as the weather warmed, Sam spent time weeding and mulching the flowerbeds. Some nights Sam and he would sit out with a bottle of wine listening to the Orioles on the radio.

While those flowers and plants were full of life, these arrangements stood lifeless around him. They smothered him.

Evrett pulled out a large black trash bag from beneath the sink. He went around to each basket and vase, pulling the condolence cards out. He read each one quickly before shoving the arrangement into the trash bag.

Bag after bag he filled. In no time the bar was clear and the kitchen table soon followed. Three collections of flowers remained. One of them was a small green vase with white lilies and yellow daisies. Evrett read the card.

"Our thoughts are with you in this troubling time. The Media Matters family."

Evrett thought back to the afternoon and night before. He remembered several coworkers of Sam attending the services. Bethany Giesinger, the office administrator had certainly been there. Logan Painter, another copywriter, also stood out in his memory, as did Henry Williams, one of the two partners at the company. A few other people he recognized from company get-togethers had been among those in attendance. But not Harrison.

The green vase shattered against the bright yellow walls of the kitchen. It was one insult too many.

He couldn't even bother to show up.

Evrett clenched his fingers in his hair.

She called at five. She never left that early. If she hadn't quit, she would still have been at work. She would have missed the accident and the man on the bridge.

The man on the bridge, he thought. *If Harrison hadn't been such an ass, she never would have been distracted by that man. Harrison couldn't even be bothered to show up.*

He looked at the clock—10:48. Evrett closed his eyes and breathed slowly. Silently he cleaned up the mess with a dustpan and brush. He carried the bags of flowers out to the alleyway behind the garage where they would sit until collection day on Wednesday. Tomorrow he would go to Media Matters and let Harrison know just how little he thought of him.

6

EARLY MORNING SHADOWS covered the brick patio behind Evrett's house when he left. If this had been any other Monday he would have been dressed in something a little more formal. Today he wore a blue polo, untucked, with khaki shorts. It was far from his usual business attire, but his destination was not the office—at least not his.

Evrett pushed open the small gate that led from his run of grass to the alleyway. The trash bags he gathered last night were piled high next to his garage. It was a small garage that barely fit his Audi. He and Sam alternated who got the garage and who had to park on the street out front of their house on Beech Avenue.

He realized he would not have to worry about that anymore.

Evrett got his car back from the parking authority over the weekend. Surprisingly nothing had been taken from it when he abandoned it last Wednesday.

Evrett decided to avoid 83 that morning. The radio had mentioned that the northbound lanes had reopened over the weekend, but it was too soon to revisit the scene. He even skipped St. Paul and drove a few blocks over and farther out of his way.

It was a little after nine when he parallel parked into a space just out front of Media Matters. Sam's office was located in a three-story brick building. Two large clay planters framed the double doors that led into the lobby of the older building, which had been converted into offices a few decades earlier.

On the second floor, the familiar face of Bethany Giesinger greeted Evrett. She was in her early forties, a mother of two boys who had gone back to work when both of her children were old enough to be in school. Evrett was surprised that she worked the front desk at the office. Surely, Harrison would prefer some fresh-faced blonde right out of college. Evrett had to remind himself that Henry Williams, the older of the two partners, was a decent guy and probably had some say in keeping Bethany around.

Bethany clearly was not expecting to see Evrett when he walked in. She choked a bit on her morning cup of tea and coughed.

"Evrett, what are you... I mean, it's good to—"

She stopped and composed herself, "How are you doing?"

"Hi, Bethany. I'm hanging in there."

It was an awkward response, but what else could he say? People didn't want to hear the truth in these situations.

"What can I do for you?"

Evrett placed his hands casually on the ledge of Bethany's desk. He peered down both directions, looking for the man he had come to see.

"I'm actually looking for Harrison. I wanted to talk to him."

"Oh, Evrett, I wish you would have called first. I could have saved you a trip down here. Harrison is off on vacation this week. He won't be back until the twenty-second."

Vacation? The thought of Harrison lying on the beach some-where while his wife lay buried only added fuel to the fire.

"Where did he go?" Evrett asked.

"Honestly, I don't think anywhere this time. He mentioned he wanted to put the finishing touches on his deck. Between you and me, these weeks are my favorite. I can get so much more done without him making some ridiculous comment every five minutes."

Bethany chuckled as she filed some papers away into a folder. There was a lull in the conversation and she realized who was standing in front of her desk.

"Evrett, I'm sorry, I shouldn't have said that. You must be dealing with so much. I'll tell you what; I'll make my chicken tetrazzini casserole and drop it off tomorrow. I'm sure the last thing you want to do right now is cook," Bethany continued nervously.

"That won't be necessary. Thanks, Bethany."

Evrett left Sam's office thinking he would probably never see that woman again.

• • •

Evrett walked toward the small amphitheater in the Inner Harbor. He watched a street performer juggle bowling pins and an elderly couple pose for a picture in front of the USS Constellation that was docked at the pier. He had left the car back at Sam's office. Rather than go back home he decided to walk around.

Sam had loved the Inner Harbor, especially the aquarium. While he preferred to stay away from the large crowds, Sam seemed to thrive on being surrounded by people. It was rare for them to go anywhere in public without her striking up a conversation with someone she had just met. All the while, she never made him feel like he was just tagging along. Even in the most crowded of places, she made him feel like there was no one else half as important.

His mind wandered in all directions as people passed by him outside the Inner Harbor shopping center. Although he stood amongst a gathering crowd of spectators, he thought of himself standing on Orleans Street again. He wasn't alone.

There he was—the man on the bridge. But it wasn't the man on the bridge. It was Harrison MacLain. He stood before Evrett, smiling smugly, smoke choking the air around them. Flames caught Evrett's eye and shocked him back to reality.

The street performer switched from bowling pins to small flaming wands. The crowd around Evrett had increased as he was lost in his revelry. Gradually his thoughts came back to Harrison.

Vacation. Evrett wondered if his lack of attendance at Sam's funeral was due to him being out of town.

No, Bethany said he was probably spending this vacation working on his house.

Evrett had been to Harrison's house a few times before. In the early years of Sam's employment at Media Matters, Harrison had held several company holiday parties and cookouts at his house in Cockeysville.

Fitting name, Evrett thought.

A fire formed deep within Evrett. It burned in the pit of his stomach. Sam was dead while Harrison and the man on the bridge lived. At least he could find one of the men who played a role in his wife's final hour.

Evrett could have ignored his disrespect if Harrison had been out of town, but to choose not to attend when he didn't even have to work the next day was inexcusable. After all Sam had to put up with, Evrett couldn't allow this to go unnoticed. Harrison had to know what type of man he was.

As the street performer caught the final wand and took a bow, the small audience applauded. Evrett had already left.

• • •

Harrison lived in a large stone and stucco house near Oregon Ridge Park. It was an excellent location for someone who didn't want to be too far from the city, but also enjoyed a rural setting. From his front yard he could see open pastures, and from his back patio, the dense forest of the park.

Evrett stopped his car at the edge of what he recalled to be Harrison's property. He remembered the long fence and the boulevard trees. This was indeed the place.

He pulled his car into the turnaround driveway, about 100 yards off the road. As far as Evrett could tell, the closest neighbor was several acres away.

Two of the three garage doors were open. Evrett could see Harrison's Lexus GX parked in one, and his BMW Z4 in the other. "Pretentious" came to Evrett's mind.

Evrett stepped out of the car and began walking to the front door. As he went to ring the doorbell he heard hammering off in the distance. It was coming from the back of the house.

There was a small walkway made of red and brown pavers that wound from the driveway to the backyard. The landscaping on both sides of the walk was a mix of small green shrubs and grasses. To the side, a little farther out in the yard, Evrett could see a personal putting green that Harrison had put in a few years ago. Two golf flags fluttered in a July breeze.

Harrison wore a backward black hat and a sleeveless University of Maryland T-shirt. He was busy hammering a long piece of wood to one of the support posts of his unfinished deck.

Half of the deck was exposed ribs, the rafters running parallel to one another. The other half had a few floorboards in place, just enough to hold a small pile of planks that would soon be added to the deck. The deck was being built high enough over an already completed patio so Harrison could still access the sliding glass door to his finished basement.

Evrett coughed to get Harrison's attention.

"Holy shit, I didn't see you there. What the hell, man?"

"I didn't mean to startle you."

"Evrett, I..."

He was surprised Harrison was so quick with his name. He hadn't seen him in almost a year. Evrett stood just out from under the deck.

"What are you doing here?"

"I wanted to talk to you. I went to the office. Bethany said you were on vacation."

"Yeah, I took the week off. You could have called if you wanted to talk. Would have saved yourself a trip."

Harrison put the hammer he was holding in his back pocket and wiped the sweat off his forehead with his shirt, exposing a slight beer belly. Even at eleven in the morning it was hot.

"You want something to drink?" Harrison asked. He took a final swig of a beer that was much too warm for his liking. He walked over to a cooler and pulled out another. He went to hand one to Evrett, who politely declined.

"Why didn't you come?"

Why beat around the bush? He came here for answers; he might as well get them.

"Come to what? The funeral?"

Evrett nodded.

"Ah, Evrett, look. Funerals aren't really my thing. The company sent flowers didn't it? Plus, let's face it, Sam wasn't my biggest fan this week."

Evrett was taken aback by how casually Harrison excused his behavior. Funerals were no one's "thing." Hearing him say his wife's name sent shivers down his neck.

"You work with someone for five years, and you can't be bothered to do more than send flowers? Flowers that weren't even personalized?"

"I'm sorry Bethany didn't have them put something more touching on the card. I'll be sure to talk to her about it when I get back."

"Screw you, that's not what this is about."

Evrett felt the heat, not from the summer sun, but from deep inside him. As he looked at Harrison he remembered all the times Sam had sat at home, venting about her day and the pig she worked for.

"Whoa, calm down, buddy."

"Don't call me buddy. She shouldn't have even been on the road. She left early because of you. You treated her like she was beneath you."

"Now, listen here, Evrett."

The two men circled one another. The distance between them had closed significantly.

"Sam should have been working until five-thirty. She would never have been near that tanker. Never seen the man on the bridge. If you wouldn't have—"

"It's not my fault the bitch quit."

"You piece of—"

It happened so fast. Before Evrett could finish his insult, he was lunging toward Harrison, thrusting forth a two-handed shove square to his chest. The force spun Harrison around, causing him to trip

38

over his own ankles. He fell forward into the corner post of the deck. The support beam lost its hold and as Harrison tumbled down, the deck came with him. Several pieces of wood landed on Harrison's neck with a sickening crunch.

The feeling of disbelief was immediate. Evrett's eyes gaped at the sight of Harrison as he lay motionless. Blood began to spurt from a large wound in his neck.

Evrett's mind was blank and full at the same time. There were too many thoughts to focus on just one. He inched closer to the body. It was obvious the man was dead. His neck was broken and crushed by the timber.

Evrett felt his stomach turn, but quickly caught hold of himself. He couldn't be sick. Not here. His gaze darted around the patio. Was there any sign that he had been there?

To an outsider it might look like it was an accident. Harrison, drinking and working alone on the deck, was a victim of an unfortunate accident. He could have tripped over anything.

Were they alone? No neighbors were close enough to have seen him drive to his house, let alone fight with the man. And if anyone were home, the crash would have brought them outside for sure.

Evrett took one more scan of the area, double-checking that no trace of him would remain. He ran back to his car and drove a casual speed away from the house of his wife's former boss. His heart throbbed inside his chest.

A creeping thought took hold of Evrett as Harrison's property faded from the rearview mirror. He glanced up and caught his own gaze in the reflection. He was surprised by what he saw in his dark blue eyes.

7

ONE BY ONE he passed them. Sometimes he was above, sometimes below. Evrett came closer and closer to the city with each over and underpass that crossed the highway.

Harrison MacLain was dead and Evrett had killed him.

Murdered him.

He couldn't shake the thought from his head.

Murderer. Never in his life had Evrett imagined he could use that word to describe himself. How could he be a murderer? He watched the evening news. He read the newspaper. He looked nothing like the men and women who were raising the crime rate in Baltimore. How could he all of a sudden be lumped in the same category?

Yet, it had happened.

Had he driven to Cockeysville to kill Harrison? Evrett didn't think so. Yes, he blamed Harrison for setting into motion the series of events that brought Sam's life to an abrupt end. But, had murdering the man been his intention? When he placed his hands on Harrison's chest and pushed, had he wanted the deck to come crashing down on him?

Still it wasn't these thoughts that surprised Evrett the most. It was how he felt.

Relief.

Satisfaction.

Evrett's thoughts of Harrison faded away and in their place he saw Sam, beautiful and alive. They were lying on the white sand of a beach near Waikiki. She was sprawled out on a towel next to him, sand sticking to her slender thighs. He smiled. He would have killed a thousand Harrisons for just one more day with that smile.

The relief and satisfaction began to fade as the memory of their honeymoon reverted into the reality of the last few days.

Evrett peered up as he drove under an overpass. He could see the roofs of a few cars crossing the road above. There was no pedestrian to distract him.

Harrison was dead, but the man on the bridge still was out there. The thought angered Evrett. He had spent so much time since Wednesday dwelling on Harrison. But what of the second man—the one actually responsible for his wife's accident?

The man on the bridge was a faceless specter in Evrett's mind. A dark phantom standing tall on the barrier of each overpass he drove underneath.

Did the man even know that he had caused Sam's death? Did he even care? Was he back at work? Having lunch with a friend? Kissing his wife?

As Evrett's mind raced, so did his Audi. The speedometer climbed up beyond ninety. His fingers tightened around the steering wheel as his foot pressed down even more forcefully on the gas. He swerved around several slower motorists who honked their horns.

The man on the bridge was alive while his wife was dead. And just as Harrison had paid for his role, so must the man on the bridge. But how could he find him?

"Shit, there's a man on the bridge, I think he's going to—" she said.

She couldn't have been the only one to see him. Someone else had to have noticed the man on the bridge. Sam wasn't the only one on the highway that day.

And suddenly there it was.

• • •

Evrett raced up the stairs of his house, his feet thundering on each wooden step. He used one of the three bedrooms of their townhouse as his home office. Framed black and white photos of unique buildings from across the globe hung on the light grey walls. His laptop was waiting for him on his desk.

He opened an Internet browser and typed frantically into the search bar. Seconds later he scrolled his pointer over the play button on the video.

The night after Sam's death, he had only seen bits and pieces of the now famous video. Evrett had been so disgusted that his wife's final moments were available for the world to see that he had pushed the existence of the video far from his mind.

Now he sat glued to every second of the clip.

This time he noticed it all: the truck driver who looked at Sam's car before deciding to save himself; the two men who ran toward Sam but turned to go the other way; the young woman who dared only to gaze at the blaze; the man who exited his car only to be pulled back in by another; and the abandoned car that blocked the roadway.

Of course, he also noticed the man behind the camera. His face was never shown, but his name was attached to his YouTube page. Chase Valenti.

As the explosion rocked him backward, Evrett cursed the man's name. How dare he do nothing.

Shortly after the explosion, the video came to an end. Evrett was surprised by its length. The clip on the news couldn't have been any longer than fifteen seconds.

In reality, it was eight minutes and forty-eight seconds.

That meant for eight minutes and forty-eight seconds, Chase did nothing.

Evrett was livid.

He watched the video again, and again, and again.

Each time, his blood boiled to the point where he had to stand up and pace before pressing the play button once more.

He could not believe it. Not one of the people on the video did anything to help his wife. He meticulously calculated the amount of time each person had to save Sam.

Evrett was convinced. They all had ample time to save her and they failed.

A minute passed as he paced around the room again.

When settled, he sat back down and watched it once more.

Those who did nothing were going to pay.

• • •

"Again, Mr. Eckhard, I'm sorry for your loss. I really appreciate you taking the time to discuss this with me."

"Thank you, I understand."

He ended the call with Judith Montgomery, his insurance agent. It was Wednesday, July 17. Sam had been dead for a week and Evrett was still dealing with the paperwork of the event. He had been on the phone with the insurance agency for more than an hour.

The news was not good.

Judith explained to him that the police report blamed Sam for causing the accident, citing the statements of multiple witnesses. Because of this, his insurance would have to cover the damages to the other motorists' cars. The silver lining, Judith told him, was that the other motorists only had minor injuries.

The silver lining, Evrett thought. It was hard to see a silver lining when your wife had only been dead for almost 168 hours.

"Who are these other motorists?" Evrett asked himself. The thought that he would have to pay for their insignificant losses infuriated him. "And what of these witnesses? Were they the same pieces of garbage who stood there and watched her die?"

Evrett had spent the last two days doing very little. He slept a lot, and walked aimlessly around the house, tracing his fingers along the walls. He also kept watching the video of the accident. By now every frame had been committed to memory. He could replay the whole thing in his head. Yet, he continued to play it, each time looking for something he had missed.

Every time he watched the video, the same burning he felt at Harrison's and at the Inner Harbor returned. What kind of world was it where people watched such horror and stood motionless, allowing the life of another human to be engulfed by the flames of fate? It saddened and angered and sickened his mind.

He would have to find them. Evrett knew that the people caught on camera, the watchers, would lead him to his destination. As far as he was concerned, each one of them was guilty—as guilty as Harrison and the man on the bridge.

But how could he find them? He had no knowledge of these people, no leads.

That was until Judith Montgomery called him.

It had never dawned on him to get the police report. He was certain the witnesses' names were on it. The document was public record, but he wasn't about to walk into a police station and request a list of the people he wanted to seek out auspiciously. He had to get his hands on it another way, and since breaking into the police station was not a viable option, that left a stealth operation into Judith's office.

This was where he would begin.

8

IT WAS AWKWARD. His office was the same as he had left it, with the addition of a few file folders that had been placed on his desk. Evrett thumbed through them before setting them off to the side. He told himself that the first day was going to be the hardest. Once his coworkers got over the initial awkwardness, they would return to normal. Until then he had to suffer through the overly polite comments and gestures. Each time someone asked him how he was doing or holding up, he was reminded of the loss all over again.

David Marks knocked on the door and entered Evrett's office. A tall man in his late thirties followed David. Evrett recognized him.

"Evrett, welcome back. I… It's good to see you."

David fumbled for the right words to say. This was his first encounter with Evrett since the funeral.

"Thanks, David. It's good to be back," he lied.

"Good. I'm sure you remember Mattias from Human Resources."

"Of course. How's it going?"

"Fine, thank you. Glad to see you," Mattias said.

"I've brought him to talk to you about your transition back to work. He has a couple forms for you to fill out. Shouldn't be too difficult."

"Sounds fine."

There was a moment where no one spoke. Taking it as a cue to leave, David patted Evrett on the back and excused himself from the meeting. Evrett motioned for Mattias to take a seat on the small sofa that lined the wall of his office. Evrett leaned on the top of his desk.

"Evrett, I wanted to talk to you about your transition back to work. Today being your first day, I want to extend our deepest condolences…"

It was more of the same thing he had been hearing, condolences and heartfelt sympathies. He had only been back to work for a few hours and already he was nauseated by it all.

His mind wandered back to the last few days. After speaking with Judith, he had been mulling over different ways to get a hold of the accident report. She would have a copy of it in his insurance file. When he had signed the insurance contract at her office he remembered a wall of filing cabinets stacked behind her desk. He'd have to get in there somehow, but he was going to take his time and plan it out. He couldn't afford to be impulsive again like with Harrison.

He wondered about Harrison. He hadn't heard anything about it yet. They would probably search for him when he didn't show up for work today. With each passing day he felt more and more confident that he got away with the crime. When his body was finally discovered, it was sure to be thought of as an accident.

"Evrett?"

His mind shot back to the moment. Mattias was looking up at him from behind thick black-rimmed glasses.

"What's that?"

"I was just saying that you might want to consider counseling to help with your coming back to work. We've found that it can be really helpful when an employee goes through something traumatic."

"Let me stop you right there."

Mattias was taken aback by Evrett's response.

"I appreciate the concern the company has for my well-being, but it's my first day back. I don't need to be told I need to go to therapy. Especially by…"

Evrett caught himself before he continued. He was surprised by his own behavior. This wasn't the way he acted at work.

"Look, Mattias. I appreciate the company looking out for me. I'll consider it."

It apparently had been enough to satisfy Mattias, who left Evrett's office rather quickly. Evrett shut the door and let out a long breath. He just needed to be alone.

By the late afternoon, Evrett was actually getting back in the groove of work again. It was a relief to let something other than Sam and the man on the bridge occupy his mind. Still, as he looked over the drafts of a future addition to a local high school, the man on the bridge slowly crept back in.

Around four in the afternoon, Evrett was sitting at his desk. No one had checked in with him all afternoon. He was thinking of Judith Montgomery's office. It was located in an older townhouse that had been converted into the Nation Trust Insurance office. It was a small branch; Judith was the only agent at the location. Two office assistants worked part-time in alternating schedules.

If the windows were old they might not be too hard to force open, Evrett thought. He absentmindedly doodled with a pencil on the draft he had been working with.

He could probably force the door open somehow. Or perhaps find a way to unlock it. Evrett knew there was a way to get into the office, it would just require a bit of planning. Luckily, he was an architect. He was a pro at planning.

Evrett looked down at his hand. He was clutching the pencil rather hard. His eyes focused quickly on the doodle he had been working on. Without realizing it, Evrett had drawn an ominous figure atop a bridge. It was beginning to sink in that he would never be free from this man.

• • •

Evrett walked into Judith Montgomery's Nation Trust Insurance office. Judith, a thin woman in her early fifties stood up to greet him. Her shoulder-length grey hair was pulled back in a tight bun.

"Good to see you, Evrett," she said, extending her arm to shake his hand. "You really didn't have to come in. I could have faxed the forms over to your office."

"Believe me, I needed an excuse to get out of there."

It was the Friday of Evrett's first week back. Actually, work was not going poorly for him. Most people had stayed out of his hair for the first few days. He figured they felt it was too soon to begin business as usual. Did they act like nothing had happened? Did they step softly around him? Unable to make up their minds apparently, his co-workers mainly left him alone. Until they adjusted, Evrett worked in his office, getting caught up with the several on-going design projects.

The alone time at work also had given him the opportunity to get started. Today was the first step. He sat down in the comfortable leather chair across from Judith.

"I'm sorry to hear that. I assume it has been hard going back to the routine of life."

Evrett nodded. Judith wheeled her chair around to the large filing cabinet behind her desk. He paid close attention as she pulled open the specific drawer that held his file.

Today's visit was not just for Evrett to sign off on his wife's life insurance. He could have easily done that through fax as Judith had suggested. Today was more important.

The first thing Evrett noticed when he pulled up in front of the office was the neighboring buildings. Nation Trust was located in a business and residential area. It was situated on the corner of a row of alternating homes and businesses. A small set of steps led up to a single door.

As he walked through the doorway he noticed the security system keypad. That was going to take some ingenuity. Evrett made sure to focus on everything. The main area of the office was divided into two rooms. The first served as the lobby and held the desk for the office assistant. In addition, a few chairs, a coffee station and a bookcase of pamphlets were really all that the first room contained.

Judith had come to greet Evrett, because the office assistant was out at lunch. As they walked to the second room, her office, Evrett looked up at the ceiling. There were two motion sensors attached to the crown molding. No security cameras were visible.

Judith opened the file and spread some papers wide on the desk. Evrett casually leaned forward. It could be so easy if the report he desired was right on top.

She continued with some small talk, but Evrett wasn't paying close attention. There was one motion sensor on the far wall. Again, no security cameras. If he could get past the alarm, pulling the file out wouldn't be incredibly difficult.

"Now, once you receive the death certificate, we will be able to send all this paperwork in. It's just so tragic. Samantha was such a beautiful woman."

"She really was."

It was weird to hear Judith talk about Sam. She had only met them enough times to be counted on one hand. Evrett appreciated that she didn't pretend to know Sam.

He signed his name on all the lines she pointed to. The death certificate would be arriving in the next few days. The funeral director had said it would not take long to receive.

The perfect reason to return, he thought.

• • •

Evrett woke up to an empty house that Saturday. This was the first weekend he'd truly be alone. Last weekend, the funeral had monopolized all his time. Dealing with arrangements and family and guests had kept him busy. Now, the silence of the house closed in around him. He had to get out.

Saturday morning runs had been a passion Evrett and Sam shared. Today was the first he'd do alone. He hadn't even thought of running in the last week. Tying the laces on his Sauconys even felt odd. He stretched his legs a bit on the front porch before quickly moving down the ivy-lined steps to the sidewalk.

He ran the path they usually took, traveling at a swift pace along side Wyman Park and then through Johns Hopkins. He and Sam would run without music, listening to the rhythm of their feet on the road. It didn't take long for them to be in unison. This time Evrett had his ear buds in. He didn't want to hear the lonely sound of his soles hitting the macadam.

The neighborhood seemed smaller to him now. Sam was the one to pick Hampden. She loved the feeling of the neighborhood, especially the row of houses on their street that faced toward the trees of the park. It was safe and secluded.

They moved in on a weekend in late October. The trees had lost most of their leaves and several of the neighbors had placed pumpkins on their porches. One of Sam's demands was to have their house be ready for Halloween. Each year she would dress up to answer the door, always complimenting each kid on their costume before placing a handful of candy in their bag.

He ran for an hour before returning to his house. Evrett caught his breath in the parking space that oftentimes would have been filled by Sam's car. He checked his watch. The mail should be there by now.

Evrett stretched a bit on the concrete steps that led to the porch. He didn't feel like doing his cool down routine today. He checked the black metal box that hung next to his doorbell.

It was here. He knew immediately that the large white envelope addressed to him contained Sam's death certificate. He would drop it off first thing Monday morning.

• • •

Evrett chose the following Friday night. It was almost midnight and Evrett was standing across the street from the Nation Trust office. He was dressed in dark clothing and carried a small black case.

It hadn't been hard to learn how to pick locks. After a few Google searches and YouTube tutorials, Evrett had the basic idea. An advertisement on Craig's List for a 12-piece precision pick and screwdriver set being sold by a man in Ellicott City provided the rest. He met the shady man on Monday at a diner and paid for the kit in cash. He wanted as little record of his actions as possible.

He practiced the rest of the week. He installed a deadbolt on his basement door and worked at it over and over again. He learned the proper pressure to apply to the wrench and the feel of the pins as the pick slid them into place. By Wednesday he could have the deadbolt unlocked in less than a minute.

Monday had also been a success. He had parallel parked a few spots down from the office and waited for Judith or her assistant, Stacy, to arrive. The office hours began at 8:30 and Evrett figured one of them would arrive a little earlier to open up.

At 8:15, Stacy parked a few spots closer to the door. As she parked her blue Corolla, Evrett got out and made his way down the street.

"Stacy!" he shouted politely.

He startled the woman. She was in her mid-twenties, probably only out of college a year or two. She had her hands full with a coffee, messenger bag and several files tucked under her arms.

"Yes?" She didn't recognize him.

"Oh, sorry. Evrett Eckhard. I have some paperwork to drop off for Judith."

He held up the death certificate envelope and smiled. Stacy reached for it. The files she was carrying began to slip.

"Here, let me help you. I figured I'd drop it off on my way to work."

It was a lie, but Stacy bought it. She smiled in relief as she handed the folders over to Evrett. If only she would have turned his file over to him as easily.

Evrett followed Stacy up the steps. Without all her items, she was now free to open the door with her key. They stepped into the office. Stacy placed the coffee and bag down on her desk and hustled over to the security keypad.

The alarm was not set to go off at the first sign of motion. It was a fact that would work to Evrett's advantage.

She looked back at Evrett, who pretended to be looking at the clock hanging above the door. His heart raced. If this didn't work he would have to figure out another scenario to get the code.

Maybe I should invest in some spy cameras, he thought.

Luckily he was taller than Stacy, and even from a safe distance of a few feet away, he was able to look over her shoulder as she typed in the passcode. Three, five, seven, two, followed by the STAY button. Evrett recited the number in his head over and over. Three, five, seven, two. Three, five, seven, two. He would only get one shot at the keypad.

"I really have to run. But here is my wife's death certificate. Can you please make sure it gets to Judith?"

An expression of pity covered Stacy's face as she took the envelope. Evrett hated to see that look on people's faces when he told them about Sam. He said goodbye to Stacy and left the office.

Three, five, seven, two.

Those four numbers remained imprinted in his mind all week. He didn't even write them down, and as he knelt in the dark in front of the office door, he recited the four digits once more.

While he spoke softly, he worked on the lock. It felt a little different than the one he had practiced on. A jolt of panic shot through his stomach. What if this didn't work? What if he got caught?

A minute passed. Should he have practiced more?

Then he felt the last pin slide up into place. He turned the wrench and the deadbolt clicked.

Step one, complete.

He felt the wall with his hands. It was too dark to see much, but the little red light of the keypad was easily distinguishable from the darkness. Evrett took out his small keychain flashlight.

THREE. FIVE. SEVEN. TWO. STAY. His heart stopped as he hit all five buttons and the red light changed to green.

He couldn't believe it. Step two, complete.

Even if the alarm was disabled, he had to be quick. A nosey neighbor could have seen him enter the office.

The door to Judith's office was locked.

"Shit," he said.

This had not been part of the plan. He used the light to guide the pick into the lock, and after another minute of twisting and pressing, he had this lock undone as well. He was good at this.

Inside the office, Evrett pulled the drawer open. He fingered through the file folders looking for his. There it was, "ECKHARD, EVRETT AND SAMANTHA," written on the tab.

Evrett saw everything as if he was watching it in a movie. It didn't feel real to him. His life had changed so much in such a short span of time. He was a widower, a murderer, and now a burglar. It wasn't his fault the universe had thrust this upon him. What choice did he have? Sam deserved better.

He found the report, which was several pages long. He had no time to read it now, and knew he couldn't take it out of the office. He took his phone and snapped pictures of it page by page. Although he worked quickly, Evrett was careful to get all the text. When the job was finished, he flipped through his photos. He had it.

Evrett retraced his steps. The file, Judith's lock, the alarm and the deadbolt were all returned to the state he found them in. He didn't waste any time once he was out of the building. Evrett sprinted away from Nation Trust.

That night Evrett sat in his bed. He pulled out his tablet and transferred each photo to his other device. With a swipe of his fingers he zoomed in on the text. It was all there.

For a moment Evrett leaned back in his bed. He looked over at the bedside table. A picture of Sam and him in happier times smiled back at him.

It really was another life ago, he thought.

He would never be able to go back. Evrett's life had been changed by the man on the bridge.

And now he was going to find him.

9

HE HAD ALWAYS BEEN A PLANNER. It had been a significant part of his personality from his earliest years. Evrett's mom was fond of telling the story about how every year Evrett laid his clothes and materials out on his bed for the first day of school. Next to the khakis and light blue polo, he placed each binder, folder, pen and pencil. He packed them one by one into his bag, and with a final pull on the zipper, he would know that he was ready for the day ahead.

Evrett had not changed much over the last few decades. Planning was ingrained in his psyche. It was who he was, a fact that came in handy in his line of work. But with the death of his wife, Evrett was suddenly faced with a life he had not planned for. He was bobbing listlessly and felt like he was always behind the current. Sam had been his guidepost and now Evrett found himself stuck.

He had felt so energized the night he broke into Judith Montgomery's office. In the days since that night, he scoured the documents, gathering as much information as he could from the forms.

But now he felt himself hitting a wall.

Evrett stood in his home office. Before him on his drafting table lay everything he had related to the accident. What had once been a list of partial descriptions based on his repeat viewings of the accident video had grown into a cache of names, addresses and testimonies thanks to the police report.

He had most of what he needed to find the eight people connected to the video. But it still wasn't enough. None of the reports mentioned the one thing he desperately wanted to find—the identity of the man on the bridge. Evrett hoped that maybe the targets would remember something if questioned.

But he couldn't just ask them about the man on the bridge without raising suspicion. How could he find what he needed? The thought plagued Evrett like an itch he could never satisfy. He had gained a lot, yet still needed much more.

Whatever his next steps were, Evrett knew they would have to be careful ones. He had acted impulsively when he accidentally killed Harrison, and while that situation seemed to work out in his favor, he could never leave his actions in the hands of fate again.

Taking a moment to glance down at his watch, Evrett saw that it was almost midnight. He needed his rest for work. With a yawn he packed everything back into a large envelope before locking it in his desk drawer and heading to bed.

• • •

Julia Ramberti was a third-year intern at GGM. She was a bright, twenty-four-year-old woman, who was full of potential. There had already been talk amongst the project managers that she would probably be offered a designer position at the completion of her internship. Evrett, who had overseen several of her projects in the last few months, was going to recommend it.

Julia knocked on Evrett's office door before she entered the room and took off her glasses as she began to speak.

"Evrett, I added the expansion schematics to the Elverson plans. Did you want to take a look at them before I send the file to the drafters?"

55

"Sure. Send them to me and I'll give them the once over."

"Thanks, Evrett."

The short exchange was over, but Julia still stood in his office doorway. Evrett sat in his desk chair. He looked up.

"Was there something else you needed, Julia?"

"Actually, some of us were going to head out for a quick lunch. Did you want to come along?"

Evrett put his pencil down.

"Oh, no. I'm fine, Julia. Thanks. I packed today."

"All right. Maybe next time?"

"Sure thing."

He smiled. Julia left having accomplished her polite task. He had almost been back to work for a month now and he had learned that his life was not going to stop simply because Sam's had. Everyone else's life appeared to have gone back to normal. No one tiptoed around him or offered sympathetic nods. It was as if they had all forgotten the nightmare that his July had been.

So Evrett decided to play along.

His days were filled with going to work, meeting with clients, supervising projects and continuing to design. He smiled at coworkers. He even made jokes from time to time. These were the things that had to happen for people to again feel normal around him.

Evrett's personal time was a different story. Any free moment at work that once would have been devoted to calling or texting Sam was now spent thinking about the man on the bridge and Evrett's list of witnesses. He now knew their names by heart.

Phil.

Chase.

Amanda.

Chad.

Andrew.

Sean.

Janine.

Gloria.

Some days he would write them over and over in different orders, always remembering to shred the lists when he was done. He wondered if they felt guilty. He wondered if they thought about Sam and the life she lost. He wondered if they would in fact lead him to the man on the bridge.

The notification for Julia's email brought Evrett's focus back to his office and the task at hand. He tore his most recent list from his yellow legal pad. The buzz of the shredder comforted Evrett as he returned to work.

• • •

On Saturday Evrett went for his usual run. Even though he now ran alone, his Saturday distance runs were still a highlight of his week. As his feet found their rhythm, his mind began to roam freely.

Evrett envisioned the list of names. He said each one to himself, keeping time with his pace. Andrew, Amanda, Chad, Janine, Sean, Gloria, Chase, Phil. They were all standing in a line. As he ran past them, he saw a silhouette a few yards ahead. Evrett couldn't make out anything specific about the figure, but he knew who it was. It was the man on the bridge, and he was only a little bit ahead of Evrett. If he could just get closer, the man would be in reach.

Evrett quickened his pace and pushed onward. He would catch him. He knew he could. It was only a matter of will. Evrett stretched out his arm, his fingers mere inches from the man's shoulder.

The blaring horn of a white Volkswagen startled Evrett. He narrowly missed being clipped by the passing Jetta. His heart was trying to tear itself out of his chest. Evrett paused to catch his breath.

He had lost himself in the run and dream. The application on his phone informed him that he ran seven miles. Evrett swore he just left his front step a few minutes ago. It had seemed so real. With disappointment weighing heavily on his shoulders, Evrett turned to start back home.

When he returned, he grabbed a bottle of water from the refrigerator. As he spun the cap open, his cellphone rang. The screen read "Mom Fielding," Sam's mother. They hadn't spoken in a few weeks. For a moment, Evrett contemplated letting the call go to voicemail. He knew what today was and didn't want to have to share it with anyone else.

At the last moment he slide his finger across the screen and answered the call.

"Hi, Mom."

The words felt like a betrayal now. When they first got married Sam had suggested that Evrett call her parents Mom and Dad. They were his family after all, she would say.

Linda didn't respond right away. Evrett chose not to read too much into the delay.

"Hi, Evrett. How are you?"

"Doing all right. You?"

"It's been hard. But you know that. Especially today. I can't believe she's been gone a month now."

"I know. It doesn't seem possible, really."

"How's work been?"

They made small talk for a few minutes. She filled him in on how the rest of the family was handling the loss of his wife. Sam's older brother Jonas was taking it particularly hard apparently. While Evrett knew her family had also suffered a devastating loss and had known Sam much longer, he couldn't help himself from feeling like no one could be missing her more than he was.

"Evrett, I was wondering if you would mind if James and I came down for a visit in a few days? Maybe next weekend? We'd really like to take a look at some of Sam's stuff. Maybe we could hold on to some of it. If you wouldn't mind."

He thought about the boxes in the basement. There were several containers filled with items and memories from her childhood and life before Evrett. Even though he had no connection to things like her high school yearbooks and other memorabilia, he cringed at the thought of another part of her being taken away from him. Still, they were her parents. They had a right to hold on to the memories of their daughter the best they could.

"No, I understand. That would be fine. Listen, I need to go. I'll see you in a few days?"

"Sure, sure. Take care, Evrett. And thank you."

He walked upstairs to take a much-needed shower, but stopped as he passed the smaller guest bedroom next to the master. Evrett and Sam had talked about converting it into a nursery when the time came. The devastating realization that it would never be a nursery crept into Evrett's head. It was a thought he couldn't stand to deal with today, so he quickly pushed it from the forefront of his mind.

Evrett zeroed in on a row of small leather-bound books displayed on the shelf of a bookcase. They were Sam's journals. She had diligently written in a journal at least three times a week for as long as he knew her. Evrett remembered nights getting ready for bed when he'd look over at Sam scribbling away. She would glance up at him and smile wryly before returning to the page. She never told him he couldn't read them, but Evrett never had. He could read her like an open book; there was no need for him to read her journals as well.

Evrett thumbed through the pages of one of the journals. Without Sam around anymore there was a sudden desire to read every page, to absorb every private thought and comment she had felt the need to commit to paper. He opened to a random page and began to read.

September 19, 2011.

This last weekend was amazing. I would have written sooner, but Evrett and I didn't make it back until late last night. We had quite the weekend.

He paused and thought of the date. It was a week before he had proposed to her. Evrett thought about the moment when he got down on one knee and asked the love of his life to be his wife. They had driven up to Gunpowder Falls State Park to hike and run on one of the wooded trails. He could still feel the nervousness deep in his gut as he pulled the ring out. Sam had thrown her hands to her mouth. Before he could even get the question out, she had said yes.

Did she have a clue he was going to ask her? He read on, learning the private thoughts of his wife.

We took a drive up to see my parents in Timonium on Saturday. Jonas and Cynthia were down as well. Suzanna is getting so big I can't believe it. It was easy to see Mom and Dad enjoyed having the whole family there for dinner. I wish we would actually get together more often. I'll have to work on that.

Evrett was great. I think Dad really likes him. They were in the garage looking at Dad's bike for a while. When they came back they were both laughing about something. I really can't believe these last few months. I haven't even known

Evrett a year yet, but it feels like it's been my whole life. I could really see this going somewhere.

Evrett recalled the conversation he had had with Sam's father in the garage. He swallowed his nerves and asked James Fielding if he could have his daughter's hand in marriage. Evrett had been afraid that since he and Sam had only been seeing each other since March of that year, the talk would have ended with rejection. James had just smiled and placed his hand on Evrett's shoulder.

"I really appreciate you asking me first. It shows character. I like that."

"You're welcome, sir."

"Do you think you can make her happy? Give her everything she deserves and then some? This is my little girl, you know. I won't give my blessing to just anyone."

"I can, sir. I know we haven't been together all that long, but I love her. There is nothing I want to do more than make her happy."

"Well, that makes two of us, son. You've got my blessing."

A pain crept up in the depths of Evrett's stomach. That time was part of a different man's life. It hurt too much to think about those happier days. Evrett closed the book and placed it back on the shelf. Perhaps someday he would read the rest of Sam's journals. Someday, but not yet. He wasn't ready to relive those moments.

10

EVRETT PREPARED FOR FALL. It was the season that held the most memories for him. September was the month he and Sam were engaged. October marked the anniversary of their move into their first, and only, house. Halloween. Thanksgiving. They would all be days Evrett would dread this year.

He somehow managed to survive Sam's birthday in August, and that left hope he could make it through the slew of special memories fall would inevitably yield.

Nevertheless, her birthday was harrowing. She would have been thirty, and Evrett had been planning a huge surprise party. No one knew this, though, as he never had the chance to send out the invites. They remained in a box in his office, and by September, they were forgotten.

As each day came and went, Evrett was surprised how fast time was moving. Work was picking up, and at the end of September, Douglas Graham, one of the senior partners and top department head at GGM, announced his plans to retire in early 2014. This would surely mean shake-ups throughout the company. While the other project managers, department heads and designers all wondered about the reorganizing of positions, Evrett continued to just go about his regular work. The Evrett that had once existed would have placed a promotion directly in his crosshairs, but that Evrett left with his wife. The Evrett that worked at GGM now only did what was required of him.

Ever since he had received the payout of Sam's life insurance policy, it had become harder for him to focus on work. At half a million dollars, the payout afforded him the luxury to stop working for a while. He had considered the option; it certainly would have allowed him time to track down the people on his list. But he wasn't ready for that just yet. He hadn't worked out a plan that felt safe and plausible.

Evrett left work early one Tuesday in mid-October. He drove down to the Inner Harbor and spent some time walking around the large promenade along the water. He saw a flyer advertising the upcoming Halloween Parade and Festival. Last year Sam wanted to attend the event in Patterson Park, but they never made it.

Halloween was going to be difficult. Sam loved the holiday and Evrett hated to turn the porch light off this year. He knew Sam would have wanted him to continue their tradition of handing out candy to trick-or-treaters, but he couldn't bring himself to do it.

As kids in costumes and masks crept door to door, Evrett sat up in his bed. He held the remote with little effort and toggled through the guide on screen. Several channels were dedicated to playing slasher film marathons in honor of the holiday. He clicked on one he had seen before. A group of teenagers trapped on an island were being hunted by a mysterious killer. It would do until he found something better.

Evrett never changed the channel. Although the movie was poorly acted, and despite the fact that he had seen it before and knew the killer would be revealed in a lame twist, he ended up watching the whole thing. As the killer's identity was finally made known, he began to think of his own list.

Gloria, Sean, Janine, Amanda, Phil, Chase, Andrew, Chad. How would he be able to approach them? He needed information from them, but they also needed to pay. Maybe he could disguise himself. Maybe he could approach each person as someone other than himself. But who? What would he say to them? And after they talked, then what? How could he make them pay for their lack of help in Sam's time of need?

Harrison MacLain's crushed and bloody image appeared before Evrett. He recalled the gruesome sight of the man's head and upper body pinned under the collapsed deck. He had gotten away with killing Harrison for one reason: It looked like an accident. And while to some extent it was an accident, it was one that hadn't appeared to involve anyone other than Harrison himself. No one suspected there was any foul play involved. If Evrett was going to be able to make these people pay, and find out what he needed to know, he would have to do so without getting caught. This meant he would have to find a way to repeat Harrison's death. The appearance of an accident would be key. For the first time in weeks, Evrett felt like he was making progress.

On a night in November, Evrett sat in his office. His workbag lay open on the floor next to the desk before him. He should have been checking over some designs Julia had done for him, but instead Evrett trolled the Internet for something that kept pushing the thought of work far from his mind.

With the Web browser open he typed in his search: "Different ways to die."

As morbid as the subject matter was, he apparently was not the only one with an interest in the topic. There were 250,000,000 results that came back within seconds of his search. Page after page of websites and YouTube videos, television shows and books littered his laptop screen. Some pages were oddly humorous accounts of ironic deaths while others leaned more toward the macabre.

Evrett clicked on a link that led him to a page that listed several ways one was likely to die. He learned that a person is more likely to die from a hernia than the accidental firing of a gun. The statistic made him smile. He chuckled to himself, an act that brought his attention to the present moment he found himself in.

Sam had died almost four months ago and he couldn't remember the last time he laughed.

Evrett continued looking at the different results, making sure he wasn't typing in anything that would be too incriminating. Most of the resulting sites listed bizarre accidents that would be nearly impossible to recreate. It was clear to him that if he did intend to harm the people who let his wife die, it would involve a lot of planning specifically related to each person. Again Evrett felt he was hitting a roadblock.

At 10:52, Evrett looked at the clock in the corner of the screen. He had spent nearly four hours paging through blogs and show clips. The files from Julia still sat untouched in his documents folder. He closed the browser and finally got to work on the designs for GGM.

• • •

Once they were engaged, Sam and Evrett alternated their holiday visits between their two families. Thanksgiving would be spent with the Fieldings followed by Christmas with the Eckhards. The following year they would switch holidays. They used to joke on the drives that when they did get around to having a child they would never leave their house on a holiday. If the relatives wanted to see them, they would all have to come to Hampden.

This Thanksgiving posed a dilemma for Evrett. This would have been their year to spend the day with Sam's family. They would have then traveled to Pennsylvania over the weekend to see his parents and sister's family. But without Sam, Evrett didn't know what to do.

Linda had called him two weeks before Thanksgiving. He hadn't answered or returned the call. A week later, his own mother phoned.

"Evrett, honey, we need to talk about Thanksgiving."

He always appreciated his mother's directness.

"I know, Mom."

"Have you given any thought to what you were going to do? I know that this was supposed to be Sam's year. Have you spoken to Linda about it?"

"Actually no. She left me a message. She said I'm obviously still welcome to come. In fact, she said they hoped I would be able to make it."

"Well, I want you to know that whatever you decide to do, Dad and I support your decision. We are fine having the two dinners like we've done in the past."

"I appreciate that."

"You just have to let us know so I can tell Molly what to do."

"Okay, I really should go to Jim and Linda's. Sam would have wanted it I think."

"All right, hon. Why don't you give Linda a call then."

"Sure thing, Mom. Love you."

So Evrett made the call and the eventual drive to Timonium. He hadn't been with Sam's whole family since the funeral. His stomach was uneasy as he pulled in front of the Fieldings' house.

You can do this.

His hands tightened around the steering wheel. Evrett peered out the windshield of his car. He took a few deep breaths before his hand found the door handle. With one final, meditative breath, he exited the vehicle.

Evrett stood on the front porch with a pumpkin pie. Sam always brought it to their Thanksgivings and he didn't want this year to be any different. He was comfortable enough with his in-laws that he didn't have to wait for them to open the door. Still, Evrett paused before making his presence known at the party. Behind the large grey shut door waited a full room of aunts, uncles and cousins, a family tree that would immediately be reminded of their shared loss by his presence.

He reached for the knob as the door flew open.

"I thought I heard a car pull up," Jonas said. "Hi, Evrett. Come in. The turkey's almost done."

Evrett followed his brother-in-law through the small hallway and into the kitchen. He could see the rest of the family in the dining room. They hadn't noticed his arrival yet.

"I made Sam's pie. I figured everyone would miss it. I hope it tastes as good as if she made it."

Jonas took the dessert from Evrett's hands and both men stood silent together. They avoided each other's eyes as they looked down at the pie.

"Wow, I…" Jonas paused.

He was a tall man in his early forties. Although there had been a large gap in age between the siblings, Jonas and Sam were close in their adult life. His voice cracked as he set the pumpkin pie down.

"I still can't believe she's gone, Evrett. It's just not fair, you know? Damn it," he said and wiped his hand over his eyes.

"I know."

Evrett couldn't think of anything else to say. He didn't really know how to comfort someone else in this situation. He was not used to being on the other end of the conversation in regards to Sam. He hoped the rest of the afternoon did not go in a similar direction.

"Okay, okay. Let's go say hi to the rest of the family. Everyone is looking forward to seeing you. I know Suzanna was really glad you were coming. What have you been up to these last few weeks?"

Evrett didn't get the opportunity to fully answer Jonas's question. He was bombarded by the rest of the family as they came up and greeted him one by one. His nervousness about dinner started to subside.

He sat next to his niece Suzanna during the meal. Evrett talked to her about junior high and how camp had been in the summer. Suzanna had taken an immediate liking to Evrett when he started coming to family get-togethers with Sam.

When dinner was over, most of the extended family left the Fieldings' home, leaving Evrett with Sam's parents, Jonas, Cynthia and Suzanna. Jonas and Evrett sat at the kitchen table while the rest of the family watched football in the living room.

Evrett ate the remaining bite of pie on his plate and took a sip of his Bailey's on the rocks.

"This year sure was different," Jonas said, calling attention to the elephant in the room.

"Yeah, it was," Evrett said, slowly. "I really want to thank you guys for still including me."

"Evrett, don't be silly. You're still part of this family. Sam loved you. You're welcome in this family as long as you want to be."

"Thanks," Evrett said.

Jonas raised his glass and cheersed.

"Evrett, I probably shouldn't bring this up. I had been debating about calling you up before. But there never seemed to be a right time to talk to you about it. About what happened."

Evrett felt his chest tighten. He had a feeling where this might be going. He managed to make it through most of the day without any one asking him about the accident or Sam. If only he had left with the rest of the family.

"And I don't mean to bring this up to depress you, but she was my little sister. I only know what the news said about the accident, and some of the bits and pieces Mom mentioned."

"I really don't know what else there is to tell you."

Evrett hoped his attempt at evading would force Jonas to realize how hard this was for Evrett. He had kept himself together for the whole day. Now he felt himself starting to unravel.

"Mom said you were on the phone with Sam when it happened."

Evrett tilted his glass and watched the thick brown liquid rise and fall.

"Yeah, she left work early that day and called me."

Evrett shifted in his chair. There was an awkward silence between the men. Perhaps Jonas had realized he was making Evrett uncomfortable. He began to steer the conversation in a different direction.

"Sam was always such a safe driver. Especially after high school. A friend of hers was in a bad accident their senior year. Sam was always extra cautious behind the wheel after that."

Evrett gulped the rest of his drink down and stood up.

"Look, I'm sorry, Evrett. We don't need to talk about it. I don't want to upset you."

"It's okay. I really need to be going anyway."

"Ah, shit, Evrett. I'm sorry. I don't know what I was thinking. I should have just kept my mouth shut. Today… Today wasn't the day to do this. I just get… I just get so angry when I think about it. You know? I think about that damn video that douchebag posted of the accident and it makes me sick to think those people all just watched."

Evrett began to feel trapped. He wanted so badly for today to go well, and it had until now. He knew Jonas meant well, and that he hurt, too, but hearing this made him feel as if he was wearing a tight collar he couldn't unbutton.

Jonas's voice rose in anger.

"Those people should have been put on trial or something. I get it was dangerous. But you mean to tell me none of them could have gotten her out? Not even the driver? Those people have to live with what they did. I hope it keeps them up at night. I really do!"

"Jonas!"

Linda stood in the entryway to the kitchen. Her hands shook and her eyes were wide. She glared at her son.

"Jonas, calm down. What were you thinking, talking about this?"

"Dammit. I'm sorry, Evrett. I'm… I just…" Jonas said.

He cupped his face in his hands.

"I need to leave. Thank you, Linda, I mean, Mom… I need to go."

Evrett grabbed his coat from the closet and hurried out of the house. He saw Linda standing at the front door as he pulled away.

Evrett drove home fast. He was a mess of emotions. There were no words to describe the combination of anger and sadness he felt, so Evrett did the only thing he could do in the moment. He screamed. It was a scream that started in the deepest depths of his chest and seethed out of him.

How dare he talk to me about that? It's Thanksgiving? If I could hold it together for one day—one damn day—why couldn't he?

As he neared home, he replayed the conversation over and over.

"I just get so angry," he recalled Jonas saying. "That damn video…makes me sick…those people all just watched.

Those people. Chad. Andrew. Sean. Janine. Amanda. Gloria. Phil. Chase.

There they were. Their inaction had not just let his wife die, but it had sent ripples through her entire family. The sight of Jonas, his face covered by his hands, flashed in Evrett's head.

As angry as he was, he agreed with his brother-in-law. They were disgusting people. Especially the one who filmed it and posted his wife's final minutes for the world to gawk at.

He went home and prepared to find Chase Valenti.

11

HE SAT IN THE CAR watching and waiting. Evrett barely recognized the man he saw in the rearview mirror. The beard he had been growing over the last few weeks was coming in nicely; however, it was still rather itchy. He ran his fingers over the hairs underneath his chin and repositioned himself in the seat of his car. It was cold in Cleveland.

Evrett took a sip of his coffee and wrapped his hands tightly around the thermos. By now the coffee couldn't even be considered lukewarm. Still, his hands were warmed slightly by the steel mug he had filled at the gas station earlier that afternoon.

It was a few minutes after seven and the sky above the suburban houses was black. Evrett yawned and looked at his watch. He had been sitting and waiting for three hours now. He hoped the man he was waiting for would emerge from the house soon. It had been a long two months getting to Chase's door.

Evrett thought about what it had taken to get here. The beard

69

was just one small step on his path to tracking down Chase. In the days after Thanksgiving, Evrett began his search. It wasn't terribly hard for him to find a starting point. Sitting in his home office, Evrett returned to the video. He watched it again, this time with the sole focus of learning all he could about the man behind the camera.

The clip itself did not offer much information related to Chase. Instead, Evrett saw what he had seen that evening so many months ago.

With the clip fresh in his memory, Evrett continued to dig. The media had done most of the work for him. In the days that followed the accident, the video went viral and spread across the social and media networks, carrying with it a vague description of the "Johns Hopkins student" who captured the tragic events as they unfolded. Clicking through links, Evrett made his way to Chase's YouTube channel. It was there that Chase posted the video that had been shared on so many other pages.

While the video of the accident was by far the most viewed, there were a few other videos listed on Chase's channel that Evrett watched. Most of them were short clips of Chase and his friends goofing around. Some must have been from when Chase was in high school. A few more recent videos showed Chase playing lacrosse. He wore a light blue jersey. It was apparent he had been on the Johns Hopkins' varsity squad.

Evrett stopped to watch a video dated October of 2012. It was only a minute long and began with Chase and a few friends sitting on a porch stoop. From the look of the building it was a brick row home somewhere in town. Chase and several of his friends were wearing Hopkins Blue Jays T-shirts. As the timer scrolled left to right underneath the video, Evrett watched Chase, with beer in hand, get up on a bench in front of the house and act as if he was surfing. Whoever was holding the camera laughed, and the shaking resulting in a blurred image. When the video refocused, Chase stumbled and landed on the ground with his beer shattering on the sidewalk.

"Party foul!" cried someone off camera.

Chase slowly stood back up and stumbled on the sidewalk. Evrett quickly paused the clip. Over Chase's shoulder, a house number was visible: 3007.

It was a start.

Finding all the houses with the number 3007 proved no hassle for Evrett. A simple Google search using the number and "Maryland" provided him a list of all the homes in the state with 3007 at the beginning of their address. Clicking on maps allowed him to even see the location of many, right down to the street view.

The wonders of technology, he thought.

By the end of the night, he found a match—a townhome a few miles away in Canton.

Planning his next move proved a bit harder. Evrett spent the weekend after Thanksgiving with his family out of state. It was a much better visit than the one he had experienced at the Fieldings'. Seeing his parents and sister was comforting. He even chose to spend the night and came home late in the day Sunday. But it was now December, and there would only be a few short weeks until the semester ended. If he didn't find some way to confront Chase, he might miss his opportunity for the year.

Work was quiet on Monday. Several employees had extended the holiday and would be back to work on Tuesday. Evrett took the day as an opportunity to get some work done without being bothered by any distractions. While he worked he let his mind deliberate about Chase.

Aside from knowing he played lacrosse and went to Johns Hopkins, there was very little that Evrett really knew. He had a hunch the college student lived in an off-campus apartment in Canton, but it could also have been a friend's party Chase had attended. Either way, it was a lead that would hopefully allow Evrett to track him down.

Part of Evrett wanted to rush out of work and drive to the house. He would knock on the door, ask for Chase, and soon be face to face with one of the people who had done nothing to save Sam. Would Evrett tell him who he was? Would Chase then apologize for his inaction? Would he know anything about the man on the bridge?

No. It couldn't go down like that. Evrett couldn't allow Chase to know who he was. He couldn't give up that control.

Once again Evrett caught himself doodling on some papers.

He had been staring out the window while his mind wandered and his hand drew. Looking down at the series of squiggles and shapes, Evrett saw he had drawn a bird. *A blue jay,* he thought.

An idea sprung up in his mind. *Lacrosse.* Somehow he knew he could use this to his advantage. He crumpled up the paper and tossed it into the trash. By the end of the week, he would be at Chase's door.

Evrett left work early on Thursday. The cold December air had settled in over Baltimore. The Inner Harbor was decorated and ready for the holiday season. In his car, Evrett changed out of his suit and into a pair of light khakis and a Nike polo and jacket. The traffic heading down Boston Street wasn't too bad yet. It had been smart to leave before the rush.

He liked Canton. It was an interesting and mixed part of the city. He remembered coming to eat at a few of the restaurants and pie shops in the area with Sam. His nervousness did not allow for much reminiscing today. It wasn't long before he parallel parked his car on a side street a block from his destination.

After a short walk, Evrett stood before a black door with the number 3007 posted on the light grey brick of the townhouse. Three knocks later, the door opened.

"Hello? Who are you?" asked a man in his early twenties. He was dressed in a dark hoodie and a pair of baggy sweat pants.

"Hello, I'm looking for a," Evrett hesitated on purpose, glancing at the note in his hand, then adding, "Chase Valenti."

"What do you want with Chase?"

Evrett's heart thumped loudly in his ears. Suddenly, he was truly aware of where he was and what he was doing. There was no turning back now.

"Well, I'm here to speak with him about a great opportunity. My name is Alex Monroe and I represent a lacrosse camp out in Essex. Is Chase here?"

Evrett tried to act naturally. He worried that he was speaking too quickly.

"Nah, Chase moved out a few months ago."

"He… He moved?"

"Yeah. Kid dropped out. You know he got kicked off the team, right?"

"Uh, no. Well, that's okay…"

Evrett could care less about Chase's lacrosse record. He had to turn the conversation back to where Chase was. The college kid in the doorway tucked his hands inside the pouch of his sweatshirt. Evrett wouldn't have his attention much longer, not in this cold.

"I'd still like to talk to him. Do you know how I could get a hold of him? Is he still in the area?"

"Nope, Chase moved back home to Cleveland. Last I heard he was crashing back home with his mom."

"Cleveland? Do you have a phone number?"

"I had his cell, but the last I heard, his phone was shut off or something."

It looked like it would take Evrett a bit more work to track down Chase. He had never been to Cleveland before. It would be much harder to track down the right Valenti family in a city several states away.

"You know, hold on a sec," the young man said as he retreated into the house. He shut the door quickly in Evrett's face. Standing on the stoop, Evrett realized just how cold it was.

The door reopened and the same hoodie and sweat pants held out a folded piece of paper.

"I remember he left a forwarding address. He moved out at the end of July before the lease was up. He wanted us to send him a re-fund for his portion of the rent. We never did get around to doing that," the man said, with a laugh.

Evrett took the paper in his hands. Could it really be this easy?

"Thank you. I really appreciate it."

"It's nothing. It better be some opportunity, if you expect to get him back to Maryland."

"I think it will be worth his while to consider what we have to offer. Thanks again."

Once Evrett was back in his car, he unfolded the paper and read the address. It appeared to have been scribbled down in haste, but the number and letters were legible. Evrett smiled as he made the return drive home; yet another step closer.

As much as Evrett wanted to leave for Cleveland that night, the responsibilities of work and the Christmas season overtook him. While the year wound down, his workload increased. It was always hard to get in touch with clients and other managers over the holidays, so whatever could be done was done. Meanwhile, Linda had called to invite Evrett to Christmas. He was relieved when he could tell her that he would be spending the actual holiday with his family. It would be one less headache.

In past years, Sam and Evrett would have set up their tree and decorated it over the first weekend of December. They would have hung garland and lights around their porch railing and placed a wreath on the front door. But Evrett skipped the festivities this year. Whatever shopping he had to complete before heading up to Pennsylvania he had done online. One by one the packages would appear on his doorstep. Whenever possible, he would even order them already gift-wrapped.

He began to get anxious about finding Chase. A trip to Cleveland would require at least a few days. He would need to find somewhere to stay as well. Evrett decided he would book a hotel room a county or two over from the address Chase's roommate had given him. He would wait until the middle of the month to avoid the possibility that the Valenti's visited family over the holidays.

The winter months are the worst time to be without a loved one. Everything that once excited Evrett about the season now reminded him of what was missing from his life. Thanksgiving, Christmas, New Year's Eve. Three big holidays in a row that were all about celebrating with family and lovers. Evrett had never dreaded them before, and didn't like that he did now.

But once New Year's had passed, Evrett made his arrangements. He informed the office that he would be taking a half a week off, and just a few days after the sixth-month anniversary of Sam's accident, Evrett got in his car and drove. About six hours later he was in Cleveland, parked just a couple spaces up from the Valenti house.

Sitting in his car, holding his coffee, Evrett thought about his next steps. He had yet to see Chase in person. Evrett kept a folder with a printed picture of Chase on the passenger seat. Evrett knew if

Chase would exit his house, he would recognize him.

The Valenti house was an average size craftsman home. A white Subaru was parked in the driveway. Evrett could tell that someone was home from the light pouring through the living room curtains.

"Come on," he said.

As he stared across the street, Evrett began to wonder what he was going to do with Chase once he found him. He needed to talk to him about the man on the bridge. He'd have to get Chase alone and perhaps comfortable enough to talk. Once Evrett was satisfied with the information Chase had to offer, then he would…

That was the tricky part.

He knew what he wanted to do. He wanted to make Chase pay, the same way that Harrison had. The long lonely drive to Cleveland had given Evrett plenty of time to come to terms with the idea that he was coming to do more than just talk with Chase. Still, the dilemma of exactly how to do it puzzled him. If he could get Chase out on Lake Erie, perhaps he could orchestrate some sort of boating accident.

It was during these malicious thoughts that the door to the Valenti house opened. The porch light was on, and even though Evrett was several car lengths away from the house, he immediately recognized the individual stepping out into the cold.

"There you are."

Chase wore a large insulated black coat. He breathed into his hands to keep them warm and looked from side to side. Evrett was so fixated on seeing Chase that he didn't notice the black LR4 pass by him. The vehicle parked in front of the Valentis' driveway. Chase nodded and hopped in the passenger side.

"Where are you heading?" Evrett asked as he put his car in drive and pulled out into the street.

Evrett relied upon a lifetime of movie memories as he trailed the dark colored Land Rover. He was careful to stay a couple car lengths behind it to avoid drawing any unwanted attention. One benefit Evrett had was the darkness that came with January evenings. Even if Chase was looking in the side mirror, it would be hard for him to distinguish Evrett's black A4 from any other car on the busy streets of Cleveland.

While following Chase and the mystery driver, Evrett noticed that the sections of Cleveland they were driving through were beginning to get a little more impoverished. With a few cars in between them now, Evrett almost missed the right turn the SUV made. He did his best to catch up.

The first stop they made was at a gas station, followed by a fast food restaurant. With each location, Evrett was sure to either keep driving or pull into another lot. Judging by Chase's body language at each place, he was unaware that Evrett was following him.

The excitement of the chase was causing Evrett's confidence to grow. Even if he couldn't get Chase alone tonight, learning everything he could about the man's life would surely help him in his path to revenge.

After an hour of stopping and driving, Evrett followed the Land Rover down the Garfield Parkway. Chase's vehicle made a quick left into a parking lot. Evrett was careful to keep driving, making no signs of turning into the lot. As he passed by, he noticed a small wooden sign that read GARFIELD PARK RESERVATION.

What could he possibly be doing at a park this late at night?

Evrett kept checking his rearview mirror to make sure he didn't miss the Land Rover. When he felt he was at a safe distance, he turned his Audi around in a driveway and doubled back toward the park entrance now with his headlights off. The parking lot was dark and he could just barely see the vehicle sitting at the back end.

As he drove closer, he saw there was another car next to the LR4. It was a blue Jetta. Both cars were turned off and it looked as if no one was inside them. Evrett looped around the lot and pulled in a few spots away from the two vehicles. There was a small trail that led into the woods.

Evrett considered what to do next. What would have brought Chase and his friends to a park long after it had closed? He thought back to when he was young, and remembered how some kids would hang out in parks and the woods to get high or drunk. Evrett recalled the video that had sent him to the townhouse in Canton. Maybe living at home had put a damper on Chase's partying.

Evrett rolled down his window and listened. The night had the stillness of a winter snow. All he heard was the muffled sound of cars in the distance. Chase couldn't have been too far onto the trail. Evrett got out of his car and began walking toward the woods.

The sound of laughter caught his attention. Evrett could tell that it was coming from somewhere on his left. He turned and looked out in the darkness. Down the path that cut through the trees, Evrett could see the glow of cellphones and flashlights. Not wanting to be noticed, Evrett stepped off of the path and farther into the trees.

With every step the sounds of the group of men became more distinct. Soon he could see there were four men all together. They stood around in a circle. Every few seconds one would move toward the center and then back out. This pattern continued over and over again.

"What the hell?" Evrett whispered.

It looked like a dance. The light from the phones rose and fell with the movement of the men. When Evrett was about twenty yards away and his eyes had totally adjusted, it became clear what was happening.

"That's the last time you fuck with us!" one of the men shouted.

Evrett could see him step forward and kick a fifth person who was lying on the ground. The fifth body shuddered as the kicker's foot made contact with its side. Evrett could hear a gasp for air between each kick.

"Come on, Jerome. Teach this bitch a lesson."

Evrett squinted into the darkness. The flashlights created a sinister glow on the faces of the men. It was then that he saw Chase step forward. Another man handed him a bat.

"Nah, Chase is gonna be the one to show this punk who's boss."

Chase took the bat from Jerome's hands and stood over the man who by now had tucked his knees close to his chest for protection.

Chase squatted next to him and placed the butt of the bat under the man's chin. He lifted his head up so he could look at Chase's face.

Evrett could see him whisper something to the man, but the distance between them got in the way. Chase stood up, took a step back and swung the bat down. The sound of wood cracking bone echoed in the night. Evrett jumped back as Chase brought the bat down a second time.

What was Evrett doing? What had he stumbled upon? Fear stiffened him. He never had imagined that he would be up against anything like this. The realization that he was outnumbered and unarmed took hold of his every sense. He had to get out of there.

Evrett took off. He knew he had to get back to his car before anyone from the other two vehicles made it back to the lot. As he ran, he could hear the sound of his feet crunching leaves and sticks below him.

"Hey! Someone's here!"

"Shit!"

Evrett knew the group of men had heard him. He only had seconds now to make it into his car and get away. Survival was all that mattered to him right now. The cars became visible as Evrett exited the woods. He quickly glanced behind him and could see several dark shadows running up the trail in his direction.

He pulled out his fob and pressed the unlock button. The interior lights of the Audi lit up, signaling that it was open. Evrett rounded the car and opened the door. As he placed the key in the ignition, he looked toward the entrance of the trail. The men were almost to the lot. Evrett floored the gas, sending the car speeding toward the road. His back tires kicked up small cinders and dirt creating a foggy cloud that shielded his car from Chase as he reached the lot. All they could see was the glow of red lights dissipating as the car sped away.

Without slowing down, he drove back onto the main road and away from the parking lot. Evrett kept checking his rearview mirror for headlights. He didn't stop, taking turn after turn for what seemed like hours until he was on the other side of Cleveland looking out at the stillness of Lake Erie.

He constantly checked over his shoulder, making sure Chase and his crew had not followed him. He watched his breath rise up into the air.

How could he have been so foolish? He hadn't brought a weapon with him, not even a knife. He had thought about finding Chase for weeks, and in one night almost threw it all away. Getting himself killed wouldn't make any of them pay, nor would it help Sam. Evrett slammed his fists against the dashboard and screamed. It was a sound filled with anger, rage and resentment.

His time in Cleveland was a failure. He played the evening over in his mind the entire drive back to Baltimore. He was ashamed to admit how ill-prepared he had been going into the evening. It could have been the end of everything. His search for the man on the bridge almost ended before it had even begun.

Finally, he was back home in his office. Although Cleveland was hours behind him now, the adrenaline was coursing through his body. The sun would soon be coming up, but it didn't matter to Evrett.

He pulled everything out and spread it across his drafting table. Pictures, maps, notes, Evrett scanned them all. Gloria, Amanda, Janine, Sean, Andrew, Chad, Phil, and Chase.

Certainly not every witness on his list would pose as much of a threat as Chase. He had underestimated him. It was a mistake he would not make again. Evrett began to scribble notes down on a piece of yellow legal pad. He didn't know how long it would take him, but he knew someday he would be fully prepared to do what he had to do. Revenge and the man on the bridge would be his.

12

THE LIGHTS OF THE AQUARIUM and World Trade Center Institute painted the surface of the water. Evrett stood by the railing of the balcony, watching the lights dance on the small waves. The harbor was calm tonight and his mind was elsewhere.

He wasn't the only one on the balcony tonight. All of the employees of GGM had gathered to celebrate the retirement of Douglas Graham at a seafood restaurant right on the edge of the harbor's south end. After dinner, Evrett had stepped outside in the cool April air. The salt of the bay filled his lungs.

"Enjoying yourself?" Julia asked.

She placed her high heel on the railing and leaned over. A slight breeze met her face and sent her brown curls a flutter.

"Sure, the dinner was awesome," Evrett said.

"Apparently GGM spares no expense."

"It's not everyday one of its founding fathers signs off. Congratulations on the new position, by the way."

"Thanks. To be honest, I'm just so relieved. I did not want to look for a new firm."

"Nah, they would have never let you go."

A brief silence fell between them. Even though Julia had worked at the firm for three years now, Evrett didn't know much about her. He knew she was a hard worker, lived in an apartment near Little Italy and had a pet Chihuahua named Jack. Julia had several pictures of the little dog spread around her cubical—what used to be her cubical now that she was promoted to a permanent position at the firm.

"Have you heard about your request to work at home?" Julia asked.

Evrett turned away from the Baltimore skyline. Julia's question took him by surprise. He should have known word would spread across the company. He had put in the request to do more work at home two weeks ago.

It was a decision Evrett made the night he returned from Cleveland. He needed to be able to focus more time and energy on his plan. First, he had to complete a few projects before he could put in the request. With those projects behind him and the reorganization of the firm after Graham's departure, April proved to be the month Evrett could finally submit the request. Now he just had to wait to see if he would get the approval he needed.

"Nope. Not yet, but I'm sure it won't be long once things settle down. The office has been crazy with Doug's retirement."

"I know. It will be weird when the dust finally settles."

Talking to Julia was nice. Besides family, Julia was the only person he talked to on a regular basis. Every now and then he would get a call from one of his or Sam's friends, but he hadn't been out with anyone in the last few months. If it wasn't work related, Evrett would have thrown the invitation for the retirement party in the trash and never given it a second thought.

But he had to make an appearance, and as much as he'd rather be back home, he was here and could at least tolerate talking with Julia.

Sam would have liked her.

"So how are things going with you, Evrett? I keep inviting you out, but you always turn me down. I'm going to develop a complex pretty soon."

He chuckled.

She smiled and swirled the glass of pinot noir she was holding. Evrett watched her bring the wine to her lips.

Julia was attractive. Evrett had no problem admitting this. At five-foot-seven and with the help of three-inch heels, she stood at eye-level with Evrett. Her eyes were the color of coffee with a little too much cream, Evrett thought, noticing them for the first time. They complemented her hair, which was usually flat and lay around her shoulders, but with the curls, it came to dangle a few inches higher, exposing the fair skin of her neck. She wore a dark royal blue sleeveless cocktail dress, cut at the knees, and accentuated the fact that she went to the gym a few times a week.

Evrett wondered if she ran.

"Things are okay," he said. "I've just been putting my mind in my work."

"You work too much, Evrett. I guess it will be a good thing that you will be working from home."

"Hopefully."

"I'll miss seeing you though. I'll never get you to go out for lunch if you aren't even coming in the office anymore."

Evrett recognized the playfulness in her voice. He was surprised by her flirtatious manner, a result perhaps, of the several glasses of wine Julia had enjoyed throughout the meal.

"I'll still be coming in, don't worry."

"I know. I know. I just really like talking to you, Evrett. You are a good guy. Definitely one of GGM's best."

He smiled and downed his fourth glass of wine. He enjoyed the compliment.

"Come on now. Thanks."

"You really do need to come out sometime. I worry about you."

"You worry?"

She nodded.

Evrett looked at Julia in the nighttime glow. The subtle way her hair framed her face reminded him of his wife.

"I have to get going. Early day tomorrow."

"Evrett?"

"I'll see you Monday."

He didn't wait to hear Julia's response. The thought of Sam had sobered him up, making him completely aware of the moment. While it was nice to feel Julia's attention, at evening's end, all he felt was longing for the touch of his wife.

• • •

By late June everything was set and Evrett was working from home. Depending on the week he would spend two to three days commuting to the office. The other days, he would wake up and do what work needed to be done from the comfort of his home.

When necessary he would contact Julia. She was always willing to help be a liaison for him in the office. Evrett knew he could rely on her.

The shift to working from home allowed him to begin tackling his greater challenge. Step one on his path to the man on the bridge was accomplished. Now he had moved on to the collection phase.

Evrett would have to find each one of his targets. He had to watch them and learn all he could about their lives. That way, he could find the perfect way to make them pay. It was settled. He would have to end the life of each person on his list.

Evrett had wrestled with the thought of revenge for some time. There was no easy solution to his problem. Each person, each target, had played a role in his wife's death. Their choice to not help her in her most desperate moments had sealed their fates. And as far as he was concerned, they each had been living on borrowed time for nearly a year now. It was time for them to pay for what they did to his wife and his world.

The tricky part in Evrett's plan was how he would be able to complete his mission. His involvement in Harrison's death had gone unnoticed for one main reason; it had appeared to be an accident. If Evrett wanted to remain undetected, he would have to find a way to "accidentally" make each target suffer the same fate. To get there, he needed tools.

He had been searching online for ways to spy on people. While always being careful to not search for anything too suspicious, Evrett had amassed a lengthy list of items he would need on his journey.

First up was a new laptop. Part of the process would be to get to know the lives of his prey. A laptop with audio software would be a must. He added to his collection a new camera, wireless mics and a few GPS car trackers. He bought five, just to be safe.

Evrett laid his purchases out in front of him as the air conditioner worked overtime due to the excessive summer heat. He was thankful he didn't have to leave the house today. He crossed items off of his checklist knowing he still would have to buy some more necessities soon.

As he began packing up for the night, Evrett gazed around the room. A few months ago, this former bedroom had been his home office. His desk and drafting table had served to help him complete several award-winning design projects. He remembered how some nights he would work until midnight on redesigns and Sam would come in with a coffee or snack and drape her arms around him. She'd kiss his neck and offer words of encouragement.

This room now served a different purpose. It would be where he did his new work—his private work.

These thoughts reminded him he had to email a few coworkers. As he typed a couple of messages on his laptop, he wondered what things would be like when he finally put his plan in motion and began hunting down his targets. Maybe he would even have to quit GGM altogether. But that was a thought he would deal with on another day.

Once the emails were sent, he closed his laptop and headed for the door. Evrett took one last look into his office. His equipment was organized and ready. He smiled, turned off the light and closed the door. Before heading down the hall, Evrett pulled out a key from his pocket and locked the door to the room. His office and all it contained was his and his alone.

Well, his and Sam's.

Evrett tested the lock one last time and walked down the hall to get some sleep.

• • •

Evrett sat on his back porch, sipping a glass of Sauvignon Blanc. An early evening thunderstorm broke the oppressive July heat. If it had been any other day, Evrett may have felt the relief that he was sure many of his neighbors felt.

Instead he imagined the heat that Sam had felt a year ago on this day.

The last few months had seemed to vanish. He thought back to one of the last nights he and Sam had shared together.

It was around Memorial Day, he couldn't remember what day exactly. It was a Friday night and they both had finished particularly daunting weeks at work. After dinner—rigatoni in homemade pepperoni sauce, one of Sam's specialties—the couple retired to the back porch, wine glasses in hand.

"Evrett, I think we should plan a trip."

Sam sat on one of their patio chairs. Her legs were draped over one another and she lazily held her wine glass.

"Oh yeah? Where to?"

"I don't know. We could go in the fall. Maybe somewhere up north?"

He sipped his wine and looked at his wife.

"What about the Finger Lakes? We could stay at a 'B' and 'B'."

"That would be great. We could go in early November. The trees might still have leaves at that point."

"Then it's decided. Let's look into making a reservation."

As he finished his glass of wine, Evrett let the memory slip from his grasp. They never made that trip, nor did they make the reservation in the first place. They lived life like they had a thousand tomorrows.

God, he missed her.

As Evrett walked up the stairs toward his waiting, empty bed, he stopped in the hallway by his office. In the darkness of the room he could just barely see the outline of his desk with his materials laid out.

He leaned against the wall and placed his head on the doorframe. Finishing a bottle of wine may not have been a good idea. He closed his eyes and tried to clear his mind.

It was then that the man on the bridge popped back into view.

Somewhere, perhaps only a few miles away, he was wrapping up his evening. Maybe he was tucking his child into bed, or out to dinner with friends, or enjoying a nice quiet night with his wife.

"Live it up," Evrett said into the dark room. "I'll find you soon."

Evrett slowly continued on into his room.

"Soon."

• • •

By October, Evrett had all the essentials on his list. Crossing off the last item filled him with a drive to get started; however, he knew that there was still much planning and organizing to be done.

While he accumulated the rest of his items, he also zeroed in on the current locations of each person on his list. It hadn't been terribly difficult to find them all. With the phone numbers, addresses and license plate numbers he gained from the police report, Evrett only needed to make a few calls to each residence. Pretending to be a doctor's office or telemarketer allowed him to ask for each person by name. With their most current whereabouts in check, Evrett had his starting points.

On weekends he began driving, learning the routes that would take him to the houses of the people on his list. Some were close by, still residing in the area around Baltimore; others were farther away, like Chase Valenti. No matter what, though, Evrett was careful not to meet or see any of the witnesses. He didn't want another fiasco like in Cleveland.

One crisp Saturday, Evrett woke up and went for his run. He followed the usual route. With each passing step, Evrett began to plan his next drive. Evrett had to stop at an intersection and wait for the traffic light to change. As he jogged in place he looked at homes around him. A few had mums on their porches, while others had pumpkins. Halloween was only a few days away. He hadn't given much thought to the holiday this year. It actually shocked him to realize how soon it would be here.

The light changed and Evrett continued on his run. Later that day, instead of taking another drive, Evrett bought a pumpkin, carved it and set it out on his front porch.

Sam would have been happy, he thought.

• • •

In November, just before Thanksgiving, Evrett went into work. There were a few things he needed to take care of before the office closed for the holiday.

When Evrett started working at home he thought for sure it would make coming to work even harder. Surprisingly, he found he didn't mind it nearly as much as before. Rather than being a piece of furniture in the office, always present and unnoticed, he drew attention and warm greetings whenever he would come in. It wasn't that bad, having the attention of his coworkers every now and then.

As he finished up for the day, Evrett walked down to Julia's office. He knocked on her door. She looked up from her desk.

"Hey, Evrett. I didn't know you were coming in today."

"I just had to drop some paperwork off in person. How have things been around here lately?"

"Oh, you know. Same old, same old. How's life in P-Js been treating you?"

"Come on. You know I do actually get dressed even though I'm working from home."

"Yeah, okay. You know if I had that luxury, I'd be in fuzzy bunny slippers all day long. It sure would beat these damn heels."

Evrett laughed.

By now he considered Julia a friend. When it began, it was weird for him to allow her in his life. It wasn't until late in the summer when he finally took her up on her standing offer to get lunch. They grabbed a couple of hot dogs from a food cart that parked near the office and talked for about an hour. Evrett had enjoyed it.

Since then, he and Julia had grabbed lunch a few more times when he would come in to work from the office. Today he had come in late and missed the lunch hour.

"Are you seeing your family for Thanksgiving?" Julia asked.

Evrett thought back to the Thanksgiving disaster from the previous year. Almost a year later, he looked back at the evening with a new set of eyes. If it hadn't been for Sam's brother, Evrett might not have rushed after Chase and would not be ready to truly begin his mission. It was funny how life worked out.

"Yeah, I'm spending the whole weekend with my parents and sister."

"You won't be seeing Sam's family this year?"

At first it had been uncomfortable for Julia to ask about Sam. After a few lunches, she finally worked up the nerve to discuss the topic so many had avoided. She had lost a close friend in high school, and while it wasn't the same, Julia had tried to let Evrett know that on some level, she understood the pain he felt.

"Not for Thanksgiving. I told them I would spend some time with them around Christmas."

"Good for you. I'm sure it will be nice to see them."

"We'll see about that. Anyway, I'm heading out. Have a good Thanksgiving, okay?"

"Thanks, Evrett. Lunch next week sometime?"

"You bet."

• • •

Evrett finished shaving and faced his reflection. He looked long and deep into his own eyes.

Was he ready?

How could he answer that question? How do you know you're ready to kill someone, let alone a whole group of people?

Evrett was a murderer. He knew this. He had killed Harrison, whether he meant to or not.

Now, after more than a year of planning and preparation, he was going to set out to end the lives of those people responsible for his wife's death.

Always, he had the man on the bridge at the forefront of his mind.

This was what it was all about for Evrett, and he was sure that his targets would eventually lead him to the mysterious man.

And here Evrett stood at the start. It was June 25, 2015, and Sam had been gone for almost two full years. During that time, he had rushed into action and regretted it instantly, and since then, he promised himself he wouldn't take care of his first target until he was 100 percent ready.

Finally, he had reached that point.

His home office was filled with detailed notes, maps and pictures. He had bought all the equipment he would need to learn about each witness's life—to learn what it would take to kill them.

He ran his hands over his face, soothing the skin with aftershave. Evrett breathed deeply. Tomorrow there would be no turning back.

"Sam, I will make them pay for what happened to you. Stay with me."

He let the towel drop to the floor and walked into his bedroom. Before climbing into bed, he took pen to paper one more time. He scribbled the names he knew all too well, this time with a map in mind.

Andrew. Chad. Amanda. Gloria. Janine. Sean. Phil. Chase. That was the order.

Once he knew how each person on his list lived, he would be ready to do what needed to be done. He had to learn their every move. He had to know all their tendencies. He had to know his prey better than they knew themselves.

And it was important for him to be smart about his actions. He couldn't make any mistakes. Every person had to die in a perceived accident. He couldn't raise any suspicion and he couldn't initiate any police investigation. That would create a risk of getting caught, and if captured, the man on the bridge would go free.

Failure. Evrett couldn't bear the thought of failing Sam, and that made him even more focused; more determined.

He would be thorough. He would be efficient. He would be successful.

He would start tomorrow.

PART III

THE LAST DAYS

13

THE BLANK WHITE SCREEN stared right back at Alec, as if it were mocking him. Words had littered the screen a few moments ago, but Alec had furiously pounded the backspace key making the last three hours of his life as meaningless as the last two years.

Another dose of writer's block had forced him to twist open a fifth of Jack Daniels, and the new bottle sat on the desk next to an empty one. A few other empties from the past week stood in poor formation on the counter of Alec's one-bedroom apartment.

The apartment's living room was sparsely furnished with a couch, a television on an old oak wood stand and Alec's matching wooden desk. All three items were surrounded by small towers of boxes.

It had been a year and a half since Alec relocated to this apartment north of the city—but it still boasted a Baltimore address. It was a short walk away from Robert E. Lee Park, where he ran and sweated out the alcohol from the night before.

The apartment was more than a thousand dollars cheaper in

monthly rent than his downtown condo, and without a daily beat at *The Baltimore Sun* and the support from his ex-wife, he had to move on.

He twirled a mechanical pencil in his right hand as he continued to stare at the screen. In the background, he heard the newscast emanating from his television—he had only recently returned to watching the news after a long hiatus. His deadline was still a few weeks away, but he had nothing to work with—and that was troublesome.

The thought of giving up had crossed his mind, but he continued to think about what else he would do. He could work in retail or perhaps pick up a blue-collar job, but that thought irked him. He just couldn't bring himself to taking such a career dive, as he viewed it.

Alec was fortunate that a good friend of his, Angela Caraway, offered him an opportunity to write for her just three days after he left *The Baltimore Sun*. He never missed out on a paycheck. It wasn't much, but along with a few other freelance gigs with local newspapers and media outlets, Alec managed to pay the bills.

Angela was a features writer at the *Sun* from 1998 to 2005 when she resigned to launch her own publication, *The Long and Short*. It was a fiction magazine that collected various short stories and published monthly. After a year of producing quality content from several well-known authors, the magazine won a few awards and took off nationally. It was especially popular among English literature teachers in high school and college. Angela noticed the online subscriptions began to greatly outweigh the print subscriptions, so in 2012, she moved the entire production online, and it continued to be a great success.

In the two years after Alec left *The Baltimore Sun*, he struggled to find his niche. Most writers for *The Long and Short* had a series or a running theme that was working for them. Alec tried to mimic that, but the reviews on his stories had not been great.

That was the bad part about having the publication online; each writer was judged on page views, comments and star ratings. Each reader could write comments and give a story a rating from one to five stars. To date, with fifteen stories published, Alec was averaging 2.2 stars, the lowest among the main contributors. Typically, Angela would let a writer go with such low ratings—and she had—but because she sympathized with Alec's situation, she had given him a longer leash.

But that leash was yanked on last week.

Angela gave Alec an ultimatum: publish a four-star story or she'd be forced to give the space to a new writer who can garner the views.

Alec understood, and when she told him this, he sensed that she dreaded the idea of having to issue such a final warning. It was the last thing she wanted to do.

So here Alec sat, in the six and a half days that followed, typing and erasing nonstop.

When he first started writing for Angela, he thought it'd be easy. He loved fiction writing and he was excited to dive into his first story. He used his experiences in journalism to write a crime drama based in the city of Baltimore, but after two editions and a sub-one-star rating on both, he scrapped the idea.

He then tried writing a series about baseball—again, another topic that he thought should be easy to write about —and the first edition told the story of a player battling through a drug addiction to eventually find success. It was a sensation when compared to his first idea, earning a 3.5-star rating, but that was the end of it. His next three cracks at writing about baseball failed miserably.

His last couple narratives jumped all over the place from an investigative journalist to a science fiction fantasy piece to a story about a homeless man.

After a while, Alec stopped reading the comments posted below his stories because they were just too painful to see. He used to take the criticism well, but as his failures mounted, the jeers began to leave mental scars.

Alec picked up his rocks glass and swirled the Jack Daniels counter clockwise to make the ice jingle on the side of the glass. It was a sound that pleased him. Mixed with the hum of the city, trains and cars, it made for the perfect July night. Even at three o'clock in the morning, it was still very warm from the ninety-five-degree heat that baked the city the prior day. Alec had a box fan churning on high, stirring up just enough air to create a comfortable atmosphere in the apartment. The chilled whiskey made it even more enjoyable.

If only he could come up with a story.

His mind wandered and he gazed out into the night sky that pulsated with a yellow and orange glow from the city. He saw a few blinking lights, most likely planes getting ready to land at BWI, traverse across the stars.

Perhaps a story on aliens? he thought, as he imagined one of the blinking lights turning sharply and taking off at light speed into the atmosphere.

He laughed and took a sip of his whiskey as the blinking light continued on its logical course.

"What's wrong with me?" he said, with a chuckle. "Aliens? Come on, Alec."

He set the glass down and looked around the room again, as if the answer was hiding behind the stacked boxes. His cellphone vibrated on the desk, creating a loud buzzing sound that startled him at first. He gave up on wishing it was Abby about a year ago, but he was still quick to grab it. He looked at the screen to see a news update, and as he read it, he noticed something else.

It was July 10.

Somehow, he had been so busy, he lost track of the days.

It was exactly two years ago he almost ended his life.

He stopped reading the news update, set his phone down and picked up his drink. He was thankful to be alive, although, with the way things were going, he sometimes wondered why. He was also saddened by the life that was lost that night, Samantha Eckhard.

He'd never forget the name. The moment her picture was shown on the local television news, he promised he'd never forget her.

Alec was sure he didn't cause the accident, but nevertheless, the thought that there was a slight chance he did weighed heavily over him during the last two years.

He thought about her again tonight. She was too young and beautiful to die like that. She had so much to live for and so much left to do. If only she knew that that was going to be her last day.

And with that thought, it hit Alec like a slap to the face.

"That's it!" he shouted.

He typed two words at the top of his Word document: "Last Day."

He decided at that moment he would write tragic stories that would motivate people to live their day like it was their last—and, in his mind, he dedicated it to Samantha, a woman he never met, but knew all too well.

Now, he just needed an idea. He didn't want to write a fictitious story about Samantha. He wanted to create a fresh one in his mind.

He sat back and closed his eyes.

"What to write?" he pondered aloud.

A few seconds passed, and as had been the case over the last two years, his mind was a chasm of darkness.

Why am I so bad at this? he thought, opening his eyes and sitting forward.

He reached for his drink, and as he did, he felt a tingling sensation in the area between his eyes. Then, like he had never experienced before, a vivid picture of a man appeared in his mind. As he watched the story of this man unfold in his head, he reached into his computer bag and pulled out a digital recorder. He hit record and started describing everything he saw.

In three hours, he had his first five-star story written.

14

THE BRIDGES MADE THE VIEW from the thirty-second floor one of the best in the nation, according to Andrew McMillan. He used what little spare time he had to absorb the scenery of his hometown city of Pittsburgh.

Bridges of all colors, but most of them golden yellow, stretched across the Allegheny, Monongahela and Ohio rivers, and from his corner office at One Oxford Centre, a forty-five story high rise in the middle of downtown Pittsburgh, Andrew could see them all.

Office? It was laughable that he even considered it an office, let alone *his office*. It was what he told his friends, but in actuality, it was a conference room where the firm stuffed part-time paralegals and interns.

Andrew dreamt of having an office to himself, but that wasn't going to happen any time soon. Not at this rate. He had failed the bar exam four times, twice in Maryland and two more times in Pennsylvania. For the foreseeable future, he was stuck in paralegal hell until he abandoned his dream.

He almost gave up a few days ago when one of his many bosses berated him over several research errors he made in a recent case. It nearly cost the firm the client, his boss said, but Andrew believed that was a lie. He wasn't trusted with such life-and-death tasks. Not anymore. The firm, Yanelli, Horwell and Associates, would never put him in charge of something that important. They knew how much of a liability he was, and the only reason he wasn't out on the streets was because Jacob Horwell was his father.

Jacob separated from Andrew's mother months after he was born. They were never married, and quite frankly, Andrew was never meant to be. He was a mistake then, and in many ways, he continued to be a mistake now. But Andrew's mother died of breast cancer when he was six, and Jacob, who was barely in his life before, stepped in.

When she passed away, the firm's founding partner was married and had another son, and even though it initially was uncomfortable for his wife, they brought Andrew in and raised him.

From that moment on, Andrew was destined to be a lawyer. He spent his summers as a teenager going to the office with Jacob, doing remedial tasks, but at the same time, learning about the business. He had watched his father try a few cases, and even though the court-room was dull—nothing like one would see in the movies—he found it exciting.

Andrew graduated with honors from the Winchester Thurston School, which he immediately transferred into when he joined his father's family. He was at the top of his class and earned several scholarships for Georgetown University, and he didn't disappoint his family in Washington, D.C.

At least not initially.

Andrew cruised through his pre-law courses, and he felt like he had an edge on the other aspiring lawyers because of his background, but nothing he saw at his father's firm prepared him for heartbreak.

Julia Brecken was his first and his last. He first saw her from across his corporate law seminar in his second semester freshman year, and after one date, he was in love.

She was too, and for the remainder of their undergrad careers, they were inseparable. Both were on a pre-law track, so they studied together and then enjoyed the off time together. They shared an apartment senior year and both sets of parents knew it was only a matter of time before they watched the two walk down the aisle, but they were equally as unprepared for Julia's indiscretion.

During her junior year, she accepted a summer internship at a large corporate firm in Austin, Texas, and one of the associates did what he did with many interns—wooed her into bed. Julia, however, stood out from all his past interns, and they quickly turned what was an office affair into a long-distance relationship. He flew in to Washington, D.C., during her senior year—on what he expensed as business trips—to meet up with her at the Westin in Arlington, Virginia.

Julia hid all of this from Andrew, who was so blinded by all his studies he didn't even notice that anything was wrong.

Then, a week before graduation, the bomb was dropped.

Julia was moving to Austin.

At first, Andrew thought this was because of a job offer. He was excited and started to tell her about how with his grades, he could easily transfer to the University of Texas School of Law, but then she cut him off.

"Andrew. I'm going alone."

A confused look on Andrew's face turned into anger and then sadness as she told him everything.

Two days later, Andrew had moved all his stuff out and into storage, and he slept on a friend's couch in Fairfax, Virginia, until he found his own place. He was slated to go to Georgetown Law before the breakup and he had no reason to leave D.C. anymore.

He started in the fall, but he struggled with the course work. If he would have put his mind to it, he would have finished in the top two percent, but he never could regain the level of commitment he had had when he was with Julia.

Still, he managed passable grades in every course and three years of mediocre work—by his prior standards—still resulted in a juris doctorate from Georgetown Law.

He remained in the D.C. region for two more years, working

in a firm northeast of the city as he prepared to pass the bar exam. But in August 2013, he packed up everything and moved home to Pittsburgh.

He had had enough of D.C.

It reminded him of Julia, the one he lost.

In actuality, it was the second woman he lost that caused him to break down, quit the firm and move home.

He and another young associate, Chad McKelvin, were driving through Baltimore, conducting a few background interviews for the firm, when all of a sudden several vehicles far in front of their company car got tangled up in a horrific accident. Andrew slammed on the brakes and safely put the car in park. Both aspiring lawyers jumped out of the car to check on the injured in a group of cars snarled up on the right side of the highway.

Everyone seemed to be okay, just shaken up, and Andrew looked farther up the highway at the tanker on its side to see another car caught up against the concrete barrier. That was when he heard the screams of the woman inside.

"Oh, shit," he said, taking off toward the car with its engine now on fire.

Chad ran, too, but he bear-hugged Andrew to stop him.

"Dude, wait!" he screamed. "Look."

He pointed toward the gas streaming out of the tanker truck.

"It's going to blow."

Chad turned and warned the others whose minor injuries weren't enough to keep them in their vehicles, and they all scrambled back about 100 yards.

Andrew turned and ran with them, but he hated it. He turned to see the woman struggling and all he wanted to do was turn around and go back, but his yearning to survive won.

He saw the fire trucks coming up the shoulder of the highway and he relaxed a bit, knowing that they could save her. That was their job. He and his firm would just represent her when she got out.

As that cruel, financially driven thought traversed through his brain, the tanker exploded, sending him and everyone around him to the ground. When he looked back, the car—what was left of it— was engulfed in flames.

He could see the woman in his mind. He could picture her crying. He had time to save her. He had plenty of time. But instead he ran away. He lost her.

That moment haunted him for weeks until eventually he quit the firm and moved home. He just couldn't take the pressure anymore. He battled insomnia nightly, sleeping only for a few minutes before the same explosion awoke him.

Sitting in his office, he thought about this nightly battle as he gazed out toward the stadiums on the North Shore. Tonight, he wasn't going to have to worry about insomnia; it was going to be self-medicated. He and a few other failures from high school who did not live up to daddy's expectations were hitting up the Rivers Casino with daddy's money. Odd how that worked, but it wasn't something for Andrew to care about.

Gambling, drinking and sex. Those were the only things that really kept him going anymore.

If only he could go back to when he was a teenager grabbing coffee at the local Starbucks for the associates.

Life was full of promise and hope then.

Now, he was stuck going through the motions with no direction, like a boat without a rudder.

He was a shipwreck waiting to happen.

15

FINALLY ALEC HAD A DRINK that wasn't meant to drown away his sorrows. Instead, it was a celebratory mix. He even livened up the evening by dropping a lime slice into the glass of rum. Why he had limes, he had no idea. Similarly, he had no clue how he wrote the piece that he was about to submit to Angela.

Nor did he care. It just needed one proofread and then he was hitting send.

It was six in the morning and Alec had a huge smile. He had just turned on the television to find a replay of the Orioles game on MASN. He took in a pair of innings before walking back to his computer to edit. It was important for him to separate himself from a story before proof reading. It was essential to clear the mind before returning to it.

It also was essential to pour another drink, and he did so before returning to the desk.

He opened up his laptop, scrolled to the top of his Word document and began to read:

• • •

The Gambler
By Alec Rossi
The Long and Short

The night was alive.

Noises of all kinds shot out from every direction, and on top of it all, a cover band rocked out a trendy top-forty hit.

For this one gambler, it was all blocked out.

He was sitting pretty with a pair of kings, same suit, and all he needed was the dealer to bust for him to win ten thousand dollars.

With a jack of diamonds already on the table and a card upside down, the dealer flipped the latter to reveal a two of spades.

The gambler knew that the odds were in his favor, and so did his friends who stood anxiously behind him.

The dealer displayed the next card.

It was another jack for the dealer and a jackpot for the gambler—a huge jackpot, and he and his friends reacted accordingly.

"Ten thousand dollars!" he screamed. "Check, please!"

High fives were shared all around, and even one of the losers who shared the table tossed him a smile.

"Rest of the night is on me," the gambler said, gathering his chips.

He cashed out and the foursome walked out of the casino and along the river. It was only nine-thirty and a club was in their future.

Fireworks shot into the air outside signifying that the Pittsburgh Pirates had just won a home game.

The gambler joked with his friends that he just made more money tonight than the Buccos' starting pitcher.

The fact was he just made more than he earned in four months at his job. But money wasn't an issue for him. He was still living off of dad's big salary. Technically, the ten thousand should go right into the hands of his old man, but it would be gone before his father could ever find out that it was won.

The quartet of over-privileged twenty-somethings loudly made their way along the Allegheny River. Their destination was a gentlemen's club downtown.

It was where they often finished their nights, but never had they had so much cash to play with. To them that was all money was, a toy.

So were women. At the club, the gambler and his friends tossed out money with ease, and with every drink and every private dance, the dreams that these young men had at one point in their lives continued to fade away.

Four hours later, the entourage found themselves back at square one, as they always did. The ten thousand was exhausted on a $3,500 bottle of Stoli Elit; $300 bottle of Johnnie Walker XR, aged 21 years; two bottles of Dom Perignon Rose 2002 at $500 a pop, and three $1,000 bottles of Magnum Grey Goose that they gifted to a bachelorette party in hopes of wooing the available ladies.

The rest of the money was spent on private, back-room dances.

The gambler was having the time of his life.

All the problems he faced in his real life were non-existent. In this moment, he was able to ignore all his failures. In the back of his mind, he knew he could correct all his mistakes tomorrow.

Right now, he was living in the moment.

And at this moment, only one-thirty in the morning, he and his friends were out of cash. It was time to go back to the casino.

They stumbled across the Roberto Clemente Bridge acting like fools. They embarrassed themselves in front of a group of beautiful single women and nearly got into a fight with a less interesting foursome of men.

As they walked along the river on the North Shore Trail, one of the gambler's wilder friends jumped onto a boat that was docked. He pulled out a set of keys and turned on the engine.

"How the hell?" the gambler said.

"I lifted them off of one of those four assholes," he said. "That's why I picked the fight. Saw him get off the boat. I picked his pocket when he pushed me."

The gambler and the other two friends laughed and jumped on the boat.

"Do you even know how to drive this thing?" the one asked, while untying the boat from the dock.

"Who cares?" the gambler said. "Let's ride!"

The pickpocket inched the boat out, and as he did, they heard the yells of the four men, and as he pulled away from the dock, the owner leapt from it and smacked off the side of the boat and into the water. The original foursome sped away, up the Allegheny.

The breeze in the gambler's long, wavy hair was amazing. He closed his eyes as he held on to the railing on the port side of the Bayliner 255 Cruiser. He could feel the boat bounce in the water as it neared thirty-five miles per hour. He heard his friends laughing over the churn of the motor.

This was perfect. The gambler always wanted to own a boat. He was at one time on a path toward riches and he could have easily had his own yacht, but he let that dream die years ago. There was still time to revive it, he thought as they cruised under one of the many bridges that he could see from his office.

The gambler opened his eyes just in time to see it. The pickpocket was pushing his friend while the Bayliner soared toward a small unlit vessel.

"Look out!" the gambler screamed, and the pickpocket quickly turned the wheel to avoid the craft.

He turned and smugly said, "I got this."

But he didn't, and the boat's new course sent it flying into a river barge. The boat clipped the side of it, flipping in the air, and the gambler smacked his head off the railing before slamming into the dark water.

He was only unconscious for a few seconds, but he wasn't aware because he was submerged in the dark Allegheny River. How far down, he did not know.

He could not see a thing.

He tried to swim to the surface, but he didn't go anywhere.

He was stuck, but on what? It felt like a hand was on his right leg, but he couldn't move his arms or kick his legs.

He gulped a mouthful of water as he struggled and panic set in. *This can't be it. This wasn't how it was meant to be.*

He was supposed to get married, have children and carry on his mother's name.

He was supposed to pass the bar exam and become an important part of the legal community.

He was supposed to live up to his father's expectations.

He had many regrets in life, and as he thought about them all, he struggled one final time to pull himself to the surface.

And with one last gasp, he realized that this was his last day.

• • •

Alec clicked the save button and smiled.

"Powerful," he said.

He looked at his empty rocks glass and got up to refill it, but in a moment of reflection, he decided against it.

He didn't want to end up like the gambler.

16

IT WAS HARD TO BELIEVE THAT IT WAS STILL JULY. It was close to fifty-eight degrees inside the hotel room as the window air conditioning unit rattled non-stop. Evrett awoke abruptly and reached for the comforter that was on the floor beside the bed. He was wearing just his boxer briefs and he could sense that his skin was ice cold.

He scanned the room to collect his thoughts. The flow of cold air from the air conditioner caught his attention and he jumped out of bed to shut it off. He scrambled to the thermostat, turned on the heat and cranked the knob around to eighty before diving back under the covers.

"What the hell happened?" he asked, noticing his clothes strewn about the room. He saw his black T-shirt next to the bed and he reached down to pick it up, but he dropped it soon after touching it.

The shirt was very damp. He noticed his jeans, hanging off the desk chair, were darker in spots. Clearly, they were wet as well. His shoes and socks were also soaked, and the boxer briefs he was wearing were not the ones he had on yesterday.

It was at that point that Evrett realized he had no clue what happened the night before. He battled the cold and walked over to his jeans. In the back pocket was his wallet, which was wet as well. He opened it and pulled out three soggy one hundred dollar bills. In his front pocket he found a green casino chip. On it read: "Pittsburgh, PA, Rivers Casino, $25."

Evrett had been in Pittsburgh for two weeks now, but he had never thought about stepping foot in the casino. He hated casinos. Why waste good money?

Looking at the chip, Evrett tried to dig deep in his mind to find out what happened. He must have had one too many drinks at the casino and taken a cab back to the hotel.

The last thing Evrett recalled doing was returning to the hotel after another full day of spying on Andrew McMillan. He hadn't yet come up with a plan to kill him, but he knew some of the information he had gathered thus far would provide him with the best answer.

He placed the chip on the dresser and walked back over to the nightstand where his phone was. Considering the condition of everything that was on his person yesterday, he feared the worst for his cellphone, but with one click, it turned on.

"How the hell did this not get wet?" Evrett asked. Based on how waterlogged his wallet was, he must have fallen into a pool. But he didn't smell any chlorine.

Then he thought about where he deduced he was the night before.

Could I have fallen into the river? he thought.

The phone lit up with the time, seven-thirty, and Evrett knew he had to get going. Andrew would show up at his downtown office around eight-thirty and he had to get down there. Today was the day he planned on stopping him on the sidewalk and sparking up a conversation. He wasn't sure how he was going to approach him, but he knew he had to do it soon.

Evrett collected all his wet clothes and draped them on the rack in the bathroom. As he hung his grey button-down short-sleeved shirt, a set of keys fell to the floor. He picked them up, not recognizing them at all. There were two silver keys and a novelty keychain with the letters "G" and "R" on a single ring.

He wondered if he should investigate his last twelve hours instead of meeting with Andrew, but he figured the investigation could wait. He'd have plenty of time after Andrew started his usual nine-hour day.

He threw on a dry pair of jeans and a grey T-shirt before running out the door.

His Audi was right where he left it when he came back from spying on Andrew the day before. He started the ignition, put the car in drive and placed his hands on the wheel. He immediately noticed the faded red stamp on his left hand. It was a triangle outline with a logo of some sort inside. The water washed enough away that he could not read it. All he could assume was that he also visited a club.

It was becoming clearer and clearer why he didn't remember the night before; but then again, he couldn't understand why he wasn't hung over.

Evrett drove the twenty miles into the city and parked in a parking garage on Forbes Avenue, a few blocks from One Oxford Centre.

He waited on a concrete bench just outside the high rise. Evrett had sat on the same bench several times, watching Andrew walk by without a care. Andrew was oblivious.

But today, he didn't come.

Evrett checked his phone for the time and he saw that Andrew was ten minutes late. This was not like him, even for a deadbeat loser. He may have slacked off on the job, but he showed up on time. He had to, otherwise his dad would fire him.

Evrett learned this from a conversation Andrew and his dad had six days ago. It was recorded on one of the many bugs Evrett had planted around the McMillan household. He also had a receiver under the conference table that Andrew sat at daily.

That bug took some serious work—and risk—as he disguised himself as a deliveryman for a local deli, bringing sandwiches to the office. He did it during Andrew's lunch hour after he saw him walk out of the building. He assumed at this point, he'd have a clear shot at getting into his office.

"Yes, I have an order for Andrew McMillan," Evrett told the receptionist at the front desk.

The rather large woman peered up from her computer screen to see Evrett wearing a bright red cap and a T-shirt for Sal's Deli. The red hat was a generic cap he bought at the mall, and he stole the shirt from the backseat of one of the real delivery drivers.

"He works in that conference room down there," the secretary said, pointing down the long hallway to Evrett's right. She was too busy to even notice that Andrew left ten minutes ago. "It's the fourth door on your right. You can't miss it."

Once inside, Evrett placed his wireless microphone in a crevasse in the wood beneath the conference table. He also placed the white bag, which held a cold meatball sub, on the table and left.

About an hour later, he heard the confusion over the sub, which Andrew wound up eating anyway. Evrett thought about how he could have easily poisoned him, but of course, poison would raise questions, and that's not the way he planned on eliminating his targets.

It had to be clean. It had to be perfect.

At this point, Evrett didn't have a solid idea. And it wasn't helping that Andrew was all of a sudden absent on the day that he planned to approach him. Today was supposed to be a big step. But now, he was missing.

Perhaps Andrew got to work early, Evrett thought, as he pulled out his iPad and logged in to his network to access his conference table microphone. He pulled out a pair of headphones and listened in.

He could hear someone tapping away on a keyboard and Evrett was sure that Andrew was just getting ahead of the game today, but he also knew it could be one of the interns hard at work. He kept listening, hoping to get some sign of Andrew, and five minutes later, he heard his father.

"Sarah, has my son arrived yet?" he asked.

"No, I sent him a text to check in. He hasn't responded."

There was a slight pause. "Yeah, he hasn't answered my calls either. Thanks, Sarah."

Evrett closed down the app and took off his headphones.

"I wonder where he is?" he asked.

Evrett contemplated sitting on the bench longer, but the need for coffee took over. He walked a few blocks to a local coffee house, ordered a large mocha latte and sat down at a table. It was just after nine and the place was still busy with people scrambling to get their caffeine fix before a long day.

As had been his task for the last two weeks, Evrett just watched. He absorbed everything around him. The woman, left-handed, pretended to do a crossword puzzle while checking out a guy in line for coffee. That man, six-foot-two with a medium build, wore a grey suit and had a bulge in his suit jacket along the waistline on his right side. A gun, Evrett assumed. Being so close to the federal building, he pegged him for an FBI agent. Or perhaps DEA. Either way, he was a fed. He was in his late twenties, and based on the piece of paper in his right hand, Evrett figured he was a rookie. That was the office's order all written down and of course they'd send the rookie to go get it.

Evrett knew in all likelihood he was correct. He had an eye for details, a skill that had helped him excel at GGM. Years of watching investigation and cop shows hadn't hurt either. Evrett found it amusing how he could analyze someone so closely and come up with such a vivid assessment. People and blueprints weren't all that different, once you knew how to read them.

He turned his attention away from the rookie to the fire on the television. The lower-third graphic on the news network read: "Fatal Boat Accident On The Allegheny." In smaller text below, it read: "Four men steal boat, crash into barge."

The video of the fire was from earlier in the morning, as it was still dark out. The scene was just a bunch of little fires floating on the water. Whatever boat had been stolen, it surely wasn't going to be returned to its owner.

The news telecast cut from the video to a reporter live on the scene. She was standing on a small hill that overlooked the crash site, next to a bridge.

As Evrett watched, he got an eerie feeling like he had seen that place before.

He quickly thought about how the last twelve hours were a mystery to him and according to the poker chip that was in his pocket, he may not have been far away from this accident. Add in the soaking wet clothes and Evrett started to panic.

He pulled out his iPad and opened the browser. He logged onto the *Pittsburgh Post-Gazette's* website and began reading the story on its front page:

> PITTSBURGH — Four men died after stealing a boat near Rivers Casino and crashing into a barge on the Allegheny River at around 3 a.m. Friday.
>
> Authorities have not released the names of the victims and will not do so until their families are notified. No one aboard the barge was injured.
>
> A third boat, also stolen, may have been involved, but police say the investigation is still ongoing.
>
> Police did say that four inebriated men lifted the keys off of another group of men after a verbal altercation. They then stole the boat and drove up the Allegheny before clipping the edge of the barge. Police believe the boat, a Bayliner 255 Cruiser, was moving an estimated forty miles per hour at impact.
>
> It flipped several times and broke apart as the engine exploded. All four men were thrown from the boat and died in the water. Autopsies will be performed Monday.
>
> The third boat, an Action Craft 1720 Flyfisher, was found adrift at the scene. The fishing boat, belonging to Grant Rentschler, of Penn Hills, was stolen earlier in the evening. Rentschler reported that he returned to his riverfront home at 7 p.m. to find the back door open, his boat keys gone along with his boat.

Evrett sat back and pieced it together.

"Grant Rentschler? … G. … R," he said. "I have the boat keys. Oh, shit, I stole a boat?"

The woman with the crossword puzzle heard him talk to himself, but she didn't make out the words.

Evrett stood up and bolted out of the coffee house. He ran to his car and quickly drove to the scene of the boat accident. When he arrived, he joined a group of onlookers. Even from this vantage point, several yards away, Evrett could see enough to know that Andrew's father was on his knees next to a few police officers.

This confirmed his suspicion that Andrew was dead.

The moment was an eerie one for Evrett. He watched a police officer place his hand on the shoulder of Andrew's father. He still knelt on the ground, his head hung low. Evrett knew the feeling of loss and hopelessness Andrew's father was feeling.

But whatever had happened to Andrew the night before was what he had deserved for his inaction.

He saw the barge surrounded by a few police boats. The boat he allegedly stole was now tied to a dock near the road. Evrett wanted to walk closer and get a better look at the scene, but he stopped himself.

If he was truly here last night, then there could be witnesses, and that meant he could be recognized. Hell, he could have already been recognized from where he was standing. It was time to go.

He jumped back into his car and casually drove away, trying to be as inconspicuous as possible. As soon as he got back onto Interstate 376 to leave the city, he picked up his speed and raced back to the motel. There, he packed his suitcase quickly and efficiently, leaving no trace of his presence. He concluded his stay by wiping down everything in the room in case the authorities somehow traced his boat theft back to this motel. He held the boat keys in his hands as he prepared to leave.

"What should I do with these?" was the thought repeating in his head.

He placed them in his pocket and decided to deal with it later.

It was more pressing that he get the hell out of town.

He paid the motel bill in cash and drove off in his Audi. While on Interstate 376, he started to think about his itinerary. He came to Pittsburgh using several turnpikes. It would be smart to avoid any tollbooths because even though he paid cash on his way out, there were cameras and he didn't want there to be any evidence that this was the day that he was heading home.

He pulled out his cellphone and searched for a way home that avoided tolls. It took him on Route 22 through Altoona, Pennsylvania, and several rural Pennsylvania towns he never imagined visiting in his lifetime.

It wasn't until he entered Northwestern Maryland on Interstate 70 that he began to reflect on his time in Pittsburgh.

He thought about how his two weeks of surveillance were a waste. But then again, were they? Andrew was dead. That was the goal. He did want to talk to him first, so there was a hint of failure in the air. Nevertheless, the end result was supposed to be his death in a horrible accident and it had happened.

For the first time since he left Pittsburgh, Evrett smiled.

As he passed through Hancock, Maryland, he noticed on the GPS that the Potomac River was flowing parallel to the interstate. He exited and drove into Fort Frederick State Park, following the signs to the river. He drove past the historical fort and to the end of the road. There he parked and walked to the banks of the Potomac. He stood there for a few minutes, looking for any sign of life. There was nobody around.

The sun was slowly disappearing below the tree line as Evrett reached into his pocket and pulled out the pair of keys. He gave them one last look before chucking them into the middle of the river, where they would sink into a forgotten world.

He watched the ripples dissipate before walking back to his car. There he sat. How did he get the boat keys? How did he do all this and not remember? How did he feasibly cause Andrew's death without even knowing it? It was his intention all along, but he never had solidified an actual plan to accomplish it.

It was a circular dialog that continued in his head, and it did not cease when he got back onto the interstate.

It was about ten o'clock when he pulled into his garage. He walked into his home and went straight to bed. He fell asleep with the sensation that Sam was behind him holding on tight.

If she was watching over him, he hoped she understood.

17

THE INCESSANT BEEPING ECHOED throughout the small grocery store. Chad McKelvin slid can after can across the scanner and dropped each one into a paper bag. He had lost count about two minutes ago and he still had a few more stacks of cat food to scan. By his guesstimate, he assumed old Mrs. Tillman must have fifty cats—or just two cats and she was preparing for the apocalypse.

When he was finally finished, he tapped a button on the register to end the sale. Mrs. Tillman pulled out her checkbook and slowly filled out all the necessary information as if she was the only person in line.

Well, she was, but that wasn't the point. Chad's shift should have ended thirty minutes ago, but she walked in ten minutes before his shift ended, which meant he'd have to wait for her to finish up to close the store.

She always did this on Sundays when the store was supposed to close at six. The last time she did it, Chad rushed her out of the store, which did not go over well with his manager.

After she complained, he was issued a stern warning and given one last chance to keep his job, so on this day, he watched her roam for thirty minutes from aisle to aisle—there were only five—and come to the register with what seemed to be a hundred cans of cat food and two gallons of milk.

She must eat the cat food, Chad thought, as Mrs. Tillman signed her name on the check. This, too, took forever. It was as if she had to remember how to construct each cursive letter before she put the pen to work. She carefully tore the check out of the booklet, gave it a once-over and handed it to him with a smile.

Chad hated that smile. It wasn't a pleasant smile; it was filled with sass. He could just feel it.

But, because of last week's debacle, he took the check, smiled and said, "Thanks, Mrs. Tillman. Can I carry your bags to your car?"

Of course, she obliged, and he carried the two paper bags to her large, light blue 1982 Buick LeSabre. He placed them in the passenger seat and kindly said goodbye to his Sunday thorn.

Back inside, Chad locked the front door, counted what little cash was accepted into the register that day and placed all the cash and checks into the safe in his manager's office. His boss would take care of it tomorrow.

For Chad, he was off until Wednesday. Being the assistant manager, he was stuck working the weekends—every weekend—while his boss sat at home.

Chad walked down the sidewalk to his car, and even as the sunlight started to fade behind the trees, the summer warmth lingered on this mid-September evening. He could hear a few children playing off in the distance, but for the most part, the small New Hampshire town of Winchester had turned in for the night.

The air inside of his Honda Civic was much warmer than the air outside of it, but relief poured in as soon as he opened the front windows.

The drive home was short, only about five minutes, and every second away from the grocery store made him feel much better about *his weekend.*

Then again, a few days off in Winchester wasn't anything special, especially for a man who despised rural living—but at this point, it was all he had to fall back on.

Chad grew up near Boston, went to college at Northeastern and then continued his education at the University of Maryland School of Law. As recent as a year ago, he was a young, hotshot lawyer handling divorce cases for a leading firm outside of Baltimore, but all of that came to a crushing end eight months ago.

It all started when he met Maddy Yalof. She wanted a divorce from her husband, Nickolai Yalof, who had selected Chad's firm to represent him. It was supposed to be an easy open and shut case, and that was why they had no problems giving it to the firm's youngest lawyer, but it turned out that there were some expensive hidden assets and the case couldn't be settled in a conference room. Instead, it was headed for a courtroom.

Chad had yet to officially step into a courtroom and nerves were getting to him, so he decided to head out to a bar the night before the first gavel tap.

What he did not know was that Maddy was following him. She was about to knock on his apartment door before he left.

She walked into the bar wearing a white dress that showed off her fit, tan legs, as well as her plus-size chest. She caught the attention of several men, but not Chad, who was staring attentively at his drink. She stealthily walked up behind Chad and whispered in his left ear, "I want you."

Chad was stunned to hear a sexy voice say such a good thing, and surely, it had to be a prank.

But it wasn't a prank, and it surely wasn't a good thing.

"Mrs. Yalof," he said with a great amount of surprise.

"Miss," she said, correcting him. "Miss Reynolds."

"No matter. Yalof or Reynolds, I cannot be speaking with you, ma'am. I will be disbarred if I say anymore."

"Then, I'll speak," she said, smiling and leaning back in closer to his ear. "I want to win. I want you to win. I'll give you five hundred thousand and a lifetime worth of, shall we say, late-night gatherings? In exchange, I'll want information and poor representation."

He looked at her in disbelief and said, "I'm not going to throw away my career like that. I have —"

She interrupted him, not with words of her own, but rather with a seductive bite on the same ear she whispered in. At the same time, she slid her hand down the front of his pants.

"Okay, Mr. Morals. I'll make it one million in an offshore account in your name that will be set up as soon as I get done with you in bed."

Maddy was a fine catch.

Chad wasn't.

He was five-foot-eleven with a round face and a balding head at twenty-seven years old. With about thirty more pounds than society expected him to have, he had never been able to attract a woman of Maddy's level, let alone have one throw herself at him.

Granted, she had ulterior motives, but as her hand did wonders, his morals began to fade.

She moved away from his ear and toward his lips. He hesitated and then went all in.

They kissed for about thirty seconds and then she pulled back.

"I have a car waiting outside. I'll take it that you're interested."

He smiled, threw down a twenty and followed her out of the bar His tab was only five dollars, but he was now a millionaire and didn't care.

As he walked out the door with the most beautiful woman he'd ever make love to, a few more pictures were snapped. Nickolai had his suspicions that Maddy was having an affair, so he had hired a private detective. He never would have imagined his lawyer appearing on the other end of the camera.

As soon as the firm was handed the evidence, it wasn't long before they tracked down the offshore account.

The evidence was overwhelming, as the private detective had followed him for two weeks. The case, which was supposed to begin hours after he woke up next to Maddy, was postponed by two weeks on the docket because the judge had to travel for a family funeral.

Chad met Maddy every night, exchanging information and planning on how to fix the trial. They knew the case would still have to go in front of a judge, because there was no way Chad could coax Nickolai into settling.

Besides, Maddy knew she could get more in court.

For Chad, it was the greatest two weeks of his life. He had never felt so alive. But then, a day before the trial's rescheduled start date, Chad was approached by his firm's managing partner and he never entered the courtroom.

He was fired on the spot, and two weeks later, he was officially disbarred.

Disbarred.

It was a word that he still hadn't said to his mother. She just believed that he had a change of heart and wanted to come home.

And Winchester was hardly home. It was the hometown of his mother, but growing up, Chad may have visited it a total of ten times. This place was foreign to him.

After his parents divorced when he was in law school, Molly Randall moved from Boston to Winchester. Chad noticed his mother's growing troubles during his college years and he sensed the move to Winchester was what she needed to recover from a tough divorce. Having Chad move home was even better for her.

Not for him, though.

Moving to Winchester meant that he was a failure. It was why he was now making less than twenty-seven thousand a year scanning cat food. He made three times that much in Baltimore, and had he not succumbed to the prospect of being an instant millionaire, he'd be building a bank account that would soon have just as much, and more.

Then, he could have used the money to lure in a prized woman like Maddy. But the idea of instantaneous gratification was too much for him to ignore—and it cost him everything.

Chad pulled into his mother's driveway and put the car in park. He got out, leaving the windows down because in Winchester, no one would even notice, and he trotted up the short concrete walkway to the front door of his mother's small one-story home.

He noticed the grass was extremely high, thanks to three straight days of rain late last week, and it needed to be cut—that of course was to be one of his many tasks for his two days off.

His mother always needed help with the usual household chores as her age prevented her from doing much of anything anymore. Chad was an only child and his mother didn't have him until she was forty-two. The doctors said it was quite a miracle that he was conceived.

A miracle.

A blessing.

A special gift from God.

She called him all of those, and he used to believe that he was put on the Earth to do something special.

Now, he understood that it was all a crock. His dreams were crushed and his future was dull.

A lame job in the middle of nowhere. Winter was coming and a deep depression was sure to accompany it.

Chad figured he had to get out of there quickly before that happened.

As he sat down to dinner with his mother, he thought quietly to himself about an escape plan.

Somehow, some way, he was leaving Winchester—the sooner, the better.

18

FALL HAD OFFICIALLY STARTED, but summer wouldn't let go of its grip. It felt more like August than the latter weeks of September. Evrett guessed he wouldn't be feeling the chill of a New Hampshire autumn anytime soon.

It was Sunday night and Evrett was parked in his Audi staring at the small storefront of a corner grocery store in Winchester. After a week and a half up North, Evrett was getting ready to make contact with Chad McKelvin.

Following his trip to Pittsburgh, Evrett had returned to the office for a few days. Working from home was still going well and it was allowing him the freedom to leave Baltimore for days at a time. Julia continued to be a great help; she was his eyes and ears at the office.

With nothing major on the horizon at work, Evrett decided he'd take a vacation. At least that was how work would see it. After the weirdness of what happened to him the night Andrew McMillan died, Evrett wanted to be able to really focus on the next target on his list.

A few weeks of scouting the area online and double-checking the information he had gathered led Evrett to book a hotel a few miles outside of Winchester in Brattleboro, Vermont. Staying in the neighboring state should help keep his tracks covered, he thought.

The drive to Brattleboro took Evrett just under seven hours with only two stops along the way. Once he checked into the hotel he unpacked his clothes and supplies. He planned to stay at least the week to learn as much as he could about the man he was hunting. The universe had stepped in to take care of Andrew, but had robbed Evrett of the opportunity to find the man on the bridge. He couldn't afford to miss out on what Chad might know.

Evrett's first day in New England started with a drive to Chad's house. The contact information Evrett had discovered placed Chad in the house of a Molly Randall. Some further detective work revealed that Molly was Chad's mother and that he had left Baltimore to live with her in Winchester.

He parked his Audi down the road from the house. Winchester was a small town filled with small houses separated by small patches of wilderness. Evrett had to be careful not to draw too much attention to his Audi. He would only be able to spend so much time parked on this particular street.

After about an hour, a Civic drove past Evrett and pulled into the driveway. A man in his late twenties stepped out of the car and walked to the front door of the rancher. Evrett recognized him at once as Chad McKelvin. At least he was in the right spot.

Chad didn't go anywhere the rest of the day. Evrett could have counted on one hand the number of cars that passed by him while he was in his. There wasn't much going on in Winchester apparently. If anyone in this town knew that there was a stakeout going on, they might join in just to escape the dullness of rural New England life.

As darkness fell, Evrett decided to drive back to the hotel room. He established that he had the right location and the right man. Tomorrow he would see what else he could learn about Chad.

In the days that followed, Evrett discovered that Chad worked at a small grocery store. He was an assistant manager and worked irregular hours. After three days of surveillance, Evrett couldn't pin down an exact schedule for the man.

There was one person Evrett hadn't seen any signs of, and that was Molly. She had not come out of the house over the three days. Evrett initially wondered if she even still lived at the house.

On his fourth day of following Chad, Evrett watched as the Civic pulled out of the driveway and drove off to work. Evrett knew he wouldn't be back for hours; Chad had left wearing his grocery store uniform. Still, Evrett wanted to work quickly. He gathered his lock picking set and wireless microphones and started off toward the house.

Evrett went to the backyard where there were enough trees to keep him hidden from the neighboring houses. He peered through the curtains knowing the only possible person who could be home was Molly. From what he gathered, she was older and relied on Chad for everything. It was rare that she would ever leave the house.

With Andrew, he found several opportunities to enter his home and hide surveillance equipment, but this scenario presented a new challenge for him.

Evrett crouched underneath the window on the back wall of the house as the early autumn sun was getting lower in the sky. Evrett had to work quickly. Standing up, he could see into the house. From his viewpoint, the kitchen was empty. He pressed himself closer to see the dining room and part of the living room. Both appeared empty, but he could tell the living room was occupied from the flickering light of the television reflecting off of the wall.

Molly must be watching television, he thought. If she was in the living room, it would mean that he wouldn't be able to break in from the back door to the kitchen. He'd have to find some place farther away from the main living area of the house.

So Evrett slithered down, trying his hardest to stay close to the exterior wall of the house. He'd need a window that would lead into one of the bedrooms.

He picked the farthest one at the corner of the house. Even if Molly was not in the living room, Evrett would be so quiet she would never know that he was breaking into her house. Breaking in would prove to be much more complicated if the window was locked. He hoped Chad or his mother were foolish enough to leave one of the windows open.

He tried the first one. No luck. The lock was turned and the only way he'd be getting in through this window would be by breaking the glass. He'd use that only as a last resort.

After peering in through the glass, Evrett could see that the adjacent wall had another window. If luck was on his side, it would be unlocked.

Evrett turned the corner, stepping over some of the plants in the flowerbed. As he got to the window, he saw that it was now open a quarter of the way.

"Odd," he said, quietly.

He could have sworn it was closed when he saw it through the other window. Nevertheless, this was going to be much easier than he initially thought.

He pushed the window up a little more, but it didn't go very far. Still, he had just enough room to squeeze through. After poking his head into the room, he tossed his bag through and then followed.

Evrett landed on the floor with a faint thud.

He looked around the room. It was clear that he was in Chad's room. Hockey sticks and memorabilia littered the walls. Even though he knew he was in the room of a man in his late twenties, he could easily have been in the room of an adolescent boy.

"Someone needs to grow up," Evrett muttered to himself.

He looked around the room for a good place to hide his wireless microphone.

There was an air return on the far wall from the window. It would be a perfect hiding place. Before Evrett went to work, he took a quick peek into the hallway. He could hear the faint sound of the television down the hall. Aside from that there was no sound of anyone coming.

Evrett pulled out the screwdriver from his kit and quickly loosened the grate on the air return. He positioned the wireless mic and then closed the grate.

He was lucky the house wasn't too big. Unlike Andrew's home, Chad's would only take a few microphones. In addition to the one in the bedroom, Evrett wanted to place one in the living room and kitchen. Of course, that all depended on Molly.

He eased the bedroom door open and looked down the hall. There were no windows in the hallway to add any natural light, and the ceiling lights were turned off.

With each step, Evrett had to remind himself to breathe. He left the bag in the bedroom, bringing with him a screwdriver, a small mirror and two mics.

At the end of the hall he stopped.

The living room smelled of cigarettes. From where he was, he could see the television. A commercial for life insurance was playing.

Evrett peered around the corner. Molly sat in a large blue recliner, her eyes closed with a cigarette dangling haphazardly from her fingers.

As far as Evrett could tell, Molly was asleep. He could hear her breathing rhythmically from across the room. If he was quiet, he'd be able to sneak past her and place his microphones with no problem.

Evrett scanned the living room. It was full of crocheted afghans and plastic ivy garland. Diagonally from where he was in the hallway was another air return grate. To get to it he would have to cross the living room, walking directly between Molly and the television.

So much weighed on Evrett. He had spent the last year gathering materials and researching each of his potential victims. He had to be careful. One wrong move and Molly would wake up. Then it would all be over.

Using the mirror, Evrett looked out into the room. Molly was asleep. He waved his hand to see if there was any response.

Nothing. She was out.

He stuck one foot out into the living room.

No reaction.

Evrett slowly walked across the floor of the living room. Luckily it was carpeted. He didn't need the sound of his footsteps echoing throughout the house.

Once by the side of the couch, he went to work unscrewing the small white grate. With one screw undone he focused his attention on the second.

When he almost had the last screw completely removed, the grate came loose and fell to the floor with a metallic thud.

Dammit.

Evrett spun his head around and looked at Molly. She shifted in her recliner, but never moved her eyes. A small cluster of ash fell from her cigarette.

Be careful, Evrett. Don't mess this up.

He situated the microphone and worked to replace the grate. Within a matter of seconds it would be impossible to detect that he had ever messed with the duct in the first place.

Now for the kitchen.

The kitchen had two entrances. There was one leading from the living room and another from the dining room.

With confidence, Evrett stood up and went for the entrance. The cabinets of the kitchen were at least a foot from the ceiling. Behind the molding on the top of the cabinets seemed like the perfect place to set up his final microphone.

He switched it on before jumping up on the counter. Evrett extended his arm and carefully set the mic behind the trim of the cabinets.

With the final microphone in place, all Evrett needed to do was get out of the house undetected. While the front door was closest, Evrett still had to retrieve his bag from the bedroom.

When he was almost back into the hallway, his foot pressed a floorboard that resulted in a loud wooden creak.

Every muscle in Evrett's body froze.

He stood motionless.

Slowly Evrett turned his head. From the corner of his eyes he could see Molly begin to reposition herself on the chair.

Had she heard him? Was she coming out of her sleep?

For a brief moment her eyes opened and fluttered. Evrett dived to the floor as silently as possible. From this position, he could still see her.

Molly yawned and rolled over slightly in her chair.

Evrett couldn't risk spending any more time in the Randall house. He hurried down the hallway and exited the way he had come in, carefully shutting the window behind him.

With the mics in place, he was ready to begin surveillance. Evrett used his laptop and iPad to listen in on Chad and his mother. After a few days of eavesdropping, Evrett felt like he was beginning to understand both of them.

It was clear from the way Chad talked inside his house that he was defeated. He would come home from work day after day depressed. Evrett could hear it in the way he responded to his mother's questioning about his day.

"How'd it go today, honey? Anything exciting happen at the store?"

"Nah, ma. Nothing ever happens at the store. Just normal people buying your basic shit."

"Chad, don't swear."

Evrett wondered what happened to the man he had first discovered from his research. Somewhere along the way after Sam's accident he had stopped being a lawyer. Now he worked at the local corner grocery. Evrett couldn't imagine the blow Chad must have taken to his ego.

After a week, Evrett could predict Chad's every move. He would wake up, lounge around the house, bicker with his mother and go to work. He would come home later in the day, bicker some more and then retreat to his room.

Listening in to Chad's private life only assured him more that there would be no great loss from Chad's demise. Yes, his mother would lose someone to harp over, but surely a nurse could fulfill that role—it was inevitable anyway.

It was after this realization that Evrett began to think about confronting Chad. This would be his first interaction with one of the people on his list. He had never gotten the chance to talk to Andrew. Evrett wouldn't let this chance go by.

And so on a Sunday night, ten minutes before he knew Chad's shift would end, Evrett sat in his Audi watching the store front of the corner grocery. Through the window he could see Chad standing by the cash register, checking out customers' groceries with as little effort as possible.

He had to act now.

Within seconds Evrett was in the store. His heart beat faster and faster with each step toward the register.

He grabbed a box of cereal from one of the end caps and proceeded to Chad's check out aisle.

Looking around the store, Evrett could see the only people there were Chad and a little old lady slowly walking up and down each aisle.

"How's it going? Paper or plastic?" Chad asked.

Evrett looked at his one box of cereal.

"Plastic will be fine," he said.

It was a simple exchange, but it felt exhilarating. This was the first instance he had communicated with one of the eight people on his list.

Chad swiped the cereal box across the scanner. As he went to hit a button to end the sale on his keyboard, Evrett snatched a pack of gum and tossed it on the conveyor belt.

"Slow night?" he asked.

"Ha. No more than usual. You from around here?"

Evrett was surprised by Chad's questioning. In a town this small, it would be easy to spot any newcomers.

"No, actually. I'm just stopping on my way up north. You can't drive forever, you know."

"You got that right."

"Hey, I'm only here for tonight. Is there anything fun to do in this town?"

Evrett hoped he didn't sound too odd. He hoped that Chad would suggest some place that he frequented after hours of working in the grocery store. Or perhaps some trail he liked to walk alone. All Evrett needed was the opportunity to get him alone. Then he could ask the questions he really wanted to ask.

"In Winchester? On a Sunday? Nope. This place has got nothing going for it. Personally, I can't wait to get the hell out. That will be $4.97."

Evrett pulled out a five-dollar bill. Chad packed his two items and receipt in the grocery bag.

"Thanks for shopping with us. Have a good night."

"Thanks," Evrett said as he walked out of the register lane. He felt it was a good first step toward communication. Sure, he hadn't asked any questions about the man on the bridge, but he at least made contact.

That night Evrett waited for Chad to leave the store. He followed him home to Molly's house and then spent an hour listening to the microphones he had positioned there. It was more of the same.

"Are you going to cut the grass tomorrow?"

"Yeah, ma. I'll get to it."

"I don't want it to get too long. You know I hate how that looks."

"I said I'd do it. Goodnight, ma."

If Evrett wanted to, he could allow himself to feel sorry for Chad. It had to be hard to be his age with his education, only to live at home and work at the local general store. But Evrett didn't let that thought last for long. Visions of Chad running away from a burning Prius wiped away any sympathy he could ever develop for the man.

As the clock in Evrett's car ticked closer to midnight, he finally decided he had gathered enough information for the day. He knew Chad would not be returning to work for at least three days. He'd have to get up early to make sure he didn't miss Chad stepping out for any reason.

Maybe he'd be lucky and Chad would go for a hike. The woods around his Winchester home would offer enough isolation for Evrett to detain Chad, ask him what he needed to, and then make it look like his death had been the result of a hiking accident.

Evrett went to bed in the Brattleboro hotel room thinking of the possibilities of tomorrow. At seven o'clock he woke up, showered, got dressed and grabbed a coffee from the hotel vending machine.

He blew on the steaming liquid before taking a sip—a sip he would never remember.

19

ALL HE COULD DO WAS SMILE as the comments poured in on *The Long and Short* website. Alec's first successful story, which bought him at least another few months at the online publication, was sitting firmly at 4.8 stars. Alec especially enjoyed the moment when Angela rounded up and called it a five-star story in front of the rest of the contributors during a video conference call.

Seven weeks after its publication, he continued to write, while working on a novel on the side. He had started it about six months ago, based off his first baseball story, but hadn't gotten too far with it. He tried to tackle a few pages while his confidence was up, but he couldn't stop thinking about his next story.

With such a long period of time in between—his series was placed on a two-month cycle due to high volume from the website's collection of authors—Angela had him earn his pay through editing and website maintenance, something he had always had a knack for. This also meant he had plenty of time to think about the second installment, and that turned out to be a bad thing. The first idea came to him so quickly and so vividly. Why could he not manage a second story? He had a few ideas, but he could not develop them enough. He didn't have the same vivid imagery that he had with the first story.

How did it come to him last time?

I was drinking, he thought.

He looked over at his liquor cabinet, which had been surprisingly left untouched since he wrote the last story.

Alec had tried to sober up many times in his life, but all attempts had resulted in failure. The fact that he somehow inspired himself through one of his own stories boggled his mind. Nevertheless, the pressure of the next deadline started to weigh on him, and he thought about how one drink wouldn't hurt.

As he stood up, a train horn sounded loudly from outside his apartment. He took a detour to the balcony instead. It was a comfortable mid-September morning with the expected high to be in the eighties later that day, but the cool of the night had yet to give up its grasp. He sat down on his patio chair that reclined for optimal comfort on a morning like this. He smiled and took in all that was great in life.

To think he once peered over a bridge and thought about jumping. There was so much he had left to do that he didn't think about in that moment. He thought about the accident and how it was a sign. Alec wasn't very religious, and he hadn't stepped foot in a church for a service in more than twenty years, but whoever, whatever, caused that accident, wanted him to live another day.

The breeze strengthened and rustled his hair. He closed his eyes and like it had before, a story came to him. Fearful that this could happen at any moment, he kept a digital recorder in his pocket at all times. He even had an extra recorder under his pillow at night. He quickly pulled it out and began reciting his next story.

• • •

The Traveler
By Alec Rossi
The Long and Short

The brochure had photos of beautiful women, beaches and aircraft carriers on it.

San Diego looked wonderful.

Much better than the cold, abysmal solitude that was not often visited by the majority of United States citizens.

For the soon-to-be cross-country traveler, he often wondered if most Americans could even tell you where New Hampshire was.

For him, it was nearly in his rearview window.

He stuffed a few backpacks and suitcases with the essentials. He had already emptied his bank account and all of the cash was in a duffle bag. A little more than forty thousand dollars wasn't a fortune, but it was enough to get him across the country to start over.

He no longer wanted the name on his driver's license, nor the memories associated with the man pictured on it.

It was time for him to start anew.

He scanned the room for anything worth taking to his new life. He overlooked pictures and knickknacks that once meant something to him. He dismissed the law degree that was long forgotten.

But his panning around the room stopped when he caught a glimpse of his old hockey stick in the corner. On the floor next to the taped-up blade was a pair of ice skates. He had played as a child, but he wasn't good enough to get a college scholarship, so he quit.

His father urged him to keep trying, and so he attempted to walk on to his college team, but after a few practices he was cut, and the stick and skates found themselves a permanent home in the corner of his room.

"It's okay, son," he said, after he was cut. "Move forward."

So he did.

Staring at the stick, he thought about how that simple advice carried him for years, until he made one crucial, career-ending mistake.

Now, instead of skating on the ice, he was trying to run on land.

He slung the few backpacks over his shoulder and grabbed the stick. He left the skates because where he was going, ice was going to be hard to find.

He walked down the hall and into the foyer. He was certain his mother was asleep and that he could slip out without her knowing.

She wouldn't understand and he didn't feel like explaining himself. Plus, goodbye was not a word he wanted to say.

He knew in a way it was cruel, but avoiding the pain was the route he chose.

As he opened the door, his mother awoke on the couch. She couldn't see her beloved traveler, but she knew he was there.

"You're going to mow that lawn, aren't you? The grass is up to my knees."

The traveler had almost closed the door when he heard this, and he hesitated.

"Okay, ma."

He shut the door and walked to his car. He threw everything inside and then looked back at the house.

His mother was old and she could barely take care of herself. He looked at the long grass and looked back at the house.

"San Diego can wait thirty minutes," he said.

He ran around behind the house and opened up the shed. Inside was an old green John Deere riding mower. He topped off the tank with some gas and began to cruise around the half-acre lot.

It was the least he could do for the mother he was about to abandon.

Abandon. It wasn't just her he was abandoning. It was him. He was leaving his life as he knew it.

As he drove back and forth in neat rows, he thought about the long drive ahead of him and a new life in San Diego. Bartending. That's what he wanted to try first. Maybe some day he could open up his own sports bar. He could just smell the barley and hops.

He turned the corner to take care of the side of the house and he noticed a large branch that must have fallen in a recent rainstorm, lying ten feet in front of his mower. He pushed on the brakes and jumped off to move it out of the way. He dragged it back onto a section of grass that was already cut and walked back toward the mower.

As he did, the brakes unlocked and the mower rolled slowly down the slight decline toward the driveway.

The traveler saw this and ran to catch up.

But then it hit him.

133

A rock the size of a golf ball ricocheted off the blades and slammed into his throat, knocking him off his feet.

While choking on what he could only assume was blood, he used his hands to feel around his neck. He could feel the gaping hole and the blood rushing out.

He tried to breathe and managed only a few breaths. He looked up into the sky and saw a few clouds passing overhead. A dizziness came over him and he had to do something.

He tried to scream, but blood just popped out of his mouth. His larynx was crushed. He swallowed some more blood and struggled to take a few more breaths.

With his hands no longer covering the wound, he looked back up at the sky once more. He felt like he was beginning to float away.

He wished he was in his car and off to San Diego.

That's where he should be.

Or, he should be back on the ice rink or in a courtroom.

There are so many places he could have been right now, but instead, he was lying face up toward the sky.

As he swallowed one last time, he closed his eyes.

It was at this moment that he realized that this was his last day.

• • •

Alec sat back in his desk chair and interlocked his hands behind his head. In the middle of reciting, he had gotten up and ran to his computer.

"Wow," he said.

He couldn't believe how fast the story came together. It just flowed out of his mind and onto the computer screen. He gave it a quick proof read and sent it in to his editor.

As planned, later that week, the fourth Friday in September, the story was published on *The Long and Short* and it was garnering multiple five-star ratings.

Alec had found his niche.

He poured an ice tea and enjoyed the final seven innings of an Orioles' afternoon game.

It was a good day to be alive.

20

THE COFFEE WAS COLD. It was sitting on the table by the window. Evrett recognized it immediately as the cup he had from the morning and it was still full. His eyes tracked slowly from one item to another, taking in the full surroundings of his hotel room. Bars of sunlight from the blinds cut the wall across from the bed into columns of increasing width.

What time is it?

He rolled over to face the clock on the nightstand. It read 4:24.

Based on the sunlight, he knew it was the afternoon.

What had happened to him?

Evrett tried to recall the last thing he remembered. A hazy picture of him standing at the vending machine came to mind. His mind fluttered back to the coffee on the table.

I took a sip, he thought.

Had he? He remembered purchasing it and blowing on the drink to cool it down. But after that? Nothing.

It happened again.

When he woke up in Pittsburgh confused with his clothing soaked, he had thought it had been just a coincidence. But a second time? Was something the matter with him?

Was he sick?

He sat up slowly.

Evrett was on top of the comforter, still in the clothes he had put on after getting out of the shower that morning. His head felt foggy, as if he had taken too much cold medicine.

But he hadn't.

He stumbled from the bed, his legs not fully under his control yet. Evrett grabbed his phone and double-checked the time. He had lost almost nine hours of his day. How could that be possible?

Yes, he was under a considerable amount of stress; the massive journey he had embarked on was certainly not an easy one. Could he be suffering from exhaustion?

He planned to make an appointment and get it checked out when he returned to Baltimore. He couldn't risk losing control anymore. Not when he had important work to do.

After collecting his equipment, Evrett was out the door. It would take him a half hour to reach Winchester. He cursed himself for missing a whole day of surveillance. Who knows what opportunities he had missed.

Evrett turned on the narrow road that led to Chad's house.

"What the—"

Ahead of him, Evrett saw flashing lights. Even in the golden afternoon sun, the red warning of the ambulance was visible. A cop car, perhaps the only one in Winchester, was parked next to it. A small group of locals had gathered in front of Molly's modest house.

His Audi came to a halt behind an old Chevy pickup that had rust around its four tire wells. Evrett got out and approached the crowd.

He worked out a quick backstory for what he was doing in Winchester, should any of the bystanders have questions for him. He was sure they would recognize him as an outsider.

"Can you believe it?"

"Probably was out there for hours. It wasn't until Doug came by and found the tractor on the side of the road that anybody knew about him."

"My word, that's just awful."

"Horrible."

Evrett listened to the conversation, trying to figure out what happened. He peered over the heads of the two women in sweatshirts and jeans. On the side of the house lay a body covered in a blue tarp. The body looked to be around six feet tall. A few fingers could be seen underneath a fold in the blue material.

"We should call in the coroner, Jared," the EMT said to the cop who then radioed the request.

Scoping out the scene, Evrett's eyes darted from the covered body to the other side of the road. A John Deere tractor sat half on the road, its front tires down in the gravel.

Chad was supposed to mow the grass today.

Evrett glanced back at the front of the house. He saw a woman with her arms wrapped around Molly. She was smoking and her eyes made it clear she had been crying. Piecing it all together, Evrett knew the body on the side of the house belonged to Chad.

Another one dead. But how?

Evrett stepped closer to the crowd.

"What happened?" he asked.

"No one's quite sure. It looks like Molly's boy was stabbed in the throat or something," said a woman in her late fifties. She spoke without fully turning to look at Evrett. Her gaze too was fixed on the body.

Stabbed in the throat? Had Chad been murdered?

His mind rushed back to his blackout in Pittsburgh. He recalled the keys he had discovered the next morning. Evrett had no recollection of stealing that boat, and yet he had apparently done it. Was it possible he had confronted Chad? Could he have killed Chad and not remember it?

No. Evrett wouldn't have stabbed him out in the open.

I couldn't have done it. Not like that.

"Poor Molly," said the other woman.

Evrett needed to get closer. He didn't want to draw too much attention to himself, but he had to know what happened to Chad, especially if he had been responsible.

Moving around the two women, Evrett stood at the corner of Chad's driveway. No one had gone beyond this part. He assumed the police officer had told everyone to keep a safe distance. From this vantage point, Evrett could see the soles of two large work boots jutting out from the tarp. He recognized them as the shoes Chad wore everyday to work.

The EMT was standing a few feet from Evrett at the back of the ambulance. He was young, probably just out of high school. A little on the heavy side, his stomach hung over his belt. He was putting medical supplies away in the back of the vehicle.

"It's just terrible what happened," Evrett said after taking a deep breath. The EMT looked up at him.

"What's that?"

"I said it's just terrible what happened. A stabbing?"

Evrett motioned to his source a few feet away. The EMT's eyes glanced over.

"Mrs. Bennett doesn't know what she's talking about."

Evrett's ears perked up.

"It wasn't a stabbing?"

"Nah, just some freak mower accident. The guy got hit with a rock. Bled to death."

"A rock?" Evrett questioned in disbelief.

"Yup. Got him right in the neck. The dude bled out. The real kicker is that his mother didn't even realize he was out there. What a way to go."

Evrett looked back at the body.

"Yeah, what a way..." he said.

He wouldn't overstay his welcome at the gruesome scene. He didn't need anyone taking too much notice of the odd man out at their gathering.

Evrett only made it a few miles out of Winchester when he got the sudden urge to pull over. He hadn't stopped thinking about what he had just left behind. The image of Molly on her front stoop, her small hand shaking as it held a cigarette precariously near her lips, kept coming to his mind's eye. Evrett could picture Chad's lifeless body lying on blood-soaked grass. He couldn't focus on the road ahead with so many thoughts on his mind.

On the other side of the road, Evrett could see the Connecticut River. The sun was setting now and the water was smooth bronze.

"What is going on?" Evrett asked.

Two of his targets were dead, and he had no recollection of their last hours. He had been so close to confronting each one.

What were the odds?

And the blackouts?

The wooziness returned to Evrett's head. He felt caged in his car and needed to escape. He opened the car door and darted across the road. He took several slow breaths, trying to force his mind to calm down.

Evrett thought back to the morning. He pictured the coffee from the vending machine. It had been so hot. Ribbons of steam floated up into the air. Evrett had blown on the drink, sending ripples across the surface.

And then nothing. It was all gone.

Failure. That's what today meant for Evrett. Again he could cross a name off of his list, but it didn't bring him any closer to the ultimate goal.

The man on the bridge was no closer today than he had been any day before.

By the time Evrett was back in the hotel parking lot, the sun had set. He packed up his clothes and equipment and then checked the room twice over to make sure he left nothing behind.

He poured the cold coffee down the sink, tossed the cup into the trash and was back on the road by nine.

• • •

Hang in there.

It was a ridiculous poster, Evrett thought. A kitten hanging from a branch with the motivational slogan hung framed on the wall behind the receptionist. The rest of the waiting room was decorated with typical doctor's office flare. Ads for various prescriptions and paintings of nondescript landscapes broke up the beige walls.

"Evrett Eckhard?"

"Here."

He followed the nurse down the hall. She showed him into a private room.

"Dr. Pascual will be with you shortly."

"Thanks."

After a few minutes of isolation, the door opened and Dr. Pascual walked in. He was in his mid-forties and completely bald. Evrett noticed the odd stain on his white coat immediately. Jelly?

"Hi, Evrett. How are you feeling?"

"Fine. I feel perfectly fine."

The doctor opened his laptop and turned it to face Evrett.

"I have the results of your tests. Everything came back normal. The blood work showed that you're in good…well, great health actually. As did the EKG. And the brain scans showed no abnormalities."

"That's good then."

"Well, yes. It is on one hand. On the other, though, we still can't say for sure why you are experiencing blackouts."

Evrett had made an appointment the day he returned from New England. He couldn't risk blacking out again. He had six names left on his list, plus the man on the bridge.

"You said work's been stressful."

"Yes, I've had some pretty important projects lately. It's kept me extremely busy. A lot of late nights."

"Have you had any recent episodes?"

"No, it has only happened twice."

"Evrett, I'm going to recommend you try to relax a bit. I know it can be hard, but stress can be a life-threatening issue. Are you still running?"

"Several times a week."

"Good, keep it up. I'm going to also suggest you talk to someone. I'm going to refer you to Dr. Kaplan. He specializes in stress reduction therapy. I think it could help you a great deal. Don't worry, he's part of our medical group."

"You're sending me to a therapist?"

Dr. Pascual closed the laptop and looked Evrett in the eyes.

"Look, Evrett. You came here with some alarming symptoms. Now, you're lucky that there is no physical malady causing it. But, our minds are dangerous organs, and they can sometimes be just as damaging as any disease."

"All right. I appreciate it. I'll make an appointment."

"Good. Georgiana will set it up for you at the front desk."

The earliest appointment Dr. Kaplan had was in November. Evrett scheduled it. Therapy? He couldn't imagine talking about his feelings to a stranger. He would never be able to tell the truth about what was really troubling him. It could end up being just another ball for Evrett to juggle. How many could he keep in the air?

• • •

The doorbell rang.

"Trick or Treat!" Julia said.

Evrett smiled and let her in. She carried a bottle of chardonnay and a pumpkin.

"I thought I'd be festive."

She handed Evrett the pumpkin. It was Friday night, the day before Halloween. It also was the first time Evrett had Julia over to his house.

"Thanks. It certainly is…festive."

Evrett stepped back outside and placed the pumpkin next to the door on the front porch.

Julia stood in the dining room with the wine in hand. She admired every little detail of the room. It was fairly clear an architect like Evrett had put his personal touch on the design.

"Did you remodel this yourself?" she asked.

"Well, I designed it," he said. "I left the hard labor to 'G' and 'B'," he said, referring to one of the local contractors utilized by GGM.

Julia peered down the hallway in curiosity.

"Here," Evrett said, grabbing the wine. "Let me take this and your coat. I'll give you the tour later."

He hung her coat on a rack in the hallway and guided her to the kitchen to open the wine.

"You won't believe the gossip at work," she said, leaning on the island counter. "Darryl totally dropped the ball on the Orlando group account. They hated the second set of designs. They're talking about taking him off the project."

"That's ridiculous. Any word who might replace him?"

Julia smiled.

"You're kidding. That's fantastic. I mean, not for Darryl," Evrett said.

"Oh, I know. I know. Nothing's definite yet. They might end up giving him another chance. But David did run a few things by me. We'll see. It would be a huge opportunity," Julia said as she uncorked the wine.

Evrett and Julia's friendship had grown over the last few months. She was becoming a larger part of his life with each passing day, as they continued their lunches when Evrett wasn't out of town.

Julia had suggested they do dinner. Evrett suggested he cook.

They finished the first bottle of chardonnay, and at Julia's suggestion, Evrett gave her a tour of the house. He skipped over the locked office and she did not seem to care. Back in the kitchen, they went for round two, uncorking a bottle of sauvignon blanc.

"You have a really clean house, Evrett," Julia said.

He chuckled.

"Does that really surprise you?"

"Not in the least. You are pretty anal."

"Hey, I just like to keep things orderly," he retorted, thinking about if she only knew how anal he really was. Behind a locked door upstairs was all the proof she would ever need.

"Whatever, you're a neat freak and you know it."

Julia looked around the room. A picture of Sam and Evrett sat on the nearby china cabinet. She took a final sip of her wine.

"Evrett, I don't mean to offend you. And this is probably the wine talking at this point. But, do you ever think you'll find someone again?"

Evrett followed Julia's eyes to the picture of Sam. He didn't know what to say.

"I mean, I know you love your wife. But, do you think she'd want you alone for the rest of your life?"

"I… I…"

"I'm not saying today, or even in the next year. But I just know that life can be hard and shitty. It's even harder to go through it alone. You're young. You have all the rest of your life…"

"Julia, I think we should talk about something else."

"Shit, I'm sorry, Evrett. I didn't mean to upset you."

He got up from the table and carried their plates to the sink.

"No, really. Don't worry about it. I know you didn't mean anything by it. I just… I'm not ready to have that conversation yet."

"I understand, Evrett. I do. You're my friend and I just want to see you happy."

"Thanks, Julia."

There was a silence between them. Evrett finished his wine.

"Coffee?" he asked.

"That would probably be good."

The rest of the night was uneventful. Evrett and Julia talked about work a bit more. She shared a few funny stories about her family and Evrett spoke of his plans to see Sam's brother and family closer to Thanksgiving.

When it was almost midnight, and the effects of the wine had mostly worn off, Evrett helped Julia put on her jacket.

"Will you be coming in to work this week at all?"

"I'm not sure. I was going to plan my month out this weekend."

"Okay. Let me know. We can do lunch. Tonight was really fun and dinner was fantastic."

"I'm glad you enjoyed it. It was fun. We will have to do it again soon."

Julia smiled and kissed Evrett's cheek.

"Goodnight, Evrett."

"Goodnight."

He opened the door and led Julia out onto the porch.

"Happy Halloween," she said. "Oh no!"

They both looked down. The pumpkin Julia had brought with her lay smashed on the porch, its innards and seeds spread wide across the porch boards in a messy web.

"Damn, kids. I hate mischief night," Julia said.

Evrett escorted Julia to her car and waved as she drove off into the night. He walked back up to his house, looking left and right for any neighborhood kids.

He stood over the crushed pumpkin.

Kids, he thought.

He listened to the sounds of the night. Everything was quiet except for the hum of cars in the distance.

Hadn't it been quiet all night?

21

ALL SHE SAW WAS RED while looking at her reflection in the mirror. It wasn't the color she had expected when Colleen convinced her to dye and cut her hair. Come to think of it, had Colleen Hampton even showed her the box beforehand? Amanda Ramirez took one last look at herself and stepped out of the bathroom.

"What do you think?" Colleen asked.

She was sitting crossed legged on the bed they shared in a townhouse Colleen rented in the city of Lancaster, Pennsylvania.

"I love it," Amanda lied.

"I think it really is your color."

Amanda smiled. What did that mean? Amanda could hardly imagine fire engine red being anyone's color, let alone hers.

Things had changed. Two years ago, Amanda was working as a receptionist at a plastic surgeon's office in downtown Baltimore. It wasn't what she had envisioned for herself growing up in rural Lititz in the heart of Pennsylvania Amish Country, but it helped her pay the bills. That, combined with her waitressing job at one of the bars at Power Plant Live, and Amanda was doing quite well for being a twenty-three-year-old college dropout.

Her sophomore year at Loyola University Maryland had been harder than she imagined. The end of the spring semester found Amanda sleeping through class and cutting out on her finals. While other students were officially declaring their majors, Amanda made the decision to leave school and make it on her own in Baltimore.

It was just too hard to know what she wanted to be, she had told her parents. That managed to buy their sympathies as well as a few months of rent money until she landed on her feet. The job at the surgeon's office came first.

It wasn't hard work, but the monotony did wear on Amanda. Day in and day out, patient after patient came in, each one hating some aspect of his or her self. This one wanted Botox to smooth out her wrinkles; another wanted a nose job to correct the "deviated septum" she had inherited from her father. Amanda handed each one their proper forms, collected their co-pays and then looked at the clock.

After a year, Amanda decided it was time to give school another shot. The medical field was calling to her, and she decided to go back to school for nursing. The waitressing gig was money on the side that Amanda put directly into the bank. She was going to turn it all around.

Then the accident happened.

That summer day in July forced her to rethink it all. Driving home from the office on Interstate 83, she barely had enough time to slam on her brakes. In front of her Mazda, a red Prius collided with another car, forcing a tanker truck to jack-knife. It took a moment for the initial shock to subside before Amanda got out of her car.

Behind her several other motorists were stopping as well. She saw a few men run toward the scene but stop. The glimmer of fire caught her eye and she froze. She could not muster the strength to move an inch. She just watched, mesmerized by the fire.

Then, it hit her. The explosion knocked her to the ground. The force was strong, but not as overpowering as the guilt.

146

It wasn't until she was home safely wrapped in a blanket on her sofa that she thought of her actions or lack thereof. There had not been one bone in her body that told her to help the woman trapped in the car, or any of the other potentially injured motorists. It was a moment of truth for her and she was a statue.

What kind of nurse would she be?

Amanda never waited to find the answer. A few weeks later, she quit the receptionist job, took the money saved up for school and moved back to Pennsylvania.

It was an opportunity to find herself.

"What would you like for breakfast?" Colleen asked.

A year ago Amanda would have asked for a ham and cheese omelet with a side of home fries and sausage—her favorite from college. But being a vegetarian, Colleen had convinced Amanda a life without meat was a healthier one.

Without waiting for a reply, Colleen went to work mixing soy milk, bananas and cinnamon, the ingredients for a vegan French toast recipe she had found online. What Amanda would give for a plateful of bacon like her mother used to make.

"Are you ready for the show tonight?"

"You know, I almost forgot."

It was true. Her mind was elsewhere this week. It always was away somewhere roaming the fields of her past this time of year.

"You've got to be joking. We've been prepping for this show since last spring. How could you almost forget?"

"It's way too early. You know I'm not a morning person. Of course, I'm ready. We just need to drop the covered bridge shot off before work today."

"This will help jump start your day. Eat up."

Colleen served the fake French toast with a smile and Amanda ate almost half her portion before deciding she had had enough.

It was delicious, as usual, but the thought that she would be serving up similar pastries and crepes later that day soured the doughy breakfast before her.

Soon after moving back home and into a rented townhouse in center city Lancaster, she was waitressing at a crepe café on Queen

Street. It was a small restaurant with a Parisian feel that many of the local hipsters frequented. It was better than the doctor's office at least.

It was there that she met Colleen.

Colleen was a year older than Amanda and worked at the coffee shop on the corner of Queen Street, a few doors down from Amanda's café. Their shifts were similar and often they would see one another on the street on their way to and from work.

One night after her shift ended, Colleen introduced herself and walked Amanda home. The walk turned into a night spent talking until the sun came up.

Amanda had never been with another woman before. In fact, she had only been with one other person, and that was Jason Baker, her high school boyfriend. She hadn't wanted to sleep with him, but after dating all fall, she finally gave in to his incessant hounding.

It had only lasted a few minutes and Amanda regretted it immediately. The next month she found out she was pregnant. Her parents convinced her that giving the baby up for adoption was the only way Amanda could have a future. Plus, Jason had a football scholarship to worry about.

Amanda sometimes wondered where she would be had she kept her daughter. Each autumn, as the holidays approached, Amanda would look back and think how things would be different with an eight-year-old waiting for her at home.

She might have been married to Jason, still living in Lititz. He would have quit school and gone to work for his father's landscaping company. They would be just scraping by, maybe with another child or two.

Would that have been so bad?

Would that have been her?

She had never told Colleen any of this.

The couple grabbed the painted canvas leaning against the door and stepped out into the autumn air.

Amanda and her freshly dyed hair walked down the street with Colleen to a small art gallery on Prince Street. It was a three-story brick townhouse that had been converted to a gallery and studio. Each room featured work from local artists, and Amanda was lucky enough to have some of her paintings displayed in one of the small rooms on the second floor.

It was Colleen who had suggested she get into painting as a hobby. Creating art was definitely something Amanda enjoyed and she was fairly good at it too. Most of her paintings were of landscapes. She would go on walks and hikes, snapping pictures with her camera. She'd then use the photos for inspiration for her paintings.

Amanda hung the painting she had carried on the last hook on the wall.

"Oh, I like that one," Colleen said.

It was a painting of a red covered bridge spanning across a small river in the middle of a field. Amanda had seen it on one of her hikes a few months ago. Standing by the bridge was a female figure facing away, hair blowing in the wind.

"I see you painted her again."

The same girl was present in all of Amanda's paintings. She couldn't say exactly where the inspiration for the figure came from, but each time, she altered the image captured with her camera to include it.

Maybe it was the daughter she gave up.

Maybe it was her from her childhood.

"Well, hon, I have to go to work. I'll meet you here after your shift?"

Amanda nodded. First Friday was always a busy day for the café. Normally a busy day would cause her to work later than usual, but she had arranged to leave early with her paintings on display for the monthly event.

Colleen pulled Amanda close for a quick peck on the cheek, and she was out the door.

Amanda looked at the collection of paintings hanging in front of her. Was this really her life?

Eight years ago she gave up her child for the possibility of a life worth living. Here she was, a vegetarian waitress moonlighting as a wannabe artist. Her weeks were filled with trips to the Central Market, open mic nights for Colleen, serving crepes and painting. Was this the life she traded her daughter for?

Amanda switched the arrangement of paintings on the wall once more and checked her watch. She had the lunch and afternoon shift, and would have to be at work soon.

Although Prince and Queen Streets were a block apart from one another, the gallery was a few blocks north of the creperie. It was just enough time for her thoughts to turn to the Dresslens.

Every year, Nicklas and Sally Dresslen sent her a picture of Elena, the daughter Amanda gave up when she was a teenager.

The photo arrived in the mail every late October from a small town in upstate New York. Amanda's mom would receive it, and without opening the envelope, forward it to her daughter. She didn't want to know anything of the granddaughter she hadn't seen in eight years. The legal agreement of the adoption kept Amanda from ever making contact with her daughter. The pictures had been her only window into the little girl's life.

Amanda kept the seven photos, each one taken on Elena's birthday, October 26, in a small wooden box locked and hidden in her closet.

The seven photos were reminders of a former self Amanda had long lost sight of.

But by now there should be eight.

This year no photo had come. Amanda had called her mom in a panic ten days ago. She listened as her mother walked to the mailbox to check if it had arrived. There was no photo.

And so she waited. Another week crept by and still nothing. A million worries had set up residence within her head.

Was Elena sick?

Had the Dresslens moved and lost her address?

Was her mom hiding it from her?

What if they had died in a car accident?

It was hard to think about anything else, let alone her first art exhibit. She had worked so hard all through the summer to be ready for tonight. As she entered work, she pushed the thoughts of Elena and the photo from her mind.

She trudged through her shift at the restaurant, as the afternoon wore on, the tables became full of couples, young and old, out to enjoy the galleries and restaurants that had special events planned for the evening. Amanda was doing well keeping her mind off of the Dresslens.

"Hello, everyone. Can I get you something to drink?" Amanda said to her newest table.

She looked up from her notepad. A young couple, she guessed at least thirty-four, sat with their daughter. She had a bob of blond hair and played with a small doll she had brought with her.

"A coffee, please. Black," the man said.

"I'll have the frozen mocha latte and she'll have a chocolate milk," the woman said.

Amanda turned to walk back to the server's station. She had served hundreds of families just like this one before. Fathers, mothers, sons, daughters; so many times before she never even took notice of them. Today, though, the image of the lovely couple and their adorable all-American child plagued her as she poured the coffee into the ceramic mug.

She returned to their table, suffered through their order, and said goodbye to another table that just finished paying their tab. It was two women, probably right around her age. Both wore business casual attire. Certainly they were coming from work before heading out into the crowds wandering the downtown city streets.

Two dollars on a twenty-five dollar check. Some tip.

It was in that moment that Amanda looked at the two single bills crumpled up in her hand. The order of the perfect family weighed heavy on her mind. All she saw was her red hair and eight years wasted.

This wasn't how it was supposed to be, she thought.

For her or Elena.

22

IT TOOK A DOUBLE-TAKE FOR EVRETT to realize that he was looking at Amanda Ramirez. Three weeks of surveilling a brunette made him completely unprepared for his target to walk out of her house with bloodstained red hair.

"Oh, man," Evrett said. "Why, Amanda?"

Evrett laughed. He honestly did not care what she did with her hair. Although, he thought it was funny that he had a small moment of disappointment for her decision.

Amanda walked alongside her girlfriend Colleen Hampton. At first, when Evrett arrived in Lancaster, Pennsylvania, he thought Amanda was still living with a roommate. But after he snuck in to place recording devices in her apartment, he found only one bedroom. He hid a device in the kitchen, the bedroom and the living room, and later that night, his suspicions were confirmed.

And this presented a new challenge. He thought his first three targets were unattached. To kill Andrew and Chad, it meant not having to rob a spouse like he was robbed. He thought he was walking into a similar situation with Amanda, but that was not the case.

He could tell they were totally in love. Through conversation and observation, it was clear.

Evrett watched the couple walk down the street, presumably to the art gallery. He got out of his Audi and slowly followed from a safe distance. He had done this several times before and knew that he could follow them without issue.

He tried to figure out what was on the canvas she was carrying, but at the distance he was at, he could not make it out. To him, it just looked like a bunch of colors mixed together.

Perhaps today would be the day. He had planned to go into the art gallery and approach her, but after meeting Chad and then finding him dead hours later, he thought otherwise.

It was still puzzling.

He couldn't completely grasp what had happened in the last five months. Andrew died in an accident that he somehow seemed to be a part of. Chad also died in a freakish accident during a time period that Evrett couldn't personally account for.

Did he succeed? Did he play a role in their deaths?

The month preparing for his trip to kill Amanda had been agonizing. Every night he went to bed wondering about the prior two targets. He had reviewed all his memories and searched deep in his mind, but he had yet to uncover the lost hours. All he knew was that in the hours that he had blacked out, two of his targets died.

He was prepared to be a murderer; however, it was scary for him to think that he may be a murderer and not know for sure.

Though that idea gave him second thoughts about everything he was doing, he decided to press on. He must. Sam wouldn't give up on him. And he did not plan to give up on her. So many stood around unwilling to help her when she needed it most, and he was not going to be like them.

He was not going to cower in the face of danger.

That is why, in spite of all the mysterious happenings, Evrett continued to pace Amanda as she walked to the gallery.

He had been inside the gallery numerous times and he had stood in front of her art. Her paintings told a story, one that his surveillance microphones could not tell.

Every single painting had a young girl depicted, and he could not figure out why. He conducted extensive research on art, and he even consulted a former professor at Georgetown.

One of his architecture professors was big into representational art, and his advice was that if a certain artist was focused on painting the same figure or person, it represented someone who was or still is important in their life.

When he said that, Evrett couldn't help but think of the numerous sketches of the man on the bridge.

He watched the two women walk into the gallery as he thought about Amanda's paintings. The girl couldn't be Colleen. The subject was clearly too young. Perhaps it was Amanda as a child, but from what he had researched, that did not fit the profile.

He waited outside while the two women took care of business inside of the art gallery. Evrett knew that in twenty minutes she would be off to the café where she was a waitress.

Her life was very structured, and that made it tough for Evrett to come up with a plan of attack.

For Andrew and Chad, it was easier. He had ideas initially before they suddenly died. Both men provided ample opportunities and Amanda did not.

He found a bench along the street a few buildings down from the gallery to sit and wait. He thought about going inside, but he had already stopped in twice and Colleen had approached him the last time. He knew it would be too suspicious if he went in again, at least while Colleen was there.

Thinking about Colleen also made him second-guess his actions. When Amanda is dead, how is she to feel? Ideally, she will find out that Amanda died in some unforeseen accident and she will never look for revenge. She will never have the opportunity to watch the evening news and see her loved one left to die.

That was how it had to happen.

Evrett had to be sure.

His phone buzzed, snapping him away from the thoughts of

Amanda and Colleen.

He reached into his pocket and swiped his index finger across the screen. It was a text from Julia.

It read: "Hey, how are you?"

Evrett hesitated, but pulled up the keyboard to type a response.

"I'm good. Out of town right now visiting the folks. Needed some time away. I'll be sending my latest schematics on the riverfront project in later this afternoon."

He pressed SEND and stared at the phone as it instantly told him that it was received. He then saw a bubble pop up indicating that Julia was typing.

He waited.

It disappeared and seconds later, her reply appeared. "I'm sure you'll have your work in. I was hoping you'd be around later. I was looking to have someone join me for dinner. When will you be back?"

Evrett knew Julia wanted more, and the thought excited him. He felt alive and wanted, but at the same time, the thought made him feel sick. He could not cheat on Sam. His mother told him a few days ago that it was time to move on with his life, but everything he did brought up some reminder of Sam.

And Julia was virtually a clone of Sam. They shared similar interests and similar looks, which just made it worse.

Perhaps it would be therapeutic to date Julia, he thought. Certainly more therapeutic than going to see a therapist. The doctor recommended that he should see one to deal with the blackouts, but he wasn't a hundred percent convinced that he needed it. Like an old man shrugging off heart pain, he trucked on.

Still, the argument in his head about dating Julia ended the same way; if Sam were to find out, he could never live with himself.

He punched up the keyboard on his phone and typed: "Sorry, I won't be home tonight. Perhaps another day."

He hit SEND and slid the phone back into his pocket. It was truly something that he would worry about another day. Today and the next few weeks were dedicated to Amanda.

The door opened to the gallery and she stepped out onto the sidewalk with Colleen. The two shared a telling embrace and went their separate ways.

Amanda walked right past Evrett. She had no clue how close she was to death.

Evrett saw her go by but pretended to be looking off in the distance. He could tell she wasn't completely with it anyway. He could have stared at her the whole way and she would not have noticed.

Clearly, there was something pressing on her mind.

After a few minutes he got up to head to the café. He had gone in once before, but he didn't get her as a waitress. Nevertheless, it provided a good opportunity for him to see how she worked.

As he walked toward the shop, he saw a mother with her daughter walking by. The young girl tripped on part of the sidewalk that was protruding in the air due to the roots of an old tree deforming the once perfectly flat concrete.

He reacted quickly, reaching down to scoop the young girl up in his arms before she smacked the concrete.

Her mother gasped and let out a small cry. She was in disbelief. She could not believe how quickly he reacted.

"Oh my God!" she said, reaching out to take her daughter from his hands. "Thank you so much. That was ... That was just amazing."

Evrett smiled while thinking about what he had just done. Honestly, he couldn't believe that he reacted so quickly, but like any hero, he was completely ready to play it off like a normal occurrence in his everyday life.

"No problem," he said, smiling. He looked the young mother in her eyes. She was in her early thirties and attractive. Evrett quickly noticed no ring on her finger and used it to his advantage.

"Would you like to get some coffee?" he asked.

The woman was taken aback, but at the same time, flattered. A handsome man just saved her daughter from injury and then asked her to have some coffee. How on Earth could she turn him down?

"Um, yes, sure," she said. "Why not?"

Evrett smiled.

"I'm Sarah," she said, extending her hand. "And this is Jamie."

"Jonathan," Evrett said, meeting her hand with his. "This place looks good enough. Shall we?"

The trio walked in and had a seat at one of the tables in the small dining area. A few minutes after the hostess seated them, Amanda walked up.

"Hello, everyone. Can I get you something to drink?" Amanda said, looking up from her notepad.

"A coffee, please. Black," Evrett said.

"I'll have the frozen mocha latte and she'll have a chocolate milk," Sarah added, as Jamie sat at the table, playing with her doll.

"I'll be right back with your order," Amanda said, disappearing into to kitchen.

After a few moments of awkward silence, Sarah looked up at Evrett. "So Jonathan, what do you do?"

"I'm an architect," he said, figuring that lying about his name was good enough. "I consult on projects for many outside companies."

"An architect," she said, sounding impressed. "I can't say I've ever met an architect before."

"Unfortunately, I've met one too many," he said, adding a laugh.

She contributed with a giggle, assuming that meeting more than one was a bad thing.

"Are you from around here?"

Evrett proceeded with caution. "No, I'm from New York. I took a job in Harrisburg and I've been living here for the last three years. There's just something nice about this area. Much different than the city, in a good way."

"I've never been."

"You've never been to New York City?" Evrett asked. He couldn't believe that someone living only three hours away from one of the greatest cities on Earth had yet to visit it.

"Nope. I've always wanted to see a Broadway play, but I just haven't had the money to do so."

Amanda interrupted and placed their drinks on the table.

"Anything else I can get you?" she asked.

"No, that will be all," Evrett said.

He took a quick sip of his coffee and it nearly burned his tongue. The flavor was unique, in a good way, and he wondered how had he not ordered one of these every day?

"This is good," he said.

Sarah took a few sips of her drink and had the same response. "Yeah, I love this place. I don't know why I don't come in here more often."

She stopped for a second and continued, "Then again, at five dollars a pop, I quickly remember why I don't come here. That's a little pricey for my salary."

Evrett took a few more sips, "What do you do?"

"Well, I work at a small dress shop down the road," she said. "It's not much, but it helps pay the bills. And they're flexible with my schedule so I can take care of Jamie."

Sarah paused again, and then continued, "Honestly, her father isn't in the picture and he doesn't help much, so I'm pretty much on my own."

Evrett was a bit surprised at how forthcoming she was, but then again, he could tell that she liked him and was willing to make him completely aware of her situation.

He took another two sips of his coffee and reached into his pocket to pull out his wallet. It was time for him to leave. He decided he'd approach Amanda tomorrow.

He grabbed a wad of cash that he had brought along with him. He loaded his wallet with five thousand for the trip knowing that he did not want to leave any trace of his presence in Lancaster.

"What are you doing?" she asked.

He sifted through and pulled out two thousand dollars. "Here. This is for the coffee. It's on me."

She looked at him crazily. "I see hundred dollar bills. Are you kidding me?"

"No," he said, standing up. "It's for the coffee, and whatever is left over, use it to take Jamie to New York City to see a Broadway show. You deserve a special trip."

"I can't take this."

"You can. I insist. I don't need it."

Evrett smiled at Jamie who was still playing with her doll. "Be more careful on the sidewalk. Accidents are everywhere waiting to happen."

"I can't thank you enough for this."

"You don't have to."

Evrett walked out of the coffee shop feeling proud of himself. Perhaps a good deed would counteract all of his future sins.

He stepped out the door and felt the crisp, late autumn cold air pinch his cheeks. All he could remember was how great it felt.

23

A GLASS OF RED WINE here and there was the only exception that Alec made during his recent dry spell. He was going on 120 days without drinking beer or liquor, a feat that may have saved his marriage many years ago.

He no longer worried about that, though. Tonight, Alec was sharing a bottle of Doña Paula Malbec with a beautiful woman.

Angela and he had grown closer over the last two years and this was officially the fifth dinner date they had gone out on in the last three weeks. They had shared dinners before, but it was usually with a group of friends. However, a few weeks back, they were alone at an Italian bar and grill, and they decided to order up a bottle of wine. After hours of talking and laughing, a few sparks flew and before they knew it, they were back at Alec's place.

They woke up the next morning with no regrets and decided to give the relationship a try.

At thirty-five, Angela welcomed the chance at a relationship with

Alec. She had been married once before, and under different circumstances than Alec, she too wound up signing divorce papers.

That was five years ago and she hadn't been with another man since. It was not that she didn't want to, she just didn't have the time to find a worthy man. She focused too much time on *The Long and Short* for her to care about her love life.

Until now.

Alec swirled the wine in his glass, sitting with his back against the chair in a relaxed position. Angela was sitting forward with her elbows on the table, running her right index finger along the outer rim of her wine glass.

She smiled and looked up at Alec, "Ready to pay up and head home?"

Alec smiled and nodded. He knew what this meant and he was just as eager to get back to the bedroom.

The last three weeks had been a blast for the sex-deprived couple. Both had been out of commission for so long and to all of a sudden be thrown back into the game was like being a college student all over again.

Alec lifted his glass and tilted it until the base was nearly level with the ceiling. In three big gulps, the delicious wine was gone. It wasn't the proper way to finish such a good wine, but when the bed sheets were begging to be displaced, speed was key. Angela did the same as Alec dropped cash on the table. He reached out for Angela's hand and they were off.

• • •

After a few hours, Angela was fast asleep, lying naked next to Alec. Her right arm was wrapped around his chest as he lay on his back staring at the ceiling.

Truly, for the first time in about ten years, he was happy. It was only three weeks into their relationship, but he was thinking about marriage. He knew it was way too soon to be thinking that, but he couldn't help but ponder it. Everything seemed perfect when with her.

This thought was interrupted as she gently squirmed in bed and then tightened her grasp on him. With his right arm wrapped around her back, he softly caressed her skin along her spine.

Alec began to think about his father and how he wished he could introduce Angela to him. They had met before, a long time ago when they were both at the newspaper, but it wasn't under these circumstances. At that point in their lives, the prospect of their current situation could not have been fathomed.

Scanning the bedroom, he watched the glow of passing car lights glide across the ceiling. He could hear their tires cut through the rain-soaked asphalt as a boom of thunder echoed lightly in the distance. Lightning flashed brightly, illuminating the room. About thirty seconds later, there was another rumble and another flash, and this time, out of the corner of his eye, Alec saw it.

A dark figure stood in the doorway and disappeared as quickly as the lightning flashed. Alec jumped up, awaking Angela.

"What is it?" she asked, looking in the same direction Alec was.

Alec said nothing and saw nothing. It was only for a split second and it was out of the corner of his eye.

"Nothing," he said. "It was nothing."

She heard another roll of thunder echo and she smiled at him.

"Scared of thunderstorms?"

Alec laughed, "Yeah, that must be it."

He laid back down and closed his eyes, and as soon as he did, he saw a vision of a woman driving. It was happening again. He reached over to the nightstand and grabbed his digital recorder. He quietly recited the details as he walked out of the room and to his desk in the living room. He then punched out the third installment of his ongoing series.

• • •

The Mother
By Alec Rossi
The Long and Short

Rain pounded the glass as the wipers worked overtime.
Mother Nature was simply hammering home her point that no

one should be out driving in this weather, especially in the dark.

The winding roads, lined with trees and filled with dead leaves, made it even worse, and for a panicked mother, the conditions were primed for disaster.

She did not ease off the pedal, though.

Onward she went at speeds that no person should even attempt when driving conditions were optimal.

She rubbed her eyes with her left hand to clear away the tears that were blackened by her Mascara. All she could think of was her daughter.

She held her once, many birthdays ago, but since that first day, her daughter had been a distant memory, carried on only through photographs.

Not anymore, she thought while swerving to regain control of the car as it hydroplaned around a sharp bend. Tonight, she was taking back what was hers for only nine months.

She knew she was getting close. Her cellphone battery died an hour ago leaving her without a GPS, but fortunately she had researched her destination online many times before.

She knew the way by heart even though this was her first trip—and it would be her last. She had no plans on returning.

The rainstorm subsided from a downpour to a drizzle as she came within a mile of the house. She slowed the car and parked it along the side of the road. As planned, she would have to walk the rest of the way. She grabbed a small black backpack and disappeared into the woods.

She checked her digital compass that she bought on the drive up to make sure she was heading in the right direction. From where she parked, she knew it was about a mile to the southeast. Dressed in all black, she maneuvered around trees and through the brush.

It was dark. Really dark. The cloud cover made it darker, although with it being a new moon, a clear sky would not have made a difference. In upstate New York, light pollution was hard to find.

She nearly slammed into a few trees, but she juked at the last second to slip past them unscathed.

The rain grew heavy again as a flash lit up the night sky. A light illuminating the backyard of her destination cut through the trees and the raindrops to give her a target. She slid the compass into her pocket and ran up to the edge of the brush.

She scanned the house, a two-story American Craftsman, with dark brown siding to give it a bit of the log cabin feel.

Inside, all the lights were off, as the family fell asleep hours ago. It was close to three in the morning and they had no clue that she was within fifty yards of their home.

The rightful mother reached into her backpack to grab her flashlight. She could not believe what she was doing, but at the same time, she could not believe she had not done it sooner.

It was a mistake to give her up and it was a mistake not to fight those who persuaded her to give away her most precious gift to the world.

Seeing the house for the first time, she planned her next move. She scanned the entire property for anything that would stop her and there wasn't a single issue. She quickly ran across the yard and up to the back door, a large glass sliding door with a deadbolt lock.

No problem, she thought. This is what she prepared for, watching countless Internet "how to" videos. She slid open the outer screen door, which was now sporting a glass pane for the approaching winter season, pulled out a pair of bent bobby pins and went to work on the lock. Twenty seconds later, she was gently sliding open the door. It was frighteningly easy, she thought.

No alarm. No dog. No one in the kitchen getting a late-night snack. All of her initial worries were calmed. Preoccupied with her mission, she left both sliding doors open as she walked into a foyer hallway toward a staircase that she presumed led to the bedrooms.

There was still no sign of life as she carefully toed each step, praying that a loose board would not scream out to the homeowners.

Once at the top, she saw four doors, and fortunately, the lone door to her left was covered in drawings that could only be etched by an eight-year-old. She approached the door and delicately turned the knob. The door popped open with a light sound that disturbed not a soul, not even her daughter.

Sleeping on her left side, her arms clutched a light brown Teddy bear that was basking in the yellow glow of the night-light next to her bed. She was so peaceful.

And her real mother smiled.

Eight years and finally, the mother could smile.

Her daughter readjusted her grip on the bear, but never awoke to see her true mother admiring the bedroom. It was clean and filled with things she could never provide. A top-of-the-line keyboard piano next to a bookshelf loaded with sheet music. Aside of that was an easel with a blank white canvas on it. Lying on the floor was a beautiful painting of a lake surrounded by pine and oak trees with a woman lying on the bank. On the other side of the room, there was a desk with a MacBook Pro and an iPad. Above the desk was a shelf overfilled with trophies from various sports and academic competitions.

It was at this moment the once-panicked mother became the proud mother. Her baby was making the most of everything she had available to her, and none of this would be accessible if her mother were to continue with her felonious mission.

"I can't do it," she said, falling to her knees, with more tears rolling down her cheeks. She stared at her daughter for a few more moments before collecting herself and standing back up. She walked over to the dresser where a picture of her daughter was taped up against the mirror. She could tell it was taken recently because her daughter looked much older than she did in any of the other seven photos her mother had suffocating in a locked box.

She pulled it off the mirror and made her way to the landing at the top of the staircase.

And that's when she was confronted by one of her biggest worries, and it was big.

The 130-pound Rottweiler growled and stared at her from the other end of the dark hall.

It was time to go.

The mother darted down the stairs with the Rottweiler sounding the alarm in the fashion true guard dogs were meant to. His barks awoke the entire family, but by the time they all shot up in their beds, the mother was sprinting toward the back door with the Rottweiler closing the gap to twenty feet.

The mother looked back to see the snarling beast pounding the hardwood with his massive paws, and she never saw the danger ahead.

The once-opened outer glass door shattered upon impact, slicing skin all over her body. She fell to the cement patio releasing a painful bellow that even scared the Rottweiler for a second, but he still launched himself at her, locking his jaw around her left ankle.

She screamed again and kicked the dog square in the face with her right foot. She wasn't proud of this, but survival instincts started to take over. The dog released her and she popped up to begin her sprint into the woods.

The rain was still falling as she ran in the direction from which she came. The adrenaline blinded her to the fact that she had already lost half a quart of blood through the gash in her right wrist. She just kept running until she came to an opening, but it was not the opening she was looking for. There was no car or pavement.

There was just a lake.

"Oh my," she said, recognizing the landscape. She looked down at her daughter's photo now covered in blood and began to cry. By this point more than a quart and a half had emptied out of her and the dizziness set in. She fell into the rain-soaked mud and rolled onto her back. Her breaths were shorter and coldness took over her entire body.

As she the rain pellets stung her cheeks, she pulled the photo of her daughter in close to her chest.

"Please don't make the same mistakes I did," she said, hoping somehow her daughter could hear her.

But she could not. And she never would.

Knowing this to be true, the mother closed her eyes and said a short prayer. She peacefully accepted that this was her last day.

• • •

It was nearly four in the morning as Alec tapped out the final words to his story. He could not believe what he had just written. It was truly the saddest of all the stories so far and he had no clue how on Earth he had gotten the idea. Nevertheless, he clicked the save button and walked back over to the bed where Angela lay on her side, hugging a pillow.

It was eerily similar to the daughter holding the Teddy bear. He shook the thought and slid under the sheets. She awoke briefly, set aside the pillow and replaced it with Alec.

He smiled, took a deep, relaxing breath, and fell right asleep.

24

WET AGAIN. EVERYTHING WAS SOAKED. Evrett rolled over in the bed and felt the damp sheets stick to his skin. As he opened his eyes, there was a bit of a blur before it all came into focus. When it did, he noticed the 1980s tan flower-printed wallpaper and the orange shag carpet. None of this made sense. He had no clue where he was.

Wearing just boxer briefs that were damp, he stepped out of bed to find his clothes strewn around the room. He noticed the breakfast menu on the nightstand and assumed that he was at some sort of motel—definitely one that was in need of a welcoming party to the twenty-first century.

He picked up the menu and read the top couple lines:

Shandy Inn, Old Forge, New York.

"New York?" he blurted out. "Where the hell am I?"

He grabbed his phone and opened up the Google Maps app. After a few seconds, the little blue dot on the screen placed him in upstate New York.

Evrett dropped the phone and sat back down on the bed. Multiple thoughts stormed through his head, so fast and so countless that he couldn't concentrate.

His head was spinning and it only came to a stop when a pair of strong knocks on the door broke the silence of the room.

"Mr. Hoffman," a female voice said.

She knocked again, "Mr. Hoffman. It's noon. You said you'd be out by eleven."

Evrett just sat there. He didn't know what to say. The only thing going through his mind was last week's phone call to Dr. James Weatherburn. He didn't actually speak to him, but it was his office.

"Dr. Weatherburn's office, how can I help you?" the receptionist asked.

"Yes, this is Evrett Eckhard. I'd like to cancel my appointment," he said.

"One moment please," she responded.

A minute passed and the receptionist returned. "Your paperwork mentions issues with blackouts. Are you sure you would like to cancel? This sounds like a very serious matter."

"Yes, I've been fine. I was under a lot of stress and I'm feeling a lot better now."

"Okay, Mr. Eckhard. Please call us immediately if anything happens."

"Sure, I will."

That response echoed through his head at this moment.

It happened yet again.

Currently, he sat in a motel room, completely disoriented and questioning everything.

"Mr. Hoffman!"

"Yes, I'm here," Evrett said. "I'm sorry. I'll be out in a minute."

After a pause, he heard her say, "Okay, thank you."

Evrett started to collect his things. It was déjà vu. His pants were soaked. His shoes were dripping wet and his T-shirt was waterlogged. The only difference was that the bottom of his jeans had heavy traces of mud.

If it weren't for that, he would swear that he had stepped into a time machine and returned to Pittsburgh.

Evrett quickly packed up his clothes and wiped down everything in the room. There couldn't be any evidence that he was ever in this room. He didn't quite understand why he was in upstate New York, but based on the last two blackout experiences, he assumed something bad happened to Amanda. He couldn't be certain, but at this point, he couldn't leave it up for interpretation. Something strange was going on.

And why was he in upstate New York?

Evrett had researched Amanda thoroughly. Her family grew up in the Harrisburg area. Her girlfriend was local. Her ex-boyfriend was local. Every part of her life was local.

He must of have overlooked something.

Evrett's shoes were no different than his jeans. As he picked away the hardened mud, he assumed the worst for Amanda. He wanted to investigate, but he decided against it. He was already in Old Forge without any explanation, so he deemed it best to get out of town immediately before he made an impression. Hopefully, the motel clerk didn't put his face to memory.

He paid the clerk in cash and got into his car to drive the seven hours back to Lancaster.

That was the location of his last memory prior to waking up in Old Forge and that was where he would begin to investigate.

If something had happened to Amanda, Colleen should know.

The drive was long and filled with thoughts of what could have possibly happened—not just with this particular incident, but with the other two blackouts.

It was three o'clock in the afternoon and he was entering Pennsylvania. On the backseat of his car in a trash bag were his soggy clothes. He had to wear his dirty shoes for a few hours until he drove through a populated area that had a small strip mall. There, he walked into a shoe store and purchased a new pair of sneakers and wore them out, leaving the old pair in the box for the shoe store to throw out.

An hour later, he stopped at a diner for dinner and he tossed the bag of clothing into the dumpster in the parking lot. With everything scattered about, if there was any evidence of a crime on his clothing, no one would ever find it.

After a four-dollar salad bar and a turkey Reuben, Evrett was back on the road. Headlight after headlight lulled him into a trance that made him lose track of the last thirty miles. He only realized it when the gaslight lit up accompanied by a ding.

Fortunately, he could see on the horizon a big Sunoco logo lighting up in the night sky. He pulled off on the next exit and drove alongside one of the many open pumps. There was only a lone pick-up truck with years worth of rust sitting quietly at one of the other pumps.

Evrett walked inside and dropped forty dollars on the counter. "I'll need forty on pump three. Thanks."

The clerk rang it up as Evrett walked back out the door. As he crossed the lot to his car, he felt his phone vibrate in his pocket. He reached into his pocket and it vibrated once again confirming that he was likely getting a phone call. On the caller ID screen, it read: JULIA.

Evrett stopped in his tracks and began the debate in his head. Should he answer or should he let it go to voicemail? As it hit the fourth ring, he knew time was running out.

Against his better judgment, he answered.

"Hey, Julia."

"Hey, Ev," she said. No one really called him "Ev" and this was the first time Julia said it, but Evrett was okay with it. She continued, "Where are you at?"

"Driving right now," he responded. "My meetings went a little later than I expected and—"

"Are you close to home?" Julia interrupted. "I want to see you."

Evrett hesitated. His plan was to return to Lancaster, but he made the mistake of telling Julia that he was driving. She knew he was away and the only reason he'd be driving would be to come home. It was already eight o'clock and there would be nothing that he could do at this time in Lancaster. He could return Monday morning and go to the art gallery to hopefully find Amanda.

"I had to swing by my parents for a bit, but I'm on my way," he said. "I can be home by eleven. Is everything okay? Would you like to come over?"

"Yes," she said instantaneously. "Everything is okay. I have a bottle of wine. I can bring it over."

Evrett hesitated again. Bottle of wine. She said nothing was wrong.

I wonder what she truly wants? he thought.

Evrett wondered if she would ever be satisfied with their friendship. He knew she wanted more, but he could not give that to her at this point. Nevertheless, he enjoyed her presence; he loved the way he felt when she was near. So with that, he decided to drive back to Baltimore.

"That sounds great," he said. "I'll see you then."

Evrett clicked off the phone and proceeded to fill his gas tank. A few minutes later, he was on the road with a mission to get home by eleven. The whole way home he thought about Sam, just hoping he was doing the right thing.

• • •

Evrett pulled up into his garage seven minutes after eleven. Julia's car was already there waiting. He quickly gathered up his things and got out of his car.

Julia was standing next to hers with the bottle in hand. She walked over to Evrett and put her arms around him.

"I missed you," she said.

Evrett put his arms around her, too.

"Me too," he said with less conviction than she displayed.

He was serious. He did miss her, but he just couldn't put it to words yet. Sam was still in the forefront of his mind.

"Let's get inside. It's too cold for you to be out here. And where's your jacket?"

Julia just smiled. She was wearing a low-cut lavender shirt that showed off a decent amount of cleavage. It was snug around her stomach proving to the world she had not an ounce of undesired fat. Evrett couldn't help but think how beautiful she truly was.

The two walked inside and Julia went straight to the kitchen to fetch a pair of wine glasses. Evrett hurried upstairs to drop his suitcase off in his office and lock the door on his way out. As he descended the stairs, he heard the buzz of the electric corkscrew and the pop signifying success.

"I thought we'd watch a movie on Netflix," she shouted from the kitchen.

Evrett walked down the hall toward the kitchen. He and Sam used to have Netflix nights all the time. He and Julia had partaken in a few over the last month, and with each one, Evrett became more and more comfortable. However, they never started so close to midnight. Typically, they were saying their "Goodbyes" at this point.

Nevertheless, Evrett went with the flow.

"Sounds good," he said, turning the corner and appearing in the kitchen.

Julia was pouring the French merlot into a large stemless bulb. She filled it much higher than any wine connoisseur would permit, but Evrett wasn't one to care.

"Here," she said, handing him the first glass. She quickly filled hers as Evrett stuck his nose into the bulb to get a whiff.

"Smells good. Really has a strong oak aroma."

Julia cocked her head and gave Evrett the "You're not a snob" look as she finished her pour. She lifted her glass in the air. "To a good night."

Evrett wasn't sure what she was going to toast to at first, but that was something he could get behind. After the last twenty-four hours, he could use some time to relax. Mainly, he just didn't want to be alone tonight.

He lifted his glass to meet hers and the cling made them both smile. Evrett tilted the glass and took a large gulp—again, another offense that would anger the connoisseur.

"How is it?" Julia asked.

"Really good," he said. "Just what I needed. Now let's go find a movie."

It took fifteen minutes for them to come to an agreement on what to watch as they sifted through the numerous categories and titles. By that time, Julia was already pouring a second glass for them both.

She returned to the couch and curled her legs up under a blanket and rested her head on Evrett's chest. She wrapped her arms around him as the movie started.

It was a comforting feeling for Evrett and he spent the majority of the first fifteen minutes of the movie thinking about Julia and Sam.

He gazed down the dark hallway toward the staircase that led to the master bedroom. He envisioned Sam standing there. Three years ago, a sight like this would have meant the end to their marriage, and it was an offense he would never commit. He loved Sam with all his heart and he never wanted to inflict pain on her. He never had the urge to cheat. Yes, he appreciated young, beautiful women, but he saw them for who they were. He never once thought that he'd love to be with any of them. Sam was his perfect match.

Was. That was the key word.

The movie they were watching broke into an action-packed scene where a few cars were speeding down the highway. They approached an underpass and the one car flipped several times and exploded.

Julia didn't think twice about it; but Evrett couldn't help but close his eyes. He imagined what it must have been like to be sitting in the car. Not the one on the television, but rather, the one his wife died in.

He thought about the heat, the smoke, the gas, the fear; it was all around him. He could see all the cowards watching. He smiled when he saw Andrew and Chad. He was glad they, too, were dead. They deserved it for giving up on his wife. He looked at Chase holding the phone and the anger built inside him. He wanted to take him out to the woods, like Chase did with that poor man.

Then he saw Amanda and he didn't know what to think. Was she dead? She, too, deserved it, and if she wasn't, he promised himself that she would be soon.

He turned around to look up at the bridge. There was no one there. He knew someone was there minutes ago, but he fled. Another coward.

The burning car started to shake and just before it was ready to explode, Evrett snapped out of it.

Julia was there shaking him. "Evrett, you okay?"

He looked around the room and suddenly realized he must have fallen asleep.

"You didn't answer me," she said. "Would you like some more wine?"

"No," he said. "I'm okay."

"Are you?"

"Yes, sorry. Just spaced out there."

Evrett looked into Julia's eyes and fell into a trance again. But this time, he saw Sam, staring at him with a smile.

Julia sat there looking at Evrett seeing Evrett.

The two mutually moved in and pressed their lips against each other. Evrett didn't resist. After a minute of heavy kissing, Julia positioned herself on Evrett's lap, straddling him and grinding seductively. Evrett let his hands wander and he slid them under the back of her shirt. Julia made it easy for him, pulling the shirt over her head and tossing it to the floor.

Evrett did the same with his shirt and the two returned to heavy kissing for several minutes. She ran her right hand down his chest to his jeans and she began to loosen his belt. Evrett went to help her when they were startled by the crash of glass breaking in the kitchen.

"What was that?" Julia screamed.

Evrett jumped up immediately. He looked at Julia with her shirt off and realized that he wasn't dreaming about Sam and that he was making a huge mistake, but that wasn't the pressing issue at this point; their safety was.

"Wait here!" he stated firmly.

He slowly crept into the kitchen with his hands in position to fight.

When he peered around the corner, he saw red wine and glass shards on the floor.

Evrett laughed. "Julia? Did you leave the bottle on the edge of the counter?"

Julia put her shirt back on and joined him in the kitchen. "I could have sworn I placed it in the center, but I was a little tipsy when I poured our second glasses."

"It's okay," he said. "I'll clean this up. What do you say we forget about the rest of this movie and call it a night?"

Julia sensed that Evrett was having second thoughts about what just had happened. She promised herself that she'd be extremely patient with him and she was going to keep that promise.

"Sure," she said. "I'll get my keys."

"Keys?" Evrett said. "You can't even put a bottle on the counter, you think I'm going to let you drive?"

She smiled.

"Why don't you head upstairs to my bedroom? I'll be up after I clean this up."

"Sounds good," she said, starting to turn toward the stairs, before Evrett called out.

"Julia," he said, with a bit of a questionable inflection.

She spun back and leaned into the kitchen, "Yes, Evrett?"

"I know we were just having some fun there, but when I get up there, can we just sleep? I don't want to be alone, but I'm not quite ready for this. I'm sorry."

"Ev," she said, walking up to him. "Don't be sorry. I understand and I'm here with you every step of the way. Talk to me, though, if there's something you need to say, you know I'll listen."

She extended upward using the tips of her toes to place a kiss on his cheek. "I'll see you in a few."

Julia walked away and Evrett continued with the battle in his head. There were so many things he wanted to say, but couldn't. Not yet. And he wondered if he'd ever be able to.

Evrett grabbed a dustpan and a broom to sweep up the glass. As he did that, he noticed a few marks on a floor-level cabinet across from the counter where the bottle was sitting. There were a few chips in the wood and wine dripping down the paneling.

He analyzed it and could only conclude that the bottle smacked against it and shattered before falling to the floor.

But that wasn't possible. The bottle wouldn't have fallen like that. It would have taken force for it to hit this cabinet and leave a mark.

It just didn't make sense.

Then again, what had lately?

He finished cleaning up and went upstairs to join Julia. She was already under the covers and sleeping. He climbed into bed and laid on his back. Julia rolled over and put her arm over his chest.

It was a safe feeling that made it seem like home. It was just like the last two years never happened.

With that, Evrett was asleep in minutes.

• • •

Evrett awoke in a dry bed, which was a refreshing moment. He could see rays of sun peering in through a few small openings in the curtains. Julia was next to him, facing the other direction. It was eight in the morning on a Sunday and Evrett heard church bells ringing in the distance.

He thought it'd be nice to make her breakfast, so he got up, put on a white T-shirt and gym shorts, and walked down stairs. He pulled out six eggs, a pair of potatoes and a box of sausage, and got to work.

He chopped up the potatoes into small cubes to make his own hash browns and he placed the sausage into the toaster oven. As he went to dice up onions, he noticed a piece of paper on the counter.

He reached out and picked it up. It was Julia's handwriting: *Hey Ev, I got up early to get home and take care of Jack. I'm around if you need to talk. See you later. Julia.*

Evrett let the letter's contents process for a second.

"What the hell?"

Why was she still here? Did she come back?

Evrett walked over to the staircase and looked up the stairs.

"Julia?"

No response.

He started to walk upstairs.

"Julia?"

As he walked into the bedroom, he saw an empty bed.

"She was just here," he said. He ran over to the master bedroom's bath, but she wasn't in there. He checked every room and there was no sign. He even unlocked the office to see if she somehow snuck her way inside there.

He quickly grabbed his phone on his nightstand and dialed her number.

She answered immediately. "Hey, Ev," she said, with a hint of grogginess. "What's up?"

"What time did you leave?" he asked.

"Around five, at least," she said. "I had to get home to take care of Jack. He and I are now sleeping in."

Evrett sat down on the bed in disbelief. Was he going crazy? He had no explanation for what had just happened. He knew for sure that he saw her, or at least her back, in bed. Someone was there.

"Ev?"

"Yes, I'm here. I'm sorry that I woke you. I just got worried."

"Aw, I'm okay."

"I know. Well, I'm sorry for waking you. Go back to sleep. Pet Jack for me."

"I will."

She hung up and Evrett just sat there for a few minutes.

Perhaps it was time to take his doctor's advice.

He planned to call the therapist tomorrow morning.

25

HAD SAM BEEN ALIVE, EVRETT WOULD HAVE SPENT the last ten minutes scraping the frost off the windows of his Audi, but the garage allowed him to get on the road earlier. He drove along Interstate 83 away from Baltimore toward Lancaster. It was time to find Amanda.

He perused a few online newspaper sites in upstate New York on Sunday, but he found nothing. All the small-town newspapers in the area were either weeklies or short-staffed on the weekends. He noticed in all of their archives that most news stories from the week-end were posted on Mondays, and he didn't have time to wait.

His phone chimed signaling he received an email, one of many that came in on Monday mornings. For the most part, they were just the typical office memos and notices that certainly didn't pertain to him, but he had to be kept in the loop.

As he quickly glanced down at his buzzing phone, he thought about what he said the day before. He told himself that he would call

Dr. Weatherburn, but second thoughts crept in again.

Truth be told, those second thoughts began the night before as Evrett sat in the Milton S. Eisenhower Library at Johns Hopkins University.

It was early evening and he was surrounded by students who were busy working toward their respective degrees. With it being a Sunday in November that meant the majority of the students were at the top of their classes. Those who didn't take college seriously didn't even know the library was open on Sundays, if they even knew it was open at all.

Evrett flipped through the pages of a medical journal with another six similar publications scattered all about the table.

He had searched through the digital database to find anything that seemed relevant. He typed in keywords such as "stress" and "blackout" and "sleep walking."

He found publications and periodicals too numerous to count. It was all too overwhelming and he was lost. This was not his element. He was more suited to critique the architecture of the library. It was built in the 1960s, Evrett assumed based on the structure's outside facade, but he knew it was renovated recently. He estimated late 1990s. He scanned the room and enjoyed the natural light that spilled in through the windows. Everywhere he went in the library had that element. He presumed it was by design to make sure that natural light touched every square inch of the building.

Evrett laughed. Lost in a world where he belonged, he knew he had to return to the unknown.

He continued to flip pages, reading about neurocardiogenic syncope, which could cause people to pass out during stressful situations, but he read nothing about a person continuing on with their actions while having no memory of it.

He read about post-traumatic stress disorder, but he didn't believe that to be the case either.

He even read all about sleep walking, but that didn't fit.

Then, it dawned on him. He didn't search for the right thing. All along he had been searching for disorders dealing with "blackouts" and "sleep," but that wasn't really what was happening to him.

He wasn't actually blacking out. He was apparently conscious and functioning; he just wasn't remembering it.

He left the books on the table and ran back to the computer where the digital catalog was. There, he typed in, AMNESIA.

He scribbled down several call numbers and went searching for the publications that would preoccupy him for the next two hours.

At around ten o'clock, he finally found something that made some sense to him. Transient Global Amnesia. He read about how this type of amnesia involved a sudden, temporary loss of memory to an otherwise healthy individual. The journal he read discussed how persons with such afflictions did not recall recent events. Those suffering from it would remember who they were and the people in their lives, but tended not to know what happened in the prior twenty-four hours and how they got to where they were.

The final part of it made him feel a bit better: "Transient global amnesia is rare and virtually harmless. It is unlikely to happen again, and episodes are usually short-lived. Afterward, the person's memory is fine."

In another journal, he found that transient global amnesia is typically a single event, but some patients can experience more than one with similar symptoms and recovery.

He then looked at the list of causes, and a few caught his eye. The first was a sudden immersion in cold or hot water. Such an occurrence seemed possible at a pair of his episodes, but not Chad's.

He continued to scan the list, which included strenuous physical activity and mild head trauma, none of which fit his profile.

But then he saw it. The final symptom: "Acute emotional distress, as might be brought on by bad news, conflict or heavy workload."

He sat back in his chair. *This must be it,* he thought. If there was one sentence that could describe his last two years, it was that. Obviously, his wife being taken from him fit the definition of "bad news." He had been dealing with several conflicts, including his more recent struggles with Sam and Julia. And the fact that he was sitting in a library for a fourth hour just to avoid a trip to a therapist proved that he was certainly dealing with a heavy workload.

He pondered for a bit on how he could cure this himself. The conflict with Julia could be solved easily, but he wasn't sure if that would be one of the biggest mistakes of his life, so he decided to think about his workload.

He would not quit his search for the man on the bridge, which meant his work away from work must continue. That left only one thing he could do—quit the firm.

Money was not an issue, so he knew he could do it and survive for a while. And he felt he was talented enough and accomplished enough to easily return to the world of architecture without a problem, even in a poor economy.

Evrett started closing up the books and returned them to a cart for some poor student worker to put away. As he left the library he decided that he would take the next couple weeks to analyze his workload and see where he could cut back. He also planned to find some more time to exercise. He read how that could ease his stress and he knew he hadn't been out running as much as he used to.

He made that change right away Monday morning, waking up at six and embarking on a four-mile run. He ate a healthy breakfast of fruit and cereal before jumping in his car and leaving for Lancaster.

It took two hours, but he pulled into town a few minutes after ten. He parked his car outside the art gallery and stepped onto the sidewalk. He dropped a few quarters into the parking meter and walked through the cool, crisp November air. The sun warmed his face, creating a soothing mix of hot and cold on his skin.

Inside the gallery, he walked up to the second floor to where Amanda's art was displayed. There, he saw a teary-eyed Colleen taking down Amanda's paintings.

Evrett knew immediately what was wrong, but he approached anyway.

"These are beautiful paintings," he said. "Are they for sale?"

Colleen turned and looked at Evrett. "Excuse me?"

"Are they for sale? I'd love to have your paintings in my home. They're breathtaking."

Colleen whimpered as more tears threatened to spill over her eyelids, but she wiped them away with her left arm and composed herself as best she could.

"I'm sorry," Evrett said. "Is this a bad time? I can come back."

"I didn't paint these," she said. "My ... My friend did."

"Oh, is it possible for me to contact her about purchasing these?" he asked.

"Look, I'm sorry," Colleen said. "I don't mean to come off as rude, but these are not for sale. The artist died Saturday and I'm taking them home to her family."

Colleen lied. She was taking them home for herself.

"Oh, my," Evrett said. "I'm so sorry. This was awful timing on my part. Please forgive my intrusion."

Colleen settled down. "It's okay. You couldn't have possibly known."

But I did, he thought.

There was about ten seconds of silence before Evrett prodded some more. "Was it an accident?" he asked.

"Honestly, I have no clue what happened. I do not believe what the police or media are saying. Amanda would not have done what they said she did."

Colleen placed the last painting in a box and lifted it up. "I'm sorry. I can't do this. Please excuse me."

She hustled out of the room, angry at his questions and angry at life.

Evrett felt bad for putting her through that, but he had to find out. Obviously the police were involved, so there was information to be found on the Internet. If Colleen knew, it's likely Amanda's family was completely notified, so her name should be available to the media.

He ran to his car and picked up his iPad. Using a free Wi-Fi connection from a corner coffee shop, he typed Amanda's name into Google. It came up right away under news. The local Harrisburg *Patriot News* had a story with the headline, "Local woman dies in apparent home invasion in New York."

He read through the article and a few details stood out. Amanda ran away from the home she broke into in the pouring rain and was found dead along the muddy banks of a lake. He quickly thought about his wet clothes and muddy shoes.

Evrett opened up his map application and typed in the address of the home she broke in to. He looked at the topography surrounding it and found the small lake not too far away from it. Then he saw the motel he stayed at, no less than a mile away.

It was clear to him.

He was there when she died.

That made it three straight targets who died while he was nearby.

It also meant he had three cases of what he believed to be transient global amnesia.

The bright side was, if this was him, Evrett knew that he was doing a hell of a job at making these deaths look like accidents. No one was on to him. He was executing his missions to perfection.

The only problem was, he couldn't remember a thing. What if during these blackouts, he had spoken to Andrew, Chad or Amanda? What if they had told him about the man on the bridge? His evidence may be lost somewhere in the darkness of his mind, never to be found.

He knew he had to do something to prevent the amnesia, but he knew a therapist was not the right route because he couldn't reveal everything.

Yes, there was doctor-patient confidentiality, but that would only apply for some of the things he would have to say about the past. He would have to hide the truth in many instances because at least five more people were in imminent danger. The whole doctor-patient confidentiality would go out the window if they knew he was about to commit a crime. And Evrett couldn't get to the bottom of his amnesia without revealing his future plans.

That was why he continued to shy away from help. Instead, it was time to get some answers of his own. Gloria, a sweet, old lady who abandoned her car and blocked first responders from saving his wife, was next on his list. Evrett decided it was time to document what happened when he hit his blackout moments.

He planned to put GPS trackers on his phone and car, and he'd set up a camera system in his home and a dash camera in his car. He was determined to find out what was happening.

If it even happens again, he thought.

The surveillance on himself was precautionary because he hoped his new stress-reducing tactics would take care of it.

He drove back to Baltimore wondering if it was better that he didn't remember this. It takes a certain type of person to be able to purposely and strategically murder another human being. Perhaps he didn't have it in him and the blackouts were a defense mechanism his brain used to prevent him from seeing the last emotions of his victims.

Thought after thought ran through his brain and before he knew it, he was in his garage. It was one-thirty in the afternoon, and he went straight inside to his den to get to work. He had numerous emails to respond to and a few projects to work on.

He put about seven hours in, caught the third quarter of Monday Night Football and went to bed early with the scored tied at 17-17. He wanted to watch more, but sleep was imperative, and exercise in the morning was even more paramount.

A train horn in the distance was the last thing he heard before he fell asleep. Six hours later, his sneakers were pounding the macadam for five miles.

He returned home, showered and got to work. He had eight hours to devote to GGM, and then he had the rest of the night to dedicate to planning his trip to see Gloria.

It was going to be a busy Tuesday.

26

EVERYTHING HAPPENED TO GLORIA, or so she liked to think. Each mundane occurrence in her daily life was an event that in turn became the topic of conversation with anyone who would listen. Today it was her eighth period students.

Out of the twenty-four pairs of eyes in the classroom, Gloria Droun's were the only ones not focused on the clock. Her twenty-three junior U.S. history students sat passively in their seats, checking off each minute that would take them closer to the end of the day and the start of their summer. Meanwhile, Gloria talked.

"You see, class, if I hadn't been there to correct the tour guide, that poor group would have left Fort McHenry believing that Francis Scott Key wrote 'The Star-Spangled Banner' only as a song, when in fact he wrote it as a poem first. And that poem was called…"

Gloria waited for a response. She had told this story before.

The class returned a defeated silence.

"The Defence of Fort McHenry," Gloria answered.

She too looked at the clock.

"Well, ladies and gentlemen, it has come to that time. After thirty-five years in the Baltimore public education system, these are the last few minutes of my teaching career."

A handful of students shifted their attention from the clock to Mrs. Droun. Behind her bifocals, Gloria's eyes glazed over with forming tears.

"It has been my pleasure to teach you the wonders of American history. You will forever be in my memory as the last class I will ever teach."

Gloria's voice cracked. It was full of pride.

"And with that I leave you with this mantra from the great F. Scott Fitzgerald, who incidentally was also named Francis Scott, just like Mr. Key."

She cleared her throat.

"There are no second acts in American lives."

She smiled and looked at the perplexed teenage faces in front of her. The quote was one she remembered from college. She could tell two or three were trying to piece the meaning together.

And with that the bell rang, marking the end of a career and another school year. The students filed out of the room, a few saying "thank you" and "have a good summer" on their way. Gloria dabbed her eyes with a tissue.

It was done.

It was hard to believe that she was really here in this moment. Thirty-five years gone in an instant. She had been twenty-two when she stepped into her first classroom, bright eyed and ready to inspire her students. To Gloria it felt like just the other week she had ended her first year. Now, she stood alone in an empty classroom. Her days of teaching students about the battles of the Civil War and the changing American dream were now her history.

In the last couple weeks, she had taken boxes home with her, hoping to avoid being left with too much to carry home on her last day. She gathered the remaining items from her desk. No more current events to discuss, attendance to take or discipline referrals to write. No more stories to tell to a room full of listeners. She grabbed her tote bag, glanced at the room one final time and left.

After dropping her keys off in the office, Gloria said her good-byes to the principal and the office secretaries. She assured each one not to worry and that she'd keep in touch. Perhaps she'd even take up subbing if retirement proved to be too slow for her. Each nodded with half smiles.

And with that Mrs. Droun left.

Her husband Russell was sitting on their back deck waiting for her to arrive home. He was a decade older than Gloria and had been retired for two years. He had a glass of white wine waiting for her.

"Welcome to the other side," he said, handing her the glass.

"Oh, Russell. It doesn't feel real. After all those years, I'm actually done."

He led her to their two lounge chairs. The deck was full of potted plants that Russell pruned and arranged in the unlimited hours that filled his retired days.

"It is going to be great, honey. You'll see."

Gloria sighed.

She wasn't sure if it was relief or resignation that she felt. Thirty-five years, and now it was time to start over.

• • •

The first month of Gloria's retirement vanished. The Drouns spent two weeks in London and Scotland, a trip they had been planning for four years. It had always been a place Gloria wanted to go.

The trip by all accounts had been a success. They toured the Scottish highlands and the city of Edinburgh. They saw all the sights one expects to see in London—the Eye, the Tower, Buckingham Palace. Their digital camera was full of photo after photo of the couple posing in front of the typical tourist hot spots.

As June simmered into July, they prepared for their annual Independence Day picnic. Family and friends filled the deck and backyard of the Drouns' home in Mays Chapel, a community north of Baltimore. Russell had placed small American flags in all the planters. He was now talking to the Drouns' eldest son, Thomas, who was grilling hot dogs and hamburgers.

Gloria was entertaining a picnic table full of guests.

"I really can't believe we got the yard all ready for the picnic. We only got back from London a week and a half ago. Can you believe it? Thank God Susan was able to water the plants. I don't know what Russell would have done if he had come back to a yard full of dead flowers!"

She raised a glass of pinot grigio to Susan, the neighbor who now sat two seats to Gloria's left.

Jane, a former fellow teacher, raised her glass as well. As Gloria sat down, she placed her hand on Gloria's wrist.

"Gloria, you look fantastic. How is everything? Are you still doing all right? The anniversary is coming up soon isn't it?"

A soft murmur spread around the table. Many of them knew to what Jane referred.

"Oh, Jane. You're right. It's next week isn't it? Two years. My goodness. Where has the time gone?"

Thomas's new girlfriend, Bethany, sat at the table. She was a slender woman in her early thirties. She worked as a vet technician at Thomas' practice.

"I'm sorry, Gloria. What happened two years ago?"

A few of the other guests discreetly rolled their eyes. A spark flashed in Gloria's.

It was a story from her history she loved to tell.

"Bethany, I'm sorry. I was sure Thomas would have told you," Gloria said, feigning modesty.

Bethany shook her head.

"Well, two years ago, I was in a horrible accident. You probably saw it on the news. It happened on 83?"

"No, I don't remember that. I'm sorry, I only moved to Maryland last year."

"Ah, that's right, dear. I better start at the beginning."

Two guests got up from the table to grab another beverage. Some shifted in their seats, well aware of the story that was about to follow. Bethany politely listened. This woman could turn out to be her mother-in-law after all.

"I had been attending a conference downtown that week. I believe it was on improving assessment strategies."

Gloria knew quite well that it was.

"After a long day of sitting through discussions and working to jigsaw ideas, all I wanted to do was make it home. Russell was making lamb shanks that evening. They are my favorite, so you can understand my excitement. Russell is an excellent cook.

"So, I was cautiously driving in the right lane on eighty-three when suddenly this red car passes me out of nowhere. I thought to myself, 'There's someone who has no respect for the road.'

"The next moments are all such a blur, I really can't say for sure what happened, but that red car swerved from their lane and into another car. That one spun out of control and into another. It was like dominoes! At this point there was this enormous truck that also was on the road and it ended up flipping on its side and blocked the whole highway."

Gloria had Bethany's full attention at this point.

"I thought for sure that this was the end for me. I slammed on my brakes and braced for impact. Thankfully, I managed to steer my car onto the side of the road and only hit the median. Still, the impact was enough to mess up my back. It's never quite been the same since."

"What happened to—" Bethany began.

"Well, without even a moment of concern for myself, I practically leapt out of my car. You see, adrenaline had kicked in. It wasn't until later that I realized I had any pain in my back at all. I raced closer to the scene of the catastrophe, hoping I might be able to help in any way that I could.

"And then boom! The truck and the red car exploded. They say it was some young woman who died in the accident. Thankfully, she was the only one. You know, typically these crazy drivers end up walking away scratch free while the innocent people they hit are the real ones to suffer."

"My goodness. That's just, such a tragic story. I'm glad you're okay."

"Thanks, dear. Some days when it rains, my back is a little tight. Now, pour me another glass, will you, hon?"

• • •

The rest of the summer was much of the same for the Drouns. They took several day trips, worked in the flowerbeds around their house, and even enjoyed a weekend getaway to New York City. Whenever possible, Russell and Gloria would lay out on the deck, sipping wine and listening to the sounds of summer evenings. It was everything she had imagined retirement to be.

Autumn found their attention turning toward the inside of the house and the couple began to organize their home office. No longer would Gloria need it to work on lesson plans and grade research papers. They removed the filing cabinets and computer desk, replacing them with two leather chairs, an ottoman and a pair of built-in bookcases. The air had turned colder, and many nights, they sat under blankets in their chairs reading.

Not once did she think of returning to the classroom.

She was content.

• • •

"I'm afraid it's cancer. Liver cancer to be precise."

The words silenced the room.

Gloria and Russell sat in two stiff, uncomfortable chairs across from Dr. Lacissi, an oncologist at Johns Hopkins. He was in his mid-forties, much too young, Gloria thought, to be handing out death sentences.

"I'm afraid it is stage four. From the results of your tests, we can see that the cancer formed a tumor in your liver, and now that cancer has also spread to your stomach."

The Drouns held each other's hands. For once Gloria was silent. She looked into her husband's eyes.

"How... How long?"

"Typically, with this kind of diagnosis and stage, most patients live anywhere from four months to two years."

The room seemed to shrink. Only a few short months earlier, Gloria had been ready to start a new and exciting chapter of her life with her husband. Now, that time was suddenly torn out of their grasp.

"You have to be wrong about this. I can't believe it. I won't believe it."

"Gloria, it's going to be all right," Russell said. He patted her hand gently.

She looked at her husband. She saw the awful road ahead. Vacations and grandchildren once dotted their horizon, now pain and missed opportunities loomed in the distance.

"No, it's not going to be all right, Russell!"

She stood up from the chair, forgetting there was a third party in the room. Gloria let go of all restraint.

"I don't even know how you can possibly say that? What about Hawaii? What about Thomas's wedding? What about all the things we said we would do when we had time? We did everything right! We planned, we saved, we waited. And for what? To be told sorry? It's not going to happen? Four months to two years, Russell? What kind of time is that?"

"It's all the time I'll have," he replied.

She looked at her husband. He seemed smaller to her now. The pains in his abdomen had only started a couple of months ago. They had ignored it, thinking it was just indigestion. Would things have been different if she had forced him to go to the doctor?

Gloria became aware of Dr. Lacissi sitting silently behind his desk. Russell took her hand and guided her back down into the chair. From behind her glasses, Gloria's eyes brimmed with tears.

"I'm sorry, Russell. I'm sorry."

"It's okay, Gloria."

She buried her face in her palms.

"What am I going to do?"

27

SO MUCH DEATH. Evrett had been surrounded by it for more than two years. Yet, he was not the only one apparently. He held a prayer card in his glove-covered hand. On the side opposite of the Virgin Mary was the name Russell Jacob Droun. He had died on December 11, 2015, a little over a week earlier.

So Gloria was a widow.

Just as Evrett was a widower.

He tucked the card back into the wooden mirror frame and continued his assessment of Gloria's bedroom. His eyes took in the various items of the room; the queen bed with mahogany headboard, a crucifix above the entryway, two alarm clocks. But even as he looked for the perfect place to hide his microphone, Evrett's mind was elsewhere.

While Sam was at the start of all of this, he instead found his mind stuck on Harrison.

It was funny how little he actually thought about the man partially responsible for his wife's death. Really, if it weren't for his accidental murder of Harrison, Evrett would probably not be standing in Gloria Droun's bedroom a week before Christmas planting surveillance equipment.

Yet here he was, and while he didn't think much about Harrison, the memories of his last three targets were always there.

It was the uncertainty.

While he knew perfectly well that he had pushed Harrison to his death on that summer day, he could not be certain he hadn't killed Andrew, Chad or Amanda. The transient global amnesia, his self-diagnosed affliction, had made sure of that.

Then he remembered. Evrett pulled out his recorder.

"Check in, two o'clock. P. M. December nineteenth. Placing bugs in target's home."

Evrett had adopted the practice of checking in after his discovery in the library. Every hour he was awake he would record the time and date. If he experienced another episode, he would notice the discrepancy in the playback.

He also thought there was a chance that he was coherent throughout the entire blackout and a final moment wiped clean his memory of the whole episode. If that were the case, he could check the recording for his updates. A traumatic event might clear his memory banks, but it couldn't destroy an audio file.

Of course, he hadn't lost track of time since the evening Amanda died. Nevertheless, Evrett continued to record himself, hoping that he wouldn't find several hours of his life missing anymore.

Gloria was not home. He wasn't quite sure where she was this afternoon, so there was no telling what time she'd arrive back. Evrett had to be quick. He placed the last microphone out of plain sight and left the house.

Once back in his car, he opened up his iPad and checked the sound from the four microphones he had placed throughout Gloria's house. White noise filled his ears.

Gloria arrived home at three-thirty carrying a few shopping bags. From his vantage point, Evrett could see that she had done some Christmas shopping.

Good for her, Evrett thought. The last thing Evrett had wanted to do these last two Christmases was suffer through shopping at the mall. Instead, he had bought his family members items online, anything to avoid the painful reminders of the season. But here was Gloria, arms full of packages.

He figured people grieve differently. Some surround themselves with people and continue pushing on as if nothing had happened. Others spend two years plotting revenge.

Evrett chuckled. When he thought about it, his life seemed so outrageous. Would anyone be able to believe all that he had done in the last few years?

What would his family say if they knew the truth?

What would Sam think if she were still here?

What would Julia do if she found out?

Through the speakers, Evrett could hear Gloria inside her house. The microphones were picking up the sound perfectly.

Evrett heard the rustling of the bags and packages as Gloria placed them down on what he assumed was the kitchen table. There was some more movement from within the house as it began to flurry outside.

Evrett was glad that this endeavor was closer to home. His last targets had all required a trip. Staking out Gloria's Mays Chapel home meant he'd be able to make the short commute and still sleep in his own bed.

He listened to Gloria's lonely Saturday night. There was no one that she talked to; no television shows that she watched. Instead, Evrett's ears were filled with the silence of a home built for two that was now filled by one.

With the flurries escalating to a steady light snow, Evrett decided he would call it an early night and make it home before the roads got too slick.

That night Evrett lay in his bed. He had recently added a fleece blanket to keep warmer as winter neared. *A Christmas Carol* was on television. It was one of his favorite holiday films.

Evrett watched as Ebenezer Scrooge was visited by the three Christmas ghosts, led by Jacob Marley. A text from Julia interrupted the final minutes of the film.

"You still up?" it read.

Evrett looked at the text and decided to just let it go until tomorrow. As he went to place his phone back on the nightstand, something stopped him. It was the thought of Gloria sitting alone in the house and the prayer card with Russell's name on the back.

His fingers moved across the screen of the phone.

"Yup. Want to come over? I'm feeling the Christmas spirit."

He looked up and caught the last few moments of the movie.

"Sure. Mind if I bring Jack?"

"No problem. He's always welcome."

"Great. We'll be over soon."

Within the half hour, Julia and Jack were at Evrett's front door. She kissed him on the cheek as they entered and Jack ran circles around Evrett's legs.

"Can I get you anything? Wine? Hot chocolate?"

Julia removed her coat and scarf.

"You know what, a hot chocolate would be great. What did you feel like doing tonight?"

"Don't laugh, but I thought we could decorate for Christmas."

Julia stared at Evrett.

"Evrett, why would I laugh at that?"

"I figured it might be a slightly unusual request."

"So you're saying this isn't a booty call?" she said, slapping Evrett on the shoulder.

Evrett laughed along with her.

"Seriously, Evrett, I'd love to. Is this the first year—"

"Yes, I figured it wouldn't hurt to put up some of the decorations we have."

"My grandmother always said, 'Don't be afraid of memories. The past is just our yesterdays.' I think putting up some decorations would be a good step."

Evrett kept the basement organized. In the corner were several red and green plastic containers filled with tree ornaments, stockings and other knickknacks to place around the house. Evrett and Julia carried the artificial Christmas tree up first and placed the base to the side of the fireplace. They assembled the tree branch by branch. Growing up, Evrett's family always had a real tree, but Sam had been allergic.

The fake one would do just fine with his schedule.

They decorated the tree while listening to Christmas music. Evrett put the lights on and Julia laid each ornament out on the coffee table. Jack slept, curled up on the tree skirt that surrounded the legs of the stand.

As they placed each ornament on the tree, Evrett felt wave after wave of nostalgia wash over him. Memories from his childhood growing up in Pennsylvania flooded his thoughts. Most of the ornaments were generic red and white globes, but some were Evrett's from his childhood. Mixed in with these ornaments were several of Sam's. When her parents had come to collect some of her things, no one had given any thought to the holiday decorations.

The last ornament to be placed on the tree was Sam's. It was a mouse that was dressed to go skiing. It even held two small poles. Evrett smiled as Julia handed it to him.

"This was Sam's favorite. I honestly don't remember the story behind it. I think she and her grandmother made these the one year when she was a kid."

"That's very sweet."

"I hope you don't mind me talking about her."

"Never. She was your wife, Evrett. I understand."

He placed it carefully on one of the highest branches. They stepped back and looked at the finished tree.

It was beautiful.

The glow of the white lights warmed the room.

"It's perfect," he said.

They wrapped up the rest of the evening by placing a few other decorations around the house. It wasn't much, but it made the home feel ready for the holiday season.

Julia sat next to Evrett on the couch. Her head rested on his shoulder. They both sipped their second mug of hot chocolate.

"This was probably the best night I've had in a while," he said.

"I'm glad I could be a part of it. How does it feel now that it's all up?"

"Weird. But at the same time, right. I actually feel good about this."

Julia yawned and pressed her body closer to Evrett's. It was well past midnight. He wanted to do more surveillance at Gloria's tomorrow.

"Are you ready for bed?" he asked.

"Sure."

Evrett and Julia walked up the stairs to his bedroom. Jack followed underfoot. As they were walking down the hallway Jack stopped at the door to Evrett's office, the door he always kept locked. The Chihuahua scratched its tiny paw against the wood.

"Come on, Jack." Julia said, patting her hand against her thigh.

What would have drawn him to that room? Evrett wondered if the dog sensed his secret, the life he kept locked behind that door.

Evrett and Julia slept with Jack between them. Again, nothing physical happened, but Evrett couldn't deny that there was an attraction there. When he was sure she was asleep, Evrett rolled over and pulled a notebook out from under the bed. A pen was jammed in the spiral that held the book together.

He wrote, "Check in. 2:15 A.M. Dec. 20. Christmas decorations up. Lying next to Julia."

He set the pen and pad back down, and felt a pair of eyes gazing at him. He turned to see Jack staring with his tongue hanging out the left side of his mouth.

Evrett smiled, as if he knew exactly what Jack was looking at him for. He quickly reached for the pen and pad, added a tail to the final period to make it a comma and scribbled in, "and Jack."

"Happy," he whispered as he patted Jack on the head.

Jack curled up close to Julia, and he and Evrett were fast asleep in minutes.

28

EVRETT STRETCHED HIS LIMBS OUT WIDE across the bed. His fingers spread open and slid across the rough sterile sheets of the double bed. Another day, another hotel room.

He slowly sat up, placing his feet on the floor. Evrett felt groggy and out of sorts. He took his recorder from the nightstand and re-played the last few seconds of audio.

"Check in. Ten-forty-five. P. M. January seventh. Ambassador Hotel. Going to sleep."

Evrett checked his watch. He had been asleep for almost seven hours. He recorded his notes and stood up.

In an odd way it felt like coming home. More than anything else, it was the smell that reminded Evrett of his honeymoon several years earlier. The Hawaiian air filled his nose and lungs as he took a deep breath of remembrance.

• • •

"This is amazing," Sam said.

She was impressed by the large open walkways of the airport in Honolulu. The airports of the East Coast were of no comparison. As Sam and Evrett walked from the gate into the balmy tropical air, she stopped at the edge of one of the breezeways.

"I can't believe we are here," she said, peering over the edge. She could see the sun shining through the leaves of a large palm tree.

"We are going to have the most amazing time here," Evrett said. He wrapped his arms around his wife and smiled. The woman of his dreams was now his wife. He couldn't imagine a better feeling in the world.

Evrett kissed Sam's cheek.

"I can't wait to do everything with you," he whispered in her ear.

"Me neither," she said. "Me neither."

They did as much as they could over the course of seven days on the island of Oahu. They toured Pearl Harbor and Diamond Head, and attended a luau. They spent whole afternoons relaxing on the white sand beaches in front of their resort. Evrett had never been happier.

On their final night in paradise, Evrett and Sam took a walk on the beach after dinner. The stars dotted the sky and the moon shimmered brightly on the waters of the Pacific. The gentle island breeze made Sam's hair dance around her face as the couple walked hand in hand.

"I can't believe this week has come to an end already," he said and sighed.

"It was a perfect week."

"Absolutely."

"Evrett, I want you to know how happy I am. This honeymoon, our wedding, all the months of planning, it has been the best time of my life."

"Well, just you wait," he said, pulling her in for a kiss. "This is only the beginning. You and I, we are going to have a great life together."

"E Hoomau Maua Kealoha," Sam said. It was a phrase a Hawaiian woman at the resort had taught her.

"E Hoomau Maua Kealoha," Evrett replied.

May our love last forever.

Yesterday, Evrett had stood looking at the palm trees alone. It was 2016, a new year, and Sam was dead for more than two years. Forever had seemed like such a possibility all those years ago.

He should have known nothing would last forever.

It was hard to believe he was back on the island, and if it weren't for Gloria Droun, he wouldn't be.

Actually, if it weren't for Harrison, Andrew, Chad, Amanda, Gloria, the Bryants, Phil, Chase, and of course, the man on the bridge, he wouldn't be here.

But at the present moment, Gloria was his focus.

After a week of trailing his target, Evrett realized his first impressions of Gloria had been very wrong. The night he had set up the microphones in her house, he had left with the image of a sad and lonely woman isolated in her own home. The days and nights of listening and following her around the greater Baltimore area had proved there was a lot of life left in Gloria.

That was, of course, until their paths would finally cross.

If there had ever been any doubt in Evrett's mind that Gloria needed to pay for her role in Sam's death, one of the first conversations he overheard had settled the issue for him.

Gloria had invited a former colleague over for tea one afternoon. Evrett had watched the rather portly woman struggle to exit her Mini Cooper and make her way up to Gloria's front door. Once inside, the guest expressed her condolences over the passing of Gloria's husband. Once that awkwardness had cleared, the two gossiped about several teachers Gloria deemed as "unprofessional." Evrett was beginning to doze off when the conversation unexpectedly turned toward the accident.

Evrett sat up in his Audi across the street from Gloria's home. His heart beat fast. It was the first time he had ever heard one of his targets speak about that day. Was this the moment he had been waiting for? Would Gloria possibly mention the man on the bridge?

"Gloria, how's your back doing? I know that the winter months are always the worst for me and my pain."

"Oh, you know, Janice, the pain comes and goes. I can't believe it will be three years this July. That's why I figured I should take this trip now. Who knows if it will get worse as I get older."

"Did you ever think to sue? It isn't like the accident was your fault."

Evrett clenched his teeth. The fact that Gloria was alive to complain about her back troubles while his own wife lay buried infuriated him.

"No, no. Believe me, I thought about it at first. I was in bed for two weeks afterward. I could barely move! And then the therapy; it was awful."

Immediately, Evrett began to recall the reports. There was no mention of her injury. In fact, it read that Gloria had abandoned her car on the side of the road. Where she went, he and officials did not know, but he knows she wasn't bedridden. She was clearly exaggerating.

Gloria continued: "I definitely had it in my mind to seek some legal counsel, but Russell talked me out of it. That man never liked to make a fuss about anything. Even with his cancer, he never complained."

"He was such a good man," Janice said.

"He certainly was," Gloria replied.

"Still, a shame you had to suffer because of someone else's recklessness."

"Oh, I agree. But at least it wasn't one of those accidents where the person responsible kills the innocent drivers and walks away scratch free. At least there is some justice in the world."

Evrett fumed.

How dare she, he thought. Any sympathy he had had for Gloria vanished. She would pay, just as Andrew, Chad and Amanda had before her. The rest of the conversation turned toward Christmas preparations and talk of Janice's grandchildren. Unfortunately, Gloria made no mention of the man on the bridge.

Evrett continued to gather the majority of his information the Monday after Christmas when Gloria was on the phone talking to her son, Thomas. He could only hear Gloria's half of the conversation.

"Your father would have wanted me to do this."

From his car, Evrett listened intently. He could surmise that Gloria had dropped the news of her vacation plans at Christmas dinner a few days before. It had shocked the family.

"We made these plans before he got sick. He told me no matter what happened, we would go on this trip. I made all the arrangements. I'm going to start in Hawaii."

Evrett held memories of his honeymoon at bay.

"I know you want to say goodbye too, but that was what the funeral was for. You have to respect your father's wishes."

Gloria's voice rose with anger.

"No, I'm not too old. I've sky dived several times. I still have my 'A' license."

Skydiving was something Sam had wanted to do. Evrett wasn't as keen on the idea, but would have done it with her.

He would have done anything for Sam.

Evrett listened to these one-sided conversations for a few days. Each day Gloria went about her routine, eventually making a phone call to some friend to tell them about the exciting months she had ahead. Within a few days, Evrett had most of the details of Gloria's trip—what flights she'd be taking, what hotels she'd be staying at, what sights she was going to see. He was lucky she liked to brag.

From South America to Asia, the Drouns planned to see it all, and although Russell had passed away, she would still have to make the journey for them both. No one was going to stop her.

So Evrett made his own plans. He told work he wouldn't be in for at least a week and that Julia would field any questions while he was away. He told her over dinner that he was going to visit a relative out in Seattle. He didn't like to lie to Julia any more than he had to, but he couldn't let her know too much.

Evrett knew going back to Hawaii would not be easy. To him it was a place frozen in perfect memory. As much as he would have liked to confront Gloria at home, he felt that he could use the change in locale to his advantage. She had never been to Oahu before, where as he had.

After a ten-hour flight, Evrett arrived in Honolulu and was met with a wave of memories. At the airport he allowed himself a few moments to reflect on times long gone. Once they passed, he had to focus himself on the task at hand. This couldn't be a trip for his memories. He was here to kill Gloria.

The only question that remained was how.

Gloria wouldn't be arriving in Hawaii until the next day. The long flight had exhausted Evrett. He checked into his hotel, had dinner, and then decided he would go to bed early. He would start fresh the next morning.

• • •

"Check in. Five-thirty-six. A.M. January eighth. Ambassador Hotel. Getting up. Slept through the night."

Gloria's flight would be arriving in twelve hours. He knew she had scheduled a pickup service and would be staying at the Halekulani Hotel on Waikiki Beach, not very far from his hotel. As he showered, Evrett thought of ways he could get to Gloria.

One of the benefits of Waikiki was the easy access to the beaches. It wouldn't be hard for Evrett to make his way into her hotel. Perhaps he could get her out onto the beach late at night. Somehow, Andrew had drowned. If Evrett was responsible for one drowning death, he could certainly be responsible for a second.

But no matter what time of night, the beach area was likely to be populated. Tourist and honeymooners would be strolling up and down the beach, just as he had with Sam.

No, he would have to find something a little more secluded.

He had heard her mention Diamond Head. He wasn't sure when Gloria's tour of the crater and military base was scheduled, but he could possibly find a way to have her take a fall down one of the narrow pathways or staircases that lead up to the volcano's top. Again, people would be the problem.

While a long shot, a simple shove or a push might serve the purpose of ending Gloria's life, but it wouldn't get him any information about the man on the bridge. He didn't have to remember the last three failed attempts. He knew Gloria would have to be different.

It was time to take advantage of the situation. He was in a state thousands of miles from home. No one knew him or his history here. He was freer to operate out in the open than he ever would be back in Maryland. Maybe it was destiny that brought him and Gloria together on this island.

Evrett walked down the main drag of Waikiki. He basked in the warmth of the sun. While not nearly as hot as his summer honeymoon, it was still a nice change of pace from the typical winter weather he was more familiar with at this time of year.

He grabbed a cup of coffee at a corner shop and stood beneath a palm tree. While it was still early, he was losing precious time. He had to figure out a plan that would allow him to finally succeed. Evrett sipped the coffee and wished he had put a bit more cream into it.

Inspiration drove by.

From his location, Evrett could see the busy traffic of Kalakaua Avenue. As he lowered the coffee, his eye caught the side of a white van. It advertised a shuttle service that would take tourists to different locations on the island.

That could work, Evrett thought.

Gloria was going to need to get around the island somehow. She hadn't mentioned any decision about reserving a rental car. He knew she planned to do some sightseeing and go skydiving while she was there. With a little bit of effort, Evrett could figure out a way to get Gloria off to a secluded place.

He would need transportation, but not the rental car he had arranged for himself during his stay on Oahu. He would need a vehicle to transport Gloria in and keep her detained until he could get her alone.

He knew he would have to steal a van. Evrett had broken numerous laws by now. He had broken into homes, invaded people's privacies and perhaps even committed multiple murders. What was one more crime added to the list?

Evrett smiled. He felt excitement. This would prove to be a new challenge for him, albeit one that would have to wait until after nightfall. Acting too soon would allow for too much time for things to go wrong.

So Evrett threw his coffee cup into the trash and began to walk toward the beach. With his mind made up, he would allow himself a few hours to simply be in Waikiki. Once Gloria arrived, it would be a different story.

• • •

Evrett checked Gloria's flight number on his phone. The website showed that the plane was still scheduled to arrive on time. In less than an hour, her taxi service would drop her off out front of the Halekulani Hotel. Once he received confirmation that her plane had landed, Evrett left his hotel and made his way to the Halekulani to wait.

This particular section of the street was surrounded by large hotels that stretched up into the air, much like the palm trees that dotted the sides of the streets. There were a few restaurants close by, and as luck would have it, there was an outdoor corner bar directly across the street.

Evrett set up shop on a stool and made sure he had a clear view of the loop that marked the entrance to the hotel.

"Aloha, what will it be?"

The bartender had shaggy hair that had been lightened by many hours out in the sun.

"I'll have a Mai Tai."

In a few minutes, the drink was placed in front of Evrett.

"Mahalo," he said.

The bartender had made the drink rather strong. Normally, Evrett wouldn't have taken the chance of impairing his judgment when trailing a target, but he knew that he would not be killing Gloria tonight. Still, it couldn't hurt to have a little increase in courage for what he planned to do.

Evrett milked the drink for another half hour until his mark finally arrived. There had been several taxis that had dropped off other guests during Evrett's watch. With each drop off, Evrett's excitement grew. At almost seven o'clock, Gloria finally stepped out of the back of a taxi. One of the bellhops from the hotel came and helped her get her bags from the taxi's trunk.

Evrett finished the rest of his Mai Tai, left a twenty on the counter and walked toward the Halekulani. He watched as Gloria strolled into the main lobby to check into her room. Evrett would allow her some time in her room before he began step one of his plan.

Gloria left the lobby and headed toward her room. He could have rushed in to follow her, but that would be too obvious. So Evrett waited outside in the Hawaiian night, pacing up and down the street. After a suitable amount of time had passed, Evrett took out his prepaid cellphone and dialed the hotel.

"Aloha, Halekulani Hotel."

"Aloha, I was wondering if you could connect me with one of your guests. A good friend of mine from the mainland should have checked in this evening."

"Of course, sir. I would be happy to transfer you. What is your friend's name?"

"Gloria Droun. I'm hoping she has checked in already. Her flight was supposed to land earlier today."

"Yes, Mrs. Droun checked in a few minutes ago. I'll transfer you to her room. Hold one moment."

"Mahalo."

There was a moment of silence as the call was transferred. Evrett felt the excitement build within him. Then the call clicked over and Gloria's voice broke the quiet.

"Hello?"

"Hello, is this Mrs. Droun?"

"Yes, who is calling?"

"Yes, Mrs. Droun, this is Craig from Shuttle Services. The Halekulani contacted us to arrange your shuttle service for the week. It is a complimentary service we run with the hotel."

"Oh, wow, that is fantastic."

"Yes, it is, ma'am. Our goal is to make your stay here on Oahu as enjoyable and relaxing as possible. Will you be needing any transportation tomorrow?"

"Actually, I already arranged a shuttle service for the morning. I'm going to be skydiving on the North Shore."

Evrett was disappointed. He had hoped he could get a hold of a van tonight and pick Gloria up in the morning. After that she would be his. But this was only a minor setback. He could still work with this.

"I'm sorry to hear that, Mrs. Droun. Well, will you be needing transportation service later in the week? Perhaps after your skydiving excursion? Planning to see any other sights while you are on the island with us?"

"Actually, I have a ticket to a luau tomorrow night. Are there any restrictions to where you can transport me?"

"No, ma'am. Our shuttle service will take you anywhere you want to go."

Anywhere I want to take you, Evrett thought.

"That's fantastic. The luau begins at six-thirty. It's the Paradise Cove luau."

"Wonderful. We will send a shuttle to pick you up at five-thirty tomorrow."

"Great. I can't wait."

With that, Gloria hung up. Evrett felt good about the progression of his plan. Even though he wouldn't be able to begin bright and early in the morning, there was potential for tomorrow night. If he could just get Gloria into a vehicle, he would be able to take her anywhere.

Back in his hotel room, Evrett organized his equipment into a black backpack. He was excited by the prospect of answers from Gloria. At the same time, he had been at this stage in his hunt before and the thought of another episode crept into his mind. Evrett took his recorder, checked his watch and logged in his whereabouts. He then placed the recorder and a prepaid cellphone into a waterproof container; he had woken up wet before.

It was three in the morning when Evrett set out on his mission. Even though he wasn't going to be able to pick Gloria up until later in the day, Evrett thought it best to acquire the van at night. He could use the advantage of darkness to steal the vehicle and park it somewhere more isolated. He planned to trail Gloria during the day and then later he could return to the van before driving to meet Gloria for the luau.

It would take him forever on foot to find a suitable van. Evrett needed an easier mode of transportation. He wouldn't be able to use his rental car for this. Luckily, an idea came to him before he left.

Evrett stumbled upon a small parking lot. There were surely to be cameras nearby, so Evrett pulled his hood up over his head. He didn't come this far to get caught on a surveillance camera. Once covered and in the lot, Evrett quickly went to work on his target.

Within a matter of seconds, Evrett had picked the lock that chained a black moped to a nearby railing. Evrett smirked at his handiwork. He had definitely mastered the art of picking locks at this point. Hot-wiring a moped, on the other hand, was a new experience for him.

Fortunately, Evrett lived in a world filled with technology. It hadn't been hard to search for how-to videos on starting a bike without its key. Thinking back to the clip he had watched earlier, Evrett located the group of wires needed to start the moped and unplugged them. He took out a small piece of wire and placed both ends into the now empty plug. The wires didn't connect as easily as he had hoped.

"Come on," Evrett said. "Come on."

He pulled the wire back out and twisted the exposed end. One quick glance around the parking lot reassured him that he was alone and still had time. Evrett inserted the wire again.

"That's it."

Evrett stood up and looked at the dash of the moped. A few of the lights had come on. He got up on the moped and pressed the ignition.

The grunt and hum of the engine trumpeted his success. Evrett backed up a few feet and drove off. He held on to his hood to make sure it didn't blow off in the breeze. His heart beat so loudly in his ears it muffled the sound of the moped. He took this as a sign that things would be different this time. Gloria and the man on the bridge finally felt within his reach.

It took about a half hour to find his next target. Evrett stopped the moped across the street from a Chinese restaurant in the neighborhood of Kalihi. He had needed to find a van that was far enough from Waikiki, and there, next to a dumpster in the parking lot was a white one. It looked clean enough from the outside that Evrett thought it could pass for a shuttle.

He drove a little closer to the lot and turned off the moped's engine. He made sure there was no logo advertising the restaurant on the van. Evrett peered into the side window to find three rows of seats and just enough space in the back for the moped. He would need it to be able to drive back to Waikiki after he hid the van.

He picked the driver's side door easily enough and soon had the back doors of the van unlocked. Evrett loaded the moped into the van and shut the doors as quietly as he could. Again, he went to work with the wiring of the automobile, and soon, the sound of the engine filled Evrett with excitement.

He traveled only a few blocks before finding another white van that was similar enough to the one he had just stolen. He pulled up alongside it, swapped the license plates and drove off into the night, reflecting on the evening's accomplishments. The successes had lifted his spirit, and within minutes, Evrett was on the highway. He looked up as he drove under an overpass. In his mind he saw the familiar phantom that had haunted him for years now.

"Soon, you son of a bitch." Evrett said to the man on the bridge. "Soon."

29

THE SOUND OF THE SPOON TAPPING against the three-quarters-filled champagne glass silenced the room faster than Alec could have ever imagined.

As soon as the thirty-some party-goers shifted their attention from the numerous conversations to Alec, he set down the spoon and placed his arm around Angela, who had a smile that made several in the room anxious for what was coming next.

"First of all, I'd like to thank everybody for coming," Alec announced, playing the role of the good host. Right after Thanksgiving, he and Angela bought a house in Pasadena, Maryland, with a backyard that touched Silver Bay, a body of water that emptied into the Atlantic Ocean. There was a small dock out back that was destined to have a boat tied to it, but the couple had decided to hold off and wait until summer to make such a purchase.

After tonight, the purchase was going to be delayed even further.

Alec continued, "We hope you've enjoyed everything so far and we're so happy to be able to spend the holiday season with our family and good friends."

Angela was still smiling, which warmed the heart of her mother, Diana, who was standing next to Angela's father, John. Her parents remember how bad the divorce was and they've enjoyed every second of their time spent talking with Alec. Angela's parents were never fond of her former husband, but they knew it was their daughter's choice. They promised themselves that the next time, they'd speak up before she made another mistake.

But there was nothing to be said in objection to Alec. John had already adopted him as the son he never had, taking him to a Baltimore Ravens game in early December. The parents were so happy for the two that their Christmas gift to them was a hefty $20,000 check to put down on the house.

Alec didn't want to accept it, but there was no way to decline it. They were insistent.

"But before we watch the ball drop and drink loads of champagne to celebrate 2016, Angela and I would like to make an announcement."

Alec turned it over to Angela as the excitement in the room grew. Alec's sister and husband were hanging on to his every word, as were his mother, Angela's sister and husband, and a large group of co-workers and good friends.

Angela laughed as Alec gave the attention of the room to her and she clapped her hands together in excitement.

"Alec and I are happy to announce that the extra bedroom upstairs will not be empty for long."

She paused to see her mother's face light up, and then continued.

"In July, my parents will become grandparents."

Several women in the room all let out screams and squeals, the kind of excited noises that no one really enjoys, while the rest clapped their hands and moved in to embrace the expecting couple.

Alec wasn't finished, though. He had a surprise of his own.

Raising his voice to regain control of the room, he said, "Now, Angela and I have talked about this before, and many of you know about our backgrounds and what we have both been through.

"I know I was always scared of moving on," he said, shifting his eyes from the room to Angela, "but I have to tell you, I can't imagine moving on without you, Angela. You rescued me with a job when *The Baltimore Sun* let me go. You took me out to dinner on the nights I felt lonely and depressed. You've been here every step of the way for the last two years and I would like you to be here for the rest of my life."

As Alec dropped to one knee, the room was in awe, knowing exactly what was coming next. Angela placed her hands together over her mouth to quell the gasp and cover part of her smile. He pulled out the traditional black ring box and opened it to reveal a one-carat solitaire with a white gold band.

"Angela Marie Caraway, will you marry me?"

"Yes, yes, yes! Oh, yes, I will!" she said without hesitation.

Alec placed the ring on her finger—it fit perfectly because he was sneaky enough to size an old ring—and they kissed and hugged as the room applauded.

John stepped forward and picked up a glass of champagne.

"Well, this has been quite an evening so far," he said, taking over. Both Alec and Angela turned because this was not in any of their plans.

"I'm so proud of these two and I want to officially welcome Alec and his family to our family. We're blessed to have such great people join our lives and let's make this New Year's party a tradition to honor this great moment."

He lifted the glass high and said, "To Angela and Alec. We love you both."

Everyone lifted their glasses and cheersed the couple.

"Okay, now who turned off the music?" John asked. "Let's get back to the party."

The room filled with laughter and everyone returned to the New Year's celebration.

Angela leaned in close to Alec and whispered in his ear, "You're the best. Crazy, but the best."

• • •

Since moving the publication online, Angela had been able to work efficiently from home. She originally had leased a small office building when she was printing a magazine, but she closed that office and allowed her employees to work from home.

Alec's stories were a big success and with several other great writers on staff, the online publication was prospering as a whole. In recent months, Alec had taken on more responsibilities, including editing, marketing and advertising.

It was much different than being a newspaper reporter, but he loved it. He enjoyed the new challenges, especially marketing. He loved working with new social media to promote *The Long and Short*. He also embraced working with high schools to get digital editions onto the iPads of English literature students.

Just the thought that English teachers and students were analyzing his works made him proud. He had even been asked to be a guest speaker at a few local high schools, and he had scheduled to make his first appearance at the end of January.

He lifted up his notes for the students and placed them in the top drawer of his desk. He cleared the rest of his desk and pulled it away from the wall in the basement.

He had just moved it out of what was soon to be the baby's room and down into the finished basement. The prior homeowners used the large basement as an entertainment room with a television, a pair of couches and a pool table. Alec saw this when he and Angela toured the home with their realtor, and he originally thought that they would do something similar.

That changed just prior to New Year's Eve when the two discussed turning it into their home office, so Alec quickly moved the desk downstairs to get started.

As soon as he got it in the basement, Angela looked around and said the red walls would have to go. They need something lighter, more soothing to work with.

"Red is angry," she said.

Alec agreed, but he had no plans to carry the desk back up the stairs, so to the middle of the room it went. Late Friday night, he laid down painting tarps, taping them in position to keep the new color from dripping onto the hardwood floors.

He awoke at six the next morning to tape around a few electrical outlets, and thirty minutes later, the doorbell rang. Dropping the roll of tape as he ran up the stairs, Alec headed to the door and opened it without looking. He knew it was Angela's brother-in-law, Ray Skaggs, who was coming to help him paint.

Ray married Angela's younger sister, Mary, in 2010, and after meeting him for the first time at the New Year's party, Alec knew the two had to hang out again soon. Ray also was an avid Orioles fan and the two soon-to-be brother-in-laws talked baseball for more than two hours after the ball dropped in Times Square.

During the conversation, Alec joked about looking to paint the basement Oriole orange, and a few seconds later, Ray offered to help him paint it. The offer still remained after Alec broke it to him that the color they actually selected was a light beige, or "Seaside Sand," as the little card at Home Depot read.

"Hey, buddy," Ray said tossing his right hand out for a handshake.

Alec met him with his hand. "Come on in. How you doing?"

"It's sixty degrees and it's January ninth," he said, chuckling. "How the hell do you think I'm doing?"

"Then it's too bad we're painting the basement and not the deck."

"Isn't that the truth?"

As they walked into the kitchen toward the basement door, Alec pointed at the refrigerator, "I know it's early, but I have a few Millers in the fridge if you'd like."

Alec still had not drank beer or liquor since July 10, but he did have several beers left over from New Year's. They weren't in any way tempting him to break his streak, but he did wish for them to go.

"Sure, thanks," Ray said. "What the hell, it's Saturday."

The two painters got to work as Angela left for her mother's home. She, along with her sister and her parents, were planning to join Alec and Ray for dinner later that night. With the above-average temperatures outside, Alec planned to use his deck and grill for the first time.

The paint job was going to be simple; the four walls included only a few obstructions, but the original red coloring would mean that they'd need at least three coats.

They had the first coat completed before nine o'clock, and as it dried, they enjoyed waffles for breakfast. The second coat was finished at one-thirty, and they ate deli sandwiches while watching a pregame show for the NFL Wild Card playoff games slated for that afternoon.

"Plenty of time," Ray said, knowing they still had to put on a third coat.

The Ravens were set to play the Broncos in the second game of the day at eight o'clock, and they had no plans on missing a play. Angela's father, John, had similar plans. He couldn't miss a snap.

"They win when I'm here," he always says superstitiously.

As they were finishing the third coat, they heard the commotion of Angela and her parents entering the home. It was three hours until game time and the two men were just about finished.

"Right on time," Ray said, tapping the face of his wristwatch.

Alec nearly acknowledged Ray's comment, but a sensation of light-headedness overwhelmed him.

"Why don't you head upstairs and check on them," Alec said. "I'll finish up here."

"You sure?"

"Yeah, get the grill fired up, too."

"You got it."

Ray wiped his hand on a paper towel and walked upstairs. Alec went over to his desk and grabbed a notepad, pen and digital recorder. He sat down in his chair as the vision began. There was an older woman and she was frantic.

It was odd because for the first time, a story idea was coming to him when he wasn't thinking about a story. In fact, with all the major life changes, he hadn't even put any thought into his next story that was due by the end of the next week.

He hit record and recited every detail.

$$\bullet \ \bullet \ \bullet$$

The Widow
By Alec Rossi

The Long and Short

The plane engine sputtered a couple times before kicking into full gear. The twin engine Cessna Caravan shook gently as it slowly began its short trek toward the small paved runway that ran parallel to the Pacific.

From where the widow was sitting, she could see people she did not know waving as the plane taxied toward the runway. They weren't waving at her.

She had no one.

Not anymore.

Her husband was supposed to travel the world with her, but she was denied that opportunity. Now, she was left all alone to embark on the adventures of her golden years.

"He would have wanted me to continue on," she told herself as she packed for her travels around the world.

A week from now, she would be in Mexico, exploring the Mayan ruins in the Yucatan peninsula. A week after that, she would be on a boat, floating down the Amazon in Brazil. Europe, Russia and Australia were all on her itinerary, too, but first she had to fly to Honolulu for one of the best skydiving experiences in the world.

It was the most anticipated trip for her husband, and it was supposed to be last on their world tour, but she made arrangements to come here first.

The plane ran over a bump as it traveled from the dirt onto the paved runway, and the widow wrapped her arms tighter around the ceramic urn containing her husband's ashes.

He wanted nothing more than to make this jump with her and she was going to fulfill his dream.

She looked out the doorway to see the waves crashing onto the sandy beach as the plane lifted into the air. She closed her eyes as the initial sensation of leaving the ground made her uneasy. She never liked taking off. It was always the initial weird feeling of weightlessness that scared her. She imagined landing would be even scarier, but she had never experienced it in a small plane. She always jumped out long before the aircraft landed.

The plane tilted slightly to the right as it flew out toward the ocean. The ascent continued and she could see for miles. It was beautiful.

A tear made its way down her right cheek as she wished that her husband was able to see what she was seeing. She loved how the bluish green water near the coast gradually faded into a dark blue abyss.

As the plane climbed to 1,000 feet, the widow watched the young couple across the plane get ready to make the same jump. The woman was scared; the widow could tell. It definitely was her first time, and from the looks of it, she would be tandem skydiving with her husband.

"Funny, that's what I'm doing," the widow said satirically in her head.

And this wouldn't be the first jump with her husband. The two were avid skydivers and they had made more than fifty jumps preparing for the "ultimate skydive," as they called it. A month ago, the couple was all set to go, but now, the second ticket for this trip was left at home on the dresser.

"If only I would have retired sooner," the widow said.

Her regretful thoughts were interrupted by the skydiving coordinator's voice, "Okay, folks. We're at fourteen thousand feet. Time to jump."

In total, five people would be jumping from the plane today— the coordinator, the married couple, a shadowy man in the back and the widow.

The couple went first, followed by the man skydiving solo. The widow stepped up to the white line as she had many times before. She got the okay and a smile from the coordinator, and she jumped.

The air rushed by her as she let out an excited scream. Regardless of where her husband was right now, to her, this was heaven. She could see the blue ocean for miles, and the neighboring Hawaiian Islands.

She took in the view for about fifteen seconds before looking down at the urn that she was holding tightly.

It was time.

She reached down to spin the cap off, but before she could, an updraft hit her and the urn flew out of her hands. She was sent spiraling several feet away from the urn and she could now see it rapidly falling away from her.

The widow immediately did as she was taught and made herself more aerodynamic to catch up to the urn.

She was panicking and crying, but she knew she had to get to the urn. The ashes were meant to fly free, not smash into the water.

As she made herself as aerodynamic as possible, she got closer and closer to the urn. She had lost it a mere fifteen seconds ago, but it had seemed like an eternity. She was still crying, but confident that she would catch up. She estimated that she was fifteen feet away.

She also noticed that this trajectory was taking her away from land where she was supposed to touch down with chute deployed.

Instead, she was heading for the sea.

She did not care at this point. She knew she could recover.

Fifteen seconds later, she reached out and corralled her husband. She held him close, giving him a big hug. She smiled as she spun open the cap and watched the ashes disappear into the air.

"I love you," she said.

She knew at this point she was well past the point of when she should have pulled her chute. She was less than three thousand feet from hitting the water just off the coast, so she quickly pulled the cord to open the chute, but nothing happened. She tried it again and again, but to no avail.

It was at this point that she knew that this was it. She tried once more to pull the chute, but she was at a thousand feet and a mere five seconds away from impact if it didn't open.

She closed her eyes and pictured her husband. She knew deep inside that she'd be with him again soon.

It was her last day, and instead of worrying about all the destinations she would miss out on, she strangely enjoyed the moment—she made the ultimate jump with the man she loved.

Seconds later, she disappeared into the Pacific.

• • •

Alec sat comfortably on the couch with his iPad in hand, as Angela lay to the right of him watching television. It was nearing one in the morning, and she was struggling to stay awake. Alec had no problem keeping his eyes open and that allowed him to finish proof reading the completed version of the next installment in his "Last Day" series.

He had written it just an hour earlier after the future in-laws departed. They had eaten dinner together and watched the Ravens defeat the Broncos in the AFC Wild Card round. It was a great game to watch, but all Alec could think about during the game was his story. He had taken all the notes earlier in the day and he couldn't wait to sit down in front of his computer.

Now that it was finished, he looked over at Angela, his bride to be. There was a deep love conveyed in his story, and he hoped that he and Angela could have the same as they grew old together. He opened the browser, and typed "Hawaii" into the Google search bar.

A honeymoon was in their future and he started to think about how he had never been to Hawaii. In fact, he had never been on the West Coast.

He searched for honeymoon packages, and he even saw a few that included skydiving lessons, but he merely laughed at those. He had no plans of putting his life into the hands of a parachute, no matter how beautiful the view may be.

As he was looking at photos, one jumped out at him. It was from a "Skydive Hawaii" website. It pictured an aerial view of a runway that looked exactly like the one he saw in his vision.

How could this be possible, he thought.

He did not recall looking at photos of skydiving locations in Hawaii, but he swore it must have been repressed deep in his memory. How else could he have been able to vividly see what was a real place on Earth?

Alec chalked it up to a strange occurrence that had a logical explanation—one that he could not figure out at this hour.

He shook Angela, who had fallen asleep, "Honey, let's go up to bed."

She greeted him with a groggy smile and reached out for his hand. He helped her stand up and they went off to bed.

30

IT WAS THE WEIGHTLESSNESS that snapped Evrett back into the moment. The rush of the free fall had forced away the veil over his mind. He could now see the blue Pacific waters churning below him, coming closer and closer.

"Oh, shit!" Evrett cried.

In the few seconds that remained, he tried to take in his surroundings to figure out where he was. His last thought had been of driving the stolen van in the darkness of the Hawaiian night. As he fell, he caught sight of the late afternoon sun.

And then he hit the water.

The rush of bubbles made it hard to see. Evrett tucked his knees to his chest for fear of hitting the bottom. There hadn't been enough time to take a good, full breath before he crashed into the water and Evrett could feel his chest struggle from the lack of oxygen. He curled over and began kicking toward the light.

He shattered the surface of the ocean and gasped for air. He got a half breath in before a wave crashed over him, sending him back below the water. Evrett fought to get a hold of his bearings. He wrestled against the next wave.

"Hey, move out of the way!"

The voice startled Evrett. He turned toward the direction of the cry expecting to see the person who had produced it. Instead, Evrett was face to face with a solid black rock.

"Come on! You're holding everybody up."

Evrett lifted his eyes up higher and higher. The rock stretched onward. At its top, he finally could see the teenage boy who had called out to him. He had floppy blond hair and was wearing a bright pair of surf trunks.

Evrett knew this place.

He wiped the water from his eyes and waved his hand.

"Sorry. Sorry."

Evrett started swimming toward the beach and away from the big rock of Waimea Bay. He could see the white shore a few yards away, and within a few minutes, he felt it beneath his feet. Evrett collapsed onto the beach just as the teenager jumped off the rock and into the water.

It had happened again. Another portion of his life lost. Judging by the position of the sun, he figured it was around four or five in the afternoon. Roughly twelve hours were missing from his memory. He couldn't believe he lost half a day. He'd have to retrace his steps and find out what happened to Gloria.

By now he knew how this worked.

He knew she was dead.

The question was how had she died?

A yellow lab ran by him on the beach. It chased after a tennis ball that landed a few feet into the water. The dog leapt into a crashing wave to retrieve the ball.

Evrett recalled the last time he sat on this beach. He and Sam had spent a day on their honeymoon driving along the North Shore of the island. On their way back, Sam had spotted the bay from the highway and requested they pull over. There were more people jumping off the big rock that day.

"Come on, Evrett. We have to try it," Sam said.

She led the way, going around to the other side of the rock. Together they climbed to the highest part of the crag, a smooth patch of the rock overlooking the water from thirty feet above. Evrett raised his hand to shield the sun from his eyes as he looked around. A few kids were climbing on the rock as well. One jumped off, laughing as he fell toward the waves below.

"This is so surreal. We sure don't have places like this back home," Sam said.

She stepped closer to the edge. Evrett was by her side.

"Let's go together. Take my hand," she said reaching for him.

"Okay, if you insist."

Their fingers interlocked and Evrett joined his wife on the edge of the rock. Even from up so high he could see the bottom of the ocean. A group of small fish dotted the image of the white sand beneath blue waters.

"On the count of three?" he suggested.

"You got it. I love you."

"I love you, too."

They kissed and then turned to face the bay. They counted together and jumped.

The moment was over so quickly. Within seconds they were under the water. As they swam toward the surface they let go of one another's hands.

"We have to do that again, Evrett!"

Evrett smiled and nodded. They would make three more jumps that day before driving back to the resort.

Evrett stood up from the beach. The yellow lab ran past him again, chasing after the same ball. It was time for him to find his van.

Time to find Gloria, too.

Evrett made the trek back to the road. He looked around for a vehicle he recognized. There was no van, no moped. Finally, he saw his rental car parked on the shoulder of the road.

All that time stealing and hot-wiring those rides, and for what? He had no idea where they were now. He hoped that the rental had his equipment at least.

When Evrett arrived at the car he found the door unlocked and the keys lying on the seat. He was lucky no one had stolen the car. It would have been a long trip back to Waikiki by foot. Evrett popped the trunk, crossing his fingers that his unconscious self had been smart enough to hold on to his bag.

"Thank God," Evrett said. He let a sigh of relief out and unzipped his black bag. Inside he found his recorder, his wallet, and a few other supplies he liked to keep on him.

He checked to make sure no one was nearby before pressing play on the recorder.

"Check in. Four-thirty-four. A. M. January ninth. Found the new vehicle."

It was the message he had recorded when he first drove the van out of the lot. Evrett looked in his wallet. Most of his cash was gone.

"Oh, come on."

When Evrett had left the hotel he had most of his cash, a little more than $1,700, on him. He never used credit cards; he wanted to leave as little of a trail as possible. Evrett counted what was left, only a few twenties and tens, along with a folded up piece of paper.

It was a receipt—for skydiving.

• • •

Evrett followed his GPS to the small airport that matched the receipt. It was also located on the North Shore. This must have been the airport that Gloria had planned to travel to earlier that day.

Evrett scanned the area. There was a jeep and a pick-up truck parked over by a small building that must have served as the office. Evrett saw a plane hanger that was large enough to fit two planes in it. A sign in the window of the office read: CLOSED.

He decided to investigate and walked toward the hanger where a man called out to him.

"Excuse me! Excuse me, can I help you with something, brah?"

The man took off his aviator sunglasses as he approached Evrett.

"Ah, yes. I was here earlier today. I think I left—"

"You? What are you doing back here? I thought we had a deal?"

The man grabbed Evrett's arm and pulled him into the hanger.

Evrett broke free of his grip. This confirmed that he had in fact been at the airport that day; however, Evrett did not like that he was in the dark about what had happened and how involved he had been in the ordeal. He had to choose his next moves carefully.

"Hey, take it easy. I just needed to come back and see if I left my bag behind? All right?"

"Oh yeah? Looking for your bag, brah? It's pretty funny that you were gone by the time we all landed. Didn't want to stay around and answer any questions, huh?"

"Questions? What are you talking about? Look, I'm missing some money and I just want to see if I left—"

"Is this a joke?"

"No, I don't know what—" Evrett began but was cut off by the other man.

"Hey, keep it down."

The man with the aviators pressed his finger up to his lips, signaling for Evrett to be quiet. He looked over his shoulder at the small building. Whoever was still in the office, Evrett could tell this man did not want them knowing he was on the premises.

Evrett whispered, "Look, I had to rush off. But in doing so, I think I left something behind, so I just wanted to come here to find it."

"Are you trying to get me fired? It's bad enough I let you bribe me."

Wait a minute. Bribe you? Evrett thought, trying to piece things together. The man clearly wanted whatever exchange they had made to remain a secret. If he had bribed him, that might explain Evrett's missing money. But what would he have bribed this man for?

"Don't think of it as a bribe, really. You were just helping me out," Evrett said, playing along.

"Helping you out? I could have lost my job. I was so stupid. And then the cops showed up."

"The cops?"

"Yeah, you had taken off by that point, brah. Pretty suspicious if you ask me."

Evrett started to get worried. What had happened? What had

he done?

"Why were the cops here? You didn't tell them about our deal did you?"

"Of course not. I didn't want to draw any unwanted attention. What do you think would happen to me if on the same day some lady dies while jumping, my boss finds out I took a bribe to let some shitty tourist skydive alone?"

There it was. Evrett had researched enough about skydiving to know that only experienced divers could make the leap without a partner. If he had gone alone, he must have used the money to bribe this man into letting him jump without an instructor.

Evrett felt a little relief. His thoughts quickly turned to the other news he had just heard.

"A lady died?" Evrett asked.

"Yeah, brah. That older lady on the plane today. She didn't get her chute open in time. They're still looking for her body out in the ocean."

"Was her name Gloria?" Evrett asked.

"Yeah, I think so. You knew her?"

"No, just... just from sitting in the office. That's horrible. I had no idea."

The man turned to look over his shoulder once again.

"Look, I want you to get the hell out of here. I didn't tell the police anything about you. Now, keep your end of the bargain and make sure I never see you again. Got it?"

Evrett nodded.

"Don't worry. You won't."

Evrett hurried to his car, heart and head pounding from the conversation. He could feel the eyes of the man in the hanger watching him the whole time. It wasn't until he was on the road again that he began to relax, letting his mind mull over the news of Gloria while trying to piece together his day.

At some point he must have ditched the van and returned to the hotel, only to leave again and follow Gloria to the airport. Somehow he then managed to get on the same plane as her to go skydiving. Once his jump was complete, he supposedly left the airport as fast as he could and drove to Waimea Bay, a place he had only been to once before.

Evrett couldn't believe it. He had let so many people see him near Gloria.

Had he made contact with her?

Did he ask her any questions?

What if she had told him about the man on the bridge and he didn't remember?

The thought of it made Evrett mad. He pounded his fist against the dashboard.

"God dammit."

Gloria was dead, and again, he had nothing new on the man on the bridge.

• • •

Evrett finished his drink and placed it down on the bar. He had one more day left on Oahu. With Gloria dead he had nothing to do on the island. Drinking had seemed like a suitable option to fill his afternoon.

The bar had a few patrons scattered about it. A couple in their early twenties flirted and laughed to his left. A larger group of friends in their forties discussed their golf handicaps to his right. Another man, alone and in his sixties sat a few stools away from Evrett.

Evrett closed his eyes and breathed in deeply. The bar sat right on the beach and he could feel the sea breeze blowing through the open walls behind him.

"What are you drinking?"

Evrett opened his eyes expecting to see the bartender standing in front of him. Instead, the man in his sixties had moved a few stools over and was now sitting next to Evrett.

"Ah, it was a margarita."

"Sex on the beach," the man said, lifting his own drink in the air. Evrett took notice of the tiny umbrella leaning on the rim of the glass.

"I always order it just for the name," he said.

The man had short grey hair that was mostly missing from the top of his head. He was tan and wore a blue and green floral Hawaiian shirt.

"It is one of the better named drinks," Evrett said.

"My name's Rupert."

"Bill," Evrett said.

The two men shook hands. The bartender walked by. Rupert raised his glass.

"Barkeep, I'll have another. As will this gentlemen here," Rupert said and turned to Evrett. "This one is on me."

"You don't have to do that."

"Nonsense. You look like you could use a drink."

Evrett had come to the bar deep in thought. Halfway through his list of targets and he felt like he was stuck at stage one. He had been at it for so long.

"Well, thank you."

Their drinks arrived quickly. The two men raised their glasses to one another.

"Cheers, Bill."

"Cheers," Evrett repeated.

"Damn, that's good. So, Bill, what are you doing in Waikiki?"

"I'm here on vacation. My wife is doing some shopping."

"A tourist, huh? Let me guess. East Coast?"

Evrett nodded.

"Ha! I knew it. You have that Atlantic Ocean vibe to you."

"Oh, yeah?"

"Yeah. We carry where we're from with us always."

"Deep stuff."

Evrett took a sip of the margarita, making sure he got some salt from the rim.

"This sure is a beautiful place," Evrett said. He looked out toward the Pacific Ocean. The water was a dazzling robin's egg blue and crashed on the white sand. He could see a woman on a paddleboard out in the water.

"It sure is. That's why I had to move out here."

"Where are you originally from?"

Rupert leaned back in his chair.

"Well, I'm originally from Grand Rapids, Michigan, but my father took a job in Connecticut when I was about seven. And then after college I moved to New York where I stayed until seven months ago, when I sold everything I had and moved out here."

"That's amazing," Evrett said.

He couldn't imagine what it must be like to start over completely fresh. A clean slate. Would he ever be able to do that?

"Eh, it's not all peaches and cream. Sadly, it wasn't a peaceful retirement I was looking for."

Rupert took a long sip of his drink.

"I came out here to die."

Evrett stopped spinning his margarita glass and looked at Rupert.

"I'm sorry to hear that."

"Thank you. It's okay. I've made peace with it. Cancer, you see."

"What kind?"

"Lung. Funny, I never smoked a day in my life either. My partner on the other hand, smoked like a chimney. He died a few years ago, though. An aneurysm."

Evrett was surprised with how casually Rupert talked about death.

"I…" Evrett fumbled for words.

"It's okay. Really. You don't need to say anything. You don't know me from Adam. We're just sitting at a bar, talking. Jeff died five years ago. He and I were together for thirty-six years, thirty-six great years."

"Wow, thirty-six years."

"How long have you and your wife been together?" Rupert asked.

"Four."

Evrett felt bad lying to this man who was being so honest with him. Still, he couldn't take any unnecessary risks. The van, the moped, the skydiving, they had all been risks. He had reached this trip's quota.

"You're practically newlyweds still. Any kids?"

Evrett shook his head. At least that wasn't a lie.

"You've still got time. You know, I'm really okay with things. I tried chemo. But I just couldn't live the last months of my life like that—getting sick, barely eating. But still, at the end of it all, that's what I regret the most."

"What's that?"

"Children. Jeff and I never had that opportunity. The world was different then. We didn't have the options that exist now. But now, looking back, I wish we would have figured something out."

Rupert grew silent. Evrett thought of the plan he and Sam had had for their future family, the one that would never exist now.

"What I've learned, Bill, is that you have to live. And live fully. Sure, you'll have regrets along the way. You'll wish you would have said something differently, or done something else. But you only get this one go at it all. You have to make the most of it."

"You're right, Rupert."

"Eh, I'm just a man drunk at a bar in the afternoon."

Rupert smiled at Evrett and patted his back. He put a few folded bills on the table and waved goodbye. Evrett wondered how much time the man had left. He played the conversation over in his mind.

At the end of his life, would he regret what he was doing? He had given so much of his life to his hunt and yet he had not come back with anything. Were Andrew, Chad, Amanda and Gloria's deaths enough? Would he look back someday and wish he had just gotten on with his life after Sam's death?

Evrett's mind turned toward Julia. And what of her? How did she fit into all of this? Was there a future there with her? And what would that mean for his love of Sam? Could he love both? *Did* he love both?

Evrett finished his margarita and walked out of the bar onto the soft hot sand. He kicked off his sandals and felt the water rush over his feet and then pull back out. Before him the ocean, full of possibility, glittered in the golden sun.

31

"I WANT YOU BOTH TO CLOSE YOUR EYES and think of the last time you were truly happy."

Sean Bryant tried to follow the doctor's orders, but found his mind fixated on one thought.

What was Janine thinking?

His wife of fourteen years sat next to him on a bluish grey couch. They had been coming to therapy together for seven months.

It didn't really seem to be helping, he thought.

He studied the lines that had begun to form at the corners of her eyes. She really was beautiful and had almost the same tight, trim body she had in college, even after having the twins. He could appreciate that. Their problems ran deeper than the surface, though.

"Now, I want you to turn to one another and tell each other when it was," Dr. Bensen said.

Her low voice interrupted Sean's train of thought. Even at close to fifty, she had a killer pair of legs that Sean couldn't help but notice.

He knew it irritated the hell out of Janine.

He faced his wife. He prayed she went first.

"Janine, you can start," Dr. Bensen said.

It was a relief. It wasn't that he was an unhappy person. There were many things in his life that he enjoyed doing. He loved his job. He loved his two boys, Jackson and Peter. He loved taking his bike out on the trails around Raleigh, North Carolina. But did he still love Janine? It was a horrible thought, but one that crossed his mind as she began her memory.

"The last time I was happy—truly happy? It was this past Christmas. The kids were playing with their new toys. The rest of the family hadn't gotten to the house yet. And I was sitting, watching them in front of the tree. It was just... It was peaceful."

Sean listened to her. He remembered the holiday as well. The moment she described was perfect. With the exception that he wasn't there in her retelling of it.

"What was Sean doing as you watched the boys play?" Dr. Bensen asked.

Janine paused for a moment.

"I don't... What were you..."

"I was in the kitchen setting up the electric griddle. The stove was acting up again and we always make pancakes after we open gifts. It's been our family tradition since we got engaged."

"Oh, that's right."

The silence that followed was awkward. He felt Dr. Bensen's attention shift to him.

"Well, Sean. What memory did you choose?"

Sean pondered the different paths before him. The straightest path was to tell the truth—that he hadn't thought of one, or perhaps that he *couldn't* think of one. Another option was to make something up. He could follow Janine's lead and choose a memory of the family. Maybe leave her out of it as well. Would that even make her feel badly anymore? Would it hurt her more to say that the last time he had been happy was a moment only the two of them shared.

No, she would see through that one.

"Sean?"

"I don't know. I think it…honestly, I can't think of one. I just know I haven't been truly happy in a while. And you know what, I thought these appointments would help, and they haven't."

"Sean, it takes time to fix a relationship that is struggling," Janine said, using words Dr. Bensen had uttered several times before.

"I know it takes time and work. But how do you know when it's hopeless? How do you know when it just isn't going to get any better?"

He implored Dr. Bensen. He knew his wife would not have the answer. Which one of them would throw in the towel? Could he? He never quit anything in his life, and he didn't want to start with his marriage. But he knew that this was not where he saw himself when he dropped to one knee and asked his college sweetheart to marry him.

"Sean, Janine. I can't tell you when you should stop trying to fix your marriage and instead seek a divorce lawyer. That is something you need to decide for yourselves. But, I can tell you that you won't get to that point as long as you are both willing to come to these meetings and put the time in. If there is still a fight left in you, there is still something worth saving."

"Good answer, Doc," Sean said.

• • •

When he wasn't around Janine, he felt like a different man. Without her as a constant reminder, he could be alive in the moment. Without her, there wasn't someone to blame.

Things weren't perfect before the accident, but afterward everything had become worse.

Sean and Janine had decided to spend the family's summer vacation visiting her relatives in Bridgeport, Connecticut. Rather than do the ten-hour drive in one day, they had decided to split it over two with a short stay in Baltimore.

They packed their Toyota Sienna minivan and left at six in the morning. Even with leaving that early, they would only make it to Inner Harbor and the aquarium around lunchtime if traffic was forgiving. Still that gave them the afternoon to spend there. The boys loved it. Sean and Janine held hands and watched as Jackson and Peter ran down the spiraling ramp in the shark exhibit. It was great to be away from the pressures of work and the unending list of chores that needed to be completed at the house. Away from all that, Sean and Janine were able to be in the moment.

After the late afternoon dolphin show, the family got back in their vehicle and began their drive again. They had found a cheaper motel a few miles outside the city and up Interstate 95 near Delaware. The traffic around rush hour was beginning to pile up as Sean piloted the van through the downtown streets. Janine was slowly programming the GPS with the address of the motel. Without knowing exactly where he was going, Sean missed the turn onto Gay Street and instead started up the ramp onto Interstate 83.

"Shit," Sean said.

"What's the matter?" Janine asked.

"We're getting onto the wrong highway. This isn't ninety-five."

"Oh, Sean! Why didn't you wait until I had the GPS set up?"

"Janine, don't start. The GPS will redirect us. It isn't the end of the world."

"The boys need dinner, and I would like to get to the room soon. Sean, look out!"

His wife saw the accident before he did. His hands quickly maneuvered the van to safety as instincts took over.

"Is everyone, okay? Boys? Janine?"

The boys both shook their heads. They both asked what was happening. Sean looked at his wife. She leaned forward in her seat. Her chest rose and fell in a rapid motion.

"Janine, are you okay?" Without thinking, he placed his hand on hers. She turned to face him, her mouth and eyes wide.

"Did you see that truck? It slammed into that car!"

Sean looked back out the windshield. About 100 yards ahead of them the tanker truck lay on its side, pinning a small red car in place. He squinted.

"There's someone in there," Sean began as he unbuckled his seat belt and opened the driver's side door.

"Sean? What are you doing?" Janine screamed.

He was almost fully out of the vehicle as his wife lunged to grab his arm.

"Janine, I have to go help that woman. She's trapped."

"Like hell, Sean!"

"Janine, let go!" Sean tugged his arm back. He couldn't just stand idly by while the woman in the red car remained trapped. Janine lost her grasp and he quickly turned back to face the accident.

"Sean, the boys!" Janine pleaded.

Sean hesitated and eventually got back into the car. A few minutes later, the flames ignited the gas, consuming the scene of the accident in an explosion that engulfed the red car. Sean's window was rolled down and he could feel the heat from the blaze.

Would he have made it in time?

He heard the cries of his family in the van behind him.

He would never get his answer.

• • •

Sean hung his scarf up on the hook in the family's mudroom. He could smell dinner cooking down the hall. The strong aroma of tomato sauce suggested it was going to be Italian again. He kicked off his shoes and entered the kitchen.

"Hey, kids. Oh, hi, Stephanie."

The twin third graders smiled at their father. They were sitting on the barstools around the family's kitchen island while the seventeen-year-old babysitter boiled water for pasta and heated up a jar of sauce on the stove. She was a pretty girl that lived a few blocks away from the Bryants. Whenever they needed someone to watch the kids, Stephanie was their first pick of teenage babysitters. The kids loved her. Sometimes Sean wondered if they had more fun with the babysitter than they did their own parents.

"Hi, Mr. Bryant. I didn't know you'd be home so early. Mrs. Bryant didn't say how late you'd need me."

Sean checked his watch. It was six, his normal time to arrive home from work. Usually Janine would pick the kids up from the after-school program by four-thirty.

"Uh, how long have you been with the boys? Did Janine pay you before she left?"

"Oh, I haven't seen Mrs. Bryant. She called me from work. I picked Pete and Jacks up on my way home from school."

Janine's been pulling this kind of shit way too much, he thought.

She worked as a supervisor in the call center claims department for a flooring company. And lately it seemed she was finding more and more reasons to stay late.

Sean wondered if she was having an affair. Their relationship had been strained over the last few years and it had been months since they had last been intimate. Even that had been a failure. Leaving the kids with their grandparents, the couple had taken Dr. Bensen's recommendation and tried to reconnect with a romantic getaway on a weekend in September. The first evening ended with them in bed with an empty bottle of champagne. He remembered thinking at the time Janine seemed distant, like she was miles away instead of right next to him.

The thought of her having an affair seemed both preposterous and reasonable at the same time.

How could the mother of his children and his wife of over a decade do that to him? There had been no evidence, only the increased time out of the house and the distance that kept widening between them. Was he just not willing to see it?

"Mr. Bryant, I totally forgot. She did tell me to give you this message."

Stephanie sailed across the kitchen to her purse. She pulled out a Post-it note with her handwriting on it.

"She asked if you could take care of some of this stuff."

Sean read the list Janine must have dictated over the phone to Stephanie. Pick up ice melting pelts for the walkway. Take the recycling out. Either fix or call someone to take care of the dryer.

Sean lost interest in the honey-do list. He didn't mind helping out around the house. He loved pulling his weight by completing various projects, such as putting in the new shelving unit in the mudroom. But whenever he was given a list of chores, he was turned off to the whole idea. He hated to be told what to do, especially when Janine was "working late."

"Thanks, Stephanie. Do you mind staying with the boys a little longer? I need to run out to get some of the stuff Janine asked for."

"No problem," she said with a smile.

She was a beautiful girl, Sean thought. Stephanie was young and had a whole life full of mistakes to make. Had he wasted his youth with Janine?

Sean paid Stephanie for the time she spent with the boys and then enough to cover the rest of the night.

He passed the grocery store in his black Cadillac SRX. It was never his intention to pick up anything that Janine had requested.

No, tonight he was on a different mission.

Sean drove slowly through the parking lot at Grayson National Flooring. He was looking for the minivan Janine had taken to work that day. As he neared the end of the lot he saw the van under one of the tall bright lights. At least she was at work and not out somewhere else.

He pulled into a space a few down from the van and put his vehicle in park. Sean envisioned the different ways this evening could unfold. In the first scenario, he saw himself backing the car out and driving home, forgetting this whole thing. Surely Janine couldn't cheat on him. Janine had made him agree to go to therapy to work on their marriage. What would be the point in just throwing it away on an affair? Maybe that was her cover.

In the second version, he saw himself storming into Janine's office to find her in the arms of some coworker. He scrolled through a list of possible candidates. Was it Jefferson, the muscular twenty-seven-year-old he had met last summer at the company picnic? Was it Darrell, her manager? Maybe it was some intern he had never even heard of.

Sean paid no attention to the soft hum of the idling engine. It soon faded away and he saw his wife in her office. A faceless man in a designer suit pressed himself against Janine's thin body. She leaned back on her large wooden desk as his hand ventured up her thigh and vanished under her skirt.

A car drove past him, catching Sean's attention and snapping him back to reality. His grip loosened on the steering wheel and he looked up over at the employee entrance of the large brick building. The double doors automatically opened and two people walked out.

Sean recognized his wife immediately. She was wearing the red jacket he had bought her at Christmas. Next to her was a tall man in a long grey coat. He carried a brief case. Sean had never seen him before.

They stopped a few feet from the door and had a quick exchange. The man had his back to Sean and he could just barely see Janine. The man bent forward and hugged her. Sean could see her arms wrap around his broad shoulders in an embrace that seemed a bit too friendly.

His heart throbbed.

Had his suspicions been correct? The duration of their goodbye seemed to tick off toward eternity.

A thousand moments flashed through Sean's mind: the first time he met Janine, smiling at the frat party at Virginia Tech; swimming with dolphins on their honeymoon in Jamaica; the night she surprised him with the positive pregnancy test; their first major fight, when he had stormed out of the house, slamming the door behind him; the accident. It was true they had had their rough spots, but could she really tear their relationship to shreds like this?

Anger fueled him now. He reached for the handle to open the door. Janine broke free from her hug and looked over toward where Sean was parked. He couldn't tell if she saw him or not, but he froze. He didn't want her to know he knew. Not yet. Not until he was sure of how to handle the situation.

He quickly threw the gearshift into reverse and pulled out of the parking space. He looked in the rearview mirror and saw Janine part ways from her mysterious companion. By the way she walked to her car, he was sure she had not noticed him.

• • •

Sean sat in the motionless vehicle. A freezing rain had started and was slowly creating a crystal covering over the windshield. The neon haze of the nearby sign sparkled through the accumulating ice.

His heart had slowed its pace a bit. He looked at the clock just as the time changed over to 9:50. Janine had called his phone seven times. Each time he sent the call to voicemail.

He knew he would have to explain himself when he got home that night. She would ask him where he had been; who he had been with. It would be a fight. A particularly vicious one he assumed.

But at 9:50 on a Tuesday night in early January, he didn't care. He looked over at the glow of the bar lights.

He slid his wedding ring off his finger and dropped it into the cup holder.

He turned the engine off and got out.

Two could play at this game.

32

"I WANT YOU BOTH TO CLOSE YOUR EYES and think of the last time you were truly happy."

Janine Bryant did as she was told. Even with her eyes shut she could sense her husband Sean's presence on the couch. Janine slyly opened her eyes and stole a glance at him. He was *actually* participating in Dr. Bensen's exercise. Janine was shocked. She closed her eyes and filtered through the memories in her mind.

She had no trouble coming up with a lengthy list of moments from their relationship when she could say she felt happy. The trouble was finding recent ones.

What is the point of this activity? she thought.

If it was to make her feel more assured in her marriage, it wasn't doing the trick. In fact, she hadn't felt better after leaving any of the last ten sessions.

Janine had suggested they try counseling last summer. She and Sean were sitting at their kitchen table, silently finishing their dinner.

The boys were done eating, and already had left the table to go build something out of Legos in the family room that served as a play-room. A few years earlier, Sean and Janine would have been sharing stories about their workdays or discussing some interesting topic they had heard about in the news. This night found them sitting in a dis-comforting silence. Sean decided he had had enough and got up from the table.

"I think we need to see someone—a therapist or counselor."

He paused halfway between the table and the sink. Sean turned and looked back at his wife.

"Okay," he said and continued across the room.

She was surprised how easy it had been to get him to agree to it.

Now she sat next to Sean, eight months after starting therapy, racking her brain for the last happy moment she had experienced. An image of the holidays popped into her head just in time.

She told Dr. Bensen and Sean about her sons opening their gifts on Christmas morning. It was true, she had been happy that morning. Janine relaxed into the cushions of the sofa.

"What was Sean doing as you watched the boys play?" Dr. Bensen asked.

She was not expecting the question. She hadn't even noticed her omission. She looked at Sean. Was he upset? Had her exclusion of him cut deep? His expression didn't change.

"I don't…What were you…"

Sean explained how he was in the kitchen making pancakes, something he did every year.

How could I forget? she thought, sheepishly adding aloud, "Oh, that's right."

She felt her cheeks flush red. Janine was certain she would leave this session feeling defeated as usual. How did this become the norm for her marriage?

At thirty-eight, she had spent so much of her life with Sean. They met at Virginia Tech, dated through college, moved in together after school and were engaged by the time they turned twenty-four. Their twenties flew by as they settled into adulthood. They both start-ed careers. He moved up through a financial investing firm, while she did the same at a company that specialized in flooring. Those were their happiest years.

Janine began to think of her early thirties—the years following her pregnancy with the twins. Motherhood had changed her. She knew that it had for numerous reasons.

Did Sean suspect how much though? If he did, it could surely explain why they were sitting there on the uncomfortable sofa.

"If there is still a fight left in you, there is still something worth saving," Dr. Bensen finished.

Janine wanted to believe.

• • •

Admittedly, she had been the one to pull away first. Sean was a great husband and father. He remembered all their anniversaries, the kids' birthday, all of it. Special occasions were always commemorated with a bouquet of flowers delivered to her office, a tradition he started a month after their first date.

No, it wasn't anything Sean did. He was everything one could hope for in a spouse.

Life is what got in her way.

Janine remembered reading the pregnancy test in disbelief. Even though children were something the couple had talked about, the discovery that she was pregnant had come as a shock to Janine.

She had just been promoted to assistant supervisor of the call center. The job came with more hours, more money and more responsibility. It was what she had been working toward.

Sean wanted to be a father in the worst way. He had been pushing the subject since they were newlyweds. Janine had worn him down to a compromise of waiting until they turned thirty-two. By that point in their plan they would be settled completely as professionals.

The boys came a few years earlier than expected.

The pregnancy went smoothly, with the exception of the other surprise—that the Bryants would be having twins. As far as either one knew, there were no previous sets of twins in the families.

Again, life had handed Janine another card she was not expecting.

Maternity leave was harder than the pregnancy. Sean was able to stay home for two weeks, which left Janine alone with the boys for six more. While Sean was at work, Janine handled everything. Conference calls and employee evaluations were replaced with feeding and pumping schedules and diaper changes. One baby would have been difficult enough, but twins were almost impossible.

More than once Janine had placed the boys in their cribs and closed herself off in the bathroom. The hum of the fan would drown out the wails of her frustration until she was ready to face motherhood again.

The return to work was a blessing. She loved her boys, but being back in the world of adults made her feel whole again. How could Sean ever understand this?

She would watch him drop his briefcase by the door and race over to the twins. He'd scoop them both up in his arms and kiss them. After work, they were his world.

That's when she started to pull away. She would ask herself at night while bathing after all the men in her house were asleep, why was it so easy for Sean to manage both lives? Why was it so hard for her?

Only Dominic Lazare had understood her then.

$$\bullet \ \bullet \ \bullet$$

It was January fifth, three weeks before her fifteenth wedding anniversary. Janine sat at her desk staring at a picture of herself with Sean and their sons. It was taken a few years earlier, while the family was vacationing on Kitty Hawk. She gazed at it. She hoped she wasn't the same woman as the one looking back at her from the frame.

She'd have to get a newer picture one of these days.

Janine grabbed the frame and popped the back off. She exposed the backside of the photo. In Sean's handwriting was the date the photo had been taken—July 16, 2012.

Almost a year before that accident, she thought.

She could still remember it all clearly: the cars, the truck, the smoke and flames. Sean had tried to act the hero and go help that poor woman, but Janine's pleading had held him back. She knew from their therapy sessions that he blamed himself for not helping the woman, but he also blamed Janine for stopping him in the first place.

How could he blame her for not wanting to lose him and to then have to raise Jackson and Peter on her own?

Would he still blame her if he knew the accident was what forced her to realize her mistakes and appreciate the family she had almost thrown away?

It was in this reverie that someone knocked on her office door.

"Come in," she said.

A tall man in a grey suit walked in. She recognized him immediately, even though it had been almost two years since she saw him. It was Dominic.

Around his neck hung the Grayson Flooring visitor badge. The last two years had been kind to him. While Sean was athletic and worked out semi-regularly, his body was no comparison to the muscular physique of Dominic. Years of bachelorhood allowed him to keep his body in top gear. His expensive dress shirt clung to his skin, creasing at the perfect places. Time had not taken anything away from Dominic. Janine couldn't help but let herself remember how it had felt to touch him and be held by him.

Quickly she scolded herself. She placed the photograph on her desk as she stood up.

"Dominic, what are you doing here?"

He smiled as he approached her. Janine rounded the corner of her desk and the two former lovers stood face to face. She extended her hand as he went in for a hug. Noticing the less familiar gesture, he corrected his course and took her hand.

"I was in town visiting my sister and I thought it would be good to see you."

She pulled back from him.

"Dominic, I thought we were clear when you left."

"It's okay! I'm not here to… You know, Jane, words seem to be escaping me at the moment."

Jane. Dominic had been the only one to ever call her that nickname. She liked it because it made her feel like a different woman.

"So…how are things going?"

Janine motioned for Dominic to sit down in the chair across from her desk.

The first few moments of their conversation were a mixture of strange emotions and memories. It was hard for her to focus on the words that came from his mouth. She had tried her hardest to forget that he even existed. Now here he was, and with his reappearance, she was reminded of the hundreds of secret meetings they had shared; the nights where she had told Sean she was working late, only to escape into the exhilaration of her affair.

She forced herself back into the moment.

"And besides that, work is going well. They have me covering the entire Northeast now."

"That's fantastic, Dominic. I'm happy to hear that."

"Thanks, Jane. In a weird way, I really owe it to you. If things had continued with us, I'd still be here in Raleigh."

"That's an odd thank you."

"But it's true. We both know if you hadn't pulled the plug, I would have never taken the transfer."

Janine thought back to when she decided to end things with Dominic. It was a moment not unlike a countless amount of other moments she had shared with her family. But this one was different because of what had happened right before it.

After talking with the police to help fill out the reports of the accident, the Bryant family had continued on their trip. They made it to the hotel safely, albeit a few hours later than Janine had originally planned. Although shaken up by the evening's events, everyone was hungry. They sat on the king-sized bed in the hotel room eating a pizza that had been delivered.

No one spoke.

Janine looked at her two boys, and then back at Sean. Who knows how close she had been to losing it all. That was when she let go of Dominic and grasped at the family she had built with Sean.

Of course, things hadn't worked out perfectly for her in that area. Janine glanced at the clock on her desk that now read 3:10.

"Dominic, I'm going to have to get the boys soon and I have a few things I need to get done before I leave tonight."

He leaned forward.

"Jane, I don't want to screw up anything for you. But I need to talk to you. I know you made things very clear when we ended everything. And a lot of time has passed. But I just need to talk before you go home. Can you give me a little time?"

Janine didn't know where he was going with this. There was something in his eyes that seemed genuine. Then again, she knew staring into those eyes could be dangerous. She hoped she wouldn't regret this decision.

"Okay, let me see if I can get the babysitter to pick the boys up. But I really do need to get this work done before I go home."

"No problem. Thank you. You won't even know I'm here until you're ready for me."

Janine made the phone call to Stephanie. Before she hung up she remembered there were a few things she hoped Sean could take care of for her. Janine soon returned to work. Dominic scrolled through something on his iPad while she sent emails and finished her one report. She was frightened by how comfortable the silence in the room was becoming. Their affair had been an on-again, off-again ordeal over the course of three years. In that time she had gotten to know Dominic very well. As they worked quietly in her office, it felt like the last two years apart had never even happened.

When she was finished, Janine powered down her computer. Dominic had just returned from the conference room with two coffees.

"Thank you."

"All done?" he asked.

She nodded.

"So, Dominic. What did you need to talk about?"

"Jane, I know you ended things with me for a lot of reasons, your family, Sean. Heck, I know part of it was just me, too. Now, it's been two years, and I've been respectful and I've kept my distance. I wanted to give you the space you needed. I changed jobs, I moved away. I dated other people.

"But, even after two years, Jane, I haven't been able to feel what

I felt for you with anyone else. Now, don't say anything yet, just hear me out. I know we were happy together. And it wasn't just the thrill of sneaking around. We had a connection. We had something. And I want that back."

"Dominic, this…I'm committed to my family."

"Yeah, but are you happy? Jane, you told me how you felt so many times. I know you love your boys, but you loved me too. And I made you happy, I know I did."

He was telling the truth. At first their relationship was just a way to feel alive and free again. She had told him once before that the affair was over when the guilt had become too much for her to bear. The reprieve had not lasted very long and she soon found herself back in the same position. She couldn't stay away then.

But things were different now. She was different. But so were things with Sean. He kept pulling farther and farther away from her. Was she denying herself a life of happiness with Dominic?

"Dominic, I…I don't know what to say. I can't move to New York."

"We could work out locations. Just tell me if you are happy now. If you are, I'll leave. I need to know if there is a chance."

By this point he was standing in front of her desk. She was looking out the window at the parking lot. It was quite dark outside. She thought back to what Dr. Bensen had said. She wanted to believe there was still a fight left in her marriage. Janine and Sean had built a life together, and although it might not be the perfect one she had dreamt of as a child, she couldn't let herself give up yet.

"Dominic, I…I have to go home. My family is waiting for me."

"Jane…"

"This is how it has to be, Dominic. This is how I need it to be."

Dominic was silent. They looked at one another. After two years, she wondered what decision he really thought she would make.

"Can I walk you out?"

"Sure," she said.

A few moments later they stood in the cold air. The warmth of her office was far behind them now. Dominic looked down at her. She saw love and disappointment in his eyes.

"Jane, if you change your mind, you know I'm only a call away."

He bent down to hug her. She took him in her arms.

"Dominic," she whispered into his ear. "Take care, okay?"

She pulled away and walked toward her minivan.

• • •

Janine was surprised to see Stephanie playing with the boys in the living room when she got home. Jackson and Peter came running up to give her a hug and for a moment the thought of Dominic seemed miles away.

"Mom!" Peter exclaimed as he threw his arms around Janine's waist. Jackson soon followed.

"Hey, guys," Janine said. "Stephanie, what are you still doing here? Where's Sean?"

Stephanie got up off of the floor.

"Oh, he came home a while ago. I told him you were working late and gave him that list you mentioned. He said he was going to get something from it, but he left it on the kitchen counter."

"Well, thanks. Did he pay you?"

"Yup, he took care of it."

Stephanie put on her scarf and coat. She said goodbye to the boys and grabbed her keys. She picked up the list she had written earlier in the night and handed it to Janine.

"Here you go, Mrs. Bryant. He didn't seem very thrilled to get it. Let me know the next time you need help with the boys."

"Thanks, Stephanie."

Janine read off the list of tasks she had requested her husband to take care of. They all seemed so insignificant in light of Dominic's revelation. How many times had Sean criticized her for nagging him? Tonight it finally sunk in. She thought back to only a few hours ago when she had called Stephanie from her office. How could she have thought these things were important enough to tell Sean when Dominic, the man she had broken her wedding vows with, sat only a few feet behind her?

Janine crumbled the piece of paper and threw it on the counter. They could wait for another day.

It was an hour later when Janine's concern grew. Sean was still not home, nor had he called to let her know where he was.

She tried calling him, but he hadn't answered. Janine handled bedtime for the boys as she would any other night. She didn't want to alarm them with the idea that she had no clue where their father was.

Janine had called Sean's phone a few more times. She could tell he was sending his calls straight to voicemail. Paranoia began to set in. What was he doing? Who was he with? Why was he punishing her? Did he know that Dominic had come to see her? Did he finally know about what she had done years ago?

A little after midnight, Janine heard the garage door open. She was sitting in the living room wrapped in a blanket. As Janine turned she saw Sean slowly walk into the kitchen from the mudroom dressed in the same clothes he had worn to work. She opened her mouth to ask him where he had been but stopped herself. The crumbled list caught the corner of her eye.

Instead she said, "I'm glad you're home."

Sean stood looking back at her. Janine thought she would drown in the silence.

"Thanks," he said finally and walked upstairs to their bedroom.

Janine wiped the tears from her eyes before closing them. That night, she slept on the couch alone.

33

ONE BY ONE, HE PLACED THE ORNAMENTS back in their respective boxes a few weeks later than most people. It was always much easier—in many ways—to put the decorations on the tree. Taking them down signified the end.

In this case, it meant the end of another holiday season without Sam.

But, in her stead, he had Julia.

And she had proven to be a nice replacement.

Replacement.

Evrett hated to call her that, but that was truly what she would be to him. Sam was his one and only, and anyone else who would try to take her spot would be second.

Julia was second.

She didn't deserve that label, either.

Evrett took down the final ornament, and it just happened to be the mouse sporting a pair of skis. He thought back to early December when Julia handed him the ornament.

That was a great night, he thought.

Evrett returned the mouse in its box and placed it in a larger box containing all of his ornaments. Looking at the bare tree, a sadness grew over him.

It had been more than a month since he had seen Julia, thirty-three days to be exact. He missed her. Not as much as he missed Sam, but he definitely yearned for her company.

He walked over to his phone, tapped on his favorites and pressed his finger against Julia's name, which sat at the top of the list.

"Hello," she said, slightly groggy.

"I hope I didn't wake you."

"Evrett!" she said. "I didn't even look at the caller ID. I was hoping you'd call."

Truthfully, she was wondering if he would ever call again, but as was her plan, she was going to be patient with him.

"You want to come over?" Evrett asked.

She, of course, obliged immediately, and with Jack in her arms, she arrived a little after midnight.

"I'm sorry it's so late," he said. "And I'm sorry it's been so long since I've called you."

"It's okay," she said. "I understand you have work to do."

"No, it's not okay," he said. "I shouldn't leave you in the dark like that."

He paused before changing the subject, "You want to watch a movie?"

"Sure," she said, wishing Evrett would have said more.

Evrett set up in the living room and they sat arm-in-arm on the couch. Julia didn't make it past the twenty-minute mark of the movie, despite the many loud scenes that caused the subwoofer to rumble and reverberate throughout the room.

Evrett watched the movie carefree, half paying attention to the story line, while at the same time reviewing the story line he was building in his own life.

Once the movie ended, Evrett tapped the power button on his television remote and the room went dark. Julia was breathing lightly and rhythmically, letting Evrett know that she was still fast asleep.

The darkness, however, was interrupted by a bright light coming from the coffee table. His iPad, for whatever reason, had turned on. He reached for it, trying his best not to disturb Julia.

On the screen, one of his browsers was open and the homepage for the *Cleveland Plain Dealer* website was displayed.

Evrett knew it was unusual for his iPad to turn on like that, and even more bizarre was that it somehow circumvented the passcode. He, however, wasn't surprised to see the website. It was marked on his favorites as he had been using it to study Chase Valenti.

As he scanned the front page of the site, he saw a red banner reading: BREAKING NEWS: WITNESS KILLED IN ROGUE SEVENS CASE.

Evrett knew enough from his research that this was important to him.

It was truly amazing what Chase had accomplished after shooting a video that became an Internet sensation on YouTube. Since dropping out of school, he had started his own gang, commonly known as the Rogue Sevens. He built a dangerous network in Cleveland, one that had drawn the attention of the authorities and now the local media.

In a story about the Rogue Sevens a few days prior, Evrett learned that the DEA had gotten involved after local authorities asked for their help. The DEA launched a small task force in Cleveland to work with local and state police to battle the Rogue Sevens.

Believed to be responsible for several murders, and more than just the gangland retaliations, Chase's group was in the limelight.

Nevertheless, for as dumb as Chase was in school, he was just as smart in the world of crime. He apparently covered his tracks well, and his influence in the community went a long way. Nobody ever saw anything, and even if they did, they didn't talk about it for fear of being the next victim.

Finally, law enforcement caught a break with a witness to a murder, but before the district attorney could convene a grand jury to get an indictment, the witness disappeared. Today, two days later, the body was found in a river, with two bullets to the back of the head; it clearly was an execution.

Still, Chase was free because the authorities couldn't prove anything.

Evrett clicked on the video of an interview with the district attorney in charge of the would-be case.

"Do you think that Chase Valenti and the Rogue Sevens were involved in this murder?" a reporter asked.

"Without a doubt. A witness places him at a murder scene and then that witness is executed a day before he is supposed to testify. You do the math."

Evrett didn't go to law school, but he knew enough that a statement like that may fly in the media, but it wouldn't hold up in a court of law.

With no witnesses to either murder, no weapon, no DNA, no evidence whatsoever, Chase was a free man.

This infuriated Evrett. Then again, he knew it would be next to impossible to kill a man in jail.

Many thoughts flew through his head.

The main one was him purchasing a gun, driving to Cleveland, knocking on Chase's door and blowing him away.

It would be the perfect crime.

No one would ever suspect him.

They would certainly be looking at rival gangs, upset and angered family members of victims, and even police and officials of the court who were fed up with his antics.

No one would ever suspect an architect from Baltimore.

Evrett took a second to breathe, and then he was calm.

"Not yet," he murmured under his breath.

Chase would get his turn.

He knew that it could mean more innocent, or perhaps not-so-innocent people, might die at Chase's hands, but Evrett couldn't deviate from his plan.

The order was important to him. He had it all planned out. In four months, Chase's reign would come to an end. He was sure of it.

Julia awoke and saw Evrett staring at his iPad.

"What time is it?" she asked.

"After three."

"Oh my. I must have passed out instantly."

"You did. No worries."

She rubbed her eyes and reached for her cellphone, confirming that it was three-eleven in the morning.

"Well, I have to get up early to do some work and it will be easier to do that at home, so I'll let you go," she said.

"You can stay, you know that."

Julia knew she could, and she wanted to, but with the long hiatus, she didn't want to push Evrett too far.

"I know. Perhaps tomorrow, or should I say, tonight?"

"Tonight? I'd like that. I can make dinner and you can try to stay awake during a movie."

She smiled and pecked him on the cheek. "It's a date."

Julia scooped up Jack and left, promising to be careful during her drive. She knew that worried him the most.

Evrett walked to his bedroom and waited until the text from Julia came through to confirm she and Jack made it home safely. He then closed his eyes and fell asleep.

The sound of the wooden bedroom window slowly grinding in its grooves as it opened didn't make him stir one bit.

34

A SHADOW MOVED SLOWLY AROUND THE BED as Evrett lay still on his back. He could see the silhouette of a woman gently step closer and closer; but he could not move. He was paralyzed.

He also was asleep.

Sound asleep.

But his brain was attentive.

Underneath his closed eyelids, his eyes were rapidly moving.

They were reacting to the alarming situation in his mind. The mysterious, shadowy woman was now leaning in toward him, closer and closer. He could not make out any facial details and that worried him. He tried to move his arms, but they remained at his side.

The shadow's head neared his and passed off to the left side, and Evrett felt a cool breeze tickle his left ear.

It was followed by a chilling voice.

Sam's voice.

"Don't give up."

Evrett, all of a sudden, could move his head and he turned to look at Sam, but he still couldn't see her in the darkness.

However, he could see her arm extend out and point down toward the open bedroom door.

"He's out there," she said, before disappearing.

Evrett looked in the direction that she was pointing, and he realized that he was no longer in his house.

He floated through what would have been his bedroom doorway and into a long white hallway. There, he could see Janine and Sean Bryant about ten feet ahead of him. A few feet beyond the couple was Phil Repin. And then, a few steps past him was Chase Valenti.

At the end of the hallway, Evrett could see the shadow of a man. He knew exactly who that was. He had sketched his portrait numerous times.

Evrett wanted to run toward him, but he was focused on the Bryants. They stepped forward and blocked out the rest of the hallway. He could tell that the man on the bridge was still out there, but he couldn't get to him without getting past the Bryants.

He felt the cold breeze on his ear again, followed by a scream. "Evrett!"

He shot up out of his deep sleep. The sheets were damp with sweat and the room was chilled with the brisk late January air rushing in from a cracked-open window to the left of his bed. How he was sweating when the room was chilled to at least fifty degrees, he did not know.

He jumped out of bed and ran to the window to shut it. He grabbed his hoodie, a pillow and a fresh blanket from the closet and ran to his living room.

It was five-thirty in the morning and he knew he had to get back to sleep. He had to go into the office early for a nine o'clock presentation. It was a project he and his team had been working on for weeks. It was finally ready for its reveal to the clients and he had to look awake for it.

He couldn't understand why he would have opened the window. Based on the condition of his sheets, he could tell that at one point, he was burning up so perhaps that led to him opening it.

After he set his pillow and blanket on the couch in the much warmer living room, he ran to the kitchen to get a glass of water. He emptied it in four large gulps and returned to the couch. Laying there, the dream he had popped into his memory.

He could remember everything, down to the extreme details of what others were wearing and the sensations he felt.

It was vivid.

Then he thought about what it meant. Every dream was supposed to have a meaning, they say.

He knew he had several dreams about Sam since her death, but not one was like this. She had never said anything to him. He always just saw her in memorable moments of his life. That, and there had been the one reoccurring dream—or perhaps nightmare—where Evrett was on Interstate 83, running toward the car trying to save her. He saw everyone watching and he always awoke suddenly right before he got to the car.

He hated that dream, and fortunately, he had not had it in a few months.

In fact, now that he thought about it, he hadn't seen Sam in a dream for a while.

Until tonight. Although, he didn't quite see her. Rather, he had heard her; he felt her presence.

"Don't give up."

"He's out there."

"Evrett!"

The latter was the last thing he remembered of the dream. It was a terrified shrill of a scream she let out. It was a cry for help. It was what he imagined he would have heard had he actually been on Interstate 83 that fateful day.

The thought gave him chills.

Then, he reflected on the first thing she said.

"Don't give up."

He knew exactly what that meant.

In the recent weeks, he had begun to question his quest for revenge. He had been trying so hard to find the man on the bridge, but had not made any progress in that department.

In the eight months since he first got in his car to drive to Pittsburgh, he had not accumulated one shred of evidence alluding to the identity of the man on the bridge.

All this time, though, he had been trying to talk to his targets to see if they could lead him to the man on the bridge. It was foolish to think that.

Perhaps, he didn't need to say anything.

He thought about the hallway. The only way to get to the man was to work his way past his next four targets.

He sat up on the couch with a sudden realization that he should not worry about what the targets knew. He now firmly believed that the questions would answer themselves, but in order for him to get to that point, he had to complete his mission.

He was now more determined than ever, and he thought about the remaining list.

Janine. Sean. Phil. Chase.

Janine. Sean. Phil. Chase.

He repeated it over and over and over until he fell asleep.

35

CAR LIGHTS PASSED AND EVRETT IGNORED THEM ALL. Eight months ago, he may have ducked in his car with the fear of being seen, but now, he realized that the world didn't care. A passer-by was not worried about the man sitting in his car, if they even saw him.

A light snow fell outside his Audi, which was parked across the street from the Bryants' home. He watched as Sean moved from room to room, and Evrett could hear him arguing with Janine on the wireless microphones he placed strategically throughout the house.

Five in all, he had bugged the living room, kitchen, master bedroom, the kids' room and the basement.

Right now, he was picking up their tense conversation, which had moved to the master bedroom. It was a Monday evening and the two bitter parents had each spent a long, frustrating day at work. They were now taking it out on each other.

In the last two weeks, Evrett had learned a lot about the Bryants. There were definitely marriage issues, those of which Evrett could

259

never imagine having with Sam.

Lies, lies and more lies.

He heard them all.

Sean was defiant in his arguments, but Evrett knew to not take him seriously. And based on what he heard from Janine, he knew he could not trust her either.

A few days ago, Sean accused her of cheating and the shit hit the fan quickly.

"You think I cheated on you?" she screamed. "What on Earth would give you that idea?"

"How about the fact I saw you with him, late in your office?"

Janine went silent. She wasn't sure what night he was talking about, but she knew *who* he was talking about. Either way, she was caught.

"Well?" Sean pushed on, and the two argued as she confessed and apologized over and over again.

All Evrett could do was laugh.

What a hypocrite, he thought.

Since he arrived in Raleigh, Evrett saw Sean have numerous sexual encounters with the teenage baby-sitter, Stephanie, and now he was ridiculing his wife.

Nevertheless, based on what Evrett had learned through the arguments, Sean deserved the affair. He was heartbroken after having been cheated on, so his affair was payback.

Well, it *was* payback.

Until it turned into love.

Sean loved Stephanie. It probably couldn't be explained, but he clearly wanted to be with her, no matter what society would say. Evrett felt like a psychiatrist with such analysis.

As he listened to the married couple argue, Evrett tapped away on his iPad researching oil heating furnaces; in particular, he was researching the exact make and model that the Bryants had in their basement.

He broke into their cozy home three times in the last week, and during the second break-in, he scouted the heating unit. He was drawn to it by a fiery conversation the Bryants had the night before the break-in. Janine was insistent on Sean having the furnace looked at because the house was not heating as warm as it used to.

Sean told her it was because she constantly toyed with the thermostat, but she pushed enough to force a phone call to a local HVAC company. Because it wasn't an emergency, they scheduled a service date for next Monday.

Perfect timing, if you asked Evrett.

In fact, it was almost too perfect based on his current research. He needed a few days to prepare and he needed a day when the children weren't home. He did not want to harm them. They were innocent in all of this.

And a few minutes prior, he heard the greatest news of all. Janine told Sean she was dropping the kids off at her parents Friday after school to give them the weekend alone.

She said they needed it, but Evrett knew it was all for naught.

Even if it somehow would help patch up their marriage, they weren't going to live to find out.

Friday was his night.

He continued to review the schematics on the furnace, researching the many causes of carbon monoxide leaks. He discovered a few days ago that the most common theme to leaks were cracks in the internal heat chamber. To do that, he would have to corrode the metal. The furnace was old, but it showed no signs of being easily tampered with. He couldn't just crack the chamber because it would be clear someone had messed with it. He had to weaken the metal and make it look natural.

After a few minutes of double-checking the materials he needed, he closed his iPad and drove off to a hardware store.

Ten minutes later, he arrived at Lowe's Home Improvement. Once inside, he avoided all of the employees who are required to ask if anyone needed assistance, paid cash at the self-checkout and walked out with a one-gallon container of muriatic acid.

He only needed two ounces to make an acidic copper solution, but this was the best he could do.

Who knows when you'll need more muriatic acid? he jokingly thought to himself.

261

Back in the car, he drove two miles down the road to a nearby Ace Hardware. There, he bought ten feet of fourteen-gauge copper wire when he only needed two feet. Same principle applied.

Lastly, he stopped at a Wal-Mart Supercenter on his way back to his motel. He picked up a pack of Rubbermaid containers, a spray bottle of Febreze and a strawberry kiwi Vitaminwater. The first two were key to his science project; the latter was because he was thirsty.

In his hotel room, he emptied the Febreze spray bottle into the bathroom sink and the fresh smell over-powered the room. He left and returned a few minutes later to rinse it thoroughly, leaving it sit on its side to dry.

Next, he poured approximately two ounces of the muriatic acid into one of the Rubbermaid containers. He then wrapped two feet of the fourteen-gauge copper wire tight enough to fit in the container. He slowly, and carefully, submerged it into the muriatic acid.

He sealed the container as the copper reacted to the acid, bubbling like an annoying kid blowing air through the straw in a soda. He placed the container in the mini-fridge. It would be ready by Thursday.

Until then, he had one other loose end to tie up. He wasn't going to let Stephanie ruin his plan.

• • •

The news media were buzzing about a large winter storm heading into the region. A March snowstorm wasn't commonplace in the south, so when a significant snowfall was predicted, the region over-reacted. Schools were already closed for Friday and fortunately for Evrett, it didn't mess with his plans. In fact, it made it easier in that Janine had just pulled out of the driveway to take the kids to her parents one night early. They lived an hour north of Raleigh and that gave Evrett at least a two-hour window.

It was seven-thirty in the evening and Evrett was ready to put his plan in motion.

He picked up one of the pre-paid cellphones he bought at the mall earlier in the day and dialed Sean's number. With Janine gone, he would surely call Stephanie to come over for a quickie. He always waited five minutes before calling to make sure that his wife didn't forget anything and come back.

Evrett preempted his dial to Stephanie.

The phone buzzed three times before Sean picked it up, answering it as anyone would when a screen displays: RESTRICTED.

"Hello?" he said, inquisitively.

"If you don't want your wife to find out about her, you'll go to the tennis courts at Jaycee Park," Evrett said. "Eight-thirty sharp. Don't be late."

Shocked and taken aback, Sean reacted, "Who is this? I will not meet you. I will—"

"Nine, eight, four. Three, seven, two. Four, five, seven, five. I'm ready to dial."

There was a silence. Evrett knew why. After hearing his wife's phone number, it was dawning on Sean that this was serious.

"You have no proof of anything," he finally retorted.

"I do. And you'll go to the park as I said. I'll see you there."

Evrett clicked off and immediately sent a picture text of a nude Stephanie riding on top of Sean on the couch in his living room. It was taken through a crack in the curtains in the back window. He knew that this would create the result he desired.

Less than thirty seconds later, Sean ran out his front door and into his Cadillac. He sped off quickly in the direction of Jaycee Park.

As the SUV rounded the corner, Evrett grabbed his lock-picking kit, along with the highly dangerous bottle of Febreze, and walked around the house to the back door. He was inside in less than a minute and he walked downstairs to the furnace. He used a screwdriver to pull off a panel to access the internal heat chamber. Once exposed, he began spraying the contents of the bottle all over.

After four days of chilling, Evrett mixed his concoction with water and poured it into the spray bottle about two hours ago. Together, this created a solution that would rust metal within an hour. He heavily sprayed the entire inside of the furnace to make sure it got the job done. He would return the next day to make sure it worked, and if needed, he would chisel away at the corroded metal to create a leak.

He hoped that it would just corrode enough to keep him from

having to physically do it. He wanted it to look as natural as possible.

Once finished spraying, he replaced the panel and left the way he came in.

As he walked to the car, he took in the cold air and felt alive. He was confident and feeling great. Interestingly enough, he was starting to enjoy it. Part of it was because he was good at it.

Everyone always talks about the dumb criminals. They rarely talk about the smart ones.

That's because they never catch us, Evrett thought.

He turned the key in his ignition and sped off to Jaycee Park. Sean had a seven-minute head start, but that was part of the plan.

When Evrett knew that he was about five minutes away, he picked up a second disposable cellphone placed on his passenger and dialed Sean's number.

"Hello. I'm here. Where are you?"

"I'm close. Across the way is a softball field. Go to the top of the bleachers on the first-base line. You'll find a phone on the top of the bleachers. Hold in the number two and it will call me."

"What is this? I will not play your game."

"You will play my game."

Sean was silent, which meant he was compliant.

Evrett clicked off and pushed down on the gas a little harder as a heavy snow began to fall.

He parked a block away from the park and walked the rest of the way. As he entered the parking lot, he could see the silhouette of a man walking up to the top of the softball bleachers. He bent down to pick up the cellphone Evrett placed there earlier and dialed.

Evrett knew it was risky leaving a cellphone out in the open, but if there was any public place that was safe, it was the top of a softball bleacher in March during the start of a winter storm.

The second throwaway phone that Evrett called Sean on moments ago began to vibrate.

Evrett positioned himself behind a large tree about 100 yards away and answered, "I'm glad you listened. Now sit down."

"Okay," Sean said, still standing.

Evrett gave him a few seconds and followed up, "I said sit down."

Sean spun around quickly, eyes darting in every direction. It was dark and quiet. He couldn't see anyone, but he sat anyway.

"Okay, I'm sitting. What do you want?"

"You're to leave Stephanie alone."

"Who are you? You can't tell me what to do."

"If you truly love her, you'll let her go. I'm someone who does not want to see her get hurt and I know all you will do is bring her pain. It cannot work. You're married. She's eighteen and your babysitter. You will call her tonight and you will tell her it's over. You will—"

Sean interrupted feeling a burst of confidence, "You will not tell me what to do. I don't know who you are and I don't care that you're really good at this Jason Bourne shit, but a few phone numbers and a sneaky picture text do not scare me. If I lose my marriage, so be it. I want to be with Stephanie."

Sean stopped and waited for a reaction, and Evrett let him soak in his moment of fury.

Then, he threw the curveball.

"How's Jackson and Peter? It'd be awfully sad if something happened while they're at your mother-in-law's. Or perhaps to your wife as she cries herself to sleep alone on the couch. Maybe it will look like a domestic argument gone awry, and based on how much you two argue, it wouldn't be hard to believe, as I'm sure your neighbors would attest to."

Stunned, Sean remained quiet and listened to every word.

He continued, "You see, Sean, I know everything. I've seen it all, I've heard it all, and I'm willing to forget everything for one simple price: Leave Stephanie alone. I'm not asking you to empty your bank accounts. I'm not asking you to commit an awful crime. I'm telling you break it off. You understand?"

After a few seconds of processing the information, Sean realized that it was in his best interest to comply. "Okay, I'll break it off."

"You'll call her right now on the cellphone you're using. She's programmed in to number three. I'll be listening. If you don't do it, I'll contact my associate who happens to be sitting outside a certain residence in Oxford. You hear me loud and clear?"

"Yes, I do."

Initially, Sean agreed because he thought he could just say he was going to break it off and then be more secretive about his relationship, but it was clear that wasn't going to happen. Oxford was the hometown of his in-laws and the word "associate" scared him to death.

He was honest when he said he didn't care if he lost his marriage, but when it came to his sons, he'd do anything for them. He clicked off the phone and held in the number three.

Evrett listened as Sean was short and to the point with Stephanie. It was ironic that he used a bunch of lies to get rid of his biggest lie of all.

After a minute, the call ended with a clearly distraught Stephanie and an equally heartbroken Sean.

Evrett heard the entire conversation through his headset. He honestly didn't care about Stephanie and the relationship. He just didn't want her luring Sean out of the house tomorrow night. He needed both of the Bryants to be at home. He needed them to die quietly in their sleep.

He watched Sean pull out of the parking lot and swerve onto the road as the snow began to pile up.

This may complicate things, he thought, knowing that he had to drive back over in the morning to finish the job.

He slushed through the fresh snow, accumulating up to an inch already, and got into his car. It was still warm inside and he enjoyed the feeling against his cold cheeks.

He recapped in his mind everything he just did. Again, he had this sense of great accomplishment, and he was just basking in the limelight after being compared to Jason Bourne. He was even more satisfied by the fact that come Saturday morning, the Bryants would be crossed off his list.

Evrett started the car and left for his motel.

He would not make it.

36

AS FAR AS NOR'EASTERS GO, this wasn't the worst storm that Maryland had had to deal with, but it was enough of a menace to shut down the entire region for the day.

That didn't matter to Alec, though. As someone who works at home, he didn't have the luxury of calling the office and telling his boss that he wasn't going to be able to make it.

Nevertheless, he spent the morning in the kitchen looking out the large bay windows, watching the snow pile up on his deck. He sat up in his chair to reach for the half-empty, half-gallon of ice tea.

It has to be at least fifteen inches, he thought.

He took another swig of ice tea and stood up, carrying the carton with him to the back door. The storm had hit a lull, as the winds died down, allowing the heavy wet snow to fall straight to the ground. He opened the door and stepped outside into a small open area of the deck he shoveled an hour ago.

Alec was wearing a short-sleeved T-shirt and jeans, but the cold did not bother him. The chill of a winter snow falling was refreshing. He took another sip of tea and closed his eyes.

It was peaceful. To Alec, there was nothing better than the silence of a snowstorm, especially in a highly populated area like Baltimore. No matter where you are, a snowstorm seems to bring out the peace—at times, at least.

His silence was interrupted by a pair of next-door neighbor kids running out their back door and into their winter wonderland of a backyard. Their father followed with a pair of sleds. The kids jumped on, and with the adjoining ropes, he pulled them around the backyard. The kids laughed and screamed throughout.

Alec smiled. Yes, his peace was disrupted, but he was now thinking about how in a few years, that would be him.

"I'm going to be a father," he said to himself.

It was a prospect that he never thought would come to fruition. After Abby left him, he was sure that a child was a dream he'd never live to see. Abby was never fond of having children and pushed back every time he brought it up.

At the time, that made him extremely upset, but looking back, he couldn't be happier that his first child was going to be with a woman who truly loved him.

He heard a tap on the glass behind him. Angela stood there wrapped in a baby blue afghan her mother crocheted. He opened the door and stepped back inside.

"You're going to catch a cold out there like that," she said.

"Ah, I'm fine. Just getting a quick hit of cold fresh air," he said.

"Are you going to come down to the office at any point today?" she asked, adding in a jesting manner, "I don't recall making today a snow day."

Alec laughed as he placed the empty carton on the table.

"It's just hard to work when all this is going on," Alec said. "I'll get working on those advertising projects in an hour. Have you had lunch yet?"

"That's what I came up for," she said.

"Go back downstairs and I'll make it for you."

"You're the best. Thanks."

Angela walked back down the basement stairs to *The Long and Short's* new office. Two months into the work-at-home initiative with all of the employees and it had gone well for all parties. For Angela, it was a huge cost-saver on infrastructure. She didn't have to rent a large business complex, pay for power, Internet, phones, office furniture, maintenance and so on.

Instead, for her ten full-time employees, comprised of writers, editors, marketers, graphic designers and web designers, she provided them with computers, cellphones and a monthly per diem for Internet. All together, it was saving her company at least a hundred thousand per year, which helped her pay for guest writers.

In the basement, Alec had set up a pair of desks for them to work at, as well as a large conference table and chairs. Weekly meetings were held online via Skype, but once a month, Angela required her employees to attend the meeting in person in the new basement office. She did not want to completely eliminate human interaction, and the employees embraced it, for it was a small price to pay to have the luxury of working at home.

Many businesses worry that the distractions at home could hurt production, but Angela was confident in her employees. She explained to them to not feel guilty if they stop working to do something around the house; she just asked that work get done on time.

Since switching to an all-online publication, the deadlines weren't as crazy as they were before, but they were still important. Before, all the work had to be done by a certain date and time each month so the magazine could go to print.

Now, there were deadlines daily and weekly. Certain writers had projects that were weekly installments, while others had monthly stories. One writer had gotten into the swing of producing a seven-part story once a month that published a new chapter every day during the span of a week.

For Angela, *The Long and Short* had become a fiction network. Fans could log on and read new content daily, and its somewhat structured release schedule allowed for promotion of upcoming stories, just as a television network would do with its programming.

The subscriptions were very inexpensive and the high school

program was growing popular throughout the Maryland region. One employee, who was the lead page designer for the publication when it was printed, was now solely in charge of producing a digital magazine each month that was separate from the online subscriptions. The Internet magazine was available to purchase on every brand of tablet, and it was a major part of the high school program.

Angela was working on a short fiction piece exclusively for the Internet magazine when Alec walked down the stairs with a tuna and cheese wrap. He placed it on her desk and walked over to his.

"Thanks, honey," she said.

"Anytime."

Alec opened up his laptop and starting working on his laundry list of to-do items for the website. Included on it was a note for him to work on his next *Last Day* story. The story idea came to him early in the morning as he shot out of bed with a sharp pain emanating from behind his eyes. The vision of his next story idea followed instantly, and he ran from the bedroom to recite it all on his digital recorder while not disturbing Angela.

It took him a few minutes to digest the story before returning to bed. It was a disturbing tale and he paced around in the kitchen debating on whether or not he should even take the next step and write it.

Angela's site had a mature section for the more graphic or more risqué fiction stories, but he wondered what she would think of him if he published this.

Eventually, he decided he had to continue with his series, but at two in the morning, he figured he could wait until later in the day to write it, especially with his deadline still seven days away.

He looked at the list and the *Last Day* story was more exciting than any of the other to-do list items, so he pulled out his recorder and got to work.

• • •

The Heartbroken Teenager
By Alec Rossi
The Long and Short

The heartbroken teenager tore the photo in half and placed it into the fireplace. It curled and charred and disappeared into the embers in a matter of seconds.

It was no longer love.

It was hate, in its purest form.

He promised her the world and took it all away faster than she could tell him that she loved him.

It wasn't the only thing he took from her, and she hated herself for it.

Her best friend told her not to get involved with a married man, yet she did it anyway; and as her friend foretold, it ended in heartbreak.

But he wasn't getting away that easily—the heartbroken teenager was sure of that.

At eighteen, she had plenty to live for, but nobody ever told her that. Her father left when she was six and her mother was absent from her life in the years that followed his departure. The teen struggled socially in high school, looking for love, but was too shy to ask a single boy out on a date.

Instead of partying with classmates on Fridays, she was babysitting and making money.

It was initiatives like that that led her to the top five percent of her high school class, but even with graduation just three months away, she had no clue which college she would attend. Several big schools came knocking, but she couldn't bear to leave her hometown, so the acceptance letters remained unanswered on her desk.

While other students were signing their letters to attend colleges in January and February, the heartbroken teen spent her nights babysitting or sneaking around town with the children's father.

From the moment she got the job when she was sixteen, there was an instant attraction to the father, but she kept her feelings to herself, until this January when he made a pass at her.

He returned home early one night while his wife was working late, and he saw the babysitter was in the middle of watching a movie on TV.

"Don't rush," he said. "You can stay and watch the rest of it if you'd like."

She had nowhere to go, so she obliged. The father sat down next to her minutes later, and after the two shared a silent stare, he leaned in to kiss her and she jumped on top of him.

He never fought it and this continued on for nearly three months before he ended it tonight.

She snuck over as she did any time she was not supposed to babysit, but he didn't answer the door. As she drove home, she called him over and over again, but he did not answer.

She entered her bedroom and her phone rang, displaying a number she did not recognize. It was him.

"It's over. We can't do this, and I won't do this anymore. Stop calling. We're going to find another baby-sitter."

She cried for an hour before throwing mementos from their relationship into the fire. First was the cheap white gold necklace, and it still was melting.

Second were the numerous movie tickets she kept from a theater all the way on the other side of the city. They never seemed to stay through the entire movie, leaving for a nearby motel.

The third was a cork from a bottle of wine they shared at a shady BYOB Italian restaurant downtown on her eighteenth birthday. It was her first alcoholic drink and it was the night he first told her that he loved her.

Lastly, she threw in the photo of the two, taken on her cellphone and printed at Wal-Mart. He didn't know she had this, but she pulled it off the mirror on her dresser and held it for a few minutes.

She didn't want to throw it in, but alas, her anger took over. That rage continued as she walked down the hallway of her mother's home and into her bedroom. She opened the closet and reached for a box on the top shelf. Inside was a Glock 19 pistol, owned by her mother's wayward boyfriend. He had taken her to the shooting range once, so she was familiar with the weapon.

She loaded it and left the house with one mission.

It was after midnight and the snow made the drive to his house a bit dangerous, but that was moot at this point.

She pulled into the driveway of the family's colonial home and walked up to the front door. She was prepared to break the glass, but oddly, the door was ajar. She pushed it open with her gun drawn, pointing ahead of her. She walked right up the stairs and into the married couple's master bedroom where they both were sleeping.

She stood at the foot of the bed and shouted, "You said you loved me!"

Both parents shot up quickly in bed.

"What are you doing here?" the father said, then realizing she had a gun.

"You said you loved me! You promised we'd be together. So tell me now, are we going to be together or not?"

"This is not the way to do this."

"What is she talking about?" the wife asked, even though she already knew the horrible answer.

"Look. I told you. I love my wife. You and I will not be together. And this is not the way to handle this. Put the gun down and we'll forget this ever happened."

"Forget!" the teen screamed. "You want to forget it all, don't you? Well, that's the wrong answer."

She pointed the gun at his wife and fired two shots, and she then unloaded the rest of the magazine into him. She continued to pull the trigger until it made only a clicking sound.

Falling to her knees, she began to cry. All she ever wanted was to be with him. Why did he have to force her to do this? Life wasn't fair, she thought.

She sobbed and stared into nowhere for about five minutes before she felt a hand gently touch her right shoulder and a woman's voice say, "Run, my sweet."

She spun quickly to see that no one was there, but she didn't stay to investigate. She ran down the stairs, out the front door and into her car. She pulled out of the driveway just as a police cruiser turned onto the murdered couple's street. She sped away and the police cruiser followed.

A second one joined in a mile down the road, and by the time she got onto Interstate 40 West, she had five police cars on her tail.

As she sped past the airport at seventy miles per hour, she saw a few more police cars ahead of her creating a roadblock.

She slammed on the breaks, and after skidding for about fifty feet, she lost control and the car spun in circles, slamming into the cement wall separating her from the eastbound lanes.

The teen never lost consciousness and felt fairly well for being in a high-speed crash. She could hear police screaming over megaphone and she knew it was over.

She grabbed the gun tucked in her pants and she reached into her pocket for the only extra magazine she brought. She loaded the gun and closed her eyes.

She cursed her father; she cursed her mother; she cursed her lover; she cursed her life—and with one pull of the trigger, she made this her last day.

• • •

Alec finished proofreading his story and looked over at Angela, who was still crafting her story. She was working on a satirical piece on pregnancy, based on experiences she had had over the last couple months.

She was ecstatic and couldn't wait to hold her precious child.

"You've never asked me how I come up with my *Last Day* stories," Alec blurted out.

She looked up with a puzzled look. "I beg your pardon?"

"I said, you've never asked how I come up with the ideas for my *Last Day* series."

"Should I?" she asked. "I just assumed you had them all planned out?"

"No. It's not that simple," he said. "They just come to me, randomly, in visions. Vivid visions."

Angela just stared at him. Alec wanted to continue on about how the accident had inspired him, but he held back. He still felt too guilty.

"I don't know. It's just weird. I can't explain it. I just have these ideas come to me and I don't know how, when or why."

"You sound a bit crazy," she said, "but then again, show me a writer who isn't?"

274

There was a pause and then Angela continued, "So, why are you telling me this?"

"Because the one I just wrote will have to go into the mature section, or at least I think it will. It's pretty disturbing. I'm not even sure why I wrote it."

"Let me see it."

He unplugged his laptop and took it over to her.

She read it as Alec stared at her, waiting to witness her reactions. She was quite still throughout, but he could tell as she got closer to the end. She was quietly shocked.

"Murder-suicide," she said looking up at him. "That's a bit different. All the others were accidents, weren't they? Why did you switch it up?"

"I told you, I don't know. The ideas just pop into my head. This was my next idea."

"I'm fine with the story going up," she said. "It's certainly nowhere close to the most controversial stories we've posted. It's got love and tragedy, everything a great fiction piece should have."

"Well, maybe I'm just getting all out of sorts for no reason," he said. "It is a good read, if I do say so myself."

"Don't let your head get too big," she said, laughing. "You won't be able to get up those basement stairs."

He laughed and took his laptop back.

As he sat down, he thought about the teenager. He felt for her. He knew what it was like to be betrayed. He just wished that she could have had a happier ending like he has had with Angela. If only she would have been rational or if she had someone there to talk to her.

"What am I saying?" he mumbled under his breath. Angela didn't hear him.

It's just a fictional character, he thought to himself.

37

THE SLAM OF A NEARBY CAR DOOR made Evrett jump in his seat. If he didn't sit so low in his Audi, he may have smacked his head off the ceiling.

He quickly took in his surroundings, trying to figure out where he was. The answer was not that simple. He was parked in front of a small brick complex with a highway behind him. From what he could surmise, he was at a rest stop. Where? He had no clue.

In his backseat, all his bags were packed, and in his passenger seat sat his lock-picking kit.

He could only imagine.

Evrett reached into his pocket and pulled out his cellphone, opening up his Google Maps app. A few seconds after he hit the locator button, the map zoomed in on Virginia and continued on to the Ladysmith Rest Area along Interstate 95 in Ladysmith, Virginia. Evrett manually zoomed out to see where he was in relation to Raleigh, and by his estimation, he was about 200 miles north of his last memory. He wasn't far off. Ladysmith was 191 miles north on Interstate 95.

Evrett was no longer surprised by events like this; he was more or less worried that something went wrong.

Looking at the time, it was four-thirty in the morning. He had planned to enter the Bryants' home in three hours to initiate his plan.

That was not going to happen now.

For starters, Evrett knew he would never make it in time, especially in this weather, and even if he could arrive on time, based on everything that had happened over the last year, he knew it would be all for naught.

The Bryants were dead.

There was no doubt in his mind, so he started the car and continued north on I-95 to Baltimore.

The snowplows were working overtime and I-95 was passable, but it still took four hours to get home. The whole time, his eyes kept latching their focus on the dash camera he set up a few months ago. He did it for moments like this and he couldn't wait to get home.

Once there, he pulled the memory card from the dash camera, ran to his den and powered up his laptop. As he waited for the memory card to load, he searched the Internet for the local media outlets in Raleigh and it didn't take long for him to find what his was looking for.

In all caps, the headline read: DOUBLE MURDER-SUICIDE ROCKS RALEIGH SUBURBS.

The headline easily drew his attention, but he wasn't sure exactly how such an event could be connected with him.

Nevertheless, he clicked on the link to find a story detailing an unidentified couple fatally shot in their bedroom by a young woman who led police on a high-speed chase on Interstate 40 before taking her own life.

Officials couldn't release names because next of kin had to be notified, but Evrett knew exactly who they were. Based on the street name for the murders, he knew it was the Bryants' street, and the make and model of the car driven by the young woman was the same car Stephanie drove.

The kicker and most disturbing information in the story was that officials were looking for a black Audi that left moments prior to police arriving.

It was at this point, Evrett shifted his attention to the memory card. He needed to see for himself what happened during the black-outs.

He double-clicked on the latest recording. He had started the recording prior to leaving for the Bryants' home the night before. He fast-forwarded through the video as he drove to their home. Evrett watched himself make the call to Sean and leave the car to sabotage the furnace.

All of this he clearly remembered.

He continued to watch as he got back into the car and drove off to Jaycee Park. Again he left the car to call Sean, and five minutes later, he was climbing back into the vehicle.

This is where his memory went blank.

But the video did not. He watched himself drive for about seven minutes and park outside the Bryants' home. He sat there for hours, lifeless, emotionless. Then, all of a sudden, at around midnight, he grabbed his lock-picking kit and left the car. He returned minutes later and returned to his sedated state in the front seat.

At the same time, he could see car lights drive up the road and stop nearby. A few minutes later, he turned the ignition and drove off.

Evrett could not believe how casual he was.

He also couldn't believe that he was there.

"What the hell did I do?" he asked, returning to the browser to read more of the story. Further down the page, he read in fear.

A neighbor reportedly saw a nondescript male get into a black Audi and speed off in the opposite direction of the young woman. The story read that the witness could not see the license plate and guessed that it was a Georgia plate.

Evrett was safe and in the clear. He also was lucky.

Raleigh Police had issued a statewide APB for a black Audi with Georgia plates, and they looked at several traffic light cameras in the area, but for some reason, the frames showing Evrett's Audi were all blurry. Police were able to trace his steps for a few blocks, but that was it. He had disappeared off their radar.

Evrett, however, was unaware of the traffic camera issues and he spent the next few days waiting for a knock at the door. He quickly destroyed the memory card and un-installed the dash camera. It was too risky to record any future trips. Meanwhile, he tore through his mind to produce a credible alibi, but every scenario he thought of didn't make sense. If asked why he was in the Bryants' neighborhood, he had no plausible excuse.

He was there to kill them.

More details were released on the double murder-suicide and it confirmed everything Evrett already knew. Stephanie fatally shot Janine with two bullets, while she unloaded multiple shots into Sean. Police found a frantic voicemail on Sean's phone and a friend of Stephanie's came forward to talk about the affair.

Police, however, did not have an answer for why Stephanie snapped.

But Evrett did.

He unknowingly put this in motion. By forcing Sean to break off the relationship, he caused Stephanie to break down.

It was not his plan. He did not want to hurt her. Guilt built up inside him. She was innocent in all of this.

Evrett sat around all night drinking whiskey. Halfway through his fourth drink, he realized that he did not check in with the office today.

He had to hand in a pair of reports, but he hadn't even started them. He went to his bedroom to retrieve his phone, which had a pair of voicemails from David Marks and another from Julia. Marks was looking for the aforementioned reports, while Julia was looking to have dinner.

It was too late for both and he figured he'd deal with the consequences tomorrow. Julia would understand; he knew that. David may be harder to deal with, but Evrett didn't care. The whiskey may have been talking, but he told himself he was almost ready to leave the firm anyway.

A strong knock at the door made things worse.

It was after nine on a Monday. He was certain this was the police. He thought about escaping through the back door, but where would he go? He could hide, but for how long?

The knock came a second time and it was more forceful.

Evrett decided to face the music. He was ready to exercise his right to remain silent. He knew there wouldn't be proof that he had contact with any of the victims. All they could do was place his car at the scene of the crime.

He peered through the curtains on the window in the door to see two patrolmen in uniform. Immediately, Evrett found it odd that it wasn't a pair of men in cheap suits, or at least business casual clothing. Certainly, a detective would interview a person of interest.

He opened the door and put on a smile.

"Hello, officers," he said. "Can I help you?"

"Sorry to bother you so late, sir," he said, giving Evrett the sense that he was in the clear, "but we are checking the neighborhood to see if anyone saw anything suspicious on Friday night. Were you around?"

"Yes, I was. I had just gotten back into town earlier that day, but I was traveling much of the night, so I slept through the early evening. Anything in particular you are looking for?"

"There was a sexual assault in an alley two blocks away," he said. "And we just got a tip that the perp ran in this direction and we're just looking to see if anyone saw anything."

"I'm afraid I didn't, officer. I'm sorry I couldn't be more helpful."

"No problem. If you do come across anything, just call the regional office," he said, handing over a card.

"I will do. You fellows have a nice night."

The officer who spoke the whole time tipped his cap and the two men went off to the next door.

Evrett closed his door and slid to the floor. He had dodged a bullet. He thought about how that was a poor choice of words, given the situation, but it was true.

His worry about having to answer to police about his whereabouts on Thursday night lessened as the week went on, and he slowly returned to his normal schedule. Julia and he went out to dinner on Tuesday—just in case the police showed up at his home—and on Thursday, they went to Holy Thursday mass.

Evrett hadn't been to church in a long time, but Julia asked if he would join her, so he obliged. She wasn't very religious, but she did feel the need to go to the important masses.

Sitting in the pew alongside Julia, Evrett zoned out. He didn't really understand what was going on anyway. Prayers, songs; stand, sit; it was all numbing. All he could do was stare at the stained glass windows. There were a multitude of colors, red, purple, blue and yellow, all of different shades, shapes and sizes. Pieced together with what seemed to be no rhyme or reason, Evrett tried to make sense of it.

There had to be a reason it was designed this way. There was a patch of yellows on the far right forming what would be a poorly drawn circle. On its edges, the yellow gradually phased to dark blue.

Evrett scanned across the panes to the other side where there was a dark blue cluster. His mind saw a man, and below the man was a bevy of reds and yellows. It was Sam's car on fire. The red and yellows started to move and Evrett could hear the screams of his wife.

As the red and yellow panes of glass burst, he let out a scream, "Sam!"

The church fell silent with all eyes on him, including Julia's. She saw the sweat beading on his forehead and could tell that he was in distress.

"Ev?" she said, putting her arm around him. "Ev, you okay?"

Evrett looked up at her and then back at the glass. Now that he looked at it, he could barely make out what he had seen just moments ago.

"I'm sorry," he whispered. "I think I zoned out there."

At this point, most of the people in the pews had turned their attention back to the priest, but there were still a few nosey persons watching.

"I'll be okay," he continued.

Mass ended and Evrett drove Julia back to her place. They said their "Good nights," and Evrett drove home.

He got caught up in a few murder investigation television series on A&E, and with each case, he analyzed all the details. He scrutinized the murderer's mistakes and assessed what he would do.

"What I would do..." Evrett said, accompanied with a chuckle.

What he would do is plan the perfect crime, black out and then regain consciousness with the target killed in some other fashion.

He laughed aloud at his current situation. Then, he started to wonder if any other murderers had ever experienced similar phenomenon.

Evrett reached for his iPad and typed in the key words into the Google search field and the first suggestion was "Dissociative Amnesia."

He started reading through the details of this form of amnesia. He had already self-diagnosed himself with Transient Global Amnesia, but now he was uncertain. The version he was reading about now sounded awfully close to what he had, too.

How the hell do doctors figure this out? he thought.

He would never find out for sure. He had already given up on the idea of getting professional help. At least not until after the man on the bridge was dead. Then, and only then, he would consider getting help. Even still, if the blackouts were only associated with the people on his list, perhaps once the list was extinguished, he'd go back to normal.

Normal. What would *normal* be after this?

Evrett pondered this and thought about his escape plan when it all was over. He didn't have one. It finally dawned on him that he had been so infatuated with his current work that he had not given any thoughts to his future. He had more than enough money to retire peacefully and quietly. Perhaps in another country; Italy, Spain, anywhere in the Virgin Islands would work for him.

He started to investigate these locations and more on his iPad, viewing properties throughout the world, but he fell asleep on the couch before he could fall in love with a new home.

It would be a duty tasked for another day.

38

JULIA ANSWERED THE QUESTION before the contestant could even buzz in. She was smart; it was one of the things Evrett liked best about her. Tonight, just like many other recent nights before, they sat on Evrett's sofa watching the evening game shows.

"What is the man in the yellow hat?"

Again Julia was correct.

"I was obsessed with Curious George growing up," she said to Evrett.

He smiled and laughed. Evrett enjoyed learning about Julia. With every evening or date they spent together he learned about one more piece of her. Looking at her he couldn't help but think there was so much that he still didn't know. He enjoyed letting Julia tell him about herself. It was a lot easier than the research he had been doing on his targets for the last year.

"I was more of a Dr. Seuss guy. *Oh, the Places You'll Go. One Fish, Two Fish*—"

"That doesn't surprise me really."

She pushed him playfully. Jack barked in Evrett's defense.

"Shush, Jack. I'm not hurting him," Julia scolded.

"Thanks for coming to my defense, buddy." Evrett said, scooping the Chihuahua up in his arms. Jack licked his face a few times.

"Do you two need a room?"

"Yeah, can you give us a minute?"

Julia got up from the couch and walked to the kitchen. "More wine, Ev?"

"Sure, the burgers should be done soon."

Julia opened another bottle of wine while Evrett went outside. He kept a small grill on his back porch. The warm weather had returned quickly to Baltimore. It had only been a little more than a month since he trudged through the snow in Raleigh. He briefly thought of Stephanie as he checked the burgers he was grilling. He never wanted her to meet the fate she did. It was another life wasted.

April had gone by so quickly. His mind turned to work. It wouldn't be long now until he closed that chapter of his life for good. Most of his projects were wrapping up and Evrett had been slowly planning his escape. Soon it would be time to tell Julia about it.

"Burgers are done. You want gorgonzola and American again?"

"You know it. I hope you wanted red," Julia said, handing him a new glass of Cabernet Franc.

"It's perfect."

They toasted and ate at the sofa, resting their plates on the coffee table. Jack sat patiently at Evrett's feet, waiting for a piece of turkey burger to fall from one of their plates. Evrett picked a small piece of the bun off and tossed it to the dog. It never hit the floor.

"Evrett, I think we should plan a trip somewhere."

The statement made Evrett stop chewing and turn toward his companion.

"A trip?"

"Wouldn't it be great to get away for a little bit? Summer will be here before you know it. It would be nice to have something to look forward to."

Evrett agreed that a trip would be a nice change of pace. However, he would soon need to make a trip to Cleveland, and Julia would not be able to come with him on that one. Chase wasn't next on his list though. Phil was, and thankfully he was closer to home.

"Where were you thinking?"

"I don't know. We could just get away for the weekend. We could go to the beach or something."

"Sure. We really should get away."

Julia smiled and took Evrett's hand. She squeezed it playfully.

He was impressed with how patient she was. Another girl might have been frustrated with the speed of their relationship. It had been about two years of spending time together—late night movie sessions, dinners and sleeping in the same bed—yet they still had not taken their relationship any further.

Evrett was sure Julia was ready for something more. Sometimes when he looked at her, all he wanted to do was take her in his arms and carry her upstairs. But with every thought like that, Evrett soon found the memory of Sam permeating his mind.

The feel of her skin.

The scent of her hair.

As much as he wanted to be with Julia, he couldn't. Not yet. It felt too much like cheating. And after watching what had happened to the Bryants, he wasn't ready to deal with those emotions, even if they were only from his own conscience.

"What are you thinking?" Julia asked.

Evrett focused on the present again.

"I'm sorry, what?"

"You seemed really far away just now. Is there something on your mind?"

"No, I was just thinking of places we could go."

"Were any of them romantic?" Julia said slyly. She placed her hand on Evrett's leg and slowly moved it up his thigh. Julia leaned toward him.

The kiss they shared was short, but Evrett could still taste the last swig of wine on Julia's tongue.

He took her hand off of his thigh and held it tightly. She nestled her head on his shoulder. Jack had curled up on the armchair across from them.

"Do you want to play Trivial Pursuit?" Evrett suggested.

It wasn't the first time they played board games together, but he could tell it wasn't exactly what Julia had wanted to hear in that moment. She sat up and looked at him slightly puzzled.

She sighed.

"Sure, Evrett. You know I love trivia. You get the game while I use the bathroom real quick."

Julia left the living room and made her way up the stairs to the second floor. Evrett could hear her footsteps above him as she walked down the short hallway. He had taken the board game off of the nearby bookcase and began setting up the pieces.

Upstairs, Julia stood looking at herself in the bathroom mirror. She ran her fingers through her brown hair to give it a little more volume and checked her teeth before washing her hands.

"One of these days, Evrett," she said to her reflection.

She flushed the toilet and left the bathroom.

Julia walked slowly down the hallway looking at the pictures that hung on the walls. They were pictures of Evrett and Sam's family and friends, mostly people Julia had never met.

Would he ever let me get that close? she thought.

There was one picture in particular that piqued her interest. It was a picture of Evrett and Sam. It was a close up shot, taken by some unseen photographer. The couple wore life jackets, and from the scenery behind them, Julia gathered that they were in one of the paddleboats down in the Inner Harbor.

She looked at Sam's face. She was beautiful.

Julia looked at Evrett's eyes. They were full of a happiness that she had never seen in him. Even when they were having the best time together, he never looked like that.

How long was she willing to be second to someone she couldn't compete with?

Her concentration was broken by the unexpected sound of a door unlatching. It startled Julia. She turned away from the picture and looked down the hallway. The door to a nearby room slowly swung open, creaking softly as it did so.

Julia was curious. She had never been in this second bedroom of Evrett's. As she stepped closer, she realized that she had never even seen this particular door open before. She knew Evrett always kept it shut.

Julia slowly stepped through the doorway. The room was dark, so she flipped on the light switch. Judging from the furniture in the room—a desk, a drafting table and a few small bookcases—Julia gathered that this must have been Evrett's office.

The room also was filled with several black duffle bags and small suitcases, each pushed neatly to the side of the room. Julia could see the desk was covered with manila file folders and papers. Moving closer, she realized that in typical Evrett fashion, they were all neatly stacked and placed. Julia counted eight separate piles as she reached her hand toward the desk. She picked up the top folder on the pile closest to the edge of the desk and opened its cover. A few sheets of paper slipped out from within the folder and fluttered to the floor.

Julia set the folder back on the desk and squatted down to collect the disturbed papers. She noticed that one sheet was a printed Google map and the next was a newspaper clipping.

"What are you doing?"

Evrett's voice caused Julia to jump to her feet, leaving the papers on the floor.

"God, Evrett. You scared the shit out of me."

"Julia, I asked what you are doing in here?"

His voice was stern and cold. A tinge of worry also hung just below the surface.

Evrett looked at the papers that were on the floor. He recognized them immediately as information he had gathered about Chase. He couldn't let Julia see them. There would be too much to explain. As she bent down again to pick up the sheets of evidence, Evrett panicked.

"Julia, you have to go."

"What?"

Her moment of confusion offered just enough time for Evrett to dive in and scoop up the papers. He snatched the file folder from the desk and quickly tucked them back into it.

"I said you have to go."

"Evrett, what's the matter? I just saw that the door was open and I—"

Open? he thought. Hadn't he made sure to lock it before Julia arrived?

"This stuff is my private…it's Sam's stuff. How dare you just go snooping through it?"

"Snooping? Wait a minute, Evrett. I wasn't snooping. I just walked in. Calm down, you aren't making sense."

Evrett placed the folder back in its rightful spot while positioning himself between Julia and the desk. She backed a few steps away from him.

How much did you see? Evrett thought.

"Who do you think you are coming in and messing with her things? You have no right to be in here. To touch these things."

Evrett could feel the moment getting away from him.

Andrew. Chad. Amanda. Gloria. Janine. Sean. Phil. Chase.

They were all here, all in this room. All Julia had to do was look into one folder and his work, his life, would unravel. And then he would never make it to the man on the bridge.

So much time, energy and work had gone into filling this room with the vital information necessary to accomplish his missions—all of the days, weeks and months of details about each one of his targets; it was too much work to let it be for nothing. He couldn't let Julia discover his secret. He had to keep Julia away from the truth.

"I need you to leave. Right now."

By this point, Jack had also made his way up into the room and was now sniffing around the edge of the desk.

"Look, Ev. This is just some misunderstanding. Just calm down. I—"

Evrett's eyes traveled from Jack to Julia. He looked into her creamy brown eyes. It broke him, but he knew he had no choice.

"Get the hell out, Julia!" Evrett screamed.

Silence followed.

The volume of his voice had made her shudder and Jack run between Julia's legs. Evrett and Julia looked at one another, her eyes wide with confusion. He could tell she was beginning to realize the enormity of the moment. Finally, Julia gave in.

"Fine. Fine. We'll go," she said and grabbed Jack. He let out a grunt.

Julia turned and walked to the door. Evrett felt his heart's pace slow ever so slightly. There was another feeling rushing in to replace the adrenaline. He couldn't tell yet it if was relief or sadness.

Julia stopped before stepping out into the hallway.

"Sam's dead, Evrett. She's dead and she is never coming back. It's time you realized that and moved on."

"Get out, Julia."

"Two years, Evrett. Two years I wasted waiting for you—"

"Just leave!"

Julia turned and left. She was too upset to muster any more words.

Evrett had nothing left to say, either, and he couldn't bring himself to look at her or Jack as they walked down the stairs. With each thundering step, Evrett felt the stab of knowing things were truly finished with Julia. They had to be.

A few moments later he heard the front door slam, and he knew she was gone. Julia wouldn't be coming back.

There would be no more late night movie viewings. There would be no more shared bottles of wine. There would be no warmth beside him in bed.

He had been foolish to think he could let someone get so close while he still had work left to finish.

As Evrett readied to leave the room he turned his attention to the lock on the door. He jiggled the handle. For two years he had made sure the room was always secured, especially when Julia came over. He tried to remember earlier in the day. He couldn't imagine he hadn't locked the door.

Somehow, though, he must have forgotten. How else could he explain Julia being able to enter his office?

Evrett turned his key and then checked to make sure the door was locked.

He would never be careless again.

39

MOSCOW SOUNDED NICE RIGHT ABOUT NOW. There was just something about the historic Russian city that Phil Repin fell in love with.

That's what he told his close friends, but the truth was, it wasn't something; it was someone.

Her name was Milena, a dark-haired beauty who stole his heart.

It was 1989 and Phil was a thriving thirty-one-year-old agent with the Central Intelligence Agency. He had just finished up eight years of service in the Navy after graduating in the top ten of the 1981 class at the United States Naval Academy. Phil joined the Navy SEALs, and for eight years he took part in numerous classified missions that no one would ever believe. He rose to the rank of Lieutenant Commander before the CIA came calling. With his Russian heritage—his grandfather on his father's side immigrated to the United States before World War I—and his fluency in the language, Phil was exactly the type of person they were looking for.

His first and only assignment was Moscow.

The Cold War was winding down, but there was still a great need for intelligence personnel in Moscow. Phil was stationed with two other agents in a flat about four blocks from the Kremlin, tucked away on a small, narrow street called Kalashnyy.

The first month was trying for Phil. It was much different than any mission he had as a SEAL. With the SEALs, it was all about speed and efficiency. In and out as quickly and as quietly as possible was what they strived for.

The need to remain stealthy was still a necessity in the CIA, but there wasn't an extraction helicopter coming in an hour. Phil was stationed there for the foreseeable future, and with the Cold War in its fourth decade, there was no telling how long he'd be there.

The job was less exciting at times, too.

Many days, he didn't leave the safe house, monitoring the thousands of wiretaps and bugs that the agency had in place for more than a decade. Phil was amazed the KGB had not found them by now.

On his forty-third night in the Russian capitol, he ventured out to a bar for a few drinks with the two other agents. The agents always went to restaurants or bars that were at least fifteen miles, or twenty-five kilometers, away from their safe house.

One, it kept them away from the locals, and two, it gave them ample opportunities to check their rearview mirrors to see if they were followed. They also never traveled in the same car and they each took different routes.

Today, Phil's route was the longest, but he didn't mind. He loved being on the road.

When he arrived, the other two agents were already halfway into their first beers. They were sitting at a table, so he went straight up to the bar to order a drink. The bar was fairly empty—understandably considering it was a Tuesday—and the bartender was waiting with a smile.

Phil gazed at her for a moment, taking in all her beauty. She had black hair that fell only a few inches past her ears, with a bright red cluster highlighting her left side. She was about five-foot-six with a body that had every curve a man looks for, especially Phil. Her white shirt was tight and it was ripped around the collar to show off the right amount of cleavage to her male patrons. She had a nose ring through the left nostril to go with the numerous piercings in both ears.

And though all of this captured his attention, it was her hazel green eyes that punched him in the face.

He leaned onto the bar and hesitated for a second before ordering a beer in perfect Russian.

The bartender hesitated to get it because she went through a similar moment checking out Phil.

At six-foot-two and with the physique one would expect of a Navy SEAL, Phil was easily one of the most attractive men that this bartender had ever served.

She gave him his beer and Phil paid before joining the other two agents. As he walked to the table, he could feel the burn of her eyes staring at him. He was trained to know who was watching him, and he could easily see her in the reflection off the glass covering a picture on the wall. He watched her watch him the whole way, and she had no clue he saw her.

As soon as he sat down in a direction that allowed him to see her without the use of deception, she turned her gaze to other remedial tasks. But even as she cleaned glasses and served the few other patrons sitting at the bar, she continued to look up in his direction. She was enamored.

Phil was too. He lost track of a few, non-agency-related conversations the other two were having.

"You okay, man," the one said. "You look out of it."

"I'm fine."

About two hours later, the three left money on the table and headed for the exit. As Phil walked out, he again felt that same burn, and this time, he turned and gave her a smile back. She was embarrassed and turned the other way.

Phil laughed as he got into his car and drove back to the safe house. The three cars went off in different directions, and after a mile, Phil talked himself into turning around. There was something more to this woman and he wasn't about to let this be the last of it. And besides, he was a single man in Moscow who hadn't been with a woman in more than a year.

He turned his car around and went back to the bar. Once in the parking lot, he pulled out his bulky satellite phone and called the safe house. He left a message saying he was going for a drive to check something out in another province and that he'd return the next day.

It wasn't uncommon for the agents to do that. Despite working out of the same safe house, they were rarely doing the same thing. The one agent had infiltrated the Kremlin seven years ago and he had been working inside ever since. The other ran a technology shop as a front, selling televisions, computers, VCRs and phones that all had CIA bugs in them. The easiest way to place bugs in Russian homes was to sell them. It was a perfect set up.

Phil didn't have a job or an undercover gig. Not yet. He was just there to run special missions as directed by Langley. For all the other two agents knew, he had just been contacted by Langley to go out on a mission.

He walked in the front door of the bar and she immediately saw him. The two men who were drinking at the bar when he left were still sitting there, as he expected they would be.

Phil strolled over to the bar and sat on a stool on the opposite end, away from the two other men.

The bartender came over to him and spoke in Russian.

"Back so soon?"

"You're beautiful," he said confidently.

This took her aback, yet she still returned a smile and an embarrassed giggle.

Phil reached out his hand for a handshake. "My name is Avdei. Avdei Lorianov. And I just had to come back to tell you that you are beautiful."

She giggled again, and said, "Milena. I'm Milena Voronova."

"Milena. Lovely. Can I get a vodka tonic?"

"Certainly."

She went to pour the drink, continuously looking back at him. She came back and set it in front of him.

"What time do you finish up? I'd love to take you out for a bite to eat."

"I'm here till close," she said.

Phil hesitated and looked around the bar, "Well, there's not many people here. Have you eaten yet?"

She shook her head no.

"Well, let's order up some food and have a seat here. I'm sure these two guys will not mind."

He stood up and walked over to the two men at the end of the bar. Milena followed along on the other side, confused at what was happening.

"Hey, guys. You mind if I steal your bartender for an hour to have dinner?" Phil threw one thousand rubles onto the bar in between the two men. "Your drinks are on me."

The two guys looked at each other a bit dumbfounded, but agreed that the best deal was to say yes.

Milena could not believe what was happening, but she enjoyed every second of it. She sat down at the same table Phil and the other agents were at earlier. She carried with her a pair of menus, including one for herself, even though she knew it by heart.

"So what's good here?" Phil said, with a laugh.

"I think it's all good," she said. "I trust our chef."

About a minute later, after Phil paged through the menu twice, he looked up and saw Milena looking right at him.

"Know what you would like?" she asked. "I'll have to be our waitress, too, you know."

Phil smiled, "Yeah, I guess I didn't think that part through."

"It's no problem. I love this date already."

And with that, the couple ordered food, ate, drank and talked over the next three hours. The two guys at the bar took the rubles and left, presumably for a bar with an available bartender.

Phil waited as Milena closed the bar and the two went back to her rented flat that was just a two-block walk away.

Milena had the next four days off and the two went on a road trip to St. Petersburg. Neither had ever been there and both wanted to go, so they decided on a whim to make the nine-hour drive.

If they weren't in love when the car left Moscow, they certainly were by the time it got back.

• • •

Two months of constant dating blossomed into a relationship that Phil never thought he could have. He was a little troubled by the double life he was leading, and the fear of losing Milena grew greater every day.

To her, he was Avdei Lorianov, an investment banker who traveled to banks all throughout Russia.

There was nothing fake about his personality or feelings; they were all sincere. Everything else, though, was a lie, and Phil hated it.

On the fifty-sixth day of their relationship, Phil nearly told her the truth; he wanted to end the lies. He was ready to quit the agency and go rogue just to be with her. But he was afraid that the United States would think he left to hand over critical information, something he would never do. They wouldn't know that, though, and he would have to walk around trying to avoid the little red laser dot searching for his head.

So for the sake of his head, the lie continued.

On the sixty-first day, it proved to be a wise decision.

Phil and Milena were driving to Staraya Kupavna, a town in the Noginsky District of Moscow Oblast. It was where Milena grew up, in a house that ran up to the banks of the Shalovka River. Her father, Zinovy, still lived there. Milena never really talked about her father, other than the fact that she had to introduce Phil to him.

Zinovy was currently cooking his favorite meal for dinner, Ossetrina pod Syrom—sturgeon baked with cheese. Phil and Milena arrived a few minutes early to watch Zinovy put the final touches on the meal.

At dinner, Zinovy prodded with multiple questions asked in such a fashion that would not scare Phil off, but at the same time garner the information desired. Phil, who planned several storylines for an instance like this, started to get the feeling that Zinovy was experienced with interrogations.

After the sixth question that was mixed in with casual dinner conversation, Phil looked up from his near empty plate and asked, "So Mr. Voronov. What is it that you do?"

"I told you, call me Zinovy," he said as he wiped a few crumbs away from his thick black mustache. "I work in the Kremlin. I'm a defense analyst. Nothing too exciting."

Phil had to use all his willpower, and then some, to hold back any sign that that information was of dire interest to him.

"Nothing too exciting?" Phil said. "You work in one of our country's most historic buildings. As a history buff, to me, that is incredibly exciting."

"Ah, yes, the building," he said. "After time, it just becomes like any old office. After a year I didn't even think about the history. I just thought about coming home to my family."

He paused for a moment, and Phil knew exactly why. Milena told him early on in their relationship about her mother, who was murdered eleven years ago. Phil never meant for his question to bring up these emotions, but it did.

After the slight pause, Zinovy asked another question. He had no clue who he was truly interviewing.

• • •

After a few more dinner trips, Phil had Zinovy's house and car completely bugged. He spent the next six months gathering from Zinovy what the higher-ups at Langley told him was critical information. Phil never told them the truth about Milena, and at the same time, his lies with her were getting deeper, especially now that he was spying on her father.

It weighed heavy on his conscious every day, because they were truly in love. Future plans were being made and Phil knew that he was going to have to make a major decision soon. Becoming a real investment banker was a real possibility.

He majored in economics at the Naval Academy, graduating with a 3.98 grade-point average, so he figured he had a good base. Unfortunately, he studied American economics, so he needed to do some self-teaching on Russian economics before he could even begin to think about disappearing off the grid.

He left the safe house one day to go to a local bookstore for economics books, and as he walked down the sidewalk, he heard a single gunshot. At first, he assumed it was an attack on him and he reached for his sidearm, concealed under his jacket, but he did not draw his weapon.

His reaction was quick, but the screams from a hundred yards ahead of him eased his fear. He scanned the rooftops to be sure, but he didn't see anyone. Even if he did, he clearly wasn't the target, and as an investment banker, he should not be playing vigilante.

He quickly turned around and went back to the safe house. It was a decision he did not think through.

He did not plan on seeing Milena that night, as she was working late, so he went to bed early in the safe house. He had recently leased a flat just outside of Moscow, but he did not have a reason to go there tonight. It was closer to Reutov and it gave him a place to bring Milena back to—the most expensive part of the lie. For Phil, it was worth every ruble.

He had a phone next to his bed at the safe house that had the same number as the phone in the rented flat, and at one in the morning, it rang loudly.

Phil grabbed the receiver quickly, "Milena?" She was the only person who had the number, other than her father.

"Yes," she said, clearly crying. "I need you. Come over. Quick."

She hung up and didn't answer when Phil called back.

Phil sprung out of bed and put on a pair of jeans and a T-shirt. He reached into his tactical bag and pulled out a pair of SIG Sauer P226 pistols secured in a shoulder holster that he quickly put on. He also grabbed a pair of night vision optics, a few extra magazines for his pistols and other trusty tools he may need for entry and assault.

As he drove quickly toward Reutov, he began running through all the scenarios in his mind. He was visualizing Milena's flat and all the entry points. He had no clue what he was walking into. It could be a trap. Could he have been played this whole time? Perhaps Milena was spying on him? The scenarios were numerous and none of them ended well.

Phil stopped a block away from Milena's flat and he got out to walk the rest of the way. He reached into the small black-clothed satchel slung over his shoulders for the night vision optics. He put them on as he got close. Ducking behind a car on the street, he had a clear view of Milena's apartment. A light was on and he saw nothing out of the ordinary. He then saw her come to the window and look out, presumably for him considering he should be at her front door by now. He scanned the rest of the area to see if he was followed, but he didn't see anyone.

He ran back to his car and put his gear in the trunk. He drew one of his pistols and tucked it in his jeans. Milena knew he had one gun for protection, so he'd be okay with that. He drove the rest of the way to where he normally parked and got out. Milena was at the window again and he could see a smile.

"What an overreaction," he said to himself.

He ran up the stairs to the second floor flat. He didn't even have to knock as she was standing there. She immediately ran through the doorway and hugged him.

"Oh, Avdei," she said, with tears running down her cheek. "My father is dead."

Phil was shocked and upset. Yes, he had been spying on the man, but he felt incredibly sad for Milena and himself. He liked Zinovy. He was funny, caring and honorable.

The KGB felt otherwise on the latter.

"What happened?" Phil asked.

"He was murdered. Someone shot him after he got lunch. Broad daylight, in the middle of the street."

She couldn't describe any more details because she burst into tears.

Phil just held her as he thought about what happened earlier in the day. He was there. He could not believe it. He was there.

Then it sunk in. There's likely only one reason someone would kill him like that. They must have found his bugs.

He then thought about his ride over. He spent so much time running through scenarios to save Milena from whatever threat was here that he did not check his six once during the drive. He immediately scanned his surroundings.

He could sense it. Something was wrong. He pulled Milena inside the doorway and slammed the door.

"What's going on?" she shouted.

He drew his pistol and held it at his side.

"Milena, I love you, and we're in danger."

She just stared at him with a confused look.

"Look, you know I love you and you know who I truly am inside. But there's more, and I've wanted to tell you and I can't tell you it all now because there is no time. If you love me no matter what, you'll come with me."

"Of course I love you, but what the hell are you talking about?"

He knew Milena was also fluent in English, and he told her before that he did not know it very well, so he switched to English to further prove his point: "Milena, I'm not an investment banker. I want to be one now, but I'm not. I'm C-I-A. I'm a spy."

At that moment, before she could react in anger, the lights went out. Phil could see the glow of a street light outside so he instantly knew the power was cut inside.

He grabbed her hand and pulled her down, "Get down."

She remained quiet and did as he said, understanding that her life was more important than her anger toward Phil.

He looked into her eyes and wiped a tear from her cheek. "Look. I'm getting you out of here alive. You can leave me after that if you wish, but I'm getting you out. I love you and I will not let these people kill you like they did your father."

She kissed him on the cheek, "Get me out of here."

"Follow me," he said.

They ran low to the floor to a second bedroom that she used for storage. There was a crawl space in the closet that Phil had scoped out when she ran out for food one day. He knew at the far end there was a large vent that led to the outside where they could escape. He led her there. As they got into the crawl space and replaced the board to close it up, Phil heard the lock of the front door to her flat being picked.

They are certainly inside by now, he thought.

Phil and Milena crawled toward the vent where he quietly pulled it open. There was a five-foot drop to a roof covering a garage that was converted into an apartment. The roof slanted down to a point where it would only be a nine-foot drop to the grass in the back.

Back there he saw no movement, but in the front, he saw a pair of men in black clothing carrying heavy-duty military weapons trying to hide while covering Phil's car. It was at this point that Phil wished he had kept his tactical bag with him.

"Do you have your car keys on you?" he whispered.

She nodded.

"And you parked in the back, right?"

She nodded again.

"Okay, I'm going to drop you down."

Phil helped Milena down onto the garage roof, and from there, he lowered her down making the drop to the grass only five feet. He then jumped with his pistol ready in hand.

Milena's car was about thirty yards away when he heard a twig snap behind them. He spun and fired two quick shots, center mass, on a KGB agent dressed in all black.

He saw another two running in from farther away and he pulled Milena down behind an old beat-up van.

"I'm going to provide cover. You get to your car and start driving. Leave. Go to our spot and I'll meet you there. Then we'll leave this place."

She stared at him for a few seconds.

"Go! Run!"

He leaned out from around the back of the van and fired a pair of shots aimlessly, causing the two approaching KGB agents to take cover. Milena, in the meantime, ran for the car.

Phil saw the two agents get up and run the other way. He then turned to see another two agents on the opposite side of Milena's car running away from it.

Milena was already inside and it was too late. Phil had been led into a trap.

"No!" he shouted running toward the car, but Milena turned the ignition and the car exploded into a massive orange ball of fire. The concussion caused Phil to fly backward against the van.

Even though all he wanted to do was fall to his knees and cry, his survival instincts kicked in. He heard a bullet soar above his head and strike the back window of the van.

Phil remained low to the ground and worked his way to the back of Milena's building. He kicked open a door and ran in. He was in someone's flat, but he didn't care, sprinting through their living room and out their front door.

In the main hallway, he heard a pair of footsteps storming down the stairs. The two men who were in Milena's apartment had just gotten word that Phil was outside. They had no idea he was back inside until he placed two perfectly aimed bullets into their heads. Both men's bodies tumbled down the stairs into the foyer. He grabbed one of their radios and a Makarov pistol. He had only two bullets left in his SIG, so he needed a backup. He didn't have time to search for more magazines, so he left.

Opening the door a crack, he could see there was no one immediately outside the door. He was trapped and it would only get worse if he waited it out, so he took the biggest gamble and burst out the front door. He sprinted across the street toward a cluster of trees, hoping that the agents out back had not come around the front yet.

As he entered the wooded area, he sought cover behind a large tree. He peeked around the tree trunk to see a pair of agents cautiously and tactically come out the front door. They must have followed him in from the back, he thought. Seconds later, another two agents came around the right side of the building.

They quickly gathered together, presumably devising a search plan, but Phil didn't let them get that far.

He stepped out of the darkness of the woods with the Sig in his left hand and the Makarov in his right. Two shots from each, four shots total, all struck the heads of the four men. Not one could react before they all were dead.

Phil ran to his car, got in and sped away. No one was tailing him this time. He was sure of it and he made the long thirteen-hour drive north to Finland where he would secretly cross the border and await his extraction.

His cover was blown the moment a KGB agent saw him change

direction swiftly after Zinovy was assassinated. It was one of many mistakes Phil made along the way and it was one of the many reasons why the CIA fired him immediately.

Depression set in fairly quick when he was jettisoned into real society back in the United States. Years of dangerous and classified missions made the adjustment an arduous one. He joined the Maryland State Police, but the daily patrols could not equal the thrill of being a Navy SEAL or a CIA agent.

After two dreadful years, he quit and took up a completely different profession, truck driving. The only thing he enjoyed about being a police officer was driving to places he had never been, but in Maryland, he ran out of those quickly.

As a truck driver, he could travel the country. He had no attachment to his home state of Maryland, so in 1995 he got his commercial driver's license, bought a Mack truck with a luxurious cabin and started running freight all across the United States.

He made several regional runs in the Northeast before his boss sent him on a cross-country trek to Seattle. Prior to driving a big rig, the farthest west he had ever traveled was Illinois—other than a flight to San Diego for S.E.A.L. training—so Seattle was an exciting venture for him.

For 900 miles, it was an amazing, unforgettable trip.

Then he saw it; the sign for Moscow.

He swerved and pulled off the road, avoiding a major accident. He took a few deep breaths and reached into his bag for his medication. He had been on several anti-depressants prescribed by his psychiatrist, but he hadn't taken a single pill in a couple months. He had felt better and he had not once thought about Milena.

Now, the word Moscow on a road sign had him on the side of the road, envisioning Milena looking right at him from the car knowing that she was going to die. He could see it in her eyes. He should have done something. He shouldn't have sent her to the car by herself. He killed the only woman he had ever loved.

Phil started to hyperventilate, and if it weren't for the fact that an Iowa state trooper saw him swerve to the side of the road, he may have died. Phil passed out just as the trooper stepped up to the driver's side door. An ambulance arrived five minutes later and he was in stable condition as he was taken to the hospital.

He never made it to Seattle, but fortunately, he was able to keep his job, and on his next cross-country trip, the medication allowed him to pass the Exit 267 road sign for Moscow, Iowa, on Interstate 80 without any issues.

Phil went nearly seventeen years without another incident until he did a friend a favor. Bill Rutledge, a fellow twenty-plus-year veteran of the trucking company who drove tanker trucks regionally in the Mid-Atlantic, needed a week off to travel to San Francisco for his only daughter's wedding. Fortunately, Phil spent two years driving tankers and still had his license to cover Bill's runs.

The first two days went well for Phil, but on Wednesday, he got lost trying to deliver gas to a station in downtown Baltimore. Trying to correct his mistake, he got onto Interstate 83 heading north, and when he got the truck up to sixty miles per hour, he saw a pair of cars collide about a hundred yards in front of him. He slammed on the brakes and lost control of the wheel causing the truck to jackknife and eventually flip onto its side. The sound of the truck's metal scratching along the pavement made his eardrums scream in pain.

After what seemed like an eternity, the truck finally came to a stop. Phil was amazed that he could move all his extremities, and other than a cut on his arm from glass, he was fine. He was sure that he would be sore the next day.

The smell of gas hit him next and he realized that he wasn't out of harm's way yet. Phil's cabin was on its side with the passenger's door now above him. He unbuckled his seatbelt and climbed up to the door, pushing it open and jumping out of the truck. When he landed on the pavement, his right knee buckled, sending a sharp pain throughout his body. It wasn't broken, but he was certain he had torn a ligament.

He could see smoke pluming into the air and he knew that an explosion was imminent. He started to run away from the truck when he heard the screams. He turned to see the car on fire.

Inside was a woman. It was Milena. He couldn't believe it. How could it be her? He saw her screaming and he wanted to help her, but he couldn't. Fear set in and he ran, faster than before. He zipped past people watching Milena scream.

He heard the explosion behind him and he stopped, spun and looked at the flames shooting high in the air. He fell to his knees, something he didn't get to do in Moscow, and screamed Milena's name.

Phil spent the next month in a psychiatric hospital before returning to his normal truck driving life with a stronger dose of medication.

It wasn't ideal, but it would get him through the next three years before he could retire and move to Moscow, Russia.

His psychiatrist strongly objected, but he didn't care. He was going back.

40

EVRETT WAS BEGINNING TO SEE THE END. His list of eight only had two more names on it. Phil and Chase, the two who had the best chance to save Sam. Evrett thought back to when he first set out on his quest. He had toyed with so many different options and paths of how he should move forward before settling on the order he did.

Would things have been different if he had started with Phil rather than Andrew? Would he now be investigating Amanda's life with more knowledge of the man on the bridge? Would any of his targets still be alive?

Evrett remembered when he set out to find Chase in Cleveland and had witnessed his gang attacking the man in the park. Evrett knew that night he wasn't ready to confront Chase. Would he be when the time finally came?

Phil and Chase. And then hopefully the man on the bridge would follow; he had to. Evrett's dream weeks ago had reassured him that this road would lead to him. All Evrett could do was continue.

And so he did.

Evrett stood in Phil Repin's kitchen. The truck driver who had left Sam to die resided in a double-wide in a trailer home community east of Baltimore, just off of Interstate 695. The kitchen table was covered in unopened bills and there were several empty beer cans stashed sporadically around the room. The home had all the signs of being owned by a man who was never home.

Phil's trucking schedule, which he kept on his refrigerator, proved to be a mixed bag for Evrett's investigation. It was hard to observe Phil when he was gone from Baltimore for such long stretches of time. However, that also allowed for several moments like this, where he could sift through Phil's life without fear of being interrupted any time soon.

Evrett had planted his surveillance equipment in Phil's home two weeks ago. His microphones had revealed a very lonely life for Phil. Listening to Phil's life reminded Evrett of the vision he had in his head for Gloria. When not driving across the country, Phil popped open a beer and sat on the couch. It was a sad, lonely existence; one that Evrett would have pitied, save for the fact that it was Phil he was thinking about.

The bedroom was in much the same condition as the kitchen. The bed wasn't made and the closet had clothes spilling out of it. Evrett had to step over a pile of jeans to be able to get to the night-stand.

As he did, he caught a glimpse of himself in a mirror above the dresser. There, he could see his fully regrown beard. Oddly, he had missed it, and after Raleigh, he decided it would be good to change up his appearance for a while. Plus, it would help him blend in if he ever had to confront Phil at a truck stop.

How that confrontation would come about, he did not know yet. And certainly his method of killing Phil also was unknown. He could use Phil's disheveled lifestyle to his advantage. He could easily create a house fire that would consume the trailer within minutes. Evrett spotted an ashtray and a crushed beer can on the nightstand. He envisioned Phil lighting a cigarette after a night of drinking alone.

His eyes would become heavy, only enhanced by the amount of alcohol he had consumed that evening. As he drifted off to sleep, the cigarette could slip from his fingers and onto the pile of clothes next to the bed. It was a believable story, and one that Evrett could set up with ease.

He crouched down next to the bed to see what Phil kept under it. There was a large black box, nearly double the size of a normal briefcase. Evrett grabbed the handle, pulled it out and placed it on the mattress. There was a lock on the lid, but just as he had done to the trailer's front door, he had it picked in seconds. Once unlocked, the lid popped open and Evrett looked inside the case.

Catching his attention right away were six pistols scattered about. Off to the side of the case were five large boxes of ammo, each comprised of 1,000 bullets.

"A little excessive, Phil," Evrett said.

He poked through the guns with his flashlight—even though he was wearing gloves, he wanted to minimize his contact with any of the items. Underneath the guns, he noticed several small booklets that were unmistakable. They were passports from all over.

On top was Phil's United States passport, and below it were booklets of many colors. A maroon colored passport that read, "Portugal." A green one that read, "Kingdom of Saudi Arabia," along with other words in Arabic that Evrett did not know. Another maroon one followed that read, "Unione Europea Republica Italiana," which Evrett easily deciphered as Italy. Below that were passports to the Netherlands, France, Britain, Switzerland, Belgium, Germany, Spain, Poland, Russia and many more that were unrecognizable.

Puzzled and curious, Evrett started to page through each one. All the stamps were from the late 1980s and early 1990s, and every passport had his picture accompanied with a different name. He studied the Russian passport, which was actually for the U.S.S.R. He knew this because of the hammer and sickle logo in the center with the letters C.C.C.P. at the top. For Evrett, it was easy to pick up because a roommate in college always wore a 1980 Soviet Union national hockey team T-shirt with both the logo and the acronym on the front.

Inside the old passport was Phil's picture; of course, a much younger looking Phil, accompanied by the name, "Avdei Lorianov."

"Avdei, eh?" Evrett said.

Underneath all the passports were dog tags. NEPIN T PHILLIP. 257-34-1345. A POS. NO REL-.

Next to the dog tags was a white I.D. card with Phil's picture on it. The CIA logo was next to it.

Evrett dropped the passports and stood up quickly, as all the information processed.

He was spying on a spy.

Bugging an old woman and a bunch of ordinary citizens was one thing, but doing the same to a man who likely knew all the tricks in the books was another.

Evrett, as he paced back and forth throughout the bedroom, immediately began to think about removing his bugs from Phil's home.

Several minutes passed by—he was awarded the luxury of time with Phil being stuck in a truck cabin somewhere in the Pacific Northwest—and finally, Evrett decided to continue with his plan.

The way he saw it, Phil had to be at least twenty years removed from a life of secrecy. Based on the current condition of his apartment and his life at this point, it was quite possible he had removed himself from that life, so much so, that perhaps he had lost his edge.

Evrett settled on that and went back to business. He returned to the case on the floor and replaced everything as best as he could remember it.

"Hopefully the drunk won't remember what order his passports were in," he said to himself.

It was a sloppy mistake, but it was one he was sure he could get away with.

Once the case was back in position under Phil's bed, Evrett continued to search the room. Phil kept a small bookcase near the closet. There were a few novels—mostly by W.E.B. Griffin and Robert Ludlum. There also were some travel publications of Eastern European countries. Evrett thumbed through them to notice an abundance of books on Russia.

Evrett did notice that there were several stamps in his passport for the Soviet Union, and with the vast array of novels and periodicals on Russia, it was clear to him that Phil missed the country. Perhaps he was looking to return someday.

Looking around the trailer, he couldn't imagine Phil as a man who had traveled outside of his delivery routes, and any return trip to Russia seemed to be wishful thinking.

However, Evrett could appreciate the thought of leaving. Only a few weeks ago he had begun looking at what life might be like for him once all this business was finished. Back then he would have said that that life might have included Julia in some way.

Things hadn't turned out that way.

Evrett chided himself for letting Julia get too close. Seeing her standing in the room he kept locked away from the rest of the world had been a much-needed wakeup call. He needed to remain focused on his mission, especially now as the endgame was beginning to take shape. Evrett couldn't take any unnecessary risks now.

It had been hard to send Julia out of the house. After so many months of companionship, he couldn't deny the feelings that had developed. But he had to finish this.

He had to finish this for Sam, and Julia simply couldn't be a part of it any longer.

Evrett shook the thoughts from his head and continued sifting through Phil's belongings. He was back in the living area of the trailer. The coffee table had a few papers strewn about it. Underneath a few old newspapers was a folder. Evrett recognized the logo immediately.

Apparently Phil had a Nation Trust retirement account that he was looking to cash in. Evrett smirked at the coincidence that the truck driver who took his wife from him just happened to have the same insurance company.

"So you're getting ready to be done with work, Phil?"

Evrett knew the freedom of being finished with a job. The week after his blowout with Julia he had finally turned in his resignation letter at work. He had been planning to leave for months, and with his relationship with Julia over, he couldn't think of a better time.

He had been missing work and meetings due to his real job, the one that took him all across the country now. Without Julia there to be his liaison and to cover for him, Evrett saw no real way for him to keep GGM and finish the journey toward the man on the bridge.

Evrett decided to call it a day. He had been snooping around Phil's trailer for almost fifteen minutes and didn't want to push it. A neighbor could have seen him enter the trailer and Evrett wasn't in the mood to deal with the police if that were the case.

Just as Evrett stepped toward his exit, he heard the creak of the flimsy screen front door. Evrett pressed himself up against the wall and held his breath.

Phil should still be out on the road. Had he misread his schedule? Was it someone coming to check on Phil's trailer? Had a neighbor called the cops?

It didn't matter who was at the door. Evrett had to be ready for what came next.

All the times he had broken into someone's house, he had managed to get away without being caught or noticed. Evrett looked around the room for something to use as a weapon. He had his flashlight, and with a well-timed and placed hit, he could do a significant amount of damage with it. Still, Evrett didn't want to leave any evidence of his visit, especially not a body.

He heard the person at the door moving and the doorknob jiggled. This was followed by a sudden burst of mail through the slot in the front door. A few white envelopes fell to the floor, spreading out like a fan. Evrett heard the creaking screen door again as the mailman continued on to the next house.

Evrett breathed again and sighed in relief. As he reached for the doorknob, something caught his attention. It was a small basket of pill bottles on the kitchen counter. Somehow he had not taken much notice of it before.

He took a closer look, examining the labels.

They all were prescribed to Phillip T. Repin. Some were antidepressants and others were to fight insomnia. It was clear Phil was dealing with some issues.

Is it over the guilt of what you did to Sam? Evrett wondered. As much as Evrett hoped his wife's death had affected Phil in some dramatic way, he figured it had more to do with his life before driving the truck.

A life that apparently had been full of secrets and lies—a type of life Evrett found himself also living now.

When this was all over, would he find himself in a similar state as Phil? Looking at the pills, Evrett imagined another path his life might have taken. Instead of filling his days with tracking down his targets, he could have wallowed away for endless hours. He could have quit work sooner, gone to therapy, allowed his grief to fester and poison his life.

No, this was the life he was meant to live now. He was driven to finish this.

Perhaps the pills would be the key to Phil's undoing. Evrett could sabotage the truck driver's prescriptions. He pictured Phil driving his big rig, fighting a drug induced sleep, only to pass out and careen off the side of the road.

Evrett couldn't do that, though. What if Phil careened into another car? He didn't want any more innocent people hurt by his actions. Stephanie started to creep up in his mind's eye and he knew it was time to leave.

"All right, Phil. When are you coming back?" Evrett said as he took one final glance at the calendar that hung on the refrigerator door. According to the schedule, Phil would be back in four days from what appeared to be his final trip. The rest of the months in the calendar were free of cities and route numbers scribbled in shaky handwriting.

"Having you home might work to my advantage. Be seeing you soon, Phil," Evrett said.

He lowered his baseball cap to conceal his face before leaving the trailer. Evrett quickly walked down the road and out of the trailer community. He had been sure to park farther away so no one took notice of his license plate.

Evrett started the Audi's engine and set out for home, a destination he would not see for several days.

41

CONGRATULATIONS, IT'S A BOY! Those four words echoed around the examination room and rushed in a great wave of emotions for Alec and Angela. After months of debating on whether or not to keep it a surprise, in the eighth month, the two changed their minds and asked the doctor to reveal the secret.

Looking at the sonogram, the doctor pointed out that they were indeed having a baby boy. Angela squeezed Alec's hand tightly. She was going to be happy either way, while Alec was ecstatic that it was a boy. He wasn't sure if a second child was in the mix and all he ever dreamed of was having a boy to play a simple game of catch with. His father was a baseball fan, but he never put on the glove in the backyard to throw with him. When he was a teenager, Alec promised himself that he would someday play catch with his son. Now, twenty-plus years later, that promise was in line to be upheld.

They stopped at a restaurant for a late dinner and then drove home, all while making plans to paint the baby's room blue and start brainstorming potential boy names. One of the names Alec threw out without explanation was Sam. He thought about honoring the woman whose death he felt guilty for, but at the same time, he was worried the name would constantly haunt him, so when Angela vetoed the name, he didn't put up a fight. They were able to narrow it down to a few names, but the final decision would be saved for later.

Once at home, Angela went right to the kitchen for more food—the baby was hungry again.

Alec went straight upstairs and continued upward into the attic. There, in the corner, were five old boxes. A decent layer of dust had collected on top of them, and Alec used his hand to clear it off to read the labels. He didn't see the one he wanted until he got to the fifth box.

He smiled as he read the label: OLD STUFF. It was generic, but he knew instantly that was the one he was looking for. He knelt down and opened the flaps that were crossed over on each other to keep the box closed.

Inside was an old orange Orioles T-shirt jersey with the number three on it below the name ROSSI. It was a customized shirt that Alec had purchased for his father, but never had the chance to deliver before he died.

The sight of the shirt made Alec choke up. He forgot it was in this box. He picked it up and held it close to his chest. He wished that his father was still around to see his soon-to-be-born grandson. He also wished he could have been there two weeks ago when in a small ceremony, Alec married the love of his life, Angela. His father was there for his first marriage, and he was there when it all fell apart. It would have been nice for him to be there the day it all came back together.

Alec let out a sigh, placed the shirt to the side and continued digging through the box. There were a lot of baseball knick-knacks, mostly giveaways he and his father had collected from their numerous trips to Camden Yards.

Beneath a playoff rally towel from 2012, Alec found what he was looking for. It was his black Rawlings baseball glove with gold lacing. He reached down and pulled it out, placing his left hand into the mitt.

"It still fits," he said, as he had expected it to.

It had been nearly ten years since he had put the glove on and it felt great. It took him back to his teenage years, playing American Legion ball with his father watching from the stands. Alec was a decent shortstop with a power arm, and his hit-for-contact skills drew the attention of a few scouts. He wasn't a major prospect, but after he led his high school team to the state finals in back-to-back years, the San Diego Padres took a flyer on him, selecting him in the thirty-third round of the 1997 MLB Amateur Draft.

It was an exciting day and his father was proud, even though the two agreed the best thing for him right now was to uphold his commitment to play baseball at the University of Maryland. After a decent freshman year, Alec tore his ulnar collateral ligament in his arm and had to get the famed Tommy John surgery. He never returned to the field as a collegiate player.

Alec had opportunities to play baseball his senior year, but he was heavily involved in news writing internships. He was a star in the media world and several newspapers came calling, but *The Baltimore Sun* inevitably won out, thus ending his baseball career.

He played in a few amateur adult leagues, but he gave that up about ten years ago when soreness in his throwing arm forced him to quit. He didn't want to have to go through Tommy John surgery and the rehab again.

But now that he had a future all-star on the way, he figured it may be time to get the glove out and hone his skills. He thought about all the possibilities. Coaching was something that never crossed his mind until now. He wondered how great it would be to coach Little League and perhaps American Legion. Maybe he could even work his way onto the high school coaching staff.

This was something that would take some investigation. It was late into the high school baseball season at this point in May, with the Maryland state playoffs in full swing. The state championship games would be played at Ripken Stadium in Aberdeen, Maryland, in about a week, Alec thought. Perhaps he should go.

He placed the glove back into the box and carried it and all its contents to his desk in the basement. He had a few shelves along the wall that were fairly bare, and he started pulling out the random bobbleheads, rally towels and baseball cards, placing them on display. On the very edge of the shelf, he placed his baseball glove next to his University of Maryland cap. He picked up his father's T-shirt jersey once more, this time without the emotional burden.

He decided right then that he was going to get it framed and placed on the wall. It was time he honored his father and not bury his memory in a box.

Alec placed the shirt on his desk in the basement before heading off to bed where Angela was waiting. Alec dreamt about his past life as a ballplayer and slept soundly through the night. He awoke early, and after a nice breakfast with Angela, he was back in the basement office hanging up his father's old jersey in a frame that was just wasting away in the corner of the basement. Alec was smiling at the framed memory when the pain behind his eyes started again.

"What the hell," he blurted out, pinching the upper part of his nose, right in between his eyes. As soon as he did that, the vision started.

He struggled to grab his recorder as the pain was stronger than it had ever been. He finally found it underneath a few sheets of paper on his desk and pressed the record button.

• • •

The Insomniac
By Alec Rossi
The Long and Short

A loud, passing horn awoke the tired truck driver as he slept in the bed in his big rig's cabin. He looked at the clock on the dash and it read three-thirty-one in the morning.

A cold sweat made him sit up in discomfort as he peeled the sticky T-shirt from his skin. He had only been asleep for about an hour, which was good for him, and he knew at this point, trying to go back to sleep was futile.

It took him three hours just to fall asleep and he had no time to try again.

For him, insomnia was never-ending.

He squeezed his way through the clutter of his cabin to the driver's seat. He turned the ignition and got his truck ready to get back onto the interstate.

Home was only three days away and he couldn't wait to get there, not that there was anything or anyone there waiting for him.

He began to pull out of the rest stop and on to a rather quiet Interstate 80. The insomniac passed a pair of trucks at another rest stop and thought about how nice it must be to sleep in.

After about an hour of driving east, hunger set in and he exited for a diner near Iowa City, Iowa. It was a diner he had stopped at several times over the last twenty years.

He pulled into the large, busy parking lot and parked in between a pair of Mack trucks.

Inside the diner, the majority of the tables were taken, but he was able to sit down at a booth against the window facing his truck.

"Can I start you off with some coffee?" the young waitress asked.

The insomniac looked up at her and took a second to answer. He was taken aback by her short black hair and nose ring.

"Um, yes, I'll have some," he stuttered. "Black, no sugar."

She smiled and walked away and he watched her every step. She was beautiful and everything he ever wanted. He could not figure out why she was stuck in a truck stop in Iowa, but then again, he knew the same question could be asked of him.

He picked up the menu and scanned the breakfast items, and when the waitress came back, she placed the coffee in front of him and pulled out her notepad and pen.

"Do you know what you would like?"

"Yes," he said, deferring to his usual. "I'll have the Southwestern omelet with hash browns and bacon. No toast."

"Is that it?" she asked.

The insomniac paused and looked up at her. He wanted desperately to ask her to sit down and eat with him, but the man who had the gall to do such a thing died many years ago.

"Yes, that's it," he finally said.

She walked away knowing she was being watched; she dealt with this every day.

As she went back into the kitchen, the insomniac sipped his coffee. It wasn't anything to brag about, but it was enough to get by.

"Kind of like my life," he said quietly to himself.

After years of traveling the country with several tons of freight, he couldn't help but be saddened by where he was today. He could have had a family to go home to. He could have had a bunch of medals on his wall. He could have had a life that others would aspire to live.

Instead, he was forgotten.

His breakfast came out as a light blue glow began to take over the horizon in the East.

Another day, he thought.

He watched a few trucks pull out, getting an early start. He poured ketchup on his plate and began to devour his meal. He realized halfway through the reason why he was so hungry was because he hadn't eaten a full meal since lunch the day before.

It must have been the excitement of getting home that made him forget about dinner.

For the insomniac, this wasn't any ordinary truck run; it was his last.

After twenty years in trucking, he was finally retiring, and he was ready for it.

It had been marked on his calendar for a year. He nearly walked away three years ago, but he powered on knowing that his retirement benefits would kick in.

"Would you like some more coffee?" the waitress asked, sneaking up from behind.

He hesitated briefly and decided retirement could wait a little bit longer. "Actually, could I get a hot tea instead? Sweetened?"

"Sure," she said.

"And could you put it in here," he said, handing over his thermal to-go mug.

"No problem."

The waitress walked into the kitchen and poured boiling hot water into the mug. She dropped a Lipton tea bag in when her boss interrupted.

"Table seven needs another order of eggs," he said, poking through the kitchen door.

The diner was understaffed, so her shift manager was waiting tables, too, but that just meant he was seating patrons and forcing her to do the rest of the work.

She struggled with anxiety and the stress of the moment started to flare up a panic attack. She put the tea on the counter and went to retrieve her purse to get the bottle of Xanax that her doctor prescribed. She spun the lid open and grabbed one pill as she filled a glass with water. She took a swig and swallowed the pill immediately.

The kitchen door flung opened, startling her and causing her to drop the lid.

"That means right away," he stated firmly.

"Okay, okay," she said. "I'm on it."

She couldn't see the lid so she set the bottle down on a shelf above the counter and left for table seven.

As she left the kitchen, she slammed the door shut to show her frustration and her bottle tipped over, spilling several pills into the tea.

She returned to the kitchen minutes later to see the bottle on its side with several pills lying on the shelf and on the counter.

"Damn it," she said, scooping the stray pills back into the bottle. She had no idea she was missing more than ten pills, all of which had dissolved in the steaming liquid.

The insomniac wasn't a stranger to Xanax. He had a prescription of his own. The waitress delivered the tea with a smile and an apology for the wait.

"No problem," he said, handing her thirty dollars. "This should cover it. Keep the change."

It was more than a forty percent tip, but she didn't feel bad taking it. She needed it more than he did.

Back in the cabin of the truck, he fired up the engine and pulled out of the lot.

"Back to the interstate," he said.

He drove more than fifteen miles before he started to feel groggy. He picked up the tea from his cup holder and finished the rest of the drink, thinking the extra packets of sugar he poured in would help.

He drove on another two miles before slumping over the wheel. His truck flew off the interstate and into a wooded area. It was traveling eighty miles per hour and sawed off a few smaller trees before the big one brought the off-road trek to a metal-crunching halt.

The insomniac slept through the whole ordeal.

He was never aware that this was his last day.

• • •

Alec grabbed two Aleve pills and water. He couldn't believe the headache he had. He had just jotted down all the details from his vision and passed out due to the pain. He had no idea why or how this was happening.

He recalled the similar pain he felt during his last vision. It was extremely odd and it had to be more than just a coincidence. Alec began to question everything.

Where are these stories coming from? That was the question running through his mind. At first, he thought it was just his brain breaking through the writer's block and piecing together ideas to formulate one story, but now, he didn't know what to think.

It *was* odd that they were all occurring about two months apart, but as he sat at his desk and looked through all his recordings and notes, the dates did not line up. The tenth of the month, twenty-first, eighth, ninth, eighteenth. There was no parallel other than the fact that he published each story bimonthly—and now the headaches.

He thought about Hawaii and how he perfectly described a place he had never seen before.

"No way," he said, as it dawned on him that he might be seeing real events. "It can't be."

He didn't believe in such things. He often joked with friends about the wackos who believe in psychic powers.

But that didn't stop him from opening up his Web browser. He typed in "Iowa City traffic" in the search line. He clicked on the live traffic view and saw that there were no backups on Interstate 80 in Iowa.

He wasn't satisfied, and he went to the local television station's website to scroll through the latest headlines, but there was no mention of a fatal truck accident on Interstate 80.

It was settled; he was just freaking out over nothing.

He returned upstairs to spend some time with Angela, chalking the headaches up to coincidence.

Later that evening, he sat down to write the story derived from his notes, and never did it dawn on him to check the Internet once more. Had he done so, he would have found the news story reporting the fatal truck accident that caused a ten-mile backup earlier that day on I-80 near Iowa City.

42

"MORE COFFEE?" said a waitress holding a glass pot of coal black liquid. It swirled back and forth as the woman placed her hand upon her hip. Evrett responded after a brief moment's hesitation.

"Yes, please."

The waitress topped his drink off and moved on to the next table.

Evrett was in a diner.

Somewhere. He had no clue.

The smell of the burnt coffee helped him come to his senses. Looking down at his plate, Evrett could tell that he had been at this particular diner for a while. Before him lay a plate with the last remaining pieces of a mostly consumed Belgian waffle.

His phone wasn't in his pocket, so he scanned his surroundings to find a shiny silver clock on the wall above the door to the kitchen. It was just after seven in the morning. His last memory was of him leaving Phil's trailer in the afternoon.

Evrett shook his head and clenched his fist tightly. He hated how he felt after a blackout. The loss of control and the missing hours of his life; it all angered Evrett. Every piece he had so carefully placed could come crashing down during one of his lost periods. Luckily, something had kept him from danger time and time again.

And now, Evrett had to put the puzzle back together.

He looked out the window of the diner. There were several cars and trucks parked out front. He could also see that it was early morning. From all this and his watch, Evrett assumed that he blacked out for about fifteen hours.

"Excuse me. Could I please have the check?" Evrett said to the waitress as she slowly passed by him.

"You betcha."

There was a Midwestern drawl to her accent. Evrett guessed that he was somewhere on Phil's delivery route. And if things went as they had in the past, Phil had joined the Bryants and the other departed targets.

Evrett left a twenty on the table and walked toward the exit. As he passed the counter, he took a peek at a menu by the hostess station.

He was in Iowa City, Iowa.

"You've got to be kidding me."

He stepped out in the summer air and pressed the key lock button on his Audi fob. The flashing headlight of his car was a beacon in the parking lot. At least that mystery was solved easily.

This blackout had been unusual in that it had come out of nowhere. Every other episode had come on when he was setting out to trail a target. While searching for a way to deal with Phil, Evrett had decided to save the trucker for when he returned home from his last job. It was as if something had decided it was time for him to go for Phil. Maybe the universe wanted Phil to pay for his past.

Evrett's Audi sped down the interstate. His GPS said he would be home in roughly fourteen hours, if he didn't stop. With the size of his tank and the miles between where he was and home, he knew that wouldn't be an option. Evrett yawned at the thought of the hours of road ahead of him.

It wasn't long, however, until he had to slow his car. The traffic in the eastbound lanes of Interstate 80 was crawling. At this speed he wouldn't be home until well into the late night hours. Evrett followed the flow of traffic and moved left into the passing lane.

"This doesn't look good," he said to himself. He figured an accident was the cause of the slow down in traffic.

After a few minutes of driving at a crawl, Evrett finally saw what slowed down his travels.

From the road Evrett could just see the back end of a tractor-trailer that had veered off the road and careened into the trees. It didn't appear as if any other cars had been involved in the accident.

Smaller trees lay tossed about like toothpicks in the wake of the truck. Deep scars in the ground led from the road to the truck's final resting place. The cab had caved almost completely in on itself, the fatal effect of a final mighty tree that helped stop the truck.

Evrett doubted that anyone had survived the crash.

And then it clicked. He knew that truck. He knew the driver. He had been brought here, just as he had been brought five times before.

Evrett knew Phil was dead.

The coroner's van next to the fire truck confirmed it. Eventually, the media would also corroborate that Phil had died on impact.

And so Evrett drove on.

He drove through Illinois and Indiana before crossing the state line into Ohio. It was here that his thoughts began to focus on Chase. After all these months of preparation and work, it was all coming back to Chase.

Evrett remembered that night spent tailing Chase around the suburbs of Cleveland. How naïve Evrett had been back then to think he could just deal with these targets in a simple manner without months of planning. Chase had shown him the error of his ways that night.

And while he may not be able to prove he played a role in the deaths of any of the targets on his list, Evrett couldn't deny there was some connection between himself and them. Every time one of them did die, he had been close by. Without his bugging and spying and trailing, he would not be here now. He knew that.

Just one left.

He would pour everything he had into confronting Chase. Perhaps he would relocate to Cleveland to make following Chase easier. There was nothing tying him down to Baltimore full time. Maybe he would rent a place for a few months.

A few miles into Pennsylvania, Evrett had to stop for gas again. He should have stopped earlier, but his mind had been elsewhere. While Evrett filled up at the pump, his stomach reminded him that he hadn't eaten in several hours.

Stepping into the convenience store attached to the gas station felt like stepping back into a different era. Evrett was more accustomed to the larger all-in-one gas stations that seemed to monopolize the market now.

A bell signaled Evrett's entrance into the store. He walked back to the far corner where there were several shelves of packaged donuts and cakes. Although Evrett usually watched what he ate, today he just felt like splurging.

The bell at the entrance jingled again, but Evrett didn't bother to look up. He was debating how many Tastykakes he was going to buy. The unmistakable crack of a gunshot demanded his attention and sent the donuts to the floor.

Evrett dropped to the floor, too, with his heart racing.

"All right, bitches! All your wallets, up front, now! You, empty the cash register! Hurry it up!"

Evrett scrambled to get himself out of the gunman's line of vision. He pulled his legs up to his chest to keep them from being seen. He had been on the road for hours. His body was stiff and his arms were sore. The last thing he needed was to be confronted in a gas station by a punk with a gun.

He heard a woman scream as the gunman grabbed at her purse. Evrett had not taken notice of how many people were in the store. He peeked his head just slightly around the corner of the shelf and looked toward the front counter.

He saw the cashier, a young kid with large gauges in his ears, frantically trying to open the cash register. There was no way that kid was going to risk his life over a few hundred bucks, so he did what the gunman demanded.

In addition to the cashier were two other patrons, a woman in her early forties and an older man. Evrett placed his age at just shy of eighty. That left the gunman.

His face was covered partially by a black hood. He was thin and Evrett thought he couldn't be much older than the cashier.

"Give me your purse, bitch!" the gunman shouted.

The woman's purse was wrapped around her arm. Her shaking hands wouldn't let her undo the strap. The gunman pulled it forcefully, tearing it and sending the woman tumbling to the ground.

"Put the cash in that," he said to the cashier and tossed the purse onto the counter. The gunman spun to the old man.

"You're next, pops. Wallet. Now."

The old man did as he was told.

"Anyone else in this bitch?" the punk with the gun asked. He stood up on his toes to peer over the shelves. Evrett jumped back. He looked forward and saw his own reflection in the glass of the refrigerator that held the dairy products of the store.

"Oh, shit," Evrett said and rolled to the other side of the shelf.

It was too late. He had been spotted.

"Thought I wouldn't see you too?" the gunman asked. He was standing next to the woman who was still on the floor.

"Look, I don't want any trouble," Evrett said with his hands in the air.

The last thing he wanted was to be involved in this altercation. He didn't want to lose his wallet, but he also didn't want to be questioned by the police once this was all over. That was if he could get out of this store alive.

"I don't care what you want. Your wallet. Now. Send it up here."

Evrett begrudgingly did as he was told. He was no longer in control and it infuriated him.

"Good choice," the gunman said.

He bent down and picked up the wallet. The lights in the gas station flickered suddenly. Everyone in the store took notice of it.

"What the hell was that?" the gunman shouted. He spun around, pointing the revolver at the cashier.

"I don't know. The store's old."

"The store's old, huh? I think you just pressed some kind of alert button. That's what you did, jackass."

"I didn't. I swear. We don't even have something like that here!"

Evrett watched the confrontation. He could tell the gunman was losing control of himself. Evrett feared things were going to get much worse for all of them. If he could surprise the gunman, he would be able to take him down. But Evrett didn't want to risk being the hero. There were more important things for him to finish.

"You've got ten seconds to finish stuffing that purse. Go!"

The cashier placed the final bills in the purse and pushed it toward the gunman's outstretched hand.

The lights flickered again as the gunman snatched the purse. He turned around, aiming his revolver at the old man, the woman, and finally Evrett.

If he was going to start shooting, it would be now.

The lights flickered one final time and Evrett saw the gunman's revolver quickly point toward the corner of the store where no one stood.

"Who the hell?" the perplexed gunman said before firing a shot. The bullet zipped through the air and lodged into the wall.

The cashier ducked below the counter and the woman let out a high-pitched scream. The gunman had been startled by something.

Again, appearing rattled, he fired at nothing and then bolted for the exit. As he did, he went flying head first into the door with enough force to shatter the glass. To most everyone, he tripped; but Evrett saw something else. The revolver and purse flew out of his hands, spilling the money from the register. Bills began blowing all over the parking lot.

Evrett didn't waste time. He got up and hurried past the woman and old man. He didn't want any of them seeing his face. He needed to get out of here.

The gunman lay where he fell, half of him in the store, half of him out. He wasn't moving. Evrett crouched down next to him. A pool of blood was forming underneath the gunman's still body. The glass from the door must have done some damage. Evrett didn't move the body to find out.

His eyes quickly focused on his wallet. It had fallen out of the purse and come to rest a few feet out on the sidewalk. He snatched it and raced to his car. Within a minute, Evrett was on the road, getting as much distance between him and the gas station as possible.

It wasn't until he was well into the next town that Evrett began to process what had just happened. His heart still beat quickly. How close had he come to death?

Evrett thought about those last few moments in the store. He had been sure the gunman was going to shoot him and the other hostages. But something had spooked the gunman. He had fired two shots at...what? As far as Evrett could tell there was no one else in the store.

Either way, Evrett was thankful. The universe mustn't be done with him yet.

He chuckled.

Get used to it, Evrett. It might not be the last time you have a gun pointed at you, he thought.

Chase was next on his list after all.

As he crossed into Maryland, Evrett's thoughts were of the surveillance cameras in the convenience store. If the cameras were working, surely the police would be looking to identify the man who fled the scene. If the station had a camera at the pump, it was also quite possible police would have his license plate. He had been under this type of stress before. If the police came knocking he would have a story ready for them.

No knock would come. Over the next few weeks, Evrett kept a low profile, just as he had done after dealing with the Bryants. Eventually, the worry of police coming to question him faded from his mind. He had no way of knowing that when police tried to view the security tapes they found nothing but swirling static. Something had interfered with the tapes.

Or in Evrett's case, intervened.

43

THE BALL SOARED RIGHT PAST the goalie's stick and into the net for the eighth time in the game. It was Chase Valenti's sixth goal and he was proving to be unstoppable, just like he was when he was wearing the light blue jersey at Johns Hopkins.

But this wasn't Division I men's lacrosse. Far from it.

It was an intramural game on a small rec field in Cleveland, and Chase was schooling everyone. After he scored his sixth goal, he did a dance and acted like he was brushing dirt off his left shoulder.

The majority of the other team ignored it, but a first-time intramural player took offense.

Thomas Whitmore, a young twenty-two-year-old who also had failed at Division I lacrosse, wasn't happy to see another failure doing better than him.

As Chase walked back to midfield, Thomas smirked at him, gave him the finger and said, "Screw you."

Chase stopped in his tracks and spun around quickly. He looked at the kid and didn't even say a word. Instead, he walked straight up to him and cross-checked him right in the throat, crushing his windpipe.

Thomas' teammates did not react in retaliation as he squirmed in pain on the ground, while Chase's teammates laughed and walked back to midfield.

A pair of players helped him off the field and called 9-1-1.

"Yes, there was an accident at the lacrosse rec fields in Garfield Heights… We believe he took an accidental stick to the neck. Come quick," the one player said calmly.

He clicked off the phone, leaned forward and whispered in Thomas's ear, "You'd be smart to tell them the same story. Those who tell the truth do not live long enough to repeat the story to a judge."

In extreme pain, Thomas didn't nod, but he understood. He knew he messed with the wrong person.

Chase didn't just own the lacrosse field; he owned all of Garfield Heights. It was his turf and if anyone messed with him or anyone in his crew, they wound up with their pictures on the HAVE YOU SEEN ME flyers that show up in everyone's mailbox.

Chase had personally put eight such flyers into circulation in the last two years. Two of the missing persons were disrespectful like Thomas, another four owed Chase money and two others were high-ranking members of a rival cross-town gang.

Thomas would later pull through at the hospital and remain silent to avoid becoming the ninth.

• • •

Chase dipped his right pinky finger into the bag of white powder and then rubbed it along his gums. He felt the tingle and knew it was the good stuff; Columbian from what the man in the white suit told him.

He placed it back into the duffle bag to complete the five-kilo order and handed over an even larger duffle filled with $300,000 in cash.

"Here's your cash, non-sequential bills, as requested," Chase said. "We'll get you your percentage of the sales when we sell out."

They shook hands and the man in the white suit walked out with his two bodyguards.

Chase sat back on his couch and opened up a bag for himself and the rest of his captains.

"Boys, let's have some fun before we get to business."

The Rogue Sevens all laughed and pulled up chairs.

Two hours passed and all seven gang leaders were out cold.

• • •

The throbbing in his head was non-stop. Chase could not believe how potent the cocaine he just bought was, and for that, he just bumped up his asking price.

He told the man in the white suit that he'd sell it for $75 a gram and $1,200 for an ounce, but after last night, Chase decided that he was going to have his men sell it for $150 a gram and $1,600 an ounce.

"This stuff is too good to be lumped in with the rest," he told his dealers.

Chase was supposed to give twenty percent of the earnings to the man in the white suit, but with his decision to charge more, he decided to pay only twenty percent of his original asking price.

"He won't know how much we actually sell it for," Chase told his second-in-command, Jerome Markus. "Just do it. Leave the rest to me."

It's a scam that Chase had pulled often on his providers. It was why he rolled around town in a black Mercedes SL550 decked out with all the latest accessories. It was why he wore the finest suits when he was not playing lacrosse. And it was why he was one of the most feared men in town.

Chase had come a long way from his days in Baltimore, selling little bags of marijuana to college students to running a menacing drug ring in Cleveland.

The narcotics squad of the Cleveland Police Department, as well as the DEA, had Chase's picture hanging on their wall, but he had been excellent at not incriminating himself. He also had a loyal group of dealers who took an oath not to talk if arrested. So far, five dealers had been busted and not a single one had pointed a finger. After they served their time, they hoped to cash in on the reward for their loyalty. One already got out of jail on appeal, and for his silence, he was promoted to the highest possible spot, second-in-command. Jerome was that man, and he was a model of loyalty. The rest of the Rogue Sevens looked up to him.

The abandoned home where Chase ran his operation was off the radar. The authorities constantly sat outside a different structure several blocks away. There, Chase had built a tunnel system from the basement to a city sewer, where he could exit onto the street via a service entrance. The police had searched the home twice, and on both occasions, a high school friend of Chase's, who was on the drug task force, told him the search was coming. That friend did not want anything to happen to his young son.

Chase remained in the house for both searches and both searches turned up empty. The tunnel wasn't discovered as it was in a secret, well-hidden passage under the basement stairs.

After a second failed search three months ago, a judge had since denied requests to search again because the circumstantial evidence was no more than what the police had before. They needed something new, something big, to catch a break against the Rogue Sevens' boss.

With the bodies piling up, the organized crime division of the FBI was about to start an investigation in cooperation with the DEA, but the task force hadn't been set up just yet. The FBI was still getting the pieces together to begin its investigation.

Nevertheless, the heat was coming.

Chase remained confident, however, in his tactics. He was sure that he would not get caught.

He was infallible.

• • •

Three months later, the man in the white suit arrived again, this time with double the order. The Rogue Sevens made more than $1.5 million on the first batch of cocaine alone. Chase reported to the man in the white suit that they made $750,000 and gave him a little more than the twenty percent with another duffle filled with $200,000.

Chase netted $1 million, while the man in the white suit, who paid only $50,000 for the cocaine to begin with, netted $350,000. He should have amassed $800,000, whereas Chase should have banked $650,000.

If the man in the white suit were to find out, Chase would be dead.

But he was, of course, infallible.

"I have brought along ten kilos this time," the man in the white suit said in a thick Columbian accent. "You think you can sell it in the same amount of time?"

Chase smiled, "No problem."

The white suit picked up the duffle bag loaded with $600,000—a wise investment for Chase, knowing he could turn it into $2 million easily—and sifted through the bills.

"This time, sell it for double what you did last time. The demand is there."

Chase was taken aback by this and stuttered out the gates in his response, "Uh, um, I'm not sure our clientele has that kind of money."

It was a bold face lie, but Chase saw his net profit cut in half. In essence, he had worked his ass off for three months for what would end up being about $700,000, even less after spreading the wealth around the Sevens.

He could jack up the prices even higher than before, but he knew inside that he'd definitely lose the majority of his clients, and first-time walk-ups were not going to fork over that kind of loot. Plus, he had already priced out a large group with the last batch.

The man in the suit stepped closer to Chase, and for the first time in a long time, he was afraid. The six-foot-three man swung his right hand onto Chase's left shoulder and assumed a firm grip. Chase heard the gold cuff links rattle as the man began to rub his shoulder.

"I know you can do it, son," he said. "So do it."

Chase didn't need to hear the "or else." It was implied.

• • •

The man in the white suit got into his car with his pair of bodyguards and drove away. Something wasn't sitting right with the man, whom his closest friends in Columbia called Humberto. Nevertheless, he decided to continue trusting Chase for a little bit longer.

Right then his car came to an abrupt stop with a loud pop and hissing sound. The front right tire deflated in an instant. He was only four blocks away from Chase's safe house and due at the airport in two hours.

He and his guards got out and assessed the damage. It was a rental car they picked up at the airport, and they hoped that there was a spare in the trunk.

"All right, boys," Humberto said. "Can you get this fixed quickly?"

Both guards exchanged perplexed stares. Humberto saw this immediately.

"Wait, do neither of you know how to change a tire?" he asked, and both shook their heads signaling no. "Estáis de broma!"

"I can do it," a voice interjected from behind them.

Humberto turned and saw a man smiling behind him. "I can change it," he reiterated. "Pop the trunk. Let's have a look at the spare."

"Grasias," he said. "Alejo, pop the trunk."

Alejo, the taller of the two bodyguards and the one who was driving, opened the trunk. The man started digging for the tire.

"What's your name, my friend?" Humberto asked.

"Rashard," he answered. "You?"

"Call me Bert," he said.

Rashard pulled out a full size spare and the jack, "I'll be done in about ten minutes."

He was precise. Exactly ten minutes later, he was spinning the last lug nut back into position.

"How can we ever repay you?" Humberto asked.

Rashard looked around and turned to him, "You have any goods?"

Humberto smiled and responded, "Whatcha looking for?"

Again, Rashard looked around, and whispered, "Crack? You got any? I'm looking for more of that good stuff."

"Well, it's your lucky day," Humberto said. "Good fortunes allowed the right car to break down in front of you today. Alejo, get him an ounce."

"Ounce!" Rashard shouted, quickly calming down, "I mean, an ounce, jeez. This will save me from dropping a buck-fifty with the Sevens."

Humberto looked at him with a puzzled look.

"One fifty?" he asked. "You don't say. For a gram?"

"Yeah, I thought it was a rip, but the shit was really good. Top notch."

There was a pause and then, "Well, young man. It appears I was mistaken. It *was* luck that allowed me to break down in front of you."

Humberto snapped his fingers and gestured for the men to get back into the car. He jumped into the back seat, rolled down the window and tossed out another ounce to Rashard.

"Sell that one, my friend, and get yourself something nice."

He rolled up the window as Alejo started to drive.

"I take it we're not going to the airport," Alejo said.

Humberto didn't say a word and Alejo knew exactly what that meant.

44

LURKING IN THE SHADOWS OF THE ALLEY, Evrett waited patiently. He's scouted this Washington, D.C., alley from the safety of his car every night for the last two weeks, and every night, a grey late nineties model Ford Taurus sedan had pulled up with a single male who handed out little bags of cocaine for large wads of cash.

By Evrett's estimation, the dealer, who went by the street name of "Two Bit," averaged ten transactions a night. Two Bit always showed up at around one in the morning and stayed for about forty minutes. Evrett also noticed that a police patrol car would drive by no later than twelve-fifty and would not appear again until at least one-fifty. The dealer knew this and used the window to his advantage.

For sixteen consecutive nights, Evrett just watched and listened. Tonight, the seventeenth night, he planned to introduce himself, informally, of course.

After a few of the dealer's regulars all made their purchases in the first ten minutes, as they did nightly, Evrett emerged from the darkness and walked toward the car parked at the end of the alley. With both hands in the pockets of his khaki cargo shorts, Evrett approached the passenger side.

He leaned over and peered into the open window, as all the junkies did.

Evrett gave a paranoid look left and right to make sure no one was around. He wasn't afraid, but he noticed that nine out of ten junkies did just that before speaking to Two Bit.

"Do you know where I can find a liquor store?" he asked, reciting an opening line used by all of Two Bit's buyers, loyal returnees and recommended newcomers. Evrett had a parabolic microphone set up in his car and he heard all the conversations, so he knew exactly how to set up a deal.

Two Bit responded after hearing the key phrase, "There's one about three blocks up Minnesota Avenue."

Evrett was expecting that response, and followed with the next key phrase. "Do they have the premium package?"

Two Bit looked Evrett over. He saw him shaking like a junkie needing a fix in the worst way.

"Who recommended you?" he asked, and Evrett sensed Two Bit's skepticism. But Evrett was prepared and he knew how to lock in the deal.

"Jay Sizz told me you could hook me up," Evrett said, picking the name of the only man that Two Bit exited his car to greet. It was three nights ago and the two shared a half-hearted hug followed by a hand-slap.

"What's up, Jay Sizz," Two Bit said to him.

That was it. As soon as Evrett had his in, he prepared for this very moment. He knew he wouldn't get past the initial greeting without a name, and his hard work paid off.

"Come over to my side," Two Bit said, motioning with his right hand. The tattoo on the back of his hand near the webbing between the thumb and the index finger indicated he was affiliated with a local gang.

This didn't scare Evrett whatsoever. Not anymore.

He slowly walked around the back of the car just so Two Bit

didn't get the opportunity to see him. If there was a chance that Evrett was going to give off any subliminal warning signs, he wanted to make sure Two Bit didn't see them.

As he came around to the window, Two Bit hit the button for it to automatically open.

"I'll need eighty," the dealer said.

"You got it," Evrett said, pulling out his gloved right hand, holding a Taser stun gun. He planted it right against the dealer's chest and let the charge go for ten seconds. The dealer flopped like a fish out of water as Evrett reached into the car with his gloved left hand. He grabbed the Glock 23 .40 caliber pistol, which was tucked into his baggy jeans.

Seventeen days ago, Evrett saw the dealer showing off the gun to friends, or perhaps associates, outside a pizza parlor about ten minutes north of where he stood now. Evrett followed him to this location later that night and began his stakeout.

Evrett slid the gun into a holster he purchased especially for this occasion and concealed it under his un-tucked button shirt.

He removed the Taser from the dealer's chest and ran for the alley. Dazed and confused, the dealer remained incapacitated before passing out, as Evrett darted down the alley. His car was two blocks away, and once inside, he drove away east out of downtown D.C.

After a few blocks, Evrett reached into his pocket, pulled out a prepaid phone he bought earlier that week and dialed 9-1-1.

"Nine, one, one, what is your emergency?" the responder asked.

"A drug dealer is very badly injured in his car parked along Minnesota Ave, near Twenty-Second."

Evrett clicked off immediately and removed the battery and sim card. He would smash all the components when he got home.

A few minutes later, a pair of D.C. patrolmen found the dealer unconscious in his car. He slowly came to as the officers pulled him out of the car, and the bag of cocaine that was in his lap and ready to be handed to Evrett fell to the ground. The officers immediately handcuffed the dealer, and an hour later, after a very tired judge signed the search warrant for the car, the police found enough drugs to put the dealer away for at least twenty-five years.

It would have been for life had Evrett left the sidearm. The Glock had been responsible for the deaths of seven people.

Evrett was determined to make that number eight.

With the unregistered firearm that could never be linked to him, Evrett smiled. His plan worked flawlessly. He got the gun he needed and he assumed the previous owner would be going to jail for a long time. The police wouldn't waste their time trying to find the man who tased a low-life junkie, and Two Bit would never dare report the unregistered gun missing. It would send him to death row. Perhaps, if Two Bit somehow eluded jail time, he'd do whatever he could to find the junkie who ripped him off, but it would be pointless. Evrett wasn't a junkie and the dealer would never look in the right place, let alone the right city.

• • •

Back at his home, Evrett ran up to his office. He placed the gun on the table and shined his desk light on it. The serial number was filed off, as predicted. He didn't have a chance to check before his getaway, and now that he could see he had the type of gun he was looking for, he knew his mission was officially a success.

Now, he could get on with killing Chase.

He was set to drive to Cleveland later the next day to begin his surveillance of Chase. He was certain it would take time to find a weakness and he was prepared to spend months in Cleveland in order to get it done. Through his research, he knew there was no sneaking into Chase's home and setting up an accident. The only way to kill Chase was to walk right up to him and blow him away with the newly acquired gun. He would toss the illegal firearm into a river and return home. No one would ever suspect him. With all the enemies Chase had made, it would be easy for Evrett to slip away undetected.

It was a crazy thought months ago, but as time passed and the realization of what kind of monster Chase had become, Evrett knew that this was his only option.

Evrett released the clip from the firearm. All thirteen bullets were in the clip, and a fourteenth was loaded into the chamber.

"One for good luck," Evrett said. He looked up at the newspaper clipping of Chase, a printout from the Internet, hanging on his wall. "This one is for you."

Evrett walked over to the wall and pulled down the picture. He was leaving tomorrow for Cleveland and he no longer had a need for this picture.

In fact, all of the materials he had collected on the prior seven targets were no longer needed, but for some reason, he had held onto them in his office.

Julia nearly stumbled across this information and Evrett knew he couldn't have anyone find it now, especially after what he planned to do in Cleveland. He began gathering all the paperwork that could connect him to any of his first seven targets and placed them into a box. He filled it rather quickly and carried it down stairs to his fireplace. He threw on a log and covered it with paper. He lit an entire packet of matches and watched the papers turn black, curl up and disappear.

He went back upstairs and filled the box three more times. After he emptied the fourth box, he retrieved his laptop and iPad. He began deleting most of the audio, video and picture files. The only thing he kept on his computer and iPad was the information on Chase. That would be deleted as soon as he was deleted.

After the last set of files were erased from his computer, he left the office for his bedroom. He would pack in the morning and leave for Cleveland.

• • •

The rent was a little more than expected, but it was the price for revenge. Evrett gave the landlord cash and he signed the lease under the name of Stephen Wallace. In a neighborhood like Chase's, background checks were often times too arduous a task for some landlords to worry about. The man standing in front of Evrett fit that profile, and with an extra hundred bucks, he was allowed to sign on the dotted line without any questions. The lazy landlord did ask for a driver's license, and the fake Ohio license Evrett prepared was passable. It took Evrett three attempts, but the how-to video online helped him produce a passable fake ID.

The apartment was a glorified studio above a small shop along Turney Avenue, yet it was perfect for everything Evrett needed. With a main "living room" section with a two-pane window that overlooked Turney Avenue, it had enough space for Evrett to live comfortably over the next few months.

Keeping a low profile was key and that made this apartment necessary—and it was just another reason for Evrett to kill Chase. He was in this situation because of him.

If it wasn't for that video, he would not be in Cleveland.

And if it wasn't for Chase being a careless human being, he may have put down the camera phone and saved Sam.

Chase could have saved Sam. Evrett analyzed the video enough to know that Chase had ample time to run to Sam's car and at least make an effort to free her before the explosion.

That video was the first thing he watched when Evrett set up his computer equipment on the desk. He then placed fresh sheets on the bed and emptied a box full of kitchen accessories. Lastly, he placed a picture of Sam next to his bed on the makeshift nightstand.

It was nothing like home, but it would do.

Once settled in, Evrett got right to work.

First things first, he had to locate Chase. Evrett wasn't lucky enough to find him at the last known address. More than a year and a half had passed since Evrett's last trip to Cleveland, and Chase had moved on to a new place, said the current owners of the former Valenti residence. Evrett questioned them earlier in the day over the phone and got no viable information on the new location of Chase. He played the role of the lacrosse director again, hoping not to draw up any suspicion.

Knowing that it was a strong possibility that he'd have to find Chase, Evrett prepared as best as he could from Baltimore.

Evrett had scoured numerous clips from online news articles on Chase, and in a few of them, he saw a man named Owen Crawford, attorney at law.

He was a crooked lawyer, but he was good at his craft, which annoyed the hell out of the district attorney's office, as well as all branches of law enforcement in the region.

Evrett figured that Crawford would eventually lead him to Chase.

It was nearing four o'clock and Evrett felt inspired to get started. It was day one of what was to be many days in Cleveland.

He grabbed a black Jansport satchel, filled with his spying equipment, and tossed it over his right shoulder. Wearing an un-tucked blue and white plaid button shirt, he made sure his Glock was concealed. He didn't plan on using it today, but he wanted to be ready for any impromptu actions.

He walked outside and down the sidewalk, passing his Audi, which was parked in an alley alongside the building. He ventured a few blocks north on Turney, with the sole intention of getting to Crawford's office before it closed for the day. It was exactly ten blocks from his apartment and the two-story residential building turned commercial was just as sketchy as the man on the sign outside. Evrett curled his nose at the smiling face of Crawford.

"Weasel," he said, wondering how any human being could willfully defend a piece of shit like Chase.

Evrett climbed the short, five-step concrete stairway to the front porch. The door had an OPEN sign hanging on the window, making it look more like a convenience store than a legal office. When he opened the door, he fully expected the stereotypical chime of a bell.

Sitting at a desk in what used to be a large foyer was a young woman. She smiled quickly and asked if she could be of any assistance.

"Yes, I'd like to see Mr. Crawford," Evrett said.

She sighed before answering with a thick Puerto Rican accent, "Mr. Crawford isn't here. He left for the evening."

Evrett had a few plans of attack for this evening, but he knew he always had to be ready for the moment when his improvisational skills would be put to the test.

This was one of those moments.

Reading the nameplate on the desk, he saw that the secretary, Ms. Sabelia Cavillo, had a set of keys with a Honda logo on it. He thought for a second as Sabelia assumed he was processing the information she just gave him.

"Okay, well, thank you," he said. "I'll just come back later."

Evrett turned to walk out as she countered, "Would you like to leave a message?"

"No thanks," he said. "Have a good night."

Once outside, he scanned the area. There were a few cars parked out front, but not one of them was a Honda. However, in the alley alongside the law firm was a pair of vehicles, one was a 1987 Honda Accord hatchback. He saw the back windows were cracked open, which meant he could leave his lock-picking set inside his satchel. Evrett estimated that new tires would cost about five hundred dollars, so he pulled out his wallet, gathered eight hundred and slid it through the crack, watching it fall to the floor of the backseat. Scanning the area for witnesses, and seeing no one, he then pulled out a Smith and Wesson switchblade—one of his many purchases prior to leaving Baltimore—and slashed the back tire on the right side.

After a loud pop and a burst of air, the tire deflated quickly. Evrett did the same to the other three tires, making sure to check his surroundings before committing the crime. No one saw him.

He ran back into the office, much to the surprise of Sabelia.

"Miss Cavillo," he said, acting a little fretted. "Do you know who parks along the alley here?"

"Well, I do."

"A white Honda?" he asked.

"Yes, why?"

Evrett could hear the level of alertness raise in her voice. "Someone must have slashed the tires. It's basically sitting on the rims."

She jumped up from her desk, grabbing her cellphone along the way, and ran outside with Evrett. She covered her gasp and muttered several curse words in Spanish.

"Did you see anyone?" she finally asked.

"No, I mean, it was like this when I got out here. I just figured you might know whose car it was. I didn't expect it to be yours. I'm sorry."

She bought the lie and dialed the police. Evrett apologized once again for something she would never blame him for and he walked away. From across the street, he watched as a patrol car pulled into the alley about ten minutes after she placed the call to 9-1-1. Sabelia was there waiting and waved the officers toward her. The two patrolmen stepped out of the car and began the tedious task of preparing a report for a crime that they knew would likely never be solved.

As the interview process began, Evrett darted across the street and into the law firm. The front door could not be seen from the alley, so it was easy for him to slip inside without Sabelia noticing. He walked past her desk and to the door with the nameplate reading CRAWFORD. He put on his gloves, and when he turned the doorknob, he found it to be locked. It was a simple lock, though, and Evrett had it picked in less than ten seconds.

Inside was an office that did not match the rest of the house. It was clear that Crawford spent thousands renovating, as the walls were comprised of dark rosewood paneling and built-in bookshelves, littered with legal literature. The desk in the center of the room looked presidential with a luxurious brown leather chair tucked nicely underneath. A few papers were scattered on the desk, but for the most part, Crawford was organized, which greatly shocked Evrett.

He locked the door behind him and quickly went to work, setting up an untraceable microphone in an air vent to the right of the entranceway, below a window that overlooked the small, fenced-in backyard. He quickly tested the microphone, because he knew he would not get back inside the room without having to break in through the front door, which included a more sophisticated lock and a state-of-the-art alarm system. It was for that same reason that he placed a second bug in the air vent on the opposite side of the room.

Once placed, he peered out the window behind the desk to see Sabelia still speaking with the police officers in the alley. His escape should have been easy, but a slam of a door in the hallway signified that he was no longer alone in the building. It also meant that his exit strategy had to change, and it had to change quickly.

He ran to the window on the right, unlocked it, slid it open and jumped into the backyard. He was fortunate that the window did not have a screen to bypass. He reached up and slid the window shut before sprinting for the fence at the end of the yard. He couldn't relock the window from the outside, so he would just have to hope that Crawford didn't notice it for a few days. Evrett scaled the six-foot chain-linked fence rather easily and he leisurely strolled down the alley and back out onto Turney. He returned to his apartment fifteen minutes later.

Evrett ordered Chinese and relaxed for the remainder of the evening. Tomorrow was set to be a big day.

• • •

The smartphone buzzed atop the nightstand, making enough noise to wake Evrett up. It was shortly after six in the morning and it was Julia's name lighting up on the screen. It was the eighth time she had called in four weeks and the seven prior calls all went unanswered. Number eight was no different.

Evrett sat up and stretched, letting out a loud groan. Five minutes later, he was lacing up his running shoes and heading out the door.

He ran about five miles, including a mile stretch through the park where he witnessed Chase kill a man, Denny Yanish, according to the news reports. After a shower and a breakfast bar, he grabbed his satchel and left. It was time to go back to Crawford's office.

This time, he took his Audi and parked in an alley on the opposite side of the road. There, he set up his audio equipment, and after Crawford staggered in at nine-forty, Evrett started recording.

Crawford was rather quiet in his office, and for an hour, all Evrett heard were papers rustling and the punching of keys on the keyboard of his computer. During this time, Evrett slipped into the alley aside the office and placed a GPS tracker under the left rear wheel-well of Crawford's maroon Lexus I 250 SC Sport convertible. He tested the signal in the car and it worked perfectly.

At eleven fifteen, when Crawford was dead silent—perhaps sneaking in a nap—Evrett decided it was time to break the silence. He picked up his phone and dialed Crawford's office number. Sabelia, who showed up in a taxi ten minutes before Crawford, answered.

"Crawford Law Offices, how may I direct your call," she said.

"Owen Crawford, please," Evrett said. "Tell him it's urgent."

"Who's calling?"

"Tell him it's about Chase Valenti. This is Sam Okanji."

She hit hold and Evrett heard silence for about twenty seconds before Crawford picked up.

"Sam? What's going on?"

Now, was the moment of truth. The only thing Evrett could not find in his research was a correlation between Sam Okanji and Owen Crawford. He hoped he only knew him by name and not by voice.

Here goes nothing, Evrett thought.

"Yes," he said, softly.

"What's going on? Why are you calling me? In fact, *how* are you calling me?"

"I fired my old lawyer and I said I was adding you, so they let me call you," Evrett said.

"And what made you do that?"

"Look, I don't have long. I did it so I could get you a message. The feds were here yesterday. They interrogated me for hours. They know I was involved in the Yanish murder. There was a witness. We chased someone in the woods and he drove away before we could find him. And, well, they found him. He's picked me and Chase out of a photo lineup. They were pressing me to give up Chase, but I never did. Still, they can't be far away from picking up Chase. I figured you'd want a heads up."

Crawford knew exactly what Evrett was talking about. Chase met with him following the Yanish murder and told him that there was a potential witness. Crawford said he'd keep an ear out and check his sources at the station to find out who it was if the brave soul ever wanted to commit what would inevitably be suicide. Crawford's sources had led to the disappearance of two key witnesses already. Now he had to start the legwork for number three.

"Thank you, Sam," he said after processing the information. "I'll get right on this and I'll work up some paperwork to become your lawyer."

"Don't waste your time. I'll tell them the lawyer I called declined and I'll find new representation. I don't want anyone to connect the dots here. Besides, they think I'm calling Harvey Tarnowitz."

"Good work, Sam. Good work."

Crawford hung up the phone and pulled out his cellphone.

Evrett also ended the call on his end and quickly picked up the head phones to start listening in on the fallout of his phone call.

It was perfect and Crawford took the bait like a hungry fish; the hook set deep into his gills.

Evrett found the name Sam Okanji in the news a few weeks after Denny Yanish was brutally beaten to death in Garfield Park Reservation. Okanji was arrested and eventually sentenced to five years in jail for drug possession. Even though it had been dark that night, Evrett recognized Sam's mug shot as one of the assholes in the park. Sam reportedly refused to give up any of his associates and quietly went to jail knowing he'd someday be like Jerome Markus.

Little did Sam know, his trusted loyalty would help lead to the demise of Chase. Evrett loved the irony.

Crawford dialed furiously and tapped his fingers on the desk. Someone answered on the other end, and Evrett could only hear Crawford's side of the conversation. He was hoping he was a speakerphone kind of guy, but that didn't pan out.

"Yeah, it's Crawford."

Pause.

"You heard anything about a witness in the Yanish murder?"

Pause.

"Well, look into it. I have a source who says there is."

Pause.

"I don't care. Look into it and get back to me."

Crawford clicked off and dialed another number. He went through a similar line of questioning and orders before dialing the number Evrett had been waiting for.

"Chase, it's Crawford."

Pause.

"We need to meet. You at the safe house?"

Pause.

"Okay. I'll be there in ten."

Crawford clicked off, gathered some belongings and darted out the door.

"I'm due in court," Evrett overheard him saying to Sabelia. "Be back in a few hours."

Evrett watched him climb into his Lexus and drive out of the alley onto Turney. Evrett turned on his car and followed at a safe distance—about five blocks away at all times—with the GPS tracker guiding him.

Eventually, the dot on the screen stopped moving and Evrett slowly pulled onto the same street. He passed the Lexus and parked about a hundred feet up the road. He didn't know which house Crawford ran into, but just being on the right road was enough for Evrett.

Nevertheless, he remained to see if he could spot Crawford leave one of the many small houses on the street. It took about thirty minutes, but eventually, Crawford emerged from the very house he was parked in front of.

Not very sly, Evrett thought.

If Chase only knew how careless his lawyer was.

Crawford sped away and Evrett remained. It was now time for him to shift his focus to Chase. He would retrieve the tracker from Crawford's car later.

Evrett drove around the block and repositioned his car so that he had a better view of Chase's apparent safe house. It was quiet for two hours until a black sedan drove up and a man in a white suit stepped out.

This piqued Evrett's interest, but he would never remember why.

45

THOMAS ROMAN ROSSI WEIGHED IN at eight pounds, seven ounces. Angela held him close as she lay in the hospital bed. She stared into his blue eyes and smiled, while Alec gently squeezed her loose hand. A happy family was born.

Two days later, Thomas was introduced to his new home. Alec carried him in his arms around the whole house giving him the tour. He told Thomas about every room as if he were a realtor trying to sell the place to him.

He took Thomas to his nursery last and placed him in the crib. Alec propped Thomas up on his side with a rolled-up towel and just stood over him. Angela snuck up behind Alec and slid her arms around him.

"He's wonderful," she said.

"Sure is. I think we did a good job," he said, adding after a pause, "Well, mostly you."

She gave him a little slap on the side. "Don't say that. He certainly has your face. Look at those perfect cheek bones."

Alec took a closer look. She was right. There was no mistaking it; Thomas was his son.

Two weeks passed and it seemed like two long days. Thomas was a screamer at night, and the couple struggled with sleep, taking turns tending to their wailing son.

Fortunately, the employees for *The Long and Short* all came together to take on extra responsibilities to give both Alec and Angela the two weeks off.

At times, both Alec and Angela had gone down into the basement office to check emails and to read the latest stories posted to the site, but outside of that, their entire time was spent hovering over their newborn son.

The vacation was soon at an end as July 4 marked the last day before they headed back to the basement full-time. Working from home meant they wouldn't be far from Thomas, but Angela's mother had planned on spending several days a week at the house watching him while they worked. She was enamored with her new grandson and wanted to spend every moment she could with him. Nevertheless, the urge to walk upstairs and play with Thomas was going to be hard to quell for them both.

Alec and Angela decided to host a cookout on the Friday before the Fourth, giving the extended family a chance to meet the baby. There was delicious grilled food, drinks galore, numerous unnecessary gifts and squealing women. Thomas was the center of attention and everyone had to hold him for at least a minute. After a few hours, Alec realized that this had been the longest time he had gone without holding his son.

He labored over the grill with his brother-in-law, Ray, and enjoyed a glass of wine. Ray tried to get Alec to share a beer with him, but he declined.

"Why are you always drinking wine?" he asked. "You don't like beer?"

"No, I love a cold beer. I just haven't had any hard liquor or beer in years and I'd like to keep it that way."

Ray dropped it right there and changed the subject, sensing the tension that could come if he pried any more.

Alec, meanwhile, started to feel a strong pain build up in between his eyes once again. The strength was several times greater than he had ever experienced.

"Can you take over?" he asked Ray, handing over the tongs.

"Sure," Ray said, watching Alec run off in pain. "You okay?"

His question went unanswered. Alec swiftly made his way through the kitchen and down the stairs to the office. Before he could get to his desk, he collapsed on the floor and passed out.

When Alec regained consciousness, he couldn't tell if he was out for more than an hour or just ten seconds. When he looked at his watch, he deduced that he had spent nearly twenty minutes face down on the floor, but he didn't waste too much time thinking about it; he just continued on to his desk and typed everything he saw while he was passed out.

• • •

The Gangland Killer
By Alec Rossi
The Long and Short

Two gunshots rang out, followed by the sound of two bodies making a loud thud as they lifelessly hit the floor.

The gangland killer was all of a sudden on the defensive.

He reached for his pistol as two of his men ran toward the staircase to see if they could find who fired the shots. Before they got to the top of the staircase a flashbang exploded right in front of them. Two seconds later, a pair of gunshots sent both men to the floor.

The gangland killer could not believe what was happening.

He was dead. He was sure of it.

But he tried to get away anyway.

He ran for a window that had a fire escape. As he got close, he fired a pair of shots to break the glass. He dived onto the steel staircase and ran down the rickety steps as fast as he could. He could hear the men shouting from above.

"It's him. He's outside! He's heading up East Twenty-First!"

The gang leader knew at that moment that he was the target. He also knew that he had made a terrible mistake somewhere along the way, but where?

He was careful, extremely careful.

How did it come to this? he thought as he sprinted down the street. He heard tires squeal behind him, so he made a sharp turn to cut through a yard. He climbed a fence and ran through a backyard.

Once he reached the end of the yard, he climbed the fence to get to the next yard. At the top, he felt a sharp pain in his left shoulder.

A bullet scorched through his flesh, making a clean hole in his shoulder that began spilling blood everywhere. He fell into the next yard in pain, dropping his weapon in the prior yard.

He didn't care to go back. At this point, his gun wasn't going to save him.

He got back up and ran toward the house. He kicked in the back door and ran through a kitchen and a hallway to the front door. He unlocked that door and ran out on to the street.

The pain in his shoulder was becoming unbearable and he groaned as he ran up the street.

With his right hand, he shielded his eyes from the sun that was low on the horizon and serving as a spotlight to mark his whereabouts. He wondered if this would be his last sunset. He knew it was only a matter of time, but he didn't think that it would come so soon.

He knew he deserved it, though. He had been the hunter on numerous occasions, but now, for the first time, he was the hunted.

He turned to look behind him and saw no one. There also was no one ahead of him, but he knew they'd be coming, so he veered off the road and found a trashcan alongside a row home. He lifted the lid and jumped in, replacing the lid over his head.

The smell of rotten food brought on a wave of nausea, but he fought it with all his might.

"I think he's down here!" a man shouted in the distance.

They were coming.

But the gang leader knew he had the advantage. No one saw him jump into this trashcan. He could be anywhere. He could be in any one of the houses on the street, or the cars or the garages. There was no way they'd find him before the police responded to the gunshots.

So he waited.

He heard footsteps run right past him and he held his breath for what seemed like an eternity.

As a man, presumably with a gun, ran past, the gang leader thought of the irony: he was a piece of garbage in a trashcan waiting to be taken out.

A few minutes passed and silence had taken over outside, but he was content on staying in the trashcan for days if he had to. He was not going to give away his position.

Never.

As he thought this, the lid opened and two men each grabbed an arm. They dragged him out of the trashcan and out into the middle of the street, where a black sedan was stopped.

The back door opened and a man in a white suit stepped out.

He pulled out a pair of gold-plated pistols and walked up to the wounded man. The two men, who dragged him to the street, pushed him down to his knees.

"He was exactly where he said he would be," the one said, pointing at a bearded man, who from the shadows on the sidewalk, continued to watch without any emotion. The gang leader could not make out a face. All he saw was a silhouette of the bearded man who sentenced him to death.

The man in the white suit nodded at the bearded man and returned his attention to his soon-to-be former business partner. He stepped forward and placed both pistols on his forehead. The gang leader could feel the cold steel press hard against his skin.

"I'm sorry. I didn't mean to do you wrong. It was business. I'll pay. I'll give you everything I earned. I'll pay."

The man in white laughed. "That time has passed. Your time has passed. And I'll get your money anyway."

The man in white pulled back the hammers on both guns and the clicks signified that this was going to be his last day.

The gang leader looked around him. Aside from the men with guns, there were people watching everywhere. A few people on porches, others on the sidewalk and a good number of frightened but nosey citizens peering out their windows.

Not one made a move to help him. Not one picked up a phone to dial 9-1-1. They all stood quietly as the man in white prepared to execute him.

"Is that what you're all going to do?" he screamed. "Somebody do something!"

Not one person flinched.

"No one cares about you, kid."

It was true.

No one cared.

His family gave up on him years ago. His friends—real friends—had given up prior to that.

"Where did it go wrong?" he asked himself.

He was a star that burned out way too soon.

"Karma," he said quietly to himself.

He had watched numerous people die in front of him. He was responsible for many, while others he just stood by and watched.

If only he had stopped one, perhaps that would have been enough to keep him from dying today.

He looked up to face his executioner one last time, but something caught his attention. His Judas in the shadows was now standing next to a beautiful woman. Both smiled as the final gunshots rang out.

It was his last day, and in that final moment, he knew exactly why.

• • •

With the final keystroke, Alec clicked save and sat back in his chair. It was now approaching eight o'clock and his head was still ringing from the vision.

He rubbed the area of his nose between his eyes and decided that a visit to the doctor was on his to-do list.

The basement door popped open and Angela called out to Alec.

"Yes, I'll be up in a second," he said, closing up the computer and running up the stairs.

"Where have you been?" Angela asked.

"Sorry, I just had some ideas I had to write down."

"Well, I just put Thomas to bed," she said, sounding annoyed that Alec had just disappeared for nearly two hours. "People are heading out. You should say goodbye."

The majority of the guests filtered out of the house by nine. Angela's parents, her sister and Ray were all who remained, and they sat with Angela and Alec in the living room discussing random topics.

John and Ray were in a heated argument over what the Ravens should do about their starting quarterback, while the women talked about Angela returning to work on Tuesday.

Alec had a few things to say, but for the most part, he listened. He was paying closer attention to what his wife was saying when he heard a crackle over the baby monitor sitting next to him. He heard Thomas let out a soft cry, and as he sat forward to get up, he heard a voice.

"Hush, my sweet," a female said.

Alec scanned the room, accounting for everyone in the house.

He jumped to his feet. "Who is still here?" he shouted running toward the foyer and to the staircase.

Everyone in the living room stopped their conversations and followed quickly. Alec sprinted up the stairs, through the hallway and into the dark nursery. He flipped on the light to see no one in the room. He continued to the crib where he saw Thomas sleeping soundly.

The rest of the family reached the room as he walked out.

"What's wrong, Alec?" Angela asked. "Is Thomas okay?"

"Yeah, he's fine," Alec said, now peering into every room upstairs.

"Did you hear something?" she asked.

Ray came out of the master bedroom. "There's no one up here. What did you hear?"

"I thought I heard a woman speak over the baby monitor."

They all stood there for a second before Ray chimed in again. "You do know that those things pick up radio waves and cordless phones and cellphones, right? Hell, it could be another baby monitor on the block."

"Yeah, it just sounded real," Alec said, puzzled.

They all returned downstairs and Angela's parents decided it was a good time to go. Her sister and husband left, too, and both Angela and Alec got an hour of sleep before Thomas started screaming.

"I got him," he said.

Thomas was still crying when Alec walked into the nursery, but he hushed as soon as he was in his father's arms. It was the same thing every night. Alec rocked him gently to sleep and laid him back in the crib.

Alec slid into bed next to Angela. Throughout the night, he replayed the vision in his head, trying to make out the faces of the couple in the shadows. It bothered him. He felt like he knew them, but he didn't know how. Could it be his mind playing tricks on him? He once read that the mind tries to make sense of what is unclear. It is why some people see a cloud shaped like a dog or a face in a smudge on a mirror or Jesus on a piece of toast. The mind wants to make sense of the unknown. Was this his mind forming familiar faces from memories deep in his past?

It took a while to shake all these thoughts, but he finally did and slept soundly.

46

BACK ON THE BANKS OF THE POTOMAC, Evrett was blind-ed by several thin sunrays piercing through the thick canopy of the forest. It took a moment for Evrett to realize where he was. In his right hand was his Glock and in his left were the keys to his studio apartment in Cleveland.

Why he was back at Fort Frederick State Park, he did not know. It was on the way home, but he had no memories of leaving Cleve-land. He pulled out the clip in the Glock, expecting to see a few bullets missing, but all were accounted for in the magazine; however, the extra round in the chamber was no longer there. Evrett, with the magazine still out of the gun, sniffed the barrel and detected the smell of burnt gunpowder. It had been fired recently.

"Oh, shit," he said.

At this point, he knew what he had to do. He ran back to his car and grabbed his cellphone. As he sat down in the front seat, he took notice of all his belongings from the apartment sprawled about his backseat. That answered one question, but he still had one big one left. On his phone, he went directly to the *Cleveland Plain Dealer's* website. It was the top headline.

VALENTI GUNNED DOWN it read in all caps.

This headline frightened Evrett. Looking at his wristwatch and seeing that it was six-thirty in the morning on Saturday, July 2, he realized he had no recollection of the last sixteen hours, at least.

Evrett was even more confused after reading the news story. According to it, a man, who no one was able to provide a description of, despite multiple witnesses, killed Chase execution style in the middle of the street. The story reported that Chase had a bullet wound to the shoulder and was killed with a pair of gunshots to the forehead. The story suggested that it was a pair of guns fired side-by-side at the same time. The story also painted the gruesome scene of the Rogue Sevens' safe house, which was at this point a misnomer. The other six high-ranking members were shot to death in a raid. The story speculated a rival gang may have been involved.

At this point, Evrett figured there was no way he could have been involved, unless he found another gun and learned how to take out a whole gang of thugs in one quick insertion.

Still, he had to have been nearby when the streets of Garfield Heights turned into a war zone, so he wondered what his role was.

Looking down at the gun and the keys to the apartment, he knew what he had to do next. He stepped out of his car and walked back to the riverbank, tossing the gun and keys as far as he could. Both sank to the bottom to join the pair of boat keys that would never be found again.

A few days later, Evrett read a more detailed story with a witness claiming that they saw a man in a white suit draw two gold-plated pistols and execute Chase. Police said they had no leads on the man in the white suit and they were asking for the public's help in catching the man. They also said they were looking for any information on another man who shot Chase in the shoulder with a .40 caliber pistol. Another witness claimed they saw Chase suffer the single gunshot wound while climbing a fence, supposedly trying to get away from the man in the white suit.

Evrett thought about the .40 caliber Glock that he once had in his possession and realized his role.

Chase was unable to hide after Evrett slowed him down.

Evrett wondered if he was aiming to hinder his escape or if he was trying to do what the man in the white suit eventually did.

It was a mystery not worth wasting time on, he concluded. The fact remained. Chase was dead. The names on his list were all crossed off.

Now, there was just one thing left to do—find the man on the bridge.

• • •

Evrett spent all of July and most of August reviewing everything he could. From newspaper articles to what memories he did have, he struggled to come up with a lead. He even watched the YouTube video another hundred times and came up with nothing.

How on Earth was he going to find the man most responsible for Sam's death? He was satisfied with all that he had done thus far, and surprisingly, he was happy that nine people were dead. He was counting Harrison.

In his moments of frustration, Evrett would sit back and reminisce on the last year and a half and how much fun he had.

Fun. He could not believe that he would actually describe it as *fun*. From spying to investigating to stealthy missions to planting microphones, he had grown to love it. He loved the adrenaline rush that came from breaking the law. To him, the ultimate moment was stealing the gun from Two Bit.

What a rush!

It was in these moments that he also felt sad that he had no one left to exact revenge on. His list of names had been exhausted.

What if he never found the man on the bridge? Where would he go from here? He still had the urge to get back out there on the road, surveilling, watching. It was addicting. It was thrilling. But he wasn't going to just go out and follow any ordinary person to satisfy his hunger. He wasn't an animal. It had to have meaning. It had to be something Sam would approve of.

He found such a reason on August 14.

Evrett came across a news story out of San Diego, California, where a woman, Sandra McIllroy, was killed when a construction company failed to follow proper protocol and a support beam fell from a high rise onto her car. The news story talked about how emails were discovered between executives who knew there was a risk, but out of sheer greed, they stormed on with the original plans. It turned out there would have been a million dollar bonus for the executives if the project was finished ahead of schedule. Had they stopped to minimize the risk of accident, they would have missed the deadline.

That was unacceptable for them.

For Evrett, it was unacceptable that a husband was without a wife and three children were without a mother.

He saved the story and started doing research on the executives responsible. It took away from finding the man on the bridge—Evrett knew this—but it got his mind off of it for a while. It was refreshing to think about something new. As he read more and more, the death of Sandra was a tragedy that needed the attention of a professional.

That's what Evrett considered himself now.

His resume was flawless in this new venture.

He wondered if Sandra's husband was already plotting his revenge. Evrett knew his pain, but he also knew that most people do not have the gall to do something about it, like he had done.

Evrett kept the information on Sandra in a manila folder tucked away in a locked drawer in his desk. He already had a short list of five people culpable for the accident. He would revisit it in a few months, he decided.

The prospect of a future list excited him, but he knew it was time to return to the task at hand.

He had to find the man on the bridge.

More than two years of planning and executing had left him sitting in his kitchen still wondering who this man was.

Someone had to know.

• • •

On a late August afternoon, Evrett, for the first time in a long time, began to display some emotion. He rested his heavy head in his hands and started to tear up.

"Sam," he said. "Sam, what have I done? Where have I gone wrong? I need to find this man on the bridge. Help me, Sam. Help me. Give me a sign. Do something. Any—"

The phone rang, interrupting Evrett's emotional episode.

"Hello?"

"Hey, Evrett. It's Linda."

Evrett strengthened his voice to hide any evidence that he was just having a meltdown. "Oh, hey. What's up, Linda?"

"We're having a cookout on Saturday. Why don't you come on over? We'd love to see you. It's been a while."

Evrett paused, and thought about it. "Sure, I'll be there."

They ended their conversation quickly after that and Evrett settled down. He asked for a sign and he believed he got one.

"Thanks, Sam," he said.

• • •

Evrett worked the cream into a dense lather in his hands before applying it to his face. He had just finished trimming his beard down to a length that would be easier to shave. He didn't want this to hurt.

As he rubbed the white froth on his cheeks and neck, Evrett thought back to when he had decided to grow the beard that was a component of his ongoing plan to reach the man on the bridge. After so many months, the beard had become a large part of who Evrett was. And while it pained him to do so, he knew it was time to get rid of it.

With each stroke of his blade, Evrett removed more and more hair, revealing the smooth skin that had been covered underneath. With each stroke, he could feel the past two years being shed from off his shoulders.

Andrew, Chad, Amanda, Gloria.

The trips to Pittsburgh, an out of state grocery store, an art gallery in Pennsylvania, and the Aloha State—Evrett let them go.

Janine and Sean, Phil, and most recently Chase.

The unfortunate turn of events that led to Stephanie's death, the thought of going up against a former spy, and the take down of a drug lord—they were now all memories floating in the dirty water of Evrett's sink. He rinsed the bowl and watched them all swirl down the drain.

Evrett pulled the warm towel away from his face. His beardless visage stared back at him. He didn't recognize himself, not at first. After inspecting his jawline for nicks, Evrett looked into the eyes of his reflection.

There he was.

Even after everything, he could still see himself there.

The last time Evrett had seen Sam's family had been before the spring. Suzanna had been in the junior high musical, playing the part of one of the townswomen. He had lucked out being able to squeeze it in between his trips. He also had enjoyed that the play left little time for awkward discussion with the Fieldings. As the years passed by, Sam had become less and less a part of their conversation. In her stead were discussions to catch everyone up with one another's lives. It had been hard for Evrett to think of topics, especially when the only two things in his life, Julia and his list, had been off limits.

Perhaps today could be a new start. He could discuss how he left GGM behind. He could talk about what he may or may not do in the future.

Well, perhaps he couldn't, he thought as Sandra McIllroy came to mind.

Evrett parked his car in front of the Fieldings' house and found a sign taped to the front door telling all guests to come in. Most people would undoubtedly be out back by now.

He managed to make it a few feet out onto the deck before anyone noticed he had arrived. Evrett had just a few seconds to place his large bowl of store-bought pasta salad on the picnic table before Linda came over to greet him; arms wide open.

"Evrett, it's so good to see you. You look great!" she said as she kissed his cheek. "I almost didn't recognize you without the beard. I like the clean look."

"Thanks. I figured it was time for a change."

"Good, good. Why don't you grab yourself a plate. There is still some chicken left. Jim's going to be grilling some more burgers soon."

"Great. I'll be fine with the chicken."

Linda smiled and placed her hand on his arm.

"I'm glad you came, Evrett. And really, you look good."

Evrett watched her walk back to a group of family members that he really wasn't well acquainted with. Most likely they had been at his wedding, but without Sam to whisper in his ear who everyone was, he thought it best to avoid the gaggle of aunts, uncles and cousins.

"Hey, buddy!" Jonas called out to Evrett.

He took Evrett's hand and shook it with a zealousness that oozed bravado.

"Jonas, good to see you."

"You too, Evrett. You too. Glad you could make it. What's new?"

"Ah, a few things, I guess."

"Really? Do tell?"

The two men made their way to a pair of empty lawn chairs, plates and Michelob Ultras in hand.

"You really quit? You left the firm?"

"I did. It just…felt right."

"Wow, I couldn't imagine. That takes balls, Evrett."

"I guess you could say that."

"What are you doing with yourself then? Are you looking for something else?"

"Honestly, I'm not quite sure what my plan is right now."

Jonas took a swig of his drink and tilted his head.

"You're kidding, right?"

Evrett looked up from his plate.

"For as long as I've known you, I don't think I've heard you say that you didn't have a plan," Jonas continued.

Evrett finished the beer and placed the empty bottle in the grass.

It was true. He didn't have a definite plan for what he was going to do next. Work was the last thing he had been thinking about. The money from Sam's life insurance would help him along for a good amount of time, but he'd eventually have to come up with something.

"Well, I think I've lived a certain way for so long, it was time for something different. When I come across it, I think I'll know it."

"You're a changed man, Evrett. Sam would have liked it, I think."

They both took a moment to let her name fill the air before starting another portion of their conversation.

"So, where are your girls?" Evrett asked.

"Suzanna is inside doing work for school. Can you believe they give incoming freshmen summer reading? Kid's not even in high school yet and she's already got a ton of work to do."

"She can handle it. She's a smart kid."

"Oh, no doubt. She just needs time to be a kid, you know? But Cynthia's always pushing her. If it isn't the musical, it's an honors class; if it's not class, it's cello practice. The girl is going constantly."

"And Cynthia? I don't think I saw her."

Jonas leaned back low in his chair. His long legs stretched out into the yard. He picked at the label of his beer bottle, trying to pull it off of the glass.

"Yeah, you won't see her. She didn't come today."

"Is everything…"

"We're…we're in a rough patch right now. She and I have had a tough year or two."

"I'm sorry to hear that, Jonas. Are you guys working it out?"

"We haven't gotten to the D-word yet. I don't think we're ready to throw in the towel. At least I know I'm not. We're just taking the summer as some time to breathe. Give each other a little space. She's actually spending time with her sister in Albany."

Evrett was overcome with the thought of how different the Fielding family was becoming. A few summers ago, Jonas and Cynthia's marriage had seemed perfect to him.

"What brought all this out?" Evrett asked.

"A bunch of things, really. Mom immediately asked if there was someone else. You know how she can be. But there wasn't. Things just…I guess we lost something. I just hope we can get it back."

Evrett thought about what his former brother-in-law had said. They had all lost something. He couldn't help but wonder if Sam's death had played a role in the fractures that had developed in Jonas's relationship with his wife.

It all reminded him of how Sam's death had impacted not only his life, but also the lives of those she had held dear.

When he finally found the man on the bridge it would be a victory—not only for him and Sam, but for the Fieldings as well.

"It's going to work out. I'm sure of it. You guys have something special. Sam and I always could see it. How's Suzanna handling it?"

"She's holding up. We've been open with her about it all. Heck, most of her friends come from divorced families. But like I said, we aren't there."

"Remember, if you need anything, you know where to find me," Evrett said. "You want me to grab you something?"

"Nah, thanks, man. I'm good. I appreciate it."

Evrett nodded and went toward the house. He was saddened by the thought of Jonas and Cynthia's marriage crumbling. While he knew marriages fall apart, he couldn't put himself in Jonas's position. Evrett would give anything to have his wife back. He couldn't fathom letting Sam go, no matter how bad their issues may be.

But he was not Jonas.

And Sam was not visiting family in Albany.

Inside, Evrett used the restroom before stepping into the living room. Linda still displayed many pictures of Sam. One of Evrett's favorites was on top of a bookshelf in the corner of the room. It was a photo of Sam taken on a Christmas morning while she was still in high school. She was surrounded by wrapping paper and had an extra wide smile for the camera. It was a simple shot, but the happiness in her eyes was so real.

Evrett reflected on the photograph before noticing Suzanna tucked in the opposite corner of the room, her back up against wall.

"Hey, kiddo," Evrett said and walked over to her. "I hear you are stuck inside doing work?"

"Hi, Uncle Evrett. Yeah. It's not so bad though."

"Well, that's good. What are you working on?"

Evrett slid down on the floor next to Suzanna. She held a digital tablet in her hands. Evrett could see on the screen that she was reading some type of text.

"English. The honors classes all have to do summer reading."

"Yeah, your father was telling me about it. We can't have you not be busy, huh?"

Suzanna giggled.

"So what are you reading? Shakespeare? *War and Peace? Moby Dick?*" he joked.

"No, it's kind of like a short story. We have to read a bunch of different types of stories and then write about them. One of them needs to be by a local author. I'm reading that one now."

"That doesn't sound so bad. What's it about?"

Suzanna swiped her finger across the screen, bringing up the story.

"It's kind of twisted. It starts out with this woman driving crazy through the rain in New York. She doesn't have a name either, which is kind of odd, but I guess that's this guy's style. Then you find out she is driving to see her daughter, but the twist is it's a daughter she gave up for adoption eight years earlier and the woman is planning to take her back. So she breaks into the daughter's house. Then the woman changes her mind, but she is chased from the house by a dog and she hurts herself by running through the sliding glass door. In the end she dies all alone by a lake in the rain. It was actually pretty interesting."

Suzanna noticed that Evrett was emotionless and in a daze at this point. "Uncle Evrett?"

He didn't respond. All he did was stare intently at the tablet in Suzanna's hands. It took a few moments for him to register that she had stopped talking.

"What's that?" he asked.

"Are you okay? You look…confused."

"Yeah, I'm fine, honey. Do you mind if I see the story for a second. It sounds really interesting."

"Sure. I was going to grab some dessert anyway."

"Thanks," Evrett said as she placed the tablet into his hands.

He looked down at the screen. When Suzanna summarized the story for him, he had felt a sudden jolt in his heart. He knew this story. It was *familiar.*

New York.

The home invasion.

The lake.

"Amanda?" he asked quietly.

Evrett read each line of the story, from the beginning to its devastating conclusion.

There was no car or pavement.

There was just a lake…

…She fell into the rain-soaked mud and rolled onto her back. Her breaths were shorter and coldness took over her entire body.

Evrett's muddy shoes and wet clothes. The lake. The conversation with Colleen. They all flooded his memory.

He pushed them from his mind and reread the story again.

She peacefully accepted that this was her last day.

It had to be a coincidence. The story was vague. It could have been about anyone.

Evrett's heart raced.

But what if it wasn't a coincidence? What if this story was indeed about Amanda Ramirez and how she died? What would that mean?

Suddenly pondering turned to panic. If this was about Amanda, how did the author know about what happened to her?

He scrolled back up to the very top of the story to find the byline. "By Alec Rossi, *The Long and Short.*"

Alec Rossi. Who was he? Was he there? Did he see her? Did he see *him*?

Evrett's head was a tumultuous sea of thoughts. He had to focus. He had to get to the bottom of this.

Evrett walked quickly outside and found his niece sitting at a picnic table next to her grandmother.

"Here," he said, handing the tablet over to Suzanna. "Thanks so much. That was a great read. I'm sure you will do well in class. You described the story perfectly."

Evrett then turned to Linda and said, "Thanks for the great time. I'm going to get going. I have a few things to take care of."

"Are you sure?" Linda said. "We still have some more food on the way."

"Thanks, but no thanks. I'll see you again soon."

She stood up and they shared a quick embrace before Evrett

disappeared around the side of the house.

• • •

Evrett's Audi sped back to Hampden while his mind raced through possibilities that could explain how Alec Rossi had been able to write a story that so closely resembled what Evrett knew about Amanda's last few hours. It wasn't long before Evrett sat at his desk in his home office. He had just feverishly opened the Internet browser and searched for "Alec Rossi" and "The Long and Short."

With the results loaded, Evrett began clicking through the information on the webpage for *The Long and Short*. He quickly gathered that Alec Rossi was a writer for an online fiction magazine. There was a page that alphabetically listed all of the writers associated with the publication. While there were many other authors besides Rossi, each contributing short pieces of fiction, Evrett didn't waste any of his time looking into them. The mystery of Alec Rossi was all he was concerned with at the moment.

Evrett clicked the link to Rossi's page. It revealed a short biography, list of published works and a picture. Evrett stared into the eyes of Alec Rossi. Evrett thought long and hard, but settled on the fact that he had never seen the man before in his life. He certainly didn't remember seeing him at any point during his investigation in Lancaster or in his sudden appearance in New York.

Reading over the biography provided a little more information on the man behind the story. Alec was close to Evrett's age and also currently resided in the Baltimore area. Evrett would certainly have to track him down. But that would have to wait.

There were too many questions that Evrett needed answered first. Evrett rubbed his temples. His mind was cluttered with thoughts.

How could he have known about Amanda?

What was Evrett missing?

Alec had more than twenty stories listed on the page. Evrett found the one he had read earlier. It was listed in a separate group from Alec's earlier entries.

"*Last Day*," Evrett said as he read the title and clicked the link to the short story called "The Mother." He reread it, searching for any additional information that he may have missed. When he finished he returned to the previous screen. He clicked on the first story in the *Last Day* set, "The Gambler."

As Evrett read each word in the short story his chest tightened. There was no mistaking it; "The Gambler" was about Andrew Mc-Millan. The Pittsburgh setting, the casino, the watery death, the rouge boat; it was everything Evrett had pieced together after his blackout.

How could Alec Rossi have known these things?

He looked at the publication date. July 24, 2015. It was the same month that Andrew had died.

Evrett looked down at his hand and noticed it was shaking.

He had been so careful to keep his tracks hidden and yet some-how this writer was publishing detailed accounts of his target's last days. In fact, Alec Rossi seemed more aware of what happened to each of them than Evrett did.

He clicked on to the next story.

In September of 2015, Rossi had published his piece entitled, "The Traveler." As Evrett read, the pieces of the puzzle began to fit together. Then he knew for sure.

A rock the size of a golf ball ricocheted off the blades and slammed into his throat, knocking him off his feet.

Chad McKelvin. Evrett's second target.

Evrett thought back to his trip to New England and all the time he took to place his microphones in Molly Randall's home. He re-membered pulling up to the crowd of bystanders discussing Chad's odd death. Again, Alec Rossi knew it all. Was he among the bystand-ers?

"The Mother" was next in the sequence so Evrett skipped ahead. He saw the date and the title and knew a recap of Gloria Droun's fi-nal moments was waiting for him within "The Widow," published in January of 2016.

"Oh, shit!" Evrett shouted.

He read Rossi's account of the skydiving incident.

In total, five people would be jumping from the plane today—the coordinator, the married couple, a shadowy man and the widow.

Evrett knew he was the shadowy man. The conversation with

the coordinator at the airport had confirmed that Evrett had been on Gloria's flight. Had Alec been there too? Was he one half of the married couple? Would he recognize Evrett if and when he would have to track him down?

But how could that be? How could Alec have been at every last moment? Evrett thought of each time he had experienced his lost time and blackouts. Somehow, Alec Rossi had been there to see what Evrett hadn't.

March brought the story, "The Heartbroken Teenager." It clearly described Stephanie, the Bryants' babysitter, as she killed Janine and Sean in a passionate fit.

"I can't believe this was published," Evrett said.

In May, Phil fell asleep behind the wheel of his truck in "The Insomniac."

Evrett took a deep breath before venturing to read, "The Gang-land Killer." He knew he had played a more active role in the death of Chase Valenti, having fired a shot that made its way into Chase's shoulder. Sure enough, Alec Rossi had captured the moment in print. At least, Evrett wasn't specifically mentioned.

Then his eyes and heart came to a full stop.

...a bearded man, who from the shadows on the sidewalk continued to watch without any emotion. The gang leader could not make out a face. All he saw was a silhouette of the bearded man who sentenced him to death.

There he was. After six other stories, Alec Rossi had finally captured Evrett. While still vague, Evrett knew Alec was referencing him.

Something else piqued Evrett's interest. He scrolled through the last few lines of "The Gangland Killer" another time.

He looked up to face his executioner one last time, but something caught his attention. His Judas in the shadows was now standing next to a beautiful woman. Both smiled as the final gunshot rang out.

Context clues had led Evrett to the conclusion that he was Chase's Judas. After all, he had been the one to give away his location. What captured Evrett's attention was the mention of the beautiful woman who smiled while standing next to him.

Who was she? Was she a piece of fiction?

There was enough truth in Alec's writing to convince Evrett that this woman had been by his side at the time of Chase's demise. Yet, he had no memory of her. What part did she have to play in all of this?

Why would she be smiling as the man in the white suit pulled the triggers that ended Chase's life?

The answer to that question wasn't clear and he couldn't let himself get distracted from the main prize.

Evrett clicked back to the *Last Day* page. Each target had a story, and Alec had written them all. Evrett's mind was exhausted. He couldn't think. Nearly two years of his life had been documented by a man he had never met.

What did Alec have to gain in all of this? What role did he play? Was he taunting Evrett? Did he want Evrett to find him?

As Evrett stared at the image of Alec, the smiling author, a familiar phantom rose up in Evrett's mind.

The man on the bridge.

Alec had written about each person involved with Sam's accident, save one, the same one who had eluded Evrett this whole time. If Alec had followed Evrett, then he too was on the same path, the path that was leading to the man on the bridge.

"That's it," Evrett said.

He let out a short chuckle, and then another. Soon Evrett was overcome with laughter. He had started the day believing the universe would point him in the right direction, and through a chance conversation with his niece, Evrett believed he found his compass.

Alec Rossi, writer for *The Long and Short*, was going to lead Evrett to the man on the bridge. All Evrett had to do now was find the author.

47

THE DEADLINE WAS FAST APPROACHING. It had been a long time since Alec had even worried about such a thing. But with three days left, he was starting to panic.

His *Last Day* story ideas almost always came to him at least a week before his deadline, but this time, he was starting to wonder if it would ever come.

He tapped a pen on the office desk to no particular beat. At one point it had the rhythm of a song he heard earlier that morning, but it quickly morphed into a nonsensical annoyance.

"Hey, Neil Peart," Angela said, looking up from her desk. "You mind ending the drum solo?"

Alec stopped abruptly. He didn't even realize how loud he was.

"I'm sorry," he said. "I'll stop."

"You okay?"

"Yeah, I'm okay," he said. After a moment of silence, he looked back up at Angela. "Neil Peart?"

She laughed. "I never told you I was a bit of a Rush fanatic in college?"

"Well, if that was the case, you would surely know that I sounded nothing like Neil Peart."

"True," she managed to say through a laugh.

Angela refocused on her computer, while Alec stared into nowhere. Finally, he decided that he had had enough.

"I'm going to head out and get some fresh air," he said. "Try and cure this writer's block at Capriati's. You need anything?"

"Sure. Bring me back a veggie sub," she said, adding, "Please."

Alec stood up and walked toward the basement stairs. "Sounds good. I'll be back in a few."

It was only eleven in the morning, but Alec didn't mind sitting down at his favorite deli for an early lunch. On his way out the door, he passed by his mother-in-law, who was holding Thomas. He kissed him on the forehead and said goodbye.

"Be right back."

As he drove away, he never noticed the black Audi shadowing his every turn.

• • •

He had to know something. This was too much of a coincidence. There were nine people on Evrett's list.

Eight had names, and those with names were no longer around to hear them called.

How? Evrett could not be exactly sure, but the man he was following surely had to know something.

And that meant he had to know the final man on the list—the man on the bridge.

Every one of his stories detailed the deaths that fell upon the unlucky eight—details that the authorities did not know, yet somehow Evrett knew them to be factually correct.

Even more interesting was the last story that clearly placed Evrett at the scene.

He had no recollection of any of the eight deaths, but based on witness reports, the clues he had gathered and now a collection of stories on the Internet, it was clear to him that he played an integral role.

But how does Alec Rossi come into play?

Evrett was determined to find out.

He watched Alec park in a lot outside a deli, one that Evrett had never seen before. It was a small place in Pasadena, Maryland, not too far from Alec's home.

Alec stepped out of his car and walked inside, as Evrett watched from his car parked along the street. Five minutes later, Alec came out with a sandwich and sat at one of the many outdoor tables set up on a covered patio.

It was a warm September day, with a pleasant breeze, and it was the perfect day to eat outside.

A couple sat a few tables away and a mother and child sat at a table on the other side of Alec.

"Okay, Alec," Evrett said to himself. "It's time."

He stepped out of his car and walked into the deli. He looked up at the menu and deliberated over its many options. His eyes stopped wandering when he saw the pastrami and provolone sub. He stared at every letter and held back.

Shortly after his engagement to Sam, they went on a three-day road trip to Myrtle Beach. They stopped at a deli along the way, much like this one, and Sam ordered the pastrami and provolone.

"Just when I thought I knew everything about you," Evrett said to Sam, before telling the kid behind the counter to make it two.

"Sir, can I help you?" a woman asked, snapping Evrett back to present day. "Sir?"

"Ah, yes," Evrett said. "I'll take the pastrami and provolone sub."

"Sure thing, be right up."

"Actually, wait," he said, causing her to spin around and refocus her attention on him. "Can you make that two?"

"You got it. To go?"

"Yes, both to go."

After about five minutes, the subs came out in a brown bag and Evrett paid the cashier.

As he walked out, he passed Alec, who without sandwich in hand was just taking in the beautiful day. Evrett reached in his pocket to get his car keys and purposely dropped them behind him.

He spun around, knelt down and picked them up. As he rose to his feet, he made eye contact with Alec.

The two shared a long awkward stare.

Alec began to look puzzled as Evrett took a step forward. "Wait a second. I know you. Yes, yes. You're that author on *The Long and Short*."

Alec laughed. "Are you serious? No one has ever recognized me."

"I love your stories," Evrett said. "They're … so real."

"Thanks," he said, now feeling embarrassed. "I appreciate the kind words."

After a short pause, Evrett continued on, "I hope this isn't too forward, but do you mind if I sit down and ask you a few questions. I'm an aspiring writer and I'd just love to pick the brain of a professional like yourself."

Alec liked the sound of that. *Professional.*

"Sure, why not," Alec said. "I honestly never knew I had a fan base. I mean, I knew people were reading my stories, but I didn't realize that anyone was interested enough to actually pick me out of a crowd. How did you even do that?"

Evrett, now sitting, looked around. "There's like five people here. Hardly a crowd."

Alec looked around and laughed, "Yeah, I guess you're right."

"Plus, I just happened to check out your bio yesterday after reading your most recent story. Riveting, by the way. But, yeah, your photo is right there and it was fresh in my mind."

"How about that," Alec said, now remembering that Angela set up biography pages a few months ago. He wasn't necessarily for it, but she wanted to personalize her writers to the readers.

"So, my biggest trouble as a writer is finding story ideas," Evrett said, jumping right into his questions. "Can you give me any pointers? I mean, how do you come up with your ideas?"

"You tell me," was what Alec wanted to say. He had no clue how he came up with his ideas. Was that the answer he should give? That

wouldn't seem *professional* at all. No, he couldn't do that. It was time to lie.

"Well, I like to say I have a wild imagination," Alec said. "I like to read the newspaper and find stories that interest me. I then imagine what it would be like if certain, unpredictable things were to happen. Basically, I like to exaggerate. I like to bend the truth. I see a drug dealer gets shot, so I think about why it happened, and I come up with a backstory. I see a man drowns so I draw up a wild night of gambling to explain why he's no longer with us. The truth is in front of us all the time. Making up the lies that get us to that truth is what makes it fun."

Evrett listened to every word and he knew something else was up. He could sense it.

Alec, on the other hand, was wondering if what he just said made any sense.

How the hell did I come up with that? he asked himself.

"That's amazing," Evrett said, playing along.

He bought it, Alec thought.

"So, what's in store for your next *Last Day* story? You have to be finishing it up soon. I saw the ad on the website saying it will be released this Friday."

Damn, Angela and her story promotions. "Well, a writer can never give away his story before it comes out," Alec said, leaving out the fact he had no clue where he was going with it. He then decided that he better cover his tracks in case he doesn't write one. "And to be honest, I think I'm nearing the end of the series. May have just one more story left in me."

"Really, just one?" Evrett asked, now with an extreme interest. "That's upsetting. But if that's the case, I can't wait to read what happens in your finale."

They both sat there quietly for about ten seconds. Evrett stared into Alec's eyes. He knew somehow, some way, this writer was going to lead him to the man on the bridge.

Would he wake up in some random city, forced to rummage through the daily news headlines to find the obituary of the man on the bridge? And then, a day later read a story online about how it happened?

When would the blackout begin? For all he knew, it had started a few hours ago and he was on a path to memory loss.

"Well, Mr. Rossi," Evrett said, standing up. "Thank you very much for your time. Good luck with your next story."

"No problem, and thank you," he said, standing as well and reaching his right hand out.

Evrett shook his hand, "Truly inspiring."

"Beg your pardon?"

"Your stories. They are inspiring."

Evrett walked away, got into his car and drove off.

Alec remained standing, replaying Evrett's words in his head. "Truly inspiring."

That's it, Alec thought.

He decided to end the *Last Day* series the way it started—with the story that inspired it all.

• • •

Evrett knew that Alec was hiding something, and he was hoping he'd find it soon. Back in his car, he pulled out the digital recorder he had in his pocket and he listened to the conversation over and over.

After the fourth time through, he started to think about what Alec said. Was it possible that he was looking at the news stories and coming up with the backstories?

This needed to be researched.

He turned the key in the ignition and sped back to his home. Once in his office, he set up his tablet and laptop and began researching every news story. He wanted to match the dates of their deaths with the date the stories were written. He jotted down all the publish dates for the *Last Day* series, but it was consistently the fourth Friday every other month.

He matched up the publish dates with dates of all his targets' death.

Andrew died on July 10, 2015, and Alec published his story on July 24. Chad died on September 20 and the story was online seven days later. Amanda's story came eighteen days later and Gloria's was eleven. It was seven days for Janine and Sean, and six for Phil, while Chase's story came twenty-one days later.

There was no rhyme or reason to it, just that it happened with enough time for Alec to research the news story and create his fictional account.

Fictional.

That's what Alec claimed it was, but Evrett knew that wasn't the case.

He also knew the publish dates were misleading. He needed to find out exactly when Alec wrote the stories. He packed his satchel with a few essential tools and he drove back to Pasadena, Maryland.

48

THE STARE LASTED A LITTLE TOO LONG FOR COM-FORT, even for his wife. Angela felt the pair of eyes on her, and after they didn't shift focus, she gave Alec a half-hearted wave to bring him back to Earth.

It worked and Alec smiled.

"You okay?" Angela said.

"Yeah, just struggling with the final installment."

"How much do you have written?"

Alec laughed and turned his laptop to display a blank Word document. Many years ago, he would have had a waste bin filled with crumbled up papers, spit out one by one from a loud, clunky typewriter. Nowadays, the delete key hid the many attempts, and the many failures, of a story.

For Alec, the blank screen represented four hours of typing gone to waste. What seemed like a great idea at lunch had turned into an arduous endeavor. He was struggling to piece together a backstory for Samantha Eckhard. He knew the ending. He just couldn't piece together a story to get her there. It had been so frustrating that his last attempt was a complete shift in philosophy, writing the story from his perspective instead of hers, but it felt too much like a confession.

"Why don't we go out to dinner and take your mind off of it?" Angela asked.

After a short pause and another glance at his blank screen, it was clear that a break may be the best idea.

"Sure," he said.

"I'll call my mother and see if we can drop off Thomas for a few hours," she said, already dialing her cellphone.

In thirty minutes, they were packed up and ready to head out the door.

From his car, Evrett watched Alec and his perfect family drive away. He saw the bags for the baby and assumed he at least had an hour to play in the Rossis's home.

After they rounded the corner, Evrett gave them an extra five minutes to make sure they didn't forget anything, and when it was clear they were gone, he went to work.

It took a few minutes to get past the lock on the back door, but he slipped inside without any neighbors noticing. The homes were close together, so he had to be careful.

Once inside, he began searching for a den. He needed to access Alec's computer, but after going room to room on the first and second floors, he was unable find a computer.

"What the hell?" Evrett said, now back in the kitchen. He scanned the room and saw a door, which he assumed led to a basement.

Perhaps it's finished? he thought.

He was right and once downstairs he realized that he had discovered the main headquarters for *The Long and Short.* The walls were littered with framed awards and cover art for fiction pieces that had appeared on the website. There were a pair of desks and a conference table.

It was fairly clear which desk belonged to Alec as Evrett used the Orioles paraphernalia as an indicator.

Sitting down at the desk, Evrett tapped the space bar on the laptop to bring the computer out of sleep mode. Once the screen awoke from darkness, a blank Word document was displayed with the saved filename of "Last Last Day."

"Hmm," Evrett said. "Are we struggling, Alec?"

He minimized the Word document and began a search for files titled "Last Day." He found a folder filled with eight documents, one for each story, including the blank document he just minimized. Evrett had hoped that the "date modified" metadata would give him a better idea of when the stories were written, but unfortunately, like every good writer, Alec gave his pieces a final read and edit a day or two before publication.

Evrett kept searching through the folders on the hard drive, trying to find any notes. He found it hard to believe that Alec just wrote these stories from scratch. There had to be some sort of research.

After a few minutes, it was clear that there were not any notes typed on the computer, so he started searching the drawers. He found a few notepads with detailed notes, but the notepads did not give him a clue on the dates.

Underneath one of the Steno reporter's notepads was a digital recorder. He turned it on and hit play. Right away, he heard Alec's voice describing the details to one of his *Last Day* stories. After a few seconds, it was clear that this audio file contained the details of Chase's last day. He scanned through the recorder and found three more recordings.

He knew the metadata on the recorder would give him the answer he'd been looking for. He dug back into the drawer, pulling out the USB cord to connect the recorder to the computer. He opened up the folder containing the recordings, as well as the evidence he was looking for.

Chase's file, default labeled as "VN300024," was recorded at 6:33 on the evening of July 1, 2016.

It was moments *before* Chase died.

About two months before that was Phil's file, labeled "VN300023," and it was recorded at 7:26 on the morning of May 19, 2016.

This threw Evrett off course for only a second before he factored in the time zones, which placed the recording at 6:26 local time in Iowa City, right around the time Phil drove his truck off the road.

The story details for Janine and Sean were recorded at 2:13 in the morning on March 18, 2016.

The fourth and final recording on this particular device was Gloria's last day, and it was recorded at 5:43 on January 9, 2016. Again, he did the quick math for the times zones, which put it at 12:43 Hawaiian time, which was about the time that he was in free fall from a plane he didn't remember weaseling his way on to.

This was all too eerie for Evrett.

At the exact time that he was in the middle of his blackouts, Alec was somehow seeing everything he didn't remember, and more.

How could such a thing happen?

Evrett was in disbelief. He didn't quite believe such things, but this was unmistakable proof that Alec had some sort of connection with the murders.

He wondered if Alec had other such visions for other murders, but an extensive search of his hard drive pulled up several stories that were nothing like the *Last Day* series.

These seven stories were one of a kind.

The only common thread between these seven stories was Evrett, but he had only met the man a few hours earlier at lunch. How could there be a connection?

Evrett sat back in the chair and reclined to collect his thoughts. As he did, he noticed the several Associated Press awards on the wall, honoring Alec Rossi for his news reporting at *The Baltimore Sun*.

The Baltimore Sun.

The Sun.

That's what's written atop the office building in big letters, "The Sun."

Evrett knew this because he'd seen it. It's visible from the bridge, a mere two hundred yards from where Sam perished.

"I wonder if he covered the accident," Evrett said aloud. "Or maybe he saw it from his office? Maybe he saw the man on the bridge?"

Evrett started a search on Alec's computer for news stories. He hoped that he still had his files from when he worked at *The Baltimore Sun*.

Hidden off the desktop was a folder filled with news stories, the last being written on July 9, 2013, the day before Sam died. He quickly went back to Alec's fiction folder where he kept all his pieces for *The Long and Short* and its first file was dated for July 28, 2013. It was a crime drama piece based in Baltimore, and it was so far-fetched, Evrett immediately knew it wasn't like the *Last Day* stories. There was no way it was real, unless he missed the news story about a police officer becoming a serial killer.

If it were about an architect becoming a serial killer, then it'd be a different story.

Evrett laughed at that thought before returning to the task at hand. He knew that something had to have happened between July 9 and July 28 to make Alec leave his long-time gig at *The Baltimore Sun* for a small fiction website.

Evrett sat quietly for a few minutes and then came up with an idea.

He maximized the Word document that was on the screen when he first started searching the computer more than two hours ago. He used his left hand to hit the keys CONTROL and Z at the same time. The shortcut for the undo function produced a byline and a title, and a second tap of the combination produced several paragraphs that Alec had typed earlier in the day. It was his last attempt at writing his final installment, and for Evrett, it was his greatest find.

• • •

The Regretful Man
By Alec Rossi
The Long and Short

The regretful man drowned his sorrows one drink at a time.
His favorite watering hole had quickly become his wake.
This was to be everyone's last chance to say goodbye, but there was no one there—no one who cared, at least. Just a bartender, an old man and his favorite drink.

"Another Jack on the rocks," he said, and the bartender begrudgingly obliged.

Sipping on the sweet poison, he wondered where did his life go wrong? How had he gotten to this point?

These were among the many thoughts that plowed through his brain at this point, and six drinks in, he struggled to process much of anything.

It was one in the afternoon and he was sloshed, but when fired from the only job he ever knew, what else was there for him to do?

Whiskey seemed to be the perfect cure for depression; at least that's what the regretful man thought at the time.

Even though it never brought his cheating wife back to his bed, he kept drinking.

Even though it had not cured the pain of missing a chance to say goodbye to his father, he continued to drink.

It would take something more to cure him.

He just didn't know it, and when the bar began to fill up at happy hour, the regretful man stumbled out the door.

He didn't belong at happy hour.

Instead, he ran toward sadness.

Walking along the bridge, he looked out toward the city skyline. He had once loved this city. From its beauty to its character, he loved everything about it.

But today, he wanted the city to end it.

Climbing to the ledge, he watched the traffic speed by. Three, two, one. He counted down a few times, but each time, he found himself standing in place. Once more, he gave it a try, but before he could get to two, the world changed below him.

Cars tangled and a fire rose.

Through the pluming smoke, he was a mere mystery on the bridge above.

Overlooking the chaos, the regretful man knew that he was meant for the mess below, but instead, he ran in the other direction. Death had fallen upon someone else that day and the regretful man knew it was too late for him to do anything about it. He had looked Death in the eyes and said not today.

You will not make this my Last Day.

• • •

Evrett was stunned.

My Last Day.

Those words reverberated in his mind, especially the word "My." Throughout the entire piece, Evrett assumed Alec was writing about the man on the bridge. And he was, but the last sentence hit home. The switch to first person had to mean something. Evrett was certain that this was Alec's confession.

He looked at the photo of Alec on the desk.

There was no doubt in his mind; his long road had finally led him to his destination.

All along there had been a certainty deep inside Evrett, one that had reassured him in moments alone and in weakness that all his work would one day lead him to the man on the bridge. Even when each target had failed to provide him any clues to the man's identity, Evrett had never given up hope that one day, somehow, he would come face to face with the man he had been obsessed with for three years.

Little did Evrett know that the moment had already happened.

"Hello, Man on the Bridge," he said, smiling. "I've got you."

If only Evrett had known Alec's true identity when he approached him at the café. He had looked into the eyes of the man responsible for all of this without even knowing it. How would that interaction have played out had Evrett had the knowledge he did now?

It didn't matter now. Evrett knew. That's all that mattered. He knew who the man on the bridge was, and finally retribution was in sight.

Outside, the slam of a car door shook Evrett from his evil thoughts, and from behind him, he heard a voice, Sam's voice, "Run, Evrett."

He quickly erased the text on the screen and returned everything to the way it was when he arrived. He retrieved a small microphone from his satchel and placed it under the desk. He jotted down the computer's IP address and shoved the paper in his pocket. Fortunately for Evrett, it takes some time to get a baby out of a car. He ran up the stairs and out the back door just as the Rossis entered their home.

It was a close call for Evrett, but it was worth the risk.

Once in his car, he let the whole situation process. Alec was a mess on July 10, 2013, and now he was living the perfect life with the perfect family. Evrett was living the perfect life until July 10 and now he was a mess.

Alec would pay.

In time, he would pay.

But first, Evrett thought, he had to feel the pain. He deserved to live with the pain of losing the woman he loved.

49

COMMITMENT. Evrett thought about the word as he rolled his titanium wedding ring over his fingers. While he did, he recalled the day he and Sam stood in front of their families and friends and exchanged vows and rings. He had never laid eyes on a woman as beautiful. He could still see her face, beaming with happiness, looking at him from underneath her veil.

That was another life and he was now a different person. He knew that. The person he had been before his wife's death would never be sitting in his office plotting the things he was plotting.

But Evrett had made a commitment to himself and to Sam that he would seek revenge for those responsible for her death. And he was finally about to fulfill his promise; however, in a way he never had really considered before.

Sitting in his home office, the room he had once kept secure under lock and key, Evrett began filling two manila folders with print outs from his computer. Even though he had recently removed every piece of evidence related to his list, Evrett was starting two new files.

While he always knew things would end with the man on the bridge, Evrett never had determined how his revenge would take shape. Yes, Alec would have to pay a price greater than all his other targets, but it had always been a vague notion in Evrett's mind. Perhaps it was because Alec's identity had remained a mystery for so long.

That had all changed only a few hours before.

Alec Rossi was the man on the bridge. And with that knowledge in mind, Evrett could now plan the perfect revenge for the man who took away his everything.

It all came back to commitment.

Angela had made a commitment to Alec when she married him. Just as Evrett believed destiny had brought him to the man on the bridge, destiny had chosen to couple Angela with Alec. If Evrett was to truly enact his revenge, Alec would have to know his pain.

Evrett would have to kill her.

It wouldn't be his first kill. That recognition went to Harrison MacLain. And while he hadn't pulled the trigger, Stephanie had also died because of his decisions to manipulate her situation. Still, she had made her own choices in the end.

No, Angela was different.

Aside from her marriage to Alec, she had no involvement with any of this. She hadn't been at the scene of the accident that day in July. She hadn't turned a blind eye to the suffering of his wife. No, her condemnation came from the simple fact that she loved the wrong man.

Earlier in his mission, Evrett might have struggled with this decision. He might have tried to find another way, one that didn't cut this woman's life short, that didn't rob a husband of his wife or a son of his mother.

But Evrett had worked too long and hard to get here to let it go now.

Sam deserved better than what she received.

And Alec deserved much, much worse.

Evrett slid his wedding ring back on the appropriate finger and then placed all his printed information of Alec in one folder, and then did the same for Angela in the other. He was about to head back out to Pasadena.

After all, Evrett was determined.

He was committed.

· · ·

For the most part, everything was the same. Alec didn't notice the minor movements of the many items on his desk. He had no reason to suspect that they were in a different position than when he left.

He sat down and pulled up the blank Word document only to stare at it for another twenty minutes. Leaning back in his chair, mostly to comfort his full stomach from a large Italian dinner, he swiveled back and forth trying to come up with a way to write his final *Last Day* story.

So much of him wished he would have made his last installment the final edition, but he was too late. As the big and little hand on the ticking clock in the basement simultaneously aligned with the twelve, Alec knew he had less than forty-eight hours to write it.

Again, he thought about Samantha and what kind of backstory he could write. He needed something with spice. Something with power.

He thought about his past and quickly, an idea hit him.

She can be just like Abby, the ex-wife that Alec had all but forgotten.

So he started typing about "The Adulterer." It had everything from the husband walking in on her packing her bags for another state to the rich asshole waiting in said state.

Alec knew his ex-wife would never read this, but the thought of her seeing it made him smile, especially considering the fact that she would die in a fiery car crash in the end.

It was the only legal way Alec could kill her, and somehow, it was therapeutic.

Alec punched the keys furiously, finishing the first chunk of the story in less than thirty minutes.

He then spent the next thirty minutes laboring over the details of her death. No matter how many times he tried, he couldn't shake the image of himself on the bridge causing the accident. Plus, there were several minutes unaccounted for between the time he ran away and the explosion. He really never knew what happened.

Alec read the initial news reports, but that was it. He refrained from reading or watching any news reports until he was certain that he would not be bombarded by any updates on the accident.

Between being fired from *The Baltimore Sun* and the guilt associated with the accident, Alec wanted nothing to do with the news for nearly eighteen months.

It wasn't until now that Alec felt the urge to find out more. For the sake of his story, he believed he had to do it.

He opened up a browser and typed in a few key words, including Samantha Eckhard's name, into the search field. Seconds later, the first link to pop up was *The Baltimore Sun's* news story on the accident.

Figures, he thought.

Despite his biases, he clicked on the link. It was the story that appeared the day after the accident, dated July 11, 2013. It included various details on the accident, most of which he knew. It didn't cover the time between the crash and the explosion.

He figured the details weren't released at this point, so he backed out onto the search results page. The second link was to a column in the *Huffington Post* titled "Innocent Bystander Laws Revisited."

Alec was extremely curious. He was a not-so-innocent bystander to this accident, so he wondered what this story could be about.

He read the article, describing how several people watched as Samantha struggled to free herself from her burning car with not one of them coming to her rescue. A few paragraphs in, it talked about the controversial YouTube video, which was embedded in the story. Without reading any further, Alec clicked the play button.

Alec watched as the video showed a man climb out of a tanker truck that was flipped on its side. He watched as the truck driver ran away from the scene, not making any effort to save Samantha.

"What the?" Alec said, hitting pause.

He looked closer at the face of the driver running away.

The Insomniac?

He clicked play and watched him disappear from the screen as the camera panned to a pair of men, one preventing the other from saving Samantha.

Any chance of a coincidence went out the window here.

Alec clearly saw the Gambler and the Traveler.

As the video continued on, he saw the Mother as well as the man who was killed by the Broken-Hearted Teenager. He could only assume his wife was in the van.

All that was missing were the Widow and the Gangland Killer.

The video came to an end with the explosion without him finding either one of them, but then it was clear to him. He looked at the name in the caption below the video: "Shot by Chase Valenti, a Johns Hopkins student."

The name rang a bell and he quickly Googled it. Chase's mug shot appeared right away and it was clear that this was the man in "The Gangland Killer."

The first link Alec found was his execution on the streets of Cleveland. He read the news story only to find out that he actually had more details than they did, but any facts they had were corroborated by his once thought-to-be fictional account.

Then Alec noticed the date and time of death. He couldn't pinpoint it, but it seemed in line with when he got his vision.

This was too much for Alec to comprehend. He quickly stood up and paced around the basement for several minutes.

Finally, he returned to his seat determined to find more. If Chase, the Gangland Killer, was dead, then everyone else must be, too.

He returned to the initial news story, only to find the name of the truck driver, Phillip Repin. He typed his name in a search field, along with "Iowa," "fatal," and "accident."

There it was. A story of a ten-mile backup. He remembered searching for this before, but he didn't find it. Now, it was here.

Similar searches, even though he didn't have names, allowed him to find stories on The Gambler, The Broken-Hearted Teenager and The Widow. Even though The Widow wasn't in the video, he figured she had to have played some role that fateful day.

He was up again, pacing.

"Why am I seeing their deaths?" he asked aloud.

The only connection was Samantha.

He started thinking about the strange phenomenon that he had been experiencing since the visions started. The shadow in the apartment. The voice over the baby monitor. He had seen his fair share of SyFy shows to come up with a few wild ideas, but they just didn't seem plausible.

Back in his chair, he calmed himself down. It was time to think outside the box. If he was seeing these deaths and they were all connected to Samantha, then what were the chances that they too were all dying in accidents?

Who would want these people dead?

Before he could finish that question in his head, he searched for Samantha's obituary.

He opened the webpage and skipped all the way to the end where it read, "Eckhard is survived by her husband, Evrett."

Back on the search bar, he typed in "Evrett Eckhard." His biography page for GGM, which had been unlinked from the website but not taken down, appeared. Alec clicked on it to find the man at the deli. The admirer of his *Last Day* stories. The man who was so interested in the final installment.

"Oh, shit," he said. "He knows."

Alec quickly deleted his final *Last Day* story. He would tell Angela that he just couldn't come up with anything. He didn't want Evrett to read this.

But it was too late.

• • •

From the safety of his car, Evrett heard it all, and from his tablet, he saw everything Alec had pulled up on his computer that night.

Over the microphone, Evrett heard, "Oh, shit. He knows."

He smiled, "You're damn right I know."

Things were a little complicated now in that Alec knew Evrett's true identity. What he didn't know was that he was several steps ahead of him.

He watched his screen as Alec deleted the story that nearly made Evrett storm through the front door. It was an atrocity, and unlike any of the other *Last Day* stories, it was a lie.

Evrett wondered what Alec would post instead. Perhaps, he would post nothing.

It didn't really matter.

Evrett knew the next chapter and he didn't need to read it on a website.

He listened to Alec leave the basement, presumably for bed, and then drove home to begin his preparation.

That was the plan, at least.

50

THREE HOURS OF SLEEP WOULD HAVE TO DO. *Sleep.* He could barely consider it sleep. Alec tossed and turned, yearning for the answers to questions that were too numerous to count.

He stared at Angela as she slept and imagined what he would do if he lost her. He couldn't imagine the pain that Evrett had endured. He wished that upon no one.

But the revelations from the night before stirred up a fear in him he had never felt. Watching Angela sleep, he thought about what Evrett was capable of. If his suspicions were correct—and based on the circumstantial evidence, he was fairly certain he was—that meant that Evrett was most likely targeting him next.

But Alec figured he was a step ahead of Evrett.

He doesn't know I know, Alec thought.

The sun began to poke through the curtains in the small basement window as Alec searched the Internet for information on Evrett. He had to find him first.

He wasn't sure what he'd do or say, but he had to find him.

Evrett was unlisted, as most people are nowadays, and every idea he had was a dead end. It was 8:33 in the morning when an idea hit him.

He picked up his phone and dialed GGM.

It rang twice before a woman picked up.

"Griffin, Graham and Marks, how may I direct your call?"

"Yes, I'm Stanley Thompson, and I worked closely on a project with an Evrett Eckhard a year ago and I wanted to send him a thank you gift basket. The project he drew up was just completed and we're so grateful for his hard work."

"I'm sorry, sir, but he doesn't work here any more."

Alec knew this, but he played along. "Oh, my apologizes. Is there any way I could send this to a home address? We really would like to pass along our gratitude."

"Well," she said hesitantly, "I guess I can do that. Let me see if I still have his home address."

After about twenty seconds, she returned to the phone. "I found an address, but I can't guarantee that he still lives there."

"That's fine," Alec said. "We'll take our chances."

"He's at three, seven, six, three, Beech Avenue, Baltimore, Maryland. The zip code is two, one, two, one, one."

Alec jotted down the info and thanked her.

Angela had left an hour earlier to drop Thomas off at her parents before heading into Baltimore to volunteer at an inner city writers' workshop. She wasn't expected to return until mid afternoon, so Alec knew he had some time to go out on his own.

He ran to his car with the address typed into his cellphone. He had to find out more.

It took nearly fifty minutes to get there as the latter part of the Baltimore morning rush wound down. He turned onto Beech Avenue and parallel parked a few houses down from Evrett's.

Sitting there, Alec thought about what he would do. Part of him just wanted to go up to the door, confront Evrett and let him know that he knew. Alec could also tell him that he would go to the authorities, unless he left him alone. Alec was sure the last thing Evrett would want is an investigation.

Blackmail. Alec couldn't believe that was the best option.

There had to be something else.

Perhaps he could just come clean with Evrett.

No, that wouldn't work. The truth would be the worst possible approach. And besides, Alec wasn't even sure what Evrett knew about his involvement. For all Alec knew, Evrett could have stumbled upon the stories and naturally had a reaction that resulted in his personal investigation of Alec.

Maybe that was why Evrett approached him. What if he was just as confused as Alec? What if Alec wasn't a target? If that were the case, Alec could apologize for his lies at the deli, justifying them with how he wasn't necessarily sure how these visions were coming to him. Alec could just sit down with him, man to man, and have a discussion. He could tell him that he had been having these visions and he had no clue that they were real until last night.

That would be a truthful statement.

He could say he didn't know that Evrett was involved until some *shocking* research unveiled the truth that these *Last Day* stories were in fact happening.

He could approach Evrett with the perception of curiosity.

This could work. He was sure that they both would like to learn more about the situation. And it was certainly a better idea than blackmail. If all else failed, blackmail could be his last resort.

Alec, now settled on this approach, took a deep breath and opened the car door. As he readied to step out of his car, Evrett's front door opened. Out came Evrett with a satchel over his shoulder. Alec ducked back into his car and gently brought the door within inches of the closed position. He watched as Evrett went straight for his car, sporting a very determined look. He was definitely on a mission.

Seconds after the car door closed, Evrett sped away. Alec did not hesitate and he quickly went in pursuit. He followed a few car lengths behind as Evrett made his way onto Interstate 83 South.

Alec was nervous being out of his element. He had seen several movies and TV shows that depicted a person following another in a car—mostly at night—so he wasn't sure if he was doing it right. He could only hope that in the daytime, Evrett wasn't paying any attention to the cars behind him.

After about a mile on the interstate, Alec began to realize exactly where he was. He'd traveled this route numerous times in his life. He was about a mile from *The Baltimore Sun*, but under the current circumstances, he was only reminded of how close he was to the accident.

"Where are you going?" Alec said, tapping the wheel nervously as he stayed in the right lane, one car behind Evrett. A half-mile later, as *The Baltimore Sun*'s office building came into view, Evrett crossed two lanes quickly to get into the far left lane. Alec adjusted quickly, maneuvering into the center lane to keep an eye on him. Evrett's left turn signal popped on and he exited for Pleasant Street. Alec did the same, crossing two lanes casually to get into the exit lane.

Everything went in slow motion for Alec as they both passed underneath the Orleans Street Bridge. He had avoided this section of Baltimore since the accident and it was eerie to be back, especially with Evrett leading the way. He followed Evrett into a parking garage on Pleasant Street, watched him park on a third level and continued on to the first spot he could find. It was on the fourth level, so Alec had to act quickly.

He darted to the closest staircase and carefully made his way to the third level. He peered around the corner of the entranceway only to find a woman pushing a stroller. He stepped out and walked closer to where Evrett parked.

As he approached the black Audi, he couldn't see anybody inside. He spun around and looked in all directions. The only movement was the woman now pushing the stroller onto an elevator.

"Shit," Alec said.

He sprinted for the staircase and ran down the several flights before exiting out on to the city streets of Baltimore. He scanned the sidewalks in all directions, but couldn't find him.

As he panned past several pedestrians, a pain in between the eyes overwhelmed him, causing him to fall to his knees.

He knew what this sensation meant.

Immediately, he was thrown into the world of another vision. It was a woman, driving a car. From the backseat, Alec saw the brown hair of the woman driving. Then, all of a sudden, he was thrust into her point of view; he now saw everything she was seeing.

The woman drove down the street, singing along to a pop hit on the radio. Alec watched as she turned on to Interstate 83 North.

Could this be Samantha, he thought?

He watched as the car traveled closer and closer to where it crashed.

Alec couldn't understand why he was reliving the accident like this. It was unlike any of the other visions. He heard the music cut out and from the woman's perspective, he could see a man standing on the bridge. He couldn't make out the face, but he knew it had to be him.

From her right, he heard another woman speak, "My apologies."

The driver spun her head quickly to see a woman in the passenger seat reach out and grab the steering wheel. Alec was stunned. It was Samantha in the passenger seat. She pulled the wheel hard to the right, causing the car to spin out.

The driver tried to fight it but it was too late. The car went flying into the concrete barrier and flipped. As it did, Alec caught a glimpse of the driver's face in the rear-view mirror.

It was Angela.

Alec immediately snapped out of his trance and his heart sunk. He was surrounded by a few concerned passers-by who were checking on his status.

"Are you okay?" an elderly man asked.

Another woman was giving him a disturbed look.

As they questioned him, he processed all the information and applied it to everything he knew.

Angela was next and he had to save her.

Without responding to any of the concerned bystanders, he took off for the Orleans Street Bridge. He whipped out his cellphone and dialed Angela. It went straight to voicemail. He dialed once again and a recorded operator said, "The cellular customer you are trying to reach is not available. Please hang up and try again."

Alec pushed even harder to run faster. He prayed, for the first time in a long time, that he was not too late.

As he ran up the sidewalk he once fled from more than three years ago, he saw Evrett climbing onto the ledge of the overpass.

"No!" Alec screamed.

Evrett did not acknowledge him.

As he came within ten feet of Evrett, Alec was relieved to see that the accident had not occurred. This confirmed to him that he was in fact seeing the future.

He screamed again.

"Stop! Don't do this! Please, do not do this!"

This time, Evrett turned his head.

"You can't stop her. You won't stop her. She hasn't failed yet."

Alec noticed Evrett's inflection was trance-like. He wasn't the same person he spoke to the other day at the deli.

Nevertheless, the message was clear.

Alec watched as traffic sped underneath him. He could not see Angela's car, but he figured it was coming soon.

"I'm sorry, Evrett!" he pleaded. "I'm sorry about Samantha! I never meant for any of this to happen! Please, I beg you. Don't do this."

Once again, Evrett turned his head to look at Alec.

"We're going to make this right. She's going to make it right."

Alec didn't know what to do. He wanted to attack Evrett, but what good would that do? It was Samantha who would somehow cause this accident. He knew Angela didn't deserve this. Thomas didn't deserve to lose his mother. And he now knew that Evrett didn't deserve to lose his wife. There was truly only one way to stop Samantha from crashing Angela's car.

It was clear. Evrett wanted him to feel his pain. He wanted to watch him suffer, and Alec wasn't going give him the opportunity.

He climbed up onto the ledge a few feet away from Evrett, and said, "Forgive me, Evrett."

Evrett looked at him, now with a puzzled expression.

Alec continued, "You don't owe me anything, but please tell my wife I love her."

With that, Alec jumped off the overpass, smacking off the windshield of a speeding pickup truck. His broken body went flying off to the side of the road as the entire flow of traffic came to a screeching halt.

Lying on his back and in severe pain, Alec heard the sound of multiple fenders crunching and horns blowing.

About five hundred yards south of him, Angela slammed on her brakes and narrowly avoided a collision with the car in front of her. All she could see were brake lights and a figure standing on the overpass.

Alec, as he lay motionless on the pavement, looked up at the ledge from where he leapt. Evrett was still there, staring at him.

And he wasn't alone.

Samantha was at his side. She was no longer a danger to Angela.

Alec's eyes slowly shut, but the lasting image of Evrett standing on the bridge was burned into his retinas.

It was at this moment he knew it was his last day.

51

EVRETT HAD GOTTEN THERE FIRST. The cemetery grass was still green with life from the warm summer and the trees were still hanging on to their leaves. Standing alone amidst all the green was a single bright yellow sunflower in an arrangement next to the gravesite. Sunflowers were Sam's favorite and it seemed fitting that after all of it, she would have a part in the day's ceremonies.

Evrett shifted his attention from the sunflower he had placed to the headstone of Alec. It read:

> Alec Mario Rossi
> November 12, 1978 – September 21, 2016.
> Loving father, husband and friend.

The man on the bridge, laid to rest, Evrett thought.

He walked away from the site as the funeral caravan entered the cemetery. From a few cemetery rows over, Evrett watched as the procession came to a halt. The funeral director driving the hearse opened the door for Angela and held her hand as she stepped out of the vehicle. A few relatives followed her, one of whom Evrett assumed was Angela's mother. The older woman cradled Thomas in her arms.

Six pallbearers waited for the charcoal colored casket to be unloaded from the back of the hearse. Another funeral employee showed them the path they would take to the grave.

Soon the pallbearers carried Alec to his funeral plot. The group of mourners followed closely behind. As Evrett watched from across the rows of graves, he remembered the words Alec had said to him only a few days earlier.

"You don't owe me anything, but please tell my wife I love her."

Evrett was amazed he remembered it, considering the fact that he couldn't say how he got to the bridge that day. The last thing he remembered clearly was waking up in the morning with the intent to track Angela for the day. What felt like only seconds had been several hours that Evrett once again couldn't account for.

But for whatever reason, the curtain had been pulled back when Alec had implored Evrett to give his wife his final message. Evrett didn't even have enough time to discern where he was before he realized what Alec was about to do. Just as the last words left his lips, Alec leapt from the ledge of the overpass.

Evrett's impulse was to reach out and stop the man.

"No!" he cried and lunged to where Alec had been standing. Alec's fall took only seconds, but it was enough. Evrett knew that he would not survive.

"Run, my love," Evrett heard from beside him. He knew the voice. He spun around, expecting to see his wife standing right next to him. Instead there was nothing but the traffic of Orleans Street, as well as a few cars that had pulled over. The drivers must have seen Alec and him standing on the ledge.

Evrett knew he needed to follow his wife's advice, but he couldn't help but linger for a few moments to watch Alec close his eyes.

It was at that point, he felt compelled to run west. He wandered several nearby streets looking for his car—he assumed he had to have driven there—but his Audi was not among the many parallel-parked vehicles downtown. He was perplexed until he remembered that there was a parking garage close to the bridge, so he walked back to Pleasant Street and into the parking deck. As sirens roared in the distance, Evrett hurried through the garage until he finally found his Audi on the third level.

"Thank you," he said, breathless.

Evrett patted his pockets for the keys, found them and hurriedly started the engine. Traffic had slowed significantly going on to the overpass, but luckily he had no trouble pulling out of the garage and driving away from Interstate 83.

As he drove, his pulse began to slow and the realization of what he had just witnessed started to set in.

It was over. Although Alec had not suffered the loss of his wife as Evrett had intended, he had paid the price with his own life. Evrett slammed his hand against the dashboard and shook his head as a smile overtook him.

"We did it, Sam," he said.

Over the next two days, Evrett watched the news closely, waiting to see if anyone reported a mysterious man fleeing the scene of Alec's suicidal jump.

But as had been the case over the last two years, there was nothing. No mention of him in the news. No mention of him in eyewitness accounts. No mention of him in video surveillance of the bridge. If it weren't for Evrett personally seeing Alec jump, he may never have known that he was there in his final moment.

His last day, Evrett thought.

Now it was time for his last goodbyes.

It was Saturday, and as the priest began to speak beside the casket, Evrett moved closer to the crowd that had gathered around Angela. Even from behind everyone, Evrett could see the sunflower he had placed amongst the lilies. Keeping one hand in his pocket, he thoughtlessly rubbed his neck underneath his chin with the other. The beard he was growing was beginning to itch.

Evrett found himself staring into the eyes of Alec yet again. His portrait was displayed on an easel to the left of the casket, and Evrett couldn't help but think that the eyes in the picture were staring right back at him.

"Hello, Alec," Evrett mustered under his breath.

Nobody was paying attention to Evrett, and it was a good thing, because they would have caught his grin.

For Evrett, it was warranted. Today was a day for celebration. More than three years after the accident and nearly two years of hard work had led to this moment; a moment he had sometimes feared would never come to fruition.

Evrett scanned the gathering of nearly thirty family members and friends, and it all of a sudden hit him that he was the only one not grieving. Most had tears in their eyes, and for those wearing sunglasses, the tears were still rolling down their cheeks.

He quickly thought about Sam and how much he missed her, and a few tears appeared from behind his sunglasses.

That's better, he thought, as the priest continued to pray.

"… Earth to earth, ashes to ashes, dust to dust; in the sure and certain hope of the Resurrection to eternal life."

The casket was lowered into the ground. The crowd was silent except for the sound of tearful whimpers and the rustling of tissues. Angela stepped forward. At this point she was holding Thomas and Evrett could see her whisper something in the baby's ear.

After looking down into the earth, Angela handed her son to her mother. One by one, the members of the crowd stepped forward to pay their final respects.

As the crowd dwindled, Evrett too stepped forward. He was the last to do so, and now stood side by side with the widow of the man he had hunted for so long. Everyone else had begun to walk back to their parked cars.

For as tall as Alec had been, the casket seemed small and insignificant lying deep in the earth.

He turned to Angela and removed his sunglasses. She took her large black glasses off as well and looked into Evrett's eyes. She could tell that he had shed a few tears. As he tried to find the words to say, he couldn't help but think of everything that was there between them. Was she aware of any of it? Did she know about the day, three years earlier, when Alec had changed the course of all their lives?

Would he have been able to go through with his plan to take her from Alec if things had been different?

He pushed those questions from his head. They didn't matter now.

"Mrs. Rossi? I'm Evrett. I knew your husband, although, I'd say he knew me better than I did him. I am so sorry for your loss."

"Oh, well, thank you. I appreciate it," Angela said.

"I know it doesn't make any of this easier, but in my conversations with Alec, he told me how much he loved you. I know he would have done anything for you and your son."

"That's very nice," she said, holding back what tears she had left. "Thank you."

Evrett nodded and began to walk away. A few feet from Angela he stopped himself and turned toward her once more. She was silent, staring deep into the granite of the headstone that bore Alec's name.

"For what it's worth, a few years ago I too lost someone very dear to me. And when things like this happen to us, it can destroy our whole world if we let it. You find yourself asking, 'Why?' The answer may not be easy to find, but you just have to remember that even though we can't see our loved ones, they are still with us. They never really leave our side. They will eventually help us answer the questions we are left with. It took me a while to see that myself."

Angela peered back at Evrett and their eyes met one last time. She wasn't quite sure what it all meant, but it was nonetheless comforting from a man who had suffered a similar loss. He held up his hand to say goodbye. She returned the gesture.

On the walk back to his car, Evrett knew what he said to Angela was true. Even though he had lost Sam, she had been with him during the whole course of his journey. All the while he was trying to avenge her, he knew now that she was there guiding him in the direction he needed to go. And with Alec gone, Evrett knew she could finally rest.

He sat in his Audi and pulled the rearview mirror to face him. In a few weeks his beard would be fully grown again. He looked into his own eyes, but in his mind he thought of his wife's eyes gazing back. He smiled.

As the engine started to hum, Evrett thought of his future. He was ready to start the next phase of his life.

He repositioned the mirror and drove away from the cemetery. After a final glance behind him, Evrett put his sunglasses back on.

The sun was too bright, he thought.

Acknowledgments

Last Day was the product of hard work and determination by a pair of friends who devoted countless hours to accomplish a shared lifelong goal of writing a novel. Family and friends of both Mark Wisniewski and Jimmy Johnson also played an integral role in making *Last Day* a published book.

MARK WISNIEWSKI

I would like to thank all my family and friends who offered their help and support over the course of this book's creation. Mom and Elizabeth Italia, thank you for reading the manuscript and offering suggestions both big and small. Brian Betteridge, thank you for traveling to Baltimore and taking the perfect photograph that is now the cover of this book.

John Tinari, thank you for constantly supporting me through this whole journey. I know I couldn't be here without your belief in me and my dreams. And Amy Rawcliffe, thank you for being my biggest cheerleader for all these years, no matter what.

I would also especially like to thank my parents, John and Christine, who have supported me in every endeavor I've decided to pursue; my co-author, Jimmy Johnson, for helping me take a lifelong dream and make it a reality; and finally, my friend Robin Albright, who long ago told me to keep writing and never stop.

JIMMY JOHNSON

I, too, would like to thank all my family and friends for their support throughout the entire process, especially my Mom, Dad and sister Betsie for being among the first to read *Last Day*. To my cousin Joceyln, my Aunt Stacy and my friend John Parsell; thank you for giving *Last Day* a close read and providing excellent feedback.

It had always been a dream of mine to write a novel, and it was an amazing nine months of writing with my co-author Mark Wisniewski. His support was key from start to finish.

And, of course, I must thank my wife, Gina, who was strong throughout the entire endeavor, even on the nights when I would disappear into my office (a.k.a., my man cave) to write, edit and market the book. She was the very first person to read *Last Day* and I'll never forget the night I awoke at 4 a.m. to see the soft glow of her iPad. She was still reading, and she turned to me and said, "I can't put this down." I didn't need to hear any more. It made this all worth it.

Made in the USA
Middletown, DE
14 May 2020